WITHDRAWN

Praise for the Shadow Police novels

'An irresistible blend of guns, gangsters, cops and monsters that grabs you by the eyeballs and never lets go. Start this book early in the day, people, because you ain't going to get no sleep until it's done'
Ben Aaronovitch

'Paul Cornell is a triple threat, the kind of writer other writers hate. He writes award-winning short stories. He writes epic television episodes for all your favourite BBC shows. He writes kickass comic books and graphic novels . . . now he's gone and written a novel too!'
George R. R. Martin

'I think it is absolutely magnificent. I loved it . . . I'm not sure I've been that gripped by a novel in . . . well, decades'
Russell T. Davies

'Tough, thrilling and unputdownable: I love Cornell's writing'
Jenny Colgan

'A much grittier vision of a gothic, fantasy London, well balanced between its depiction of the city's criminal underworld and a horrifying fantasy reality that for most of the novel lurks just at the edges of sight. Its take on the crime genre is less *The Bill*, more *The Sweeney*. Cornell's undercover coppers and plain-clothes detectives are a thoroughly seedy bunch of repro-bates'
Guardian

'*The Sweeney* to Aaronovitch's *The Bill*, perhaps – which shows Cornell to be a master of yet another discipline' *Independent*

'Realistic banter, original twists; a nifty debut' *Daily Telegraph*

'Pacy, smart and revels in London mythology. It's especially clever in that our heroes don't stop being coppers just because they now realize there are more things in heaven and earth (and elsewhere) than dreamt of in our philosophies. *London Falling* might not be on the Booker longlist, but crikey it's good fun'
Scotland on Sunday

'The team's continued struggle to understand the dark and terrifying side of London is gripping. This book is a strong follow-up, a good standalone story, and an excellent read for fans of dark urban fantasy'
Publishers Weekly

'*London Falling* enters at the very top rank of London Gothic novels. It is grittier and harder-edged than Neil Gaiman's *Neverwhere*, more coherent and less esoteric than China Miéville's *Kraken*, less pedestrian and harder-hitting than Ben Aaronvitch's *Rivers of London*. Cornell is a fantasy novelist to watch'
SFX

'Cornell is breaking new ground with his group of urban magicians and the uncanny threats they face. Readers will surely want to jump on board. Recommended'
SFRevu

'Paul Cornell is a very good writer indeed . . . another accomplished piece of work from Paul Cornell's ever bubbling mind-cauldron. Fans of police drama or those familiar with Ben Aaranovitch's *Rivers of London* will find themselves in their element, and if you're a *Being Human* viewer you'll appreciate the sense of urban unease'
CultBox

WHO KILLED
SHERLOCK HOLMES?

PAUL CORNELL has written some of *Doctor Who*'s best-loved episodes for the BBC, as well as an episode of the hit Sherlock Holmes drama, *Elementary*. He has also written on a number of comic book series for Marvel and DC, including X-men and Batman and Robin. He has been Hugo Award-nominated for his work in TV, comics and prose, and won the BSFA award for his short fiction. Paul has written two previous Shadow Police novels, *London Falling* and *The Severed Streets*.

By Paul Cornell

London Falling
The Severed Streets
Who Killed Sherlock Holmes?

WHO KILLED SHERLOCK HOLMES?

PAUL CORNELL

TOR

First published 2016 by Tor
an imprint of Pan Macmillan
20 New Wharf Road, London N1 9RR
Associated companies throughout the world
www.panmacmillan.com

ISBN 978-1-4472-7326-4

1 3 5 7 9 8 6 4 2

A CIP catalogue record for this book is available from the British Library.

Typeset by Palimpsest Book Production Limited, Falkirk, Stirlingshire
Printed and bound by CPI Group (UK) Ltd, Croydon, CR0 4YY

Visit **www.panmacmillan.com** to read more about all our books
and to buy them. You will also find features, author interviews and
news of any author events, and you can sign up for e-newsletters
so that you're always first to hear about our new releases.

For Deborah Stanish

PROLOGUE

Christopher Lassiter pinched the top of his nose and closed his eyes. Quiet desperation is the English way. This situation had taken him by surprise. He'd never imagined that he could be seen as a scrounger. God, hadn't he paid his way? Wasn't that the bloody idea, that you paid your way, then if you fell on hard times, they helped you out? Yet here it was, open on the table in front of him, a form asking him about his 'fitness for work'. The language used wasn't so much cold as downright harsh. He'd almost called the phone number on here right away – there must be some mistake – until he'd realized it wasn't free to call, and of course they'd keep you hanging on listening to Mumford & Sons, while some Indian call centre watched the clock tick away before finally deciding they'd squeezed you enough and would deign to—

He carefully put down the form. He'd been in the RAF, damn it – that's what he wanted to say. He hadn't been an actor all his life; he'd done something useful, for a jolly long time, before the chronic fatigue syndrome. His journalism had been useful after that too, before the BBC had decided that they could make up news broadcasts from press releases on the Internet. Being in this bloody chair was not his fault. Having a spare bedroom, in which was piled everything from a life that had been too big for this tiny flat, well, he was going to be

1

blamed for that now too, wasn't he? You should get a Polish lodger in, squeeze him like we're squeezing you! Where was he supposed to *put* everything? Did they think he could afford storage? Wasn't the totality of his life, his character, worth more than a mere collection of data points?

The sudden headache made him wince. It was that that had finally done him in, so he couldn't concentrate, couldn't develop a train of thought, couldn't present to camera without making the viewers aware of pain, couldn't remember his lines. The pain had taken his ability to make money, and now here they wanted everything else, wanted him to work for nothing, even. Where would he live? He wouldn't mind getting out of London, the way the place was going, but his only social life was the pub round the corner. He was all right here, tucked away, though you sometimes got kids wandering around the side streets, drunk, on their way home from the Brixton Academy. There was even a bit of green nearby if you inclined your head at the kitchen window at just the right angle. Didn't he deserve these small, last comforts? These days, every comfortable shape you felt you could lean on just seemed to have fallen away.

The ring on the doorbell came as a blessed relief. It also surprised him. Who would that be? Some arse with a collecting tin. He'd ask *them* for money. He wheeled himself over to the answering device and saw a shape behind the frosted glass. He pressed the button. 'Who is it?'

'Old friend of yours!'

Chris was sure he recognized the voice, but couldn't put his finger on where from. He hit the other button and in strode . . . Oh, what a welcome sight!

'Well,' he said, 'what brings you here?'

Christopher Lassiter's body was found eight days later. With the warm early autumn weather, it had taken that long for Mr Peng, who owned the shop beside the flat, to notice the smell, and to realize he hadn't seen Chris coming and going. The

2

door was knocked upon by Jackie Dorney, a community support officer from Coldharbour Safer Neighbourhood Team, and finally opened with a duplicate key provided by the landlord, who'd been bloody elusive.

She found Lassiter lying beside his wheelchair, his face contorted in agony. He'd obviously been dead some time. She took one long, careful look at the room, then stepped back out of the flat without touching anything, closed the door behind her, took out her Airwave radio and called it in as a suspicious death. The civilian Metcall centre worker went through her script as she had for all the more ordinary times Jackie had contacted her, finally told her to wait there, and she acknowledged. She made herself stay standing upright, though she wanted to lean against the wall in shock, because she was aware of passers-by starting to look. This had to be a murder. There'd been no sign of any wounds on the body, no blood near it, except . . . the memory of it got to her only in some deep way that let her conscious mind stay calm above it . . . except the walls had been daubed with blood, a single word written in it above the corpse, a word that wasn't in English, but that, even so, Jackie found weirdly familiar.

Within a few minutes, local uniforms and CID arrived to secure the scene and make initial enquiries. Within an hour, crime scene examiners and detectives from SC&O1, the Homicide and Serious Crime Command, had arrived, and Jackie was questioned at the scene, then released to write up her notes, which would become a witness statement. She saw the story on the news that night. A man in his sixties had been found dead, they said, and police were seeking witnesses who'd seen anyone calling at the flat in the past two weeks. So there couldn't have been any useful CCTV footage of his front door. The circumstances of his death were suspicious.

Jackie felt she now understood her job a little more. All the horror she'd seen in that room was regularly reduced to words like that. She worried for the coppers who encountered such things on a regular basis.

That same day, a detective constable on the Major Investigation Team talked to a reporter off the record and soon the resulting story was all over the media. They were still waiting for the post-mortem and the toxicology tests, but the lack of any other apparent cause of death suggested Lassiter had been poisoned. The blood on the wall wasn't his, but that of an as-yet-unidentified third party. The simplest research had revealed that the word that had been written there was an obvious reference, but that didn't mean other possibilities as to what it might mean were being ruled out. That word had now been seen by the world, in a grainy long-lens photo taken through the window of Christopher Lassiter's flat, when, for reasons perhaps influenced by money, someone inside had just for a moment pulled aside the curtains.

The word was *Rache*.

ONE

Three imperial stormtroopers strode into Chilcott's bank on Park Street in Mayfair, brandishing their weapons, 'The Imperial March' playing from concealed speakers somewhere on their person. They got a chuckle from the three or four people sitting in the foyer, waiting to go back into the meeting rooms. One broad-shouldered chap in an expensive suit saluted them with his designer cup of African coffee, but Lacey Fitzherbert, through her own fear, could feel the awkwardness. Chilcott's was not Barclays on the high street. This marble and teak foyer was more like the entrance of a hotel; nothing so infra dig as tills for a bank as rah as Chilcott's. It smelt of some sort of polish that Lacey had only smelt otherwise at stately homes. Someone, these customers would be thinking, was going to have to tell these fine fellows they'd find no opportunity for a charity collection here, not from the rich. Unfortunately, the customers' thoughts were irrelevant, because Lacey knew exactly what was about to happen.

The stormtroopers turned slowly, checking where everyone was. Oh God, this was it; this was what they'd paid her for; this was what her dad had begged her about at the kitchen table. 'Nobody will ever know,' he'd said. 'We would never put you in danger unless it was . . . It's just that they . . . they came to us, and . . .'

She was suddenly very aware of the new guy standing beside her. What was his name? Kevin, that was it. He had a concerned look on his face. She'd noticed him as soon as he'd arrived, a week ago, those rugby-player muscles under his jacket, and she had a thing about black guys. He set off her gaydar a bit, but these days who didn't? She stepped away from him, just a little closer to the desk she'd been hovering near all morning. Now she thought about it, she'd noticed him glancing over at her a few times.

'What are they—?' he started to say.

The lead stormtrooper swung round, pointed his gun at a corner of the room with no people in it and fired a burst. A piece of modern sculpture exploded into fragments. It was the loudest noise Lacey had ever heard. 'Stay fucking put!' he bellowed, his voice amplified and distorted by what must be a microphone under his helmet. His two mates had swung to cover the customers with their weapons, and the fine ladies and gentlemen had leaped up and were shrinking back, screaming, their hands in the air. One of them, the woman nearest to the door, was hesitating, Lacey noticed. Had the stormtroopers seen that she was thinking about going for it? Should Lacey say something? Suddenly, she kicked off her shoes and ran.

Lacey shouted – she didn't know who to – and half put up a hand to prevent herself from seeing what was about to happen, or stop it from happening, or something. The loudest possible noise roared again, but as she looked, the door was slamming back against its frame. The woman had made it.

'You do *not* do that!' the lead stormtrooper bellowed again at the customers. 'If anyone else tries that, I will fucking kill *all* the rest. Do you understand? Do you understand?!'

There were nodded assents. One of the stormtroopers was running to the door, where he started quickly and expertly locking it.

'Why didn't they do that on the way in, do you reckon?' said Kevin. He sounded really bloody calm about all this.

The lead stormtrooper swung his gun in Lacey's direction, and Lacey knew, horribly, that she'd already disobeyed; she'd already left it too long to do what she had to. She jerked out her hand and found the silent alarm button under the counter.

'What are you fucking doing?' The lead stormtrooper marched over, snatching up his gun to aim at her head. She thought of her mum and dad, and hoped desperately that she wasn't the victim of some huge lie. He was about to grab her round the throat, shove his gun to her head. That was what she'd been told he'd do. She'd thought about it many times, but she hadn't had that enormous sound in her head and stomach then. Still, she was going to let it happen.

But then Kevin moved between them. Dear God, no, was he going to try to be a hero?

The stormtrooper swung his gun away from her to cover him. 'Step away.'

Kevin raised his hands, looking concerned and careful, not taking any risks. 'Listen,' he said, 'there's no need for anyone to get hurt. You've come for the safe deposit boxes, right? That's all we have of value here. Well, I can show you where they are. I know where the two sets of keys are. I can even get you the list of who owns which box.'

The stormtrooper paused.

Lacey felt panic start to take over. What the hell was Kevin talking about? Why would he lie? Only staff of her level of seniority could get hold of that list. That was one reason she was in this mess. She'd already given that list to her parents, to pass on to whoever was behind all this. To get the keys, you'd need to be a couple of pay grades higher. Today, that would be only . . . No, looking around the staff here today, she couldn't actually see anyone else she knew: it must all be guys from the other shifts in today, which was weird, now she thought about it. Her thoughts snapped back to the here and now. Not only was Kevin putting her family's life in jeopardy with this mad offer, so was the bloody stormtrooper by thinking about it. She had to demonstrate her willingness to go along with the plan, to show them that her hesitancy about the alarm hadn't been deliberate. She pushed her way past Kevin and lunged at the stormtrooper, falling into him, the bravest thing she had ever done. She hoped it looked like she was having a go at getting his gun or trying to escape or something.

'Tell me who can open the safe deposit boxes!' he yelled into her ear, back on script, trying to make it obvious that he was addressing her and not Kevin. He grabbed her throat, which hurt like fuck. No, she wanted to say, not that hard. I can't breathe! He remembered and let go enough for her to speak.

'I won't tell you!' she shouted.

'I can!' Kevin insisted, pointing at himself.

The stormtrooper paused awkwardly again. He obviously had as little idea as she did what Kevin's weird willingness to help was about. Lacey looked over her shoulder into those blank eye sockets, willing whoever was under there just to follow his orders.

Kevin looked perplexed. 'Look,' he said, 'do you want to rob this bank or not?'

'Don't listen to him!' Lacey gasped. 'He doesn't know what he's talking about!'

One of the stormtroopers yelled from the front door, 'Police! Fucking loads!'

The stormtrooper holding Lacey let go. He looked around as if making his mind up under pressure. He was, just from the body language, a terrible actor, but that in a stormtrooper outfit looked somehow authentic. 'All right,' he finally yelled, 'this is now a hostage situation!'

Lacey closed her eyes in sheer relief. That was what she had been told to expect. She had done her part. She, Kevin and the handful of other staff and customers were yelled at and rushed back into the meeting rooms by the three stormtroopers, who shoved them into corners, told them to sit and slammed the doors on them. Through the big panel windows, Lacey watched as they started to arrange the seating into a rough barricade, pulling out unfolding metal sheets from their backpacks to add to their defences. Presumably they weren't worried about anyone thinking, at this point, that they seemed to have come very well prepared for a siege they weren't expecting.

'They let us keep our phones,' said a voice from beside her. It was, of course, Kevin. He still sounded strangely calm. 'So hey, we can tell the world we're in a siege.' He took his phone out and typed a very quick text that seemed to consist of a single word.

Few people knew that the private home that stood next to Chilcott's bank on Park Street in Mayfair had two levels of cellars. In London, there were strict ordinances about building upwards, so if one had no elbow room sideways and one wanted, say, a new pool, or, in this case, a new home cinema, one applied, with the aid of solicitors who specialized in that sort of thing, for planning permission, hoping all the while that the underground railway wasn't too close to the surface. Having got said planning permission, one got the builders in, and they got the excavators in, and they started to chew downwards. Much too noisy to stay put during all that, of course, so one pissed off to one of one's other houses, somewhere abroad, which was where, Mark Ballard knew, the owners of this abode were once again, oblivious to what he was doing in the home cinema they'd had built several years ago.

What he was doing at this very moment was standing in a newly excavated area to one side of the cinema, looking up at an incongruous mechanical digger. It was standing part in and part out of an excavated concrete wall. Some of it, where it had got in the way of what Ballard's team were doing, had been sawn off and piled nearby. It was as if they'd unearthed a dinosaur.

It had been a news story about the presence of the digger down here that had first alerted him to the possibilities this building next to Chilcott's bank had to offer. Big construction companies, making millions on underground developments such as this, had initially gone to the bother of bringing in cranes to lift mechanical diggers, once their work was done, out of their excavations. Then they'd realized that the cost-benefit analysis actually tipped in the direction of just finding somewhere to hide the digger and leaving it entombed in a wall, the company sometimes going just a little bit beyond the planning permission they'd been given for the few days it took to do so. Ballard had slipped someone at City Hall some cash to get a look at the plans and realized that, yes, the only place the digger could have been entombed was right up against the bank.

Its presence, leading to structural weaknesses in the concrete, had made his team's initial drilling a lot easier. He had, once again, found a little crack in reality and had grabbed it and ripped it open like . . . well, like pulling apart a chicken. He often thought of the moment he'd really done that. He'd been fifteen, on some outing with a bunch of other kids from 'deprived backgrounds' or whatever the term had been back then. He'd needed to show the girl he was with what he could do. He'd climbed over the gate at a city farm, and had grinned back at her, and had been quick enough to catch the chicken, and had hauled its legs both ways in a second. The shriek it had made had stayed with him. He'd known from that moment that he was someone who could and would do *anything*.

He wondered, as he looked up at the digger, what future archaeologists would make of these buried machines that had dug their own graves. They'd think of them as some sort of offering. Ballard knew how the power of London worked. The buried diggers would, after a few years, create ripples in the currents of force that could make the impossible happen. To deliberately bury something that would swiftly accrue stories from folk memory, as people in pubs told others what was down there . . . He wondered how many of London's builders still knew what their ancient guilds had taught. All those secrets he'd wheedled out of sloshed retired bastards in the right bars. He'd done it all himself, like always, the self-made man. He was here with only four employees, the minimum needed for this job. He checked the news on his phone. There we go: first reports of a siege situation at Chilcott's bank . . . quotes from texts of loved ones within. Excellent. It was beautiful that that team had decided they'd dress up as stormtroopers. They'd put themselves into the role of action figures, as if they were going along with how he thought about them. People never seemed quite real to Ballard, not real like he was. They were just a rather-too-small cluster of predictable reactions.

'OK.' He stepped forwards to where Tony was supervising the work crew. The tall black lieutenant looked up expectantly. He had that blank expression again. He was so fucking sad all the time, so weighed down by something he never talked about. Still, he'd been an excellent find, a bloke with not just gang soldier experience, having been part of Rob Toshack's crew, but also someone who actually had the Sight. So he wouldn't freak out when Ballard produced one of his little toys. When Ballard had asked how Tony had got the Sight, the man had just shaken his head, the truculence of which had made Ballard think that maybe after this gig he'd take Tony out drinking and arrange for him to be carted off in a van to somewhere that Ballard and some muscle could tease that secret out of him. Yeah, that was a pleasure to be saved for later, making a macho bloke squeal, and by the end of it, he'd get from him what he needed to know. Oh, that would be satisfying.

'Go for the bank wall, chief?' asked Tony.

Mitch had the drill at the ready. They'd been down here for a month, cutting past and through the digger, until they were now at the point where Mitch's electric sensor indicated the bank's security system was threaded through what was surely much tougher concrete, mixed with proprietary additives and reinforced with steel bars.

One of Ballard's artefacts had altered the flow of power

through this building so that the noise and the vibrations didn't reach the outside world, as Ballard had confirmed with some delightful early autumn strolls round the block. Ballard had used his 'white blanket' rings to get the team in and out without being noticed. Tony was firm with the others, didn't allow any slacking, but didn't strut around showing off his authority. Ballard appreciated that professionalism. That and the stoic suffering the man already seemed to be enduring made him think he would actually try to hold out against the tortures Ballard had planned for him. Brilliant.

'Wait a sec.' Ballard went to the hole in the wall that had become so familiar and took the metal bracelet from his jacket. To him, its power was only a slight tingling, but that tingle had led him to precious and powerful items at auction houses all over the world. Ballard placed the bracelet on his wrist and put his palm to the concrete wall of the bank. Alarms might even go off at that slight contact, but such alarms were to be expected, weren't they, when one's bank was in the middle of a siege situation? The police would assume that the robbers were now trying to breach the secure cell at the centre of the bank, but they would also assume that by controlling the siege they were controlling the robbery. He whispered the words that had been written phonetically on a photocopied document that had come with the bracelet, words that he suspected weren't actually from a language but were just precise noises, attuned to the shape of the metropolis. He'd got both the bracelet and the document from the back room of an undertaker's in Chesham that had a sideline in the dark stuff. They'd also, for a hefty price, provided the sacrifices, small personal injuries like the cutting of gums and the pulling of nails, that gave him the power he was using today.

There was a satisfying feeling of something huge moving around him, impacting on the wall, invisibly altering it. He felt his will change the world, again. He was pleased at the idea that Tony might be actually seeing it. Ballard himself didn't have the Sight, so everything he did using the power of London remained invisible, intangible, to Ballard himself, when for the Sighted, he'd been told, it was about watching luminous tendrils do their work, being able to sense the presence of the supernatural, learning about an object of power simply by looking at it.

Getting the Sight was a goal for the future, but not a tremendously urgent one. He was doing fine without it. Ballard suspected that what he was doing on this job was close to the intent, centuries ago, of those that had formalized the power of London into a matter of holding particular items or making particular noises. He was now in the business of building and demolition, as had been many of those practitioners. They had created a culture of architects that had kept these procedures a trade secret, formalized them and swiftly ceased to enquire further into how they worked. They had merely repeated what had been done before, and been content to see it done again. Ballard felt that he was the last person who studied as a science something that had, years before, become the mumbled repetitions of a religion.

He realized his work was done, stepped back and waved for the drill crew to get to work. Tony consulted with Mitch and marked a place on the concrete. The engine started up, the drill bit surged forwards, and the team lurched with it, having to steady themselves, surprised at how easy its passage had been. Tony looked over to Ballard and dourly nodded. Ballard allowed himself a grin in return.

PC Isla Staverton sat in the unmarked van on Reeves Mews, wondering about the intelligence analyst. Staverton's job was to liaise between said analyst and the teams of SC&O19 specialist firearms officers standing by in unmarked vans on several side streets. She herself was SC&O19, number two to Sergeant Tom Stennet, who was Bronze leader on this operation, in charge of the third tier of the organizational structure, and also waiting in one of those vans. The analyst, whose name was Lisa Ross, had seemed, at the initial briefing, to be narked at the standard structure of an op like this to the point of being all eye-rolly. Typical bloody specialist, looking down on your everyday lid, simply because she was from this weird unit of just four people that everyone in the canteen talked about but about which nobody really knew anything.

Ross was here to record the timeline of what went down as it happened, her laptop open and an i2 Analyst's Notebook application ready on it, displaying a colourful diagram of the organized crime network they were aiming to bring down today, with 'Operation Dante' in red at the top. Staverton had at least hoped that the analyst's narkiness wouldn't extend to Ross attempting to give her orders. The analyst technically outranked the PC, but she'd never met a copper who'd accept that situation. As it turned out, the analyst had been silent and distant to the point of rudeness, not just focused on her task but staring into space in the long stretches between. Something that was normally there in a person seemed, in her, to have been switched off. She displayed none of the anticipation Staverton had felt around officers on the verge of a major score. At least, as had every other analyst Staverton had met, she hadn't objected to Staverton using her first name rather than calling her 'ma'am'. Let her try and see how far that got her. Staverton got the feeling that party girl here just didn't react to much anymore. God, what sort of trauma had made her like that? The analyst's DI, James Quill, who was Silver leader for this operation, and about whom Staverton had heard happier stories, had also seemed pretty out of it at the briefing, curt and angry at any question. Only Lofthouse, the detective superintendent, Gold leader for this op, had seemed straightforward and professional.

Now, Ross looked up from her phone, which had just got an alert for an incoming text, as she was typing. 'That was a text message from second undercover, saying, "Siege." So the bank robbery team are sticking with Ballard's original plan and haven't been lured away from it by the promise of easy money.'

'I'll relay that to the front-of-bank team.' There was a van of specialist firearms officers parked directly across from the bank in case the stormtroopers had opted to ignore their chief's plan, open a few tasty safe deposit boxes and scarper before, they thought, the police had got there. To take them in a prepared bottling at the front of the bank had been judged by Lofthouse to be less dangerous than letting the full plan play out, so they'd been offered this temptation by the second undercover.

'Noted. I'm now texting back that second undercover should work on Fitzherbert.' Staverton remembered from the briefing that Lacey Fitzherbert was the junior manager who'd been turned to the dark side through family pressure. She'd passed on to Ballard's people the list of which safe deposit boxes belonged to which customers. Her testimony, it was said, would help in making sure the charges against the patron stuck, though Staverton was still puzzled that the weird little squad feared they might not. Ballard was here personally, wasn't he, actually supervising a drilling team? He was being that stupid. What sort of conjuring trick did they think he was going to pull? At the briefing, they'd been told how this operation had come about. One of the undercovers, a detective sergeant, had his previous criminal life maintained by SC&O10, with contact details such as phone numbers and email addresses with someone always briefed to answer correctly at the other end of them. He'd thus been approached by one Mark Ballard, who'd been a suspect in the funding of a couple of high-end robberies. The DS, now the first undercover in Operation Dante, had met with Ballard, who had offered the DS certain subcultural cues about the nature of which DI Quill had been strangely vague. That contact had been spun, by this incredibly small team, whose lack of official mission statement must mean they were something to do with intelligence, into Operation Dante.

'OK, Lisa,' she said, noting a new message on her own laptop.

'I just got an email from Silver saying they've given the order to start moving in the cordon, putting all the expected details of a siege situation in place, so Ballard's going to hear all the right things from the media.'

'Noted,' she said. The tone in her voice was not an invitation to conversation.

'Why the stormtrooper thing, do you reckon?' asked Kevin.

Lacey knew stress affected different people in different ways, but she was now wondering what she'd done in a previous life to meet, at this point of sheer terror for her, someone who reacted to it by getting laid-back and chatty. 'I don't know,' she said. 'Maybe they're into *Star Wars*.'

'I think it's something you could sell to the media,' said Kevin, 'as a thing a group of experienced bank robbers might do. It sounds kind of smart, because we've all seen those guys who make their own stormtrooper outfits out and about, collecting for charity. They can just walk into a bank carrying guns and nobody blinks an eye.'

'But . . . ?' There was something about the sheer calmness of him now that was deliberate, wasn't there?

'But they're also memorable,' Kevin continued. 'SCD7 – sorry, that's the Serious and Organised Crime Command – will be able to fill in the CCTV trail of how they got here with witness testimony. Also, how many of those costumes exist? The hobbyist community and specialist shops would be able to trace all the buyers within, let's say, two days.'

Oh God. Oh God, who was he? 'Well, we already know this lot are a bit shit, don't we? They panicked and went into siege mode when—'

He shook his head and sighed. 'Don't do that, Lacey. Don't lie to me. You're no good at it.'

'I'm not!'

'They turned down my kind offer of a guided tour and folded

at the slightest resistance from you. They could have used me to get at least a couple of specific items on their shopping list and got out before the first marked cars arrived. That's what almost any gang would have done.' Lacey felt a horrible tightness in her guts. She hoped he knew all this because he read a lot of true crime. 'We think this lot are either being paid a great deal of money to take some jail time or they're expecting to get out of here in some extraordinary way.'

'We?'

'You realized I was a copper a few moments ago, but you didn't call one of the stormtroopers over to blow my cover.' Lacey felt her breathing get faster at the thought that just by sitting here she'd made a decision, a decision to let down the people who could hurt her mum and dad. She tried to keep her expression steady. 'That's a good sign. You probably haven't been paid to take a fall.' Lacey closed her eyes and shook her head. She wanted to scream. She was being crushed between enormous forces she hadn't summoned. 'So you're doing this out of love – we get that.' She was going to snarl at him that he had no idea when she felt his hand on her arm. She opened her eyes and saw that he was offering her his phone. 'Here,' he said, 'text your mum.'

Lacey saw a text balloon already on the screen, just a 'Hello?' She recognized her mum's number. 'How—?' she began.

'She and your dad are heading for an undisclosed location, in the back of a heavily armoured police van,' he said. 'I think she could use some moral support.'

Ballard watched as Tony and the team quickly shovelled enough of what remained of the wall out of the way to let him pass. Tony straightened, nodded to him. Go on, mate, crack a smile, while you still can. No? No.

Ballard walked to the metal edge of the vault itself, took the chalk from his pocket and drew the shape of a door there. He stretched out an arm, felt a terrible dreamy need to close his eyes, as if an adult shouldn't see things like this, and pushed his way through into what now felt to him like soft fronds of . . . Christmas. The inside of the wall of a bank vault smelt of Christmas. Perhaps that was just the associations in his head, ideas of plenty and panto scenes of Aladdin's cave, when to the Sighted, well, who knew what extra dimensions such an experience held for them? That was all he had time to think before he was pushing his way out of the other side and calling for the others to follow. Ballard opened his eyes to see Tony coming through immediately, at a run. The other three took longer, and the look on their faces was deeply scared. They'd seen something that made them wonder about the fundamentals of the world in which they lived. Ballard would have lied to them, given them a cod-scientific explanation, but he wanted them to stay in awe of it. If he was doing this by mere gadget, their thoughts might have gone, then it must be the most valuable gadget in the world, and why were they bothering about a bank when he was right there and vulnerable, and they could raid him instead?

Ballard took a look around. The interior of the space was lit by motion-sensor lights, which were now just coming on. Literally every alarm in the building would be silently blaring. The vault interior, as he'd known from pictures he'd bought from a source at the architect's, resembled nothing more than a high-end self-storage facility, metal boxes on shelves, all requiring two keys. Inside each was a further locked casing that would slide out as a drawer. There were metal boxes with ladders leading to them, and a handful of metal boxes that could be walked into as small rooms. 'Targets,' he said. The team had each memorized two numbers, and had all seen the plans. They headed off towards their targets and Ballard followed. He'd left the biggest target for himself.

Lacey looked up from the phone and rubbed the tears from her eyes. 'I didn't have any choice,' she said.

'We know,' said Kevin, if that was his real name. 'Your family are safe now. You can be too. We can keep people safe. I'm proof of that, OK? I've been half a dozen different people, all around the country, but I'm still here.'

There was something incredibly reassuring about him, now he'd dropped the acting. It was like he'd seen terrible things but was still hanging on, still a nice guy. 'What do you want me to do?'

'We know who's behind this. He's in the building now. Once we've got him into an interview room, we need to be able to threaten him with your testimony on an honest basis, because—' He was silent suddenly as one of the stormtroopers ran past, grabbed a desk, then ran back to add it to the barricade. 'Because he might be able to tell if we're lying.'

'What?'

Kevin waved that aside. 'But we're hoping this won't come to court. We're hoping to turn him, and if we can do that, then even if they could ever find you, you'd have nothing to fear from his organization.'

Lacey had heard a tone of relief in her mum's texts, that this was over. Even if her father was yelling and denying everything, like he so would, he'd still got into the back of that van. She looked up to where the stormtroopers were now lined up behind their barricade, aiming at where police would come crashing through the doors.

The phone on one of the desks rang. 'Right on time,' said Kevin.

'Is that a negotiator?'

He just smiled in response, watching for what happened next. The leader of the stormtroopers had gone to the phone and was awkwardly looking between it and a CCTV camera.

'He doesn't want to take his helmet off to answer that,' said Kevin. 'So they're hoping to get out of here. Which is good news. Also, they hadn't anticipated still being here when the police got to the negotiation stage, which seems to have happened really quickly, so they're hoping to get out of here *soon*. Also good news.' He started texting again.

The stormtrooper finally just smashed the phone off the desk, stuck one finger up to the CCTV camera and ran back to the barricade.

'Why did the negotiator call so early?' whispered Lacey.

'It wasn't the negotiator,' said Kevin; 'it was a mate of mine called Lisa, who wanted to learn those two things.'

Ballard stood in front of his target safe deposit box – one of the large, walk-in ones – the diamond drill in his hand. He possessed an object that could use London's power against concrete, but not against aluminium and twelve-gauge steel. He was also at the stub end of his stick of chalk and wanted to keep some in case he needed an emergency getaway. Still, doing this the old-fashioned way, with only two boxes per worker, they'd be out of here within the hour. The police, following standard negotiating practice, would keep the robbery team waiting longer than that before even making contact. He started up the drill and began to cut round the first lock.

Alex Kyson was getting bloody hot under the stormtrooper helmet. He was a career criminal in his thirties, the sort of lad who lived in the sort of pubs where if you worked out and had a steady nerve in the back-room poker, you got offers to step over the line. Each step took you further, and hopefully none of the steps were anything you couldn't step back from. This bank job was the furthest he'd ever stepped. He knew blokes who'd turned it down, because they didn't trust the patron, but, as a result of how difficult recruiting for this gig had turned out to be, the patron had given him a little demonstration of what he could do, and from that moment, Alex was in. The stormtrooper bit had been his idea, the sort of flourish that got you talked about by the right blokes, got you into the true-crime books. It had been going great, apart from that unexpectedly helpful bank worker, but now the timeline was getting a bit dodgy.

He leaned heavily on the barricade, glancing back to the hostages every now and then to make sure they were busily texting away. That phone call coming so early was worrying. It wasn't as if it could have been someone calling about their mortgage: all the regular calls to the building would have been blocked. He looked to the doorway that led to the stairwell down to the safe deposit vault. That was the direction from which salvation would come, and it was meant to be coming soon.

'You reckon the boss has burned us?' said Van, his Dutch accent making the concept sound almost gentle, even through the helmet.

'We don't have any reason to start thinking like that. Not yet.' He looked back to the front door and saw through the glass that a figure was standing outside, a small woman in a business suit. She had her hands up.

'More negotiations?'

'Let her in.' They could buy time by talking.

Van did as he was told. With the other stormtroopers covering the move, a slight, smart woman was pulled inside the building and over to the barricade and the doors locked again behind her.

She regarded Alex with a sighing detachment. 'Aren't you a little short for a stormtrooper?'

Alex stifled a laugh. 'Who are you, then?'

'Metropolitan Police Detective Superintendent Rebecca Lofthouse. I believe I used the *Star Wars* quote wrongly, though.'

Alex knew his movies. 'I don't think so.'

From behind him, he heard the sound of doors swinging open. He looked over his shoulder to see that every bank worker he'd had chucked into one of those offices was now standing or crouching, holding in firing postures the guns he hadn't found, because, having planned to leave these guys with their phones, he'd had no call to search them. The odd one out was the cooperative one, who was standing back with their inside woman. The shooters had the drop on every one of his men.

Alex also knew that plastic stormtrooper armour wouldn't protect him and his team from real-life gunfire. He swung back to cover Lofthouse.

Her sigh had become a benevolent smile. 'I mean,' she said, 'that *I'm* here to rescue *you*.'

Ballard felt the second lock give and heaved out its mechanism. Where were the others? They should have achieved their targets and returned by now. It wouldn't be long before they'd have to go fetch the stormtroopers and get them out down here, the final move in the trick, like pulling the tools out of the bottle in which he'd made this elegant model ship. It was always the fucking *people* that let you down. He'd finish this, then go to help them. He pulled the crowbar from his coat, shoved the sharpened end into the third lock and started to throw his weight against it.

Mitch Daniels, who was enough of an old jailbird to have taken this job because it didn't have 'business as usual' written all over it, looked over his shoulder from his second target safe deposit box, also one of the walk-in ones, as Tony appeared, a lever-arch file, presumably the contents of one of the smaller boxes, in his hands.

'You had a look inside?' Mitch asked with a laugh. He hadn't done so with the similar file he'd found in the box he'd already opened, but he'd been tempted. More things in heaven and earth, my son. Who'd have thought it?

'Nah. Want a hand?'

'No, this one was bloody open.' He indicated by swinging the door back and forth. 'That could be bad news, if they was transferring stuff when we came in. Won't be a sec.' Mitch ducked inside the small metal room and went to the sack that lay in one corner. The top of the sack was open.

'Best take a look, then,' said Tony.

Mitch laughed again and pulled open the sack. He looked inside. Nothing. He looked up, with a sudden sinking feeling inside him, to see Tony coldly meeting his gaze as he swung the door closed.

Ballard marched into his target safe deposit box. There, sitting in the middle of the floor, exactly as he'd seen it in his mind's eye, was a golden goblet. He squatted and picked it up. His heart sank as he realized something was very wrong. The paint on the goblet was flecked. It wasn't made of gold, or even metal. He plucked at a bit of it. This thing was made of . . . *papier mâché*!

'Here's one we made earlier,' said a voice from behind him.

Ballard spun round, panting, his hand going into the pocket of his jacket. Stepping into the metal room was a rumpled white man in his mid-forties. He wore a suit that looked like he'd slept in it, and his eyes had a terrifying lack of moderation. Ballard found himself taking a step back. It had been decades since he'd met anyone he hadn't immediately felt able to take on. This bloke, though, had seen shit, and was only just holding on. Ballard now had his hand on something he could use to attack, but had no faith in his ability to get away with it. He'd heard whispers that the Met now had someone like this. 'Who are you?'

'To quote your mates in the other building, Luke Skywalker . . . I'm your daddy.'

Ballard realized he could hear the sound of running boots, converging on this place. If he was going to get out, it had to be now. He threw out his hand towards the man, ripping the air straight at him, making the wall of the metal box boom with the impact.

The man staggered, but to Ballard's astonishment, leaped

forwards again, unharmed. Before Ballard could find another weapon, one fist went into his stomach, and another smacked him sidelong across the jaw, and the next thing he knew he was lying in unaccustomed pain, brought down for the first time since he was a kid, staring up at the figure who was now squatting above him, his hands on him, actually going into his jacket, actually touching him. He tried to move, but was slammed back down and cried out in pain.

'My name,' said the man, 'is Detective Inspector James Quill. You do not have to say anything, but it may harm your defence if you do not mention, when questioned . . .'

Ballard realized he was being arrested. He wanted to bellow at the man, to sob, to say he would rather fucking die. He ground his teeth together and made himself breathe. 'How did you know?'

Quill didn't even smile. He finished the caution. 'The force has been with you,' he said. 'Always.'

TWO

The next morning, Detective Constable Kevin Sefton drove into work with hope in his heart. He had the car radio on, expecting to hear, as the lead item on the news, about the bank raid his team had foiled. That'd be an obvious continuation of the narrative of success that the Metropolitan Police was feeding to the population in press release after press release, and to be fair, backing up with a surprising number of results, high-profile crimes being solved all over the place. The public, it was felt, had to be reassured that the summer of riots was behind them, that order was being restored. His team in particular had needed this big success. They'd needed something to save the other three from their brooding silences, the accusatory looks, the anger that the Ripper case had left them with. Sefton was annoyed, therefore, to find the news reports leading with a story that had been brewing for the last couple of days: the '*Study in Scarlet* murder'. A man called Christopher Lassiter had been found dead in his home in Brixton, apparently poisoned, the word 'Rache' written on the wall in blood other than his own.

'I'm just someone who makes television,' said a plummy voice Sefton recognized. He turned up the volume on his car radio and heard it identified as Gilbert Flamstead, the actor who played the BBC's Sherlock Holmes. 'The three of us, myself, Alice and Ben—'

'The three actors who play Sherlock Holmes? I heard you got together now you're all filming in London at the same time. Do you have a message for the murderer?'

'No. We *don't*.'

'So you refuse to condemn the killing?' Typical bloody journalist. Sefton had always liked Flamstead: too smart ever to give a quote that didn't have some side to it; horny as fuck. The idea of him getting together for drinks with Alice Cassell, who played the US TV version of Sherlock Holmes, which was normally set in Los Angeles, but was also filming three episodes in London at the moment, and with Ben Speake, the Shakespearean actor who was the star of a series of knockabout comedy Sherlock Holmes movies out of Hollywood, the latest of which was also filming in London now, to talk about the murder . . . well, he saw why the news was leading with this, but come on, at this length? Bank raiders actually caught, *Star Wars*, all that?

'Being just some bloke, I do not have the *authority* to condemn the killing. I feel desperately sorry for Mr Lassiter's family. I never want murders to happen. OK?'

A week ago, the same media outlets had been saying that 'Holmesmania' had been 'gripping the capital', with groups of fans of each of the three versions location-hunting across London and gathering to scream at a press call with all three actors in deerstalkers. (Flamstead and Cassell had been rolling their eyes at theirs, which their characters never wore.) The media had immediately made the connection: 'Rache' had also been scrawled on the wall in blood in the first Holmes novel.

Sefton had followed the case distantly, certain SC&O1 would have someone they fancied for it and were just taking the time they needed to put the case together. If killers, in the wake of the Ripper murders this summer, had taken to scrawling things on walls again, especially in what could well be their own blood, so much the better, because it provided an immediate supply of DNA.

The next item on the news was something about an injury to

a footballer. The foiled bank raid was mentioned fourth, by which point Sefton was making amazed gestures at the radio. He sank back in his seat as he heard the bare details. It all sounded kind of puny now. Damn it. He'd been hoping this small success would be the hammer he needed to start fixing his friends.

'Wasn't that great?' Sefton, trying to project a sense of pride and accomplishment, strode into the Portakabin across the road from Gipsy Hill police station. This served as the ops room for the four-person team that everyone in the Met who didn't work at Gipsy Hill assumed were an elite unit. 'Successful operation.' He gestured at the makeshift ops board made of cork. Every point on the operational objectives list had been circled as having been achieved. 'Suspect in custody, being left to stew, waiting until we officially offer him a deal, because his team thoroughly ratted on him. We're saying to the Met mainstream, "Hey, our existence is justified, here's a crime you can understand, and oh, by the way, it's solved." What could be better?'

The three other members of his team were standing apart from one another, looking off in different directions, like they were an indie band posing for an album cover. They all looked as if they had a long list of things that could be better.

Sefton sighed. Costain and Ross he could understand. They'd had a relationship, and, because of an extraordinary betrayal of trust by Costain, it had fallen apart. Costain looked guilty; he moved guilty; he seemed angry with himself about that guilt, all the time. Ross, on the other hand, had frozen. Through occult means, in a fruitless attempt to get hold of something that might be able to free her dead father from Hell, she had sacrificed her future happiness, lost the basic ability to feel joy. Sometimes she'd pause for long moments after she was asked a question, as if the effort of answering might be too much. She and Costain came in every morning and didn't speak to each other.

Ross had recently been away for a week, taking a training course in statement analysis at the Dallas police academy. She'd been doing a lot of that, upskilling to be more of a tactical analyst, putting the team first as they got more and more into the detail of the London occult underworld. When she'd got back, Sefton had asked her about Dallas, what it had been like to be in a city where the Sight didn't work. Surely, he'd asked, it must have been a relief to get a break? The look on Ross's face as she'd just shrugged had told him that for her, there was no longer any such thing as a break.

Those two Sefton might have been able to deal with, had it not been for Jimmy. Detective Inspector James Quill, immediately following a vastly successful operation, was currently rubbing his face, as if he was again dealing with a vast anger that Sefton had seen too much lately. He'd literally gone to Hell, and Sefton understood the fear that sometimes crossed his boss's face, the stress that made him jerk at an unexpected sound. However, Sefton couldn't shake the feeling there was something more to Quill's pain. It was as if, for Quill, looking at the rest of them these days made his stress worse. A couple of times, when he'd been alone with Sefton, he'd started to say something and then stopped himself. It was as if he carried knowledge he couldn't share, despite having briefed the rest of them on all the details of Hell. Whatever his secret was, it was a burden.

OK, then. Moving forward. 'We need to start looking for a new operation,' said Sefton. 'We need to at least start working out what we want to ask Ballard.'

There was silence again. Nobody knew where to start. Nobody wanted to be here.

Sefton walked with Lofthouse down the corridor that led to her office in Gipsy Hill police station. He was grateful as always that the four of them tended to get immediate access to their boss.

'It's not like Quill's not talking,' she said. 'He told me about what he saw in Hell. Dear God.' She led him in and closed the door behind them. 'I debriefed Quill about Operation Dante – and now it occurs to me that he named the bank job that and

I never even called him on it.' She put her hand on her desk as if to steady herself. Was Sefton wrong, or was there a burden on her shoulders too? Of all of them, their boss should be the one with the least tension, not having the Sight herself, but benefiting from their success, getting good word of mouth across the Met, but . . . no, this was also someone who wasn't sleeping too well.

He waited for her to sit before doing so himself. 'I wanted to, ma'am.' He had something big to ask of her, and he felt the need for formality. 'Thing is, in the old days he kept up such a brave face I thought maybe it was a good thing he'd made a joke out of it.'

'Such jokes do not ease his pain now, though, do they?'

'That's what I wanted to meet with you about, ma'am. This unit might have just had a major success as far as the mainstream Met is concerned, making it, I'm sure, a lot easier for you to defend our funding, but I can't see how we can go forward. I can't see how we're going to work together again. Dante basically fell into our laps. We separated into our specialities, and we didn't have to interact much beyond stuff we'd done a hundred times before. The next time something from *our* world comes along, something that pushes us, that demands we rely on each other . . . excuse my French, ma'am, but' – and there went the formality – 'we'll be fucked.'

'I had rather begun to realize all the above myself. Do you have some new options for me?'

Sefton took a deep breath. 'You've been helping us all this time without sharing the experiences that got us here. You believe us when we tell you about impossible things. You've asked us not to question you about it. Clearly you know something about hidden London. Clearly you knew the Continuing Projects Team, the guys who, we presume, used to be our sort of law in this town.' He remembered the personnel file with her name on it they'd found in the ruins of the CPT's headquarters in Docklands. Since then, Lofthouse had refused, incredibly, to discuss the matter with them. Quill had said she'd intimated that was the price of her continuing to let them operate. 'We're at the end of our tether, ma'am. Anything you can add to our knowledge would help.'

Lofthouse closed her eyes.

'It's time for you to come clean with us, ma'am.'

He thought for a moment that she was going to yell at him, but no. She was fighting some internal battle. Finally, she managed to look at him again. 'Do you know,' she asked, 'when the temple building you found in Docklands was destroyed?'

Sefton felt bemused at this sudden turn. She sounded like she didn't know. Which was contrary to what he'd assumed about her involvement with the CPT. 'We can only say it was after a certain date, five years ago, when the records cease. Everyone who talks about the old law says the CPT seem to have stopped presiding over London around then.'

'I gather, from what you've all told me about previous operations,' said Lofthouse, 'that it must take a great deal of energy and concentration on someone's part to make everybody forget the Continuing Projects Team?'

'That's correct. We haven't been able to discover anything else about them. It's like they've been erased from history, except for their pictures, left at the site, we think, as a demonstration of that power.'

'Right.' She seemed to have decided something, but it wasn't a pleasant decision. From the look on her face, it meant a whole world of tough choices. 'That'll be all, Detective Constable.'

Sefton was amazed. 'But—'

She gave him a look that dared him to make her repeat herself.

When Sefton had left, Rebecca Lofthouse let out a long breath and put both hands on her desk. She did the breathing exercises to make herself calm, the ones she'd been using since just before she'd visited Quill's team in Docklands, when they'd been exploring the ruins of the 'temple' of the Continuing Projects Team. That had been the point when horror had entered her life.

That horror had known what she was going to discover when she visited them. She had already made attempts to do something about her situation: slightly; quietly. She'd thought she'd moved covertly, but if, as she'd been told during the Russell Vincent case, MI5 had noticed what she'd been up to, then, she was sure, so could the terrible power that was watching over her.

Now things had to change. Sefton's visit had crystallized a feeling she'd had herself. For the sake of James Quill and his team, she had to start taking some risks.

A week later, at the end of another working day that had been devoted to tidying up the loose ends of Operation Dante, Quill stopped his car outside his semi-detached house in Enfield and shut off the engine. He hesitated, as always these days, before going inside. He just needed to take a moment, to prepare for the role he had to play at home. He had to appear to be a jolly daddy for Jessica and reassure the continually worried Sarah that he was OK.

It's everyone who ever lived in London.

That was what the sign above the entrance to Hell had said. He saw it in his memories every day. He had so many questions. He worried about what that meant in practice. He'd seen, in Hell, people from all time periods. Did 'everyone' include visitors to London? Was one night at a Holiday Inn in Clapham enough to sentence you to eternal damnation? Better act like that was the case. Some of those in Hell had thought, in their confused way, that there'd been other sorts of afterlife before, that this was a recent change. Could it change back?

He hadn't told anyone. He couldn't bring himself to. On his journey home tonight, he'd seen the usual horrors of hidden London. They seemed obvious now, meaningless. They were nothing compared to what was waiting.

He got out of the car, went and unlocked his front door, and when he heard Jessica calling from inside, he made himself not think about what the things in Hell would do to her. He made himself not think, as he did, over and over, that there was nothing he could do to prevent it. Instead, he forced himself to smile.

'Laura called.' Sarah had that expression on her face again as they made dinner: busy, happy engagement. It was one she'd held on to for weeks. When Quill had first come back to life, had literally returned from Hell, she'd waited for a while, then had gently begun asking lots of questions, trying to get him to talk. He'd burst into tears, the first time, then yelled at her to stop. The tears hadn't come back, but the yelling had. Over the weeks, her questions had fallen away, and she was now being supportive, hoping he'd come to her. She would wait forever. He was angry all the time. He was full of fight or flight, waiting, every moment, for a blow that might kill him, might send him to Hell again. He had thought he was brave. He wasn't. His depression . . . well, he didn't know where that began and actual sanity ended now, because now there genuinely *was* no future. The previous evening, she'd carefully asked him about the end of the operation, and he'd done what he'd started to do instead of yelling, played the part of himself to talk to her, talked about how pleased the team all were.

'Oh,' he said now, 'how's she doing?'

Laura was Sarah's sister, who lived in Inverness and worked in computers. Quill had known her, when he'd first met Sarah, as Derek. There had been an awkward phone call before the wedding. 'Mate, listen, I've got a favour to ask. I want to come to the wedding as . . . OK, this is complicated, so I'm just going to say it. I'm having a sex change. That's not what they call it these days, but that's what I call it. By the time the wedding comes round, I'm going to be living as a woman. Is that OK?'

Quill had thought for a moment that Derek had been joking, but no. 'Does Sarah know?'

'Not yet. I wanted to talk to you first.'

'It sounds,' Quill had said, 'like you and I are going to need a few pints of therapy.'

When they went out, Quill had asked loads of questions, as coppers did, interested in someone who was doing such an extraordinary thing. He'd had a bit of awareness training back in the day, but this was a mate. Derek had finally told Sarah everything. Sarah had been angry about Derek talking to Quill first, but Quill had seen the situation as a sign that he was getting on with her family, and had talked and talked about it, to the point where the siblings had told him he could stop. He'd made sure Laura, as she now was, was welcome at the wedding.

Now, they went out for a pint when Laura was in London, though Laura's capacity for alcohol had declined a bit, and largely talked about Scottish soccer, of which Laura had an extraordinary knowledge. Every now and then, though, Laura would, a bit deliberately, move the conversation to wider topics, in a way that Derek hadn't. Quill had got the feeling she'd been freed, and did his best to join in, though there were times he wanted to say that maybe Sarah should have come along too. He'd started to refer to her, a couple of pints in, as his 'best mate', which she probably was now that Harry had gone, but at one point, Laura had corrected him and said, 'Best *friend*?' Quill had nodded. So he now had a best friend who wore dresses and make-up, and sometimes tried to get him to appreciate fabrics. He hadn't seen her since he'd got the Sight, and the idea of going out with her and talking about her stuff and not at all about the depth of shit he'd got lost in seemed like it could be a blessed relief.

'She's fine,' said Sarah. 'She's had a promotion. She's coming down at the weekend.'

'Great.' There was that momentary ache about the possibility that the sign over Hell's doorway also referred to visitors to London, but no, he could choose not to believe that.

'Yeah,' said Sarah. 'She's house-hunting. She's moving to London.'

In his tiny flat above a shop in Walthamstow, Kev Sefton had finally managed to get to sleep, his boyfriend, Joe, snoring soundly as always beside him. The background noise of London at night strayed in through the window, which was still open, just about, the first cool of autumn making the curtain flap.

Sefton was dreaming tension dreams, his legs working at the duvet. Behind his eyes, he was looking up into the pleading face of . . . It wasn't quite the actor who played Sherlock Holmes, with the posh accent and the dextrous fingers. Sefton knew, in the way one knows things in dreams, that this was no actor; this was something from the heart of London itself, something with the weight that sometimes crashes into dreams. This man had crashed in, desperate, panting, and was scrabbling at Sefton's shirt, not trying to get it off – this wasn't going to be that sort of dream, no matter what his mind tried to make it. The man was trying to make Sefton understand something. Oh, it was Sherlock Holmes, the real Sherlock Holmes! (Was Sherlock Holmes real?) He needed him; he was crying out. Sefton couldn't understand what he was saying. He was desperate; he was looking for help. The man turned and ran, down darkening streets, streets full of fog, shadows suddenly falling over him. Sefton pursued him. He ran round a corner and collided with . . . with nothing. There was a gap, a gap where Sherlock Holmes should be, a gap in the air!

Sefton fell through it and found himself *falling—*

He woke up with a start, tense, his arms still flailing. Joe mumbled something beside him. Sefton let his breathing slow. When he'd been an undercover, he'd grown used to that sort of dream. He'd ignored them as obvious, not indicative, but now he was on the path to being . . . something else, something he didn't have a name for, now he was always looking into the fine detail of hidden London, trying to find ways to leverage it for his team, maybe he should start paying more attention to what his unconscious was saying. He got out of bed and rubbed his forehead. What had that dream said? That Sherlock Holmes had gone. Well, you could interpret that as saying there was something missing in terms of the law. The dream could have been about the way Lofthouse had hustled him out of that meeting without providing him with anything that could help his friends.

No, that was reading it like someone in a magazine advice column would read it, adding one too many layers of awake interpretation. The dream had said Sherlock Holmes had gone. A fictional character had . . . Oh, oh, now, wait a sec.

Sefton went into the other room and found the holdall in which he kept all the gubbins he experimented with that was 'very London'. He was hoping that soon Ballard's collection would be added to it, if they could make a deal with him. All those lovely items yelling with the Sight that they'd found on him, all out of Sefton's reach now, in evidence boxes. Sefton found a pendulum made of lead from a Roman sewer. He swung it gently. Sefton had been pondering, lately, what it was about the London-ness of an object that could possibly lead to it having any sort of power. It was ancient thinking, against science, that mere association could alter a physical object. So far, everything his team had found, while mind-boggling, had surrendered to rationality, in the end. Some sort of reason, some sort of natural law, must work for hidden London, or they wouldn't have got as far as they had with the business of deduction, with logic. It was still their only way to salvation.

He found a map of the Underground, unfolded it and spread it out on the carpet. He held the pendulum above it and let it swing. He closed his eyes, feeling for the tiniest deviation from the lean of the floor, and was sure, after a moment, that he felt something. He'd done this many times before, in many locations, to establish a norm. He always sat in the same way, programming his muscle memory to feel when there was any influence on the pendulum. Now there was something that was making his body recall that lurch in the dream, that moment of falling, as if . . . something or someone was indeed missing from London. He opened his eyes and watched the pendulum slowly subsiding and . . . glitching, by the tiniest jerk every time. He folded the paper several times, each time starting the lead swinging again, each time watching as it swung towards the same general area, until he thought, Yeah, it's pretty obvious where I should go, isn't it?

He grabbed some clothes and went to find his car keys.

Baker Street was still busy close to midnight, with people wandering from the Greek nightclub down the road, street sweepers clearing up, deliveries being made, the cold and the neon in the dark making Sefton think of approaching winter. The Sherlock Holmes Museum, which was actually at 237–41 Baker Street, but said 221B on the door, was a couple of shopfronts along from a pub called the Volunteer, which had only night lights on, the staff clearing up.

Sefton had never been here before. The museum itself was a neat little frontage with Victorian lamps, a sign, a blue plaque visible beside a balcony on the second floor. It was so obviously artificial on this big, busy, modern street, a house conversion the fictional aspects of which dated back only to 1990, the point at which it had been decided that the chance to make a profit should take precedence over the reality. From Sefton's Sighted point of view, it was like the mass consciousness of London had demanded the building exist.

There was, thank God, a single light burning on a higher floor, otherwise, he realized, he'd have no way of getting in. He went and rang the doorbell, several times, and when a face appeared at the window above, he held up his warrant card.

The interior of the museum was exactly what he'd expected, a ticket booth followed by a narrow staircase, with captions pointing out exactly how authentic every piece of bric-a-brac was. Sefton felt uneasy as one of the assistant curators, a petite young woman with a ponytail, who identified herself as Ann Stanley, led him upstairs to 'Holmes's flat' on the first floor. Clean-up today, she'd told him, had taken longer than usual, so, exhausted, she'd made use of the small room the museum kept for staff to stay over. This was the sort of building Sefton and his team were getting used to exploring, with every detail of its history shouting at them because they had the Sight. Only, this one had been designed that way for ordinary people and had nothing of the actual Sight about it. No real home, even of an eccentric Victorian detective, would have this much significant detail. They'd laid it out like nobody ever threw anything out or cleaned up. The items on display were props, fakes. That was why it all felt so . . . nauseating, to someone with the Sight. None of these items sang with it as they should. The house felt . . . vulnerable, compromised, as if by laying out all these things that should have the weight of the Sight to them, it was inviting something terrible to happen that would lend them that property for real.

The curator unlocked and let him into the 'consulting room', asking lots of questions, which suddenly Sefton couldn't hear, because now all his attention was taken up with what was in the centre of the room. Between a settee and a bearskin hearthrug there lay the body of a man. He wore a deerstalker and one of those short capes. He lay on his back, one arm stretched out in what looked like a helpless plea towards the smaller of two desks in the corners of the room. Sticking out of his chest was a straight knife with some sort of decoration on the blade. The weapon tugged at Sefton with the gravity of the Sight. It was the only thing here that did. Around the body had formed a pool of blood.

'What's that knife doing there?' asked the curator, puzzled. She obviously couldn't see the body, or her reaction would have been much more urgent.

Sefton dared to take a step nearer and looked down into the face of the dead man only he could see, a face that was changing, shifting, continuously as Sefton watched. This was what had suddenly gone missing from London. His dream hadn't required any interpretation. He was at a crime scene, and the crime was the murder of Sherlock Holmes.

THREE

It took little persuasion for the curator to accept that this was a crime scene. She'd seen enough procedural TV shows to understand that evidence could be invisible to the naked eye, and the knife in the floor had startled her. Everything had been normal, she said, when she'd locked up this room at around 11 p.m. Sefton got her to call her bosses, which meant her leaving a message on their answerphone. That was perfect, because it meant that, in the early hours, after first Quill and then Ross and Costain had arrived, and Sefton had interviewed the curator, taken her contact details and sent her home, the team had the place to themselves.

Quill stared at the body, as if this was some mad joke being played on him. He looked, if possible, more burdened than ever. Before Sefton could ask if something had happened, he was all business. 'Is he solid?'

'No, Jimmy.' Sefton demonstrated, sticking the toe of his shoe right through the body's head. They all knew that the 'ghosts' formed by London 'remembering' a real or fictional character had varying degrees of solidity. This time, they couldn't examine the corpse, couldn't even turn it over. Sefton had already taken a lot of photos, using his phone, then checked that, to a Sighted person, the body did show up in them. The image of the body was still multifaceted, changing as you looked at it, changing with the angle. It was, Sefton had realized, a combination of all the different Sherlocks, all the different actors, including Speake, Flamstead and Cassell, loads he didn't recognize, some in modern dress, many wearing the deerstalker and cape, which thus had a regular shape compared to the flickering of the rest of the image, and also a sort of pencilled version, which Sefton realized must be the strong memory created by the original illustrator of the Holmes stories, whose name Sefton couldn't remember. That added a flavour that, after a moment, he realized reminded him of an ancient A-ha pop video. That thought had led to him filming the body on his phone, until he was sure he'd caught the full cycle of incarnations as they flickered by.

'No habeas corpus, then,' said Ross, which might have been a joke except there was, as ever, no humour in her expression.

'How is this even possible?' asked Costain, who looked like he might have wanted to make a few dark jokes himself, but was, as always now, restraining every expression of who he was for Ross's sake.

'Well,' said Sefton, who'd had a while to think about this, 'if you mean "How is there a Sherlock Holmes?", then I think it's obvious that there would be, or was, in our version of London. London remembers things that happened, but like we saw with the "most haunted house" at Berkeley Square, it equally remembers stuff that was just made up. Sherlock Holmes: a very popular fictional character with a huge link to London. A lot of people even think he's real.'

'There's been "Holmesmania", with the three versions filming at once in town, getting everyone thinking about it,' said Ross. 'It's actually kind of obvious he'd be one of our "ghosts".'

'If you mean "How do you kill a ghost?"' Sefton continued, 'you've got me there.'

'Why haven't we seen him before?' Costain had stepped closer to the body.

'Where's he associated with?' said Ross, a rhetorical question, talking to herself, though Costain had looked up hopefully for a moment at the thought she might actually have addressed him. 'Just this building. The ghost of Jack the Ripper was in Whitechapel. Every other place associated with Sherlock Holmes . . . Is it Dartmoor in *The Hound of the Baskervilles*?'

'Yeah,' said Quill, 'and there's the Reichenbach Falls, wherever that is.'

'Not in London,' said Ross.

'Yeah, I fucking knew that,' said Quill, startling her. Then he visibly chided himself. 'Sorry.'

Sefton found himself frowning. That wasn't the Quill he knew. He'd hoped . . . but later for that.

Costain was shaking his head, like he fundamentally didn't believe what he was seeing. 'Ghost body, but not a ghost weapon.' He gently tapped the dagger with the toe of his shoe.

Sefton nodded. 'To kill a ghost, you'd need a special weapon, and that'd have to be a real object. Makes sense.'

Ross stepped to the edge of the blood pool and, with a reluctance born of many tangible crime scenes, put her finger in the liquid. 'Blood isn't real,' she said. She stepped into it to squat by the blade, and waved aside the start of a warning from Quill. 'We can't disturb something that isn't there. This weapon, though, is solid evidence.' She took out her phone to take some closer photos of what Sefton had initially taken for decoration, but now could make out as a tiny row of what looked like stick men, engraved on the blade. 'There's an obvious question here: is this coincidental to the *Study in Scarlet* murder, or some sort of weird copycat case, or is there a link?'

'You said you felt like something had gone missing from London,' Quill said to Sefton. 'That Holmes came to you in a dream. Did someone do this? Is this murder?'

'Now we're wondering if ghosts commit suicide,' murmured Costain, as if someone had to say it.

'What do you mean, Jimmy?' asked Sefton. He didn't like that sound in Quill's voice, familiar from his own experience.

He was used to the voices of organized crime network bosses, that edgy mix of authority and paranoia.

'I mean, maybe it's London saying something to us. Maybe this is, you know, symbolic.'

'That's the first time I have ever heard you use that word,' said Costain. He was looking as uneasy as Sefton was, trying to find some banter here.

Quill slowly shook his head. 'The death of Sherlock Holmes? He's deduction; he's the idea you can . . . you know, pick apart something that's happened, find meaning to it, solve it. Maybe we're getting to the end of that being possible. Maybe soon nothing'll mean anything.' He suddenly, artificially, laughed, as if he'd realized how unlike his old self he sounded. 'Cheerful thought, actually. Then we can retire. Go somewhere nice.' His smile faded again.

Ross made an audible clicking sound with her tongue, as if adding an annoyed full stop to an idea she wasn't willing to entertain. She got out her notebook. 'I'm going to start recording all the details,' she said, as if Quill hadn't spoken. 'What about the rest of the room?'

Sefton was glad of her moving things on. He took the evidence gloves from his pocket and put them on, which made Costain and finally Quill do that too. They examined the crime scene. Sefton had taken it to be undisturbed, but they swiftly found quite a few worrying changes to what the guidebook photo indicated was the norm. It was hard to see, but on one of the walls was drawn, in chalk, an upright rectangle, as if someone was planning to build a doorway there. 'Look at this,' said Costain. 'Like Ballard used to get into the bank.'

'So other people have something that can do that,' said Sefton. 'That speaks of a suspect leaving the scene. Oh, wait a sec.' He made a phone call and checked quickly with some bemused officers on night shift, finding that Ballard was still in his cell and his piece of chalk was safe and sound in evidence. No, he hadn't drawn anything on the cell wall.

'The things,' sighed Costain, 'we have to worry about.' They went back to work.

In front of the grate of the fireplace, there was a strange, rather theatrical shoe, bigger than anyone could comfortably wear, with faded blue, gold and red details, the toe of which was upturned. There was a hole in it, and from its side had poured a trail of what, with a sniff and the withholding of a sneeze, Sefton identified as tobacco. A pile of the stuff, beside it, had been formed into a spiral shape.

'Bloody spiral,' said Quill, sounding suddenly like he'd solved the case.

Ross immediately came over and said it didn't look anything like the spiral patterns the witch Mora Losley had left behind her in their first case together, and besides, those had been made of soil. She sounded like she wanted to add that Quill should have already noted those things.

'That'd be a Persian slipper,' said Costain, looking at the guidebook and diverting Quill from Ross's glare.

The hole in said footwear looked like it had been cut. Sefton took a picture. As he did so, he glanced up and noticed something else. On the mantelpiece above the fireplace, there was a drawing of a woman in Victorian costume. There was something about her eyes. He stood and looked more closely. They'd each had the tiniest of pinpricks made in them. It made it look like the woman's gaze was following you, but in a disturbing, askew way. Under the drawing was a caption: 'Irene Adler.' Sefton pointed the holes out to Ross, who was now writing at high speed. 'The woman in Holmes's life,' said Costain.

'You ever read any of the stories?' asked Sefton.

'When I was a kid. She's in a lot of the films and TV shows, isn't she?'

Beside the photograph, a large knife was embedded in the mantelpiece. It had caught Sefton's gaze on his first inspection of the room, but it was pictured in the guidebook, so he gathered it was a feature of the room as it should be. It held a bundle of letters, with the 221B address at the top of the first one. Sefton leafed through them and noticed something. 'Here, look at this.'

The others gathered round. Only the first two letters were complete, the top one being an appeal for help from someone who'd lost their cat, the second one a letter from someone complaining to Holmes about the noise of his violin playing. Both of them had a series of tiny holes punched in them, sometimes cutting out letters from words, sometimes not. The holes were also present in the blank sheets that made up the rest of the pile, not going through from the letters above them, but cut out in different patterns, after which they must have been put back under the knife.

'What the living fuck?' said Costain. He was shaking his head. He checked the guide again, but couldn't find any reference to this being something from one of the Holmes stories. Sefton let his gaze drift to the right and realized that what he'd thought was a globe of the world was something entirely different. On top of another cabinet in the corner, beside lots of objects that were souvenirs of particular cases, sat what had once been – he took the guide from Costain and checked – a wax bust of Holmes's head. However, it was now just about unrecognizable. The features had been melted, the eyes now streaks of colour down the pale face, the nose a stalactite connecting to the wood below. Sefton reached out and found no heat near it. Raising a hand to keep the others back, he put a finger on the wax itself. It wasn't even warm.

'We can get an expert opinion on that cooling,' said Ross, 'get a time frame.'

'The curator,' added Sefton, 'said everything was normal at eleven p.m. That's the last time she looked in here. I had that dream . . . maybe five minutes later. I was here by midnight. Maybe the dream was actually the moment Holmes . . . "died"? He seemed to be desperately asking for help.'

'Over here,' said Ross, moving on. She was pointing to a

series of bullet holes in the wall, above a pile of books beside Holmes's desk, which formed the letters 'V.R.' 'I think *that's* an original feature.'

'It is,' said Sefton, consulting the guide.

'But this isn't.' She was pointing at a series of thin red lines that connected several of the holes, sometimes crossing each other. 'Looks like biro, not blood.' She moved lights to photograph the lines clearly. Her brow had furrowed into a look Sefton appreciated. She had seen several patterns now, and, though that brought her no pleasure, for both her and the rest of them that was equivalent to her having seen a lock to which she would surely subsequently find keys.

'What's he pointing at?' said Quill, who had kept glancing back at the body.

Indeed, now Sefton looked closely, the outstretched hand was flickering through some gestures that resembled pointing. He looked up in the same direction as Quill and found the smaller desk in the corner opposite, with pictures of two men above it, one in military uniform, the other a man of proud appearance with white hair whipped back from his brow like a mad composer.

'General Gordon, a contemporary of Holmes, died in a siege in the Sudan, and Henry Ward Beecher, an American anti-slavery preacher,' said Costain, consulting the guidebook. 'Or, as I suppose we can now refer to them, suspects.'

'What was he working on?' Quill had wandered to Holmes's own desk, to the left of which was pinned a map of the night sky, a diagram of the solar system and an astronomical photo of lots of stars.

'He wasn't *working on* anything,' said Ross; 'he's a fictional character in a museum. His ghost might have *looked* like it was working on something, but nothing remembered by London has . . . agency, volition.'

'And yet,' said Quill, 'those charts and that photo aren't in the guidebook. And you just made an assumption based only on the limited amount of shit we've seen.'

Ross looked relieved to be corrected. She glanced to Sefton. This was definitely more like the Quill they knew. 'Yes, boss.'

Quill unpinned the astronomical map, diagram and photo, and inspected them more closely. On the back of the photo was something that made him call them over to see. In an elegant, precise hand, there was written:

The ultimate crime. I must solve it.

'That,' said Sefton, 'would be a motive for murder. Holmes got too close to something.'

'Considering all the books and stuff,' said Costain, 'what would he think of as "ultimate"?'

Ross was looking annoyed again. 'I can't get used to the idea of him "thinking",' she said. 'If he was, that's such an anomaly it must mean something.'

'Maybe a ghost like Holmes *would* work on crimes,' said Sefton. 'That's what he was remembered for.' He checked the handwriting on his phone against what Google could find. 'Quite a few people have had a go at doing Holmes's handwriting. They all look a bit like that, but we sort of know what his writing would look like, don't we?'

'Where's Watson?' said Costain.

Sefton wanted to smack himself on the forehead. The sheer density of information in this murder room made seeing what was right in front of you bloody difficult. 'Yeah, good point. If Holmes was well known enough to be a ghost, and pinned down to this location, wouldn't Watson be too?'

'Probably,' said Ross. 'Damn it. I *hate* "probably".'

They all took a closer, Sighted look around the room, Sefton remembering what Costain had said to him about how hard to find some of the Ripper victims' ghosts had been. Of Watson, however, there was no sign.

'The curious case,' said Costain, 'of the Watson who wasn't there.'

'Moriarty,' said Ross, seemingly the instant the idea came to her. 'Got to be suspect number one, surely? If you ask anybody the question "Who killed Sherlock Holmes?", that's the answer you'll get.'

'Maybe,' said Sefton. 'Except that Moriarty isn't as huge in the public imagination as Holmes is, and isn't linked to a London location. I don't think he'd have a ghost.'

'Wait a sec.' Quill had been looking off into the distance, the photo still in his hand. He was breathing hard, as if he'd just finished running. Sefton watched as Quill searched the desk beside the photo and found something else. 'I think this was sent to him,' he said. He picked up an empty envelope from the desk, compared the size of it to the photo and showed them the card backing. The stamps on the front were modern, and carried a London postmark. The letter was addressed to Sherlock Holmes at the famous address.

'He must get a lot of mail,' said Sefton. 'Some fictional characters do. I wonder where it's kept.'

'We need another word with that curator,' said Ross.

'Whoever killed Holmes,' said Ross, 'left a room full of deliberate clues. That's a strike against Moriarty. His big thing was that you wouldn't suspect he was a criminal, wasn't it? He took care *not* to leave clues.'

Sefton went back to the other side of the room, which held a bookcase containing volumes such as a reverse telephone directory, and several bound collections of Holmes's own monographs. Sefton opened one of them and was momentarily surprised to find the pages blank. These were, of course, like the letters, just props. There were some gaps in the rows of books. He looked on the desk for them, then around the room. He couldn't find them, and indicated that to the others.

Ross photographed the shelves and noted the placing of the gaps. 'Why would someone nick fake books?' she asked.

'Maybe it was an opportunist, robbery gone wrong,' said Costain. She looked incredulously at him, then realized he was joking and turned away, took a couple of steps away from him, angry at him all over again.

Sefton watched Costain's face fall; another small attempt to reach out, another indication that the connection between them had gone forever. He looked back to Quill, who was leaning on the wall, his expression far away. It was like he'd had an idea but he'd lost it.

Sefton was suddenly angry, with himself and with them. 'Don't just – don't *do* that!' he yelled. The others all turned to look at him. 'You've stepped right back into going through the motions, filling your roles, and that's great, that's what we should be doing, but if we keep doing only that, we will run ourselves into the ground, like you've already been doing for weeks now!'

'Kev—' began Quill, a sigh in his voice.

'But look at this, look at it! It got to you when you saw that handwriting, I know it did! That's Sherlock bloody Holmes lying dead right there! This is . . . This has to be a change in how London remembers stuff, if he doesn't just regenerate like a video game character or something like that. This is huge. Wait a sec.' He checked his evidence gloves weren't torn, marched over, looked to Ross to check what he was about to do was OK, and, a nod from her confirming that it was, pulled the blade from the flickering 'body'. He half expected Holmes to flash back into existence and become once again what he must have been before, the wraith of an idea haunting these chambers, but he didn't. Sefton straightened up and held the murder weapon high in the air. 'This is the ultimate murder mystery, and this room displays a ton of evidence. What more do you need to get excited about what only *we* do?! What more do you need to bloody snap out of it, work together and be . . . *us* again?!'

Costain was grinning at him, he realized, obviously relieved by what had been said, but still, Sefton was immediately a bit embarrassed at having made the closest to a stirring speech that he'd ever heard from anyone in the Met. 'Kev—'

'I mean it. Enough with the jokes from you.'

'No, I agree, and that's great, that's the best thing, but I just looked at the BBC news page.' He held up his phone. 'Another body's been found with "Rache" written on the wall. Do you want to say it or will I?'

'What?'

'Mate . . . the game is *afoot*.'

FOUR

The next morning, while still at home, Lofthouse got a call from Costain to go over the events of the previous night, and to ask her to help them get an in on what had now become the '*Study in Scarlet* murders', plural. Lofthouse had called up the DI on that operation, Anita Clarke, and, with much more ease than would previously have been the case, got Quill's team folded into the op. She wondered why Quill hadn't called her himself, but this morning she had other things to worry about, things she had kept secret from everyone. It was time for her to take action, but, above all, she had to do it without being noticed.

She'd already made her first move by checking out her own bank accounts online. It had been a lot more stealthy to do that than to make an appointment to go and see her account- ant, who held the paper versions. She'd had to contact the bank about seeing the older statements, and that had been more risky, but she'd now seen all the transactions from seven years ago, adding a margin of error to the five years Sefton had mentioned. She'd checked through them by area, looking for businesses and cashpoints in places she didn't usually go.

She'd realized something was wrong with her memories at the instant Quill's team had told her about her own name being on that empty folder recovered from those ruins in Docklands.

She'd been primed to discover something impossible, because just before she'd left . . . No, she didn't want to think about that terrible moment, about the first appearance in her life of the awful threat that still hung over her.

It was strange to speak of 'gaps' in one's memory, because surely one's memory was mostly gaps: one forgot almost everything one experienced, unless one made an effort to remember. That was why police officers kept records. If she had understood what Quill's team had told her about their experiences correctly, however, the process by which the memory of the Continuing Projects Team had been erased from the minds of all who knew them extended to people not being able to perceive records of the erased persons' existence. Quill and his people could see the ruins of the CPT's former headquarters, and a document that listed their names, with photos beside them. She herself, not having the Sight, of course could see neither. The sounds of their names, however, when read out to her, immediately haunted her. She *knew* she'd known them, she was *sure* of it, but there was simply no information in her mind to back up that gut feeling. The names seemed apt for them, but imparted no further layer of meaning: Sir Richard Chartres, RIBA, KCBE; Patrick Kennet-Fotherington, LLB; Felicity Saunders, permanent secretary; Adam Fletcher, senior producer current affairs; Rev. Michael Watson.

Even if she hadn't been got at before going down to Docklands, she would have been sure at that moment that to restore the memories of those people to her mind was the most important thing she could do to help Quill's team. However, got at she had been, so she had to do what she had to do now without Sefton's help. She so wanted to talk to him, to any of them, about what she was going through. Instead, she'd made the decision to keep up her poker face, to help them as she felt called to do, but also not to risk the most important thing in her life. The power that was watching her didn't seem to mind her helping Quill's team. That was frightening in itself.

Her bank accounts were not direct records of the existence of the forgotten people, so presumably hadn't been erased from all human memory. Therefore, she'd hoped they might provide her with indirect evidence of where she might have met with those people. She had been both troubled and excited to see that there were indeed two places in London where she seemed, five years ago and before, to have often been, without now remembering anything of it. Before she'd made that discovery, she'd made a few, limited, excursions to other places where she might have met people who matched those names, places to which it was not extraordinary for her to go: the Houses of Parliament; the BBC; the Inns of Court. She had walked randomly, hoping to find some clue, some smell even, that might ignite her memories. That slightly strange behaviour had been what the MI5 people had noticed. Her more fearsome watcher, however, didn't seem to have.

One of the odd places her bank accounts said she'd spent time in was Docklands, which was obvious. If she'd known the CPT, she'd have visited their headquarters. The other . . . the other was where she was going to go today. She left her house, raised a hand to her husband, who was standing at the window, a shadow on the glass, and headed to the car she'd ordered.

She got in and greeted the driver, let him pull out of her driveway and head for the M25. She looked carefully out of the windows, then turned urgently back to him. 'All right,' she said, 'we're not going to the meeting, and you're *not* going to call ahead to tell them I can't make it. OK?'

Lofthouse strode out of Golders Green Underground station at speed, feeling as off piste as she'd ever gone, a prey animal who had got away from the hunter. She spent a moment looking around, past the bus station, with its rows of double-deckers, to the clock tower and the three-storey shops. It was drizzling; a welcome cold was on the breeze. She'd hoped to recognize something. She did not.

She found the two different cashpoints from which she had made withdrawals, in that unknown dreamtime. There was nothing memorable about them, of course. Nor was there, and this had been a greater hope, about the two restaurants where she'd paid for meals. She went inside both, looked around, was asked by staff, who bloody obviously wouldn't remember a single customer from a single occasion five years ago, if she wanted an early lunch. She walked out in both cases without replying. She got out her map, wishing she could use her iPad, and worked out where the boundaries of the suburb could roughly be said to be. She headed north on the Finchley Road, all suburban houses and gardens. She was going to walk the leafy avenues, as far as it was possible to do so, in disciplined squares.

She had no idea what she was looking for. She'd asked James once or twice what having the Sight was like, and just from his descriptions of it, she felt blind now, blind and desperate. She was throwing the dice every moment she was here. Though she had no obligation to be there, the regular intelligence-sharing meeting she was meant to be attending right now might have already decided that it was unlike her not to show up and called her nick, who would call her mobile, which she of course had to keep switched off, and then, worried, call home. She could not, however, call the meeting to make excuses, or have anyone else in her circle call them. It was like one of those nightmares in which one was running with one's legs bound.

She looped eastwards towards the park, and after a while realized everything was becoming more Hampstead, and turned back towards the centre again. She marched up onto Golders Hill Park and looked down on the suburb, sheltering under a tree as the rain started to really come down. Meaningless green. Suburban nothing to do with her. There was something nearby, the map told her, called Leg of Mutton pond. Surely she would remember that? She didn't.

She went back down and headed off along Golders Green

Road itself, towards Brent Cross. She was getting more and more afraid, more certain every moment that she was going to be caught. She should run to Quill, or at least to Sefton, burst in on them and say they had to help her. But no, they would only have seconds to do so, because her unexpected arrival would be noticed. She couldn't take that risk. Every time she thought about the threat that had been made, she reeled inside at the idea of what she could lose.

Stop, Rebecca. Don't think about the fear. Continue what you're doing. Just a bit longer. You're a professional and you do not allow yourself to be a slave to fear.

She stopped at a cafe in a side street and sagged into a chair. She ordered a pot of tea without milk or sugar, and left the teabag to stew while she checked out on her map which places around here she hadn't gone to yet. Hopeless, hopeless.

'Superintendent!' She looked up to see a man she didn't know, who'd just walked in carrying a greengrocer's box full of fruit. He was smiling at her. 'Long time no see!' He put the box down on the counter and came over, rubbing his hands on his apron. 'What brings you back here?'

She felt like leaping up to embrace the most welcome stranger she had ever met. She did not. She slowly stood, one hand on the back of the chair to support herself. 'You'll have to forgive me,' she said. 'You see . . . I've lost my memory.'

The man's name was David, he was the owner of the cafe, and they'd had a few conversations on the subject of her work, while never really becoming friends. He'd wanted to talk to her about getting more police on foot through here. It had become a running joke between them. She'd stopped by often, until . . . Wow, it must have been five years back; how time flies, he said. He was concerned about her condition, eager to help out. It took a desperately long time to get past reassuring him that she'd had medical attention. She'd always sit in the window if she could, he said, watching the people go past. She'd always said she was here visiting friends. Nearby? He supposed they must be. She'd never said who.

'Oh, wait a sec, come on now . . .' David put a hand to his brow. 'You once left your stuff here, asked me to look after it, 'cos you'd forgotten something, left it wherever you were visiting. You popped out, and you was back literally just a minute or two later.'

'*A* minute? Or *two*?'

He laughed at that, then stifled it. 'More like two.'

She went out into the street, looked at her watch and walked for ninety seconds at her normal fast pace. From what David had said, it didn't sound like she'd run. That gave her a radius. Then she looked again at her map and used her fingers to make a circle. She doubted she would have been visiting a shopkeeper. The only houses within that distance were a cluster of upmarket apartments, a square of them on the map, behind the street here, set aside in their own bit of green. That sounded like the sort of place heavy-hitters like the people on that list might live. She worked out where she had to go, rushed round a corner, and now she was trying not to run.

She turned the corner and there the building was. It was a square of apartments, built round a courtyard, something of the 1920s about it. The lawn was well kept, and the trees that baffled the wind and rain were neat. Lofthouse had visited homes like these before, grace-and-favour apartments given to the great and the good, retired civil servants who wanted to live in town. There was no sign naming the place. That would have been gauche. She went to the main gate, which was open, cars parked inside. Wheelie bins of rubbish were neatly lined up beside a little pile of junk mail with a brick on top of it. There was a security office, but it was closed at the moment; this wasn't a gated community. She still half expected to recall something, but no. The erasure had been complete.

She put a hand, as she so often had in recent months, to the charm bracelet on her wrist. This was something else that she could tell nobody about. The key on her charm bracelet. The impossible key that seemed to have a mind of its own. She was wondering if, now she was here, it would react. But no, she would have felt it by now. It wasn't like she could shake it to get a reaction. The key was the second powerful force that influenced her life. A positive one? Perhaps you could call it that. She'd come to trust it, anyway, and now it was silent.

Stairwells were inset in each of the four walls. She chose one at random, went up it and walked the cloister-like corridors. She could see how something as scholastic as this building would appeal to someone who'd, presumably, worked in the 'temple' at the Docklands site. Would all of them have lived here? No, not people as large in the world as that: they would have had big lives in all sorts of places. She was looking for the home of one person. An old friend. Probably not someone, with an apartment as small as these must be, with a family living at home.

She quickly walked all four quarters, on both levels. At times she held up the key, hoping it would oblige her with a inclination in one direction or the other, but got no reaction. A part of her had hoped this building might provide the solution to another mystery: was there a lock somewhere her mysterious key fitted? Perhaps in one of these doors? It didn't seem likely, given their relatively modern design. The key looked ancient, rounded by so many fingers, though its teeth were miraculously sharp.

She returned to the gatehouse, frustrated. Now there was a caretaker inside, reading the paper. She knocked on his window, showing him a forced smile and her warrant card. He looked alarmed as he came to the door, but she quickly calmed him. 'Just background on a case – nothing to worry about. Could I see a list of your tenants, please?' The proffered list didn't include any of the names she was after; of course it didn't: the records of them had been erased from the world, James had said. But . . . hold on.

'There are eight corner apartments and four apartments along each side of each floor, right? So why are there only thirty-five flats on this list?'

The caretaker shrugged. 'That's all we have. I should know.' He looked complacent about it when, in any normal situation, that would have been the cue for an interesting fact, a demonstration of his familiarity with the building.

Lofthouse was seized with sudden hope. She went back into the courtyard. She would walk each corridor again, counting doors this time. She headed for a stairwell, again passing the rows of wheelie bins. A thought struck her. A caretaker wouldn't take it upon himself to spare any apartment its junk mail. What had James told her about this process of forgetting? That it seemed to leap from mind to mind across everyone who knew about the thing that was being forced out of the public consciousness. So, an automated process, once it had started up . . .

She went to the pile of letters and took the brick away. They were all from apartment 23. She ran back to the gatehouse, grabbed that list off the caretaker again, looked up and down it. No apartment 23. She returned the paper to him, but was suddenly sure there *must* have been one, so she took it back and examined it again. She found the names and addresses sliding away from her gaze in a way that made her eyes hurt. She couldn't see what was being concealed, but she could just about perceive the concealment itself, now she was deliberately seeking it. She handed the list back again to a now thoroughly bemused caretaker and jogged over to the appropriate stairwell.

Lofthouse walked the corridor past apartments 22 to 25 without noticing anything strange, then swore out loud and walked back, this time making herself stand in front of each flat in turn. It was as if this power sent her brain into the mode where one is doing something one does every day, and so finds oneself thinking consciously of something else and can't remember the familiar action in the gap. Now she purposefully walked past apartment 22 and made herself stop before she got to 24, and yes, she could feel . . . something, as she turned to look in what must be the right direction. The feeling was very powerful, now she focused on it, but it was very localized. It was like finding an enormous wind blowing through a tiny crevice, like something one read about on the science pages, a force inside the smallest spaces of the universe. She still couldn't sense anything between these two apartments, but she was just about aware now of something buffeting her mind aside, getting between the light in her eyes and her knowledge of it. She made herself step forwards and reach out. Her hand stretched further and further into nothingness. She didn't know what she was hoping for. It was impossible, she knew, for her to be aware of encountering a door.

The key on her charm bracelet jerked urgently. She didn't know if that was in anticipation or warning. It was enough, though, to make her halt.

She moved quickly aside, suddenly afraid that, should she stay here too long, pushing against this power, the one who had set it here would notice.

OK, she'd achieved something. She knew where her target was. She'd known there was a hole in the world, but now she had experienced it herself. That was terrifying, but so was what had pushed her to come here. Now she had to get back to where she should be and work out her next move, work out some way to get through a door she'd couldn't perceive.

On the way out of the apartment block, Lofthouse decided upon another experiment, to check in with the more positive of the two powers that were ruling her life. Would the key react as it had in the past, to push her in one direction or the other? Time to find out. She started to deliberately consider the idea that, having come this far, she would go no further, that this discovery had been enough. She *felt* the key on her charm bracelet react, and had a moment to brace herself before the wave of depression and misery hit her. She stumbled, had to put a hand on the wall beside her to steady herself. No, she thought; actually, I'm going to pursue this to the end. I'm going to get inside that apartment and find what's hidden. The torment left her like a chemical reaction, and she breathed deeply for a moment, enjoying the rush of freedom from pain. The key was certain about what it wanted. Though she still had no idea why it wanted anything.

She made her way back to Paddington Green and arrived for the end of the meeting, saying she'd just popped in to make sure there was nothing urgent that would surprise her in the briefing notes she'd be sent later, got reassurances that this was the case, then, having thus made sure she'd killed off almost all possibility that comment would be made about her absence, exited like she'd been there all the time, switching on her iPad and phone as she did so. She had a different driver on the way back to Gipsy Hill, thank God.

She'd been expecting him to appear, but it was just as big a shock as it always was. As she was reading the *Telegraph* on her iPad in the back of the car, he walked into the frame of the tablet, that familiar face with a look of slight suspicion on it. A few months ago, on the face of the man himself, she'd have taken that look to be teasing, joking. Now it made her stomach tense up and her face freeze.

'Been anywhere nice?' he asked.

'The regular meeting.' The driver would assume she was using FaceTime. She knew from previous experience that others couldn't see or hear him.

'You don't normally switch off your gear in the meeting.'

'I wanted to get away from you for a few minutes. Or can't I do that now?' The driver would now be assuming they were having a row. She understood where MI5 had come by their suspicions, though she didn't like their implied penetration of her security. Still, she had bigger problems.

'You can do whatever you like, as long as you're willing to

accept the consequences.' With a familiar little nod, he headed off the page again, and she wanted to bellow, to kick the floor, to throw the iPad aside. She did none of those things.

'Could we stop at my house?' she asked the driver.

The car pulled into the driveway. Lofthouse got out, with as much calm as she could project, and marched to the door. She fumbled with keys, managed to get the damn thing open, stepped inside.

'In here,' said the familiar voice. Oh, thank God. She found him in the kitchen, the person she'd seen walk onto her iPad, the most familiar person in the world to her, her husband, Peter. He was standing in the kitchen with his hand in a pan of water, which was sitting on the hob. Now he calmly reached over and switched on the heat. 'I wonder how long it'll take,' he said, 'before this body starts feeling the pain.' He had done something similar just before she'd gone over to see Quill's team in Docklands – walked into her office unexpectedly, carrying a pair of shears from the garden, and put them round his little finger. Whatever had literally possessed him had quickly convinced her that it was a genuine threat, that this wasn't some form of mental illness on Peter's part, by letting Peter go for a few moments, resulting in her husband asking her why he was at her workplace. Then the possession had resumed. Her remaining doubts had been swept aside when she recalled the bizarre element that had entered her life already in the form of the key, that impossibility to which she'd already become accustomed.

She could see now that Peter's brow was sweating, that somewhere inside there was the man she loved, despite this control by something alien, despite the smile on his face.

'I haven't done anything,' she lied.

'I think you've been thinking about doing something.'

'I have, but I haven't done anything!'

'Hmm.' He was sizing her up. He had all of Peter's mannerisms, but she wasn't sure if she could guess what he was thinking in the same way she could with her husband. She had come, since Quill had told her about the impossible things that he and his team had experienced, to associate this evil spirit with what Quill called the Smiling Man. Perhaps they were one and the same. He certainly kept a grin on Peter's features most of the time.

'I wouldn't do anything to let you hurt him. I wouldn't.'

He considered, then decided. 'Kneel,' he said. 'Beg.'

Without a moment's hesitation, Lofthouse knelt and started to ask piteously for no harm to come to Peter. In the back of her mind, she kept repeating to herself the address that could save her husband. The spirit let her keep going until the sound of bubbling was audible from the pan, then finally, with a familiar little laugh, lifted his hand from it. It was reddened, but not yet scalded. 'Amazing,' he said, 'what you'll do for him. I really must experiment further.'

FIVE

Quill watched as the other three examined this new crime scene. Following Sefton's call to arms, they seemed to have a new energy about them. It was Sherlock Holmes's writing that had done it, that urgent tone. The ultimate crime, which they had to solve. Had that got the ghost 'killed'? Had he been murdered when he got too close to a solution? Why all the clues? He deeply wished he could share in the energy of his team, in the urgency of Holmes. He wasn't concentrating enough, knew he was missing something.

The same thought kept rolling round and round in his head. Assuming nights in a hotel didn't count, and he was now making that assumption based on the fact that when he'd been in Hell, he'd met relatively few people who didn't have London accents, then the only person he knew he could save from damnation was Sarah's sister, Laura, who'd never lived in the capital. How, though? How could he persuade her not to do something as seemingly harmless as move here? How could he do it without telling her what her sister and her sister's child were already sentenced to? His body's continual fear that something would leap out at him was making him physically tired, what felt like a literal weight around his shoulders, arms and chest. It was wearing him out. He couldn't imagine what would happen when he was worn out.

He'd decided, at Baker Street, that surrendering the scene to a crime scene examiner might well yield new data, so he'd asked Costain to call it in to Lofthouse, getting Anita Clarke's *Study in Scarlet* investigation involved on the basis that someone seemed to have purposefully vandalized the Holmes Museum, leaving deliberate clues that were perhaps relevant to Clarke's investigation. He hadn't met Clarke before, but when she turned up, he found her to be smart and straightforward, and was pleased to be able to let her people deal with the representatives of the company that owned the museum as they arrived at the start of a working day. 'What have your lot found?' she'd asked.

'Just this,' he'd said, gesturing to the room around him. 'No idea as to motive. No idea if it's actually anything to do with your . . . two murders now.'

'It looks indicative, specific vandalism and that knife, maybe taunting us.' Quill could see what she couldn't, that she was walking in blood. 'How did you get on to this?'

Quill had glanced to Sefton and considered, like he giddily considered so many career-ending decisions these days, telling the truth. 'I'm afraid we're not allowed to say.' One of the museum officials had arrived, and Clarke had had to deal with that. She'd asked a sergeant to show Quill's team what they had, and they'd all had a bit of a kip in the back of the cars on the way to the first of the crime scenes, in Brixton.

Sefton had given that house a quick once-over, using his pendulum and his nose to search for any sign of spilled silver or knotted gold, any hint of something that could only be sensed by those with the Sight. He'd found nothing. There'd been no sign of a struggle, the sergeant had said. Christopher Lassiter had trusted his killer enough to calmly have tea with him, having let him into the house. It had almost certainly been someone he knew.

Then they'd been taken to see the body, which had also yielded nothing from their side of the street. Lassiter had lain on the gurney looking oddly tense, his muscles locked, a look of strain on his face. Quill had wondered if he himself had looked like that when he'd been in this same situation, had imagined once again Sarah seeing him like that. Lassiter's body had had its every muscle paralysed, the medical examiner had explained to them. Cause of death was asphyxiation as a result, which had taken about half an hour. Had Lassiter lain on the floor, watching his killer write that word on the wall? The poison had probably been curare. There were no puncture marks on the body, and the main investigation had found tiny pieces of what looked like the shell of a pill in the teeth. It might have been incompletely dissolved in hot tea.

'We were working on the basis,' said the sergeant, 'that the killer or killers were trying to recreate the first murder in *A Study in Scarlet*. The second crime scene supports that, as you'll see.'

In the Conan Doyle story, Quill was told, it had been a pill and had been identified by Holmes as being 'a South American alkaloid'. The tea hypothesis was based on two cups that had been left on the draining board in the kitchen, both immaculately cleaned. No DNA other than the victim's had been found at the entire crime scene. None from friends, even. The matter of the blood, though, was ongoing. Lassiter had, in recent years it seemed, lived an isolated existence. Had he watched, dying, even that careful washing-up? Had he gasped and fought for air, perhaps expecting the good life he'd lived would get him to Heaven? Almost certainly not, not these days.

Then, with thankfully more sleep in more cars in between, the team had been brought here. It was now late afternoon, dark outside, and they were in a hotel next to Euston Station, in a second-floor room that was utterly bland. Beside the open window lay the body of a man in the uniform of a cleaner, with a deep stab wound in his left side. On the wall above the body, as at the Brixton crime scene, the word 'Rache' was written in blood.

'The time frame,' said Ross, 'puts this murder at ten p.m., *before* . . . I'm going to call what was done to Holmes a murder.

So the sequence goes Brixton, here, Baker Street. If they *are* associated, and that's a big assumption, noted as such, maybe the first two killings are to somehow, I don't know, power up that blade that killed Holmes?'

'Using sacrifices associated with Holmes to create a weapon to kill Holmes,' said Sefton. 'That feels right, and in my area of study, that often means it could *be* right.'

'There are no more murders in *A Study in Scarlet*. So if that is what the MO was, this is over.'

Quill squatted to look at the very real body and read from the report that the crime scene examiner had handed him. 'Stabbed through the heart. This is almost precisely the location of the second murder in *A Study in Scarlet*, which wasn't the case with the first killing. In the book, that took place in Lauriston Gardens, a real street that is a lot closer to the Brixton Road. The cause of death, though, in both cases, looks to be precisely the same as in the book.'

'So the deaths don't have to be correct in every detail,' said Sefton.

'The difference could be indicative,' said Ross. 'Why were the killer or killers content with the general area for the first murder, but were so specific with this one?'

'No sign of a murder weapon,' said Quill.

'Could be the same one as killed Holmes,' said Ross. 'But why would that be necessary when the first murder was by poison?'

'They're waiting until we're done before they remove the body. Nothing was taken from the room. The window was open when the body was found.'

'Any connection between the victims?' asked Costain.

'The main investigation hasn't unearthed anything yet. This is Richard Duleep, forty-six, lived in Rickmansworth, wife and three kids, a few counts of petty theft and aggro when he was younger, seen as a bit of a risk by the cleaning company, but they say he'd obviously turned over a new leaf. His workmates say he was just cleaning the room like always. Guest checked out hours before.'

Costain looked out of the window. 'The bird shit on the ledge is smeared. Someone got a ladder up here, right?'

'That's the line the main investigation are pursuing.'

'That's bizarre,' said Ross, 'and also maybe indicative. If you're aiming to just kill someone, anyone, in this building, then why not simply walk in, pick a floor and wait? Or break in downstairs or something?'

'You need time to write the word,' said Sefton.

'Yeah, but to actually bring a ladder, to do it in full view . . .' Ross was shaking her head, annoyed at the world.

'We'll get access to nearby CCTV camera footage after they've examined it,' said Quill. 'We're told they have a clear view of the front of the building.'

'If you're going to climb up a bloody ladder right in view of everybody,' said Costain, 'there'll be witnesses. We're going to find out what suspect or suspects looks like. Unless they're invisible, which is always a possibility.'

Sefton was looking up at the word scrawled on the wall. 'There are spatters between this and the body. I think this time that's the victim's blood.'

'Fits with the book,' said Ross. 'In the story, the killer had a nosebleed at the first murder and wrote on the wall in his own blood. Then he used the victim's blood the second time. He didn't have to worry about DNA evidence.'

'Spoilers,' said Costain. Which still got no reaction from Ross. 'Here, could this be that obvious? Could the killer be the ghost of whoever it is in the book? He's got a motive for killing Holmes.'

Sefton considered for a second. 'I don't know what the name of that character is, so I don't think he's anywhere near well known enough for London to remember him. From what I remember, none of the three adaptations filming in town are doing *A Study in Scarlet*, or maybe that'd be different.'

'His name's Jefferson Hope,' said Ross, 'and I agree, but he goes on the ops board.' She said it like she was answering Sefton.

Quill found himself looking once again at the body. This Richard Duleep was in Hell now, experiencing the torments Quill had experienced – more, because Quill was pretty sure he'd been spared some of it. It didn't matter how kind Richard had been to his wife and three kids, how much he'd reformed; he'd fallen victim to the ultimate postcode lottery. It seemed almost bizarre to *care* who'd killed him.

He looked up at the others, thinking he'd just blurt it out, share the burden. Seeing their faces stopped him. There was no help to be had. He'd just be putting weights round their necks. He made himself play his role once more. 'Let's take all this back to the Hill.'

They got back to the Portakabin late in the day. As soon as they entered, Ross went to the ops board, which was now bare, the details of Operation Dante having been unpicked from it. She pinned a piece of blank paper on the wall beside it, took a marker and offered it to Quill. 'Name of the operation and list of operational aims.' She was aware that she was being brusque with a senior officer, but she was getting enormously pissed off with Quill's strained silences. It wasn't as if he was the only one suffering from what had happened during the Ripper case. She herself had lost the ability to feel happiness, but beyond that, her father was in Hell. Previously she'd got slight comfort from him being able to make desperate attempts to visit her. Unfortunately, those had been discovered, and ceased. She shared, however, Sefton's conviction that they had here a new case that could get them working together like they'd used to, though maybe not all of them. Costain could piss off outside London, where he wouldn't have to worry about the Sight, for all she cared.

Quill paused before taking the marker. He'd sometimes indicated, after he'd had a few, that he had occasionally suffered from depression. He'd talked about their new vocation as a revelation that there was a point to life after all, as if there could be a cure, but this current malaise went further than anything she'd seen from him.

She now had a vague idea of how he felt. She sometimes needed to find logical reasons to do everyday things like choosing a different shirt in the morning. Her problem, however, was specific. Quill these days seemed to keep getting stuck thinking there was something he should do or say, decide not to say it, then have to be forced back into the moment. He needed someone to keep trying to jump-start him.

Quill caught her look and finally nodded. He went to the paper and began to write.

1. *Ensure the safety of the public.*
2. *Gather evidence of offences.*
3. *Identify and trace subject or subjects involved.*
4. *Identify means to arrest subject or subjects.*
5. *Arrest subject or subjects.*
6. *Bring to trial/destroy.*

'Generic,' said Costain, 'but yeah. We can't bundle killing a fictional character with the other two murders, not if we want a jury to keep a straight face. What are we going to call it?'

Quill picked up a piece of card and looked at it. 'One of you,' he said, and held it in their direction.

Sefton took the pen and the card from him. 'Something bloody positive,' he said. Then he started to write, turned and pinned the name of their new operation at the top of the ops board.

OPERATION GAME.

'What, like . . . the game Operation?' said Costain.
'I couldn't call it "Afoot", could I?'

'It'll do,' said Quill.

They began, between them, to build the board. Ross felt herself relax as they did so, and she was sure Sefton and Costain felt the same way. They put up pictures of the victims, including, taken from the Internet, a Sidney Paget illustration of Holmes in his deerstalker. They linked a photo of the Holmes murder weapon to that image, with a close-up of the detail on the blade, and a picture of a generic pill to that of Lassiter. What was inscribed on the blade had been the easiest detail to find: the stick men were from another Holmes story, 'The Dancing Men', where they'd been a sort of code. In the story, the messages were much longer, and when translated were a mixture of imploring stalker notes and threats. Ross had found some complete alphabets for the figures online, but they differed, and having consulted the story itself, she found there weren't enough letters given to construct a definitive version. However, one of the online versions had yielded a translation for what was on the blade that made sense, and now she wrote the word on the board beside the weapon: *Ghostkiller*. She would have added as a suspect a picture of the Holmes expert who'd written the online alphabet, but he'd died in New Zealand fifteen years ago.

The word 'Rache' was pinned up and connected to the two non-fictional victims. Ross printed out images of the lines between the bullet holes in the wall, the gaps in the bookcase, the gaps in the letters, the pinpricks in the eyes, the melted head, the spiral on the hearth, the chalk doorway, the astronomical charts and photo, and the envelope it had arrived in. The charts had been interesting: a map of the heavens circa the 1960s, the sort of thing you might buy in a junk shop; a chart of the solar system that was similar, with a 1973 date on the copyright; a picture of a very general star field, with index numbers at the edges that presumably indicated what part of the sky this was. She pinned photos of all of them, and of the message on the back of that particular picture, onto the board. She sent the photo and envelope to be fingerprinted. Costain printed out pictures of Jefferson

Hope, as drawn on what looked like a cigarette card, Moriarty, a drawing from one of the books, General Gordon and Henry Ward Beecher and added them, with a look on his face that was continually hoping to get either a laugh or an order to bin them, to a suspect line above all the rest.

Then, more seriously, he added a picture of the assistant curator, with her name, Ann Stanley, under it. 'She was there alone,' he said. 'We shouldn't just trust her version.'

Ross found herself wanting to nod, but made herself not do so. Any positive gesture in his direction could be the start of a slow slide towards him wheedling his way back under her guard. She knew what he was capable of. She put up a blank card with the question 'Watson?' on it. She ran a line down separating the Holmes murder and the other two, because a connection had yet to be found, and Costain had to divide up his 'suspects' as a result. He gave no indication of being annoyed at that. 'We have two killings like those in Holmes's stories,' she said, 'and one that isn't. That's got to be the main indicator here. Let's not start trying to make the death of Holmes *into* a Holmes story.'

'You know,' said Sefton, 'one of the Continuing Projects Team was called Watson. The memory of him is missing like the ghost of this Watson is missing. Can anyone think of another Watson?'

A quick look at Wikipedia confirmed they could. 'I'm relieved these days,' said Costain, 'when it turns out there *are* still co-incidences.'

As they were working, Quill got an email through from DI Clarke's office. The crime scene examiner had decided the wax head could have been melted, by a sufficiently intense flame, in five minutes, so that didn't give them any help with the time frame. They looked at the plans and found that the chalk door-way would lead into the stairwell of the building next door, which one could exit without setting off an alarm. So if the killer had had the same resources Ballard did, they had an obvious means of escape.

After they'd finished, they stepped back and looked at what

they had. So much noise. Not unusual for this stage of an operation. She'd wanted there to be something straight away for the sake of the team. 'Reasons why someone might have done all that at the Holmes crime scene,' she began.

'As ritual,' said Sefton, 'necessary for the sacrifice, if that's what this was.'

'As a message,' said Costain, 'a taunting puzzle hidden in all that detail, like Jimmy said.'

'We still don't know exactly how the process of London remembering stuff works. According to what Jimmy saw' – she didn't want to say 'in Hell' – 'the memories of the dead seem to matter as much as the living. If Sherlock Holmes, the remembered fictional character, is now somehow dead, then how are they still filming movies about him?' She held up her phone showing news footage of the three Holmes productions carrying on today despite the media screaming about the new murder. 'Shouldn't they have forgotten who their central character is, or lost enthusiasm for him or something? What exactly does it mean to have "murdered Sherlock Holmes"? If we can find out what's changed because of the murder, then we might get some idea of motive, because at the moment that's completely lacking.'

'Maybe,' said Costain, once again back to being Mr Funny with that fake-jaunty sound in his voice, 'there's a serial killer going after fictional Londoners. We stake out Mary Poppins and bring Paddington in for protective custody.'

Ross thankfully realized she'd just got an email alert and looked at her phone. 'They've got a DNA match from the blood on the wall in the first murder,' she said. 'It's someone who was in custody at the time. Which these guys are referring to as obviously a mistake, impossible, but—'

'Yeah,' said Sefton, 'but the "I" word is where we come in.'

Quill's phone rang, a call from DI Clarke. After a moment, Quill put her on speaker. 'We've now got someone we'd normally fancy for this, big time, but as you've heard, he's got the perfect alibi. That CCTV footage from outside the second murder scene shows a black male, early twenties, around six foot, about a hundred and forty pounds, scaling a wooden ladder. We've got a clear shot of his face, which we've put through facial recognition, and he resembles to a degree that would satisfy any jury the suspect already in custody whose DNA matches that of the blood from the first scene. I've just sent Lisa the files.' Ross clicked on her phone and found the image of a young man. 'Suspect's name is Albert Bates, known as Albie.'

After Quill finished the call, Ross played the video. The figure climbing the ladder, with a calm, professional look on his face, was clearly the same man. 'We need to talk to him,' she said. 'If he's guilty of one or both murders, we have to find out how, and if he's got anything to do with the Holmes murder.'

Sefton pointed to the photo of the murder weapon on the ops board. 'We can also make use of an asset we have in our pocket. An occult London expert like Ballard might be willing and able to tell us something about the blade and about that chalk, if he's looking to make a deal.'

Ross automatically looked to Quill, seeking for him to split their forces. He stared back at her for a moment, then clicked again into the role he was meant to be playing. 'Right,' he said. 'We've had a long day, so let's get back to this tomorrow. If Clarke lets us play through, Costain interviews the suspect in jail, Sefton will talk to Ballard, and Ross will interview the Holmes Museum curator.'

'What about you?' said Ross.

'I'll be . . . here,' he said, once again lost.

SIX

Costain felt HM Prison Wandsworth before he saw it. Driving his car along Trinity Road, he felt that old grumbling sensation in his gut again, like when he'd first got the Sight and attempted to leave London. Up ahead on the right, a big beast was coming, full of shit and history. He turned off and drove slowly towards the low, square fortress that actually had a portcullis visible over its doors. There were leafy little houses all around, pensioners out in their gardens. This monstrosity loomed over them.

He'd been inside 'Wanno' once before, as an undercover placed to obtain information on drugs getting into the prison. He hadn't found out very much, hadn't had a chance to. There'd been a whisper that he'd been compromised and they'd got him out of there. Given the sentences of the offenders he'd mixed with, and the brevity of his stay, he doubted anyone would recognize him. Still, it gave him pause. This place had given him nightmares way before the Sight.

He went to the staff entrance and found an office with thick glass and an intercom that was always on, no button to push. He slipped his warrant card through the slit and waited in this space that made him itch, made him feel like an animal in a net, just the bleached smell of it, the same smell you got in sandwich shops after some homeless person had wandered in and they'd cleaned up. It seemed like it took an age while they checked his appointment and identity against their lists.

They finally found his data, and asked for his phone, which he handed over, annoyed despite knowing about this stage in advance, looking into the face of the office worker who was regarding him with a horrifying blandness that could mask . . . anything. Who knew what the people in a bureaucracy like this thought about him? He was sent to the social visits side of the entranceway, had to actually go out and come in again, and there he was asked, again with that blank look, to allow himself to be patted down, to see if he was carrying contraband, and scanned for explosives and drugs. He found he was breathing hard as it was done, wanted to say he was a fucking police officer, but that's you protesting too much, eh, mate? All by the book, sir. He hoped the man would say that, but he didn't. Costain took small pleasure in indicating the officer should stop. 'Wait a sec.' He took from his pocket an evidence bag, in which was a most unusual item. 'Evidence to show the prisoner.' The man took it, looked inside it without opening the bag, finally gave it back to him and nodded.

He was sent back out again and into the staff side once more to await his escort. The middle-aged man in prison officer uniform arrived ten minutes later, but, walking swiftly through the bleached corridors, making the man keep up, Costain managed to arrive on time for his appointment with the officer in charge. He asked to see what had been in the suspect's pockets when they'd brought him in, and quickly sifted through a tray containing a mobile phone, a wallet in bright purple with a tiny coke spoon attached, which was surely a statement that said the opposite of what this kid thought it did, a little cash, crumpled, some condoms past their expiry date. Costain switched on the phone, found nothing blazing to his extra senses from the screen. None of these items had anything of the Sight about them. 'What's he like?' he asked.

The officer in charge shrugged.

Costain was led into the Heathfield Centre, as the main body of the prison was called, and then towards B Wing. He walked down corridors painted pale green and cream with a new prison officer beside him. She made little sighing jokes, her face set into a calm lack of expression. The place smelt of guilt and denial. The feeling was ground into the walls. There were little cracks in the edifice of hurt, flashes of light that Costain glimpsed out of the corners of his eyes as he walked, actual visible hope, which only served to make the cloak of cynicism and self-defeat more obvious. The building felt like the waiting room for the Hell he'd himself once glimpsed.

Thinking about it suddenly made it almost too much to take. He nearly turned back. He would have done had it not been for a questioning look from the prison officer. He was the wrong person to come here. In the past, perhaps Quill would have picked someone else. Or he'd have sent Costain deliberately to rub his nose in it. Even that would have been easier to handle. The guilt of this place was making him think of Lisa. He associated any sort of guilt with her, because of what he'd done to her.

He thought of being inside her, of the passion on her face, and then killed that thought. That was the guiltiest thing of all, the thing she must think of all the time, that she and he had just been about sex, when being with her had been for him the first time in his life when sex had felt like coming home. He thought about how there was such stark silence every time they had to work together, how every time they talked it felt as though they might just suddenly start talking like they once had.

It must take such effort on her part to keep her guard up when he was around, not to let herself relax in his presence for even a second. No, who was he kidding? His crime against her had been so big that it took her no effort at all, because she felt it again every time she saw him. He realized his thoughts had distracted him from what he was seeing. There were impossible shadows moving on the walls. The motions were the raising and lashing of a whip. With the shadows now came sounds. Screams began echoing and re-echoing, bouncing back from the ends of every corridor in this part of the prison.

He felt the whip on his back, damn it; he actually felt it through his jacket like the sting of a wasp and flinched.

This place had been where they'd once kept the national stock of the birch and the cat-o'-nine-tails, as though there might be a shortage. The prison officer, oblivious, led him round a corner and Costain jumped at a new sudden noise, the release of a catch, something falling, a crack of wooden machinery. The new shadow fell down the corridor towards and over him: the gallows.

He couldn't remember how many it was, over a hundred people, who had been executed here, including Lord Haw-Haw and Derek Bentley. The death penalty for murder had been abolished in 1965, but they'd kept the gallows here in good working order, it was said, until 1993. Just in case the powers that be changed their minds. He'd read about Oscar Wilde being kept in here, his only crime being that he was gay. Costain wondered about whether there was a memory of that kept by the building, or rather by all the living and the dead who kept a memory of the building, and then, of course, in the way of the Sight, all of a sudden Costain could see him, a hunched figure, trying only to cling on to something of himself, stumbling ahead, looking suddenly agonized sidelong as small children were marched in a line past him. He was worried entirely for them, not at all for himself.

Costain wondered about that for a moment. Partly to get rid of an incredulous expression on the face of the prison officer, who was probably wondering what sort of a loony she was escorting, with all his sudden twitches and winces, he asked her if children had ever been kept here.

'Oh yes, tons of them, back in the nineteenth century. You know, sensible policies for a happier Britain.' She led him into a corridor of interview rooms at the end of a cell block. He was shown into one of the rooms, provided with coffee by another prison officer, and then the young man familiar from the scene-of-crime video was led in, in prison uniform. His face didn't wear the same purposeful expression as it had on the camera footage, just a sort of calm boredom. The escorting officer left and closed the door. They were alone. No CCTV, even.

Costain took a long breath and was immediately a professional, his game face on. 'Are you Albie Bates?'

The kid nodded.

'Don't just fucking nod to me, son – you're in shit here.'

The basic intimidation didn't get to the kid. He'd been interviewed by the main investigation earlier this morning. He'd claimed ignorance throughout. Easy to do when you had the perfect alibi. He'd never read any Sherlock Holmes stories because he'd never read anything, and didn't remember seeing anything with the word 'Rache' in it on telly. Now he leaned back in his chair, opened his legs, folded his arms, resigned to this latest waste of his valuable time.

'Yeah.'

From what Costain had read, the kid was like most repeat offenders, adapted to life inside. He kept himself fit enough to avoid trouble, made small sums of money off jail work to pay for his cigarettes, relied on the regularity and stability in here. As soon as he'd been released, on three previous occasions, he'd gone straight back into pissed-up violence and theft. He was in this time for GBH, having delivered a serious kicking to an old lady while still failing to get her purse off her. This was the sort of boy the gangsters only signed up once, the sort of boy who found life out there to be just too fucking complicated. The good news about that was he was no criminal mastermind. The bad news was he looked a very bad fit for a masterplan to assassinate Sherlock Holmes.

Costain took the item from his pocket that Sefton had chosen and put it on the table between them. It was something the

DC had found in a second-hand shop, a tiny bell, with a London manufacturer's mark on its handle. He hadn't managed to discover anything about it, which was a little worrying, because, to those with the Sight, it screamed its existence; it bellowed. It had taken weeks for Sefton to conclude that it didn't seem able to do anything else, at least not without precise instructions he couldn't even guess at. Costain had carried it in his pocket this morning feeling like he was hauling a bowling ball, until the bell's feeling of significance had become eclipsed by that of the prison itself. You put this thing down in front of someone with the Sight, they were going to react.

Bates laughed, didn't flinch. 'What the fuck?'

Costain pointed at the bell. 'Made in London.'

Here was something. A tiny reaction. 'Fuck off.'

'Oh, what, did you think the law didn't know about all that stuff, that it was a whole world of freedom for shit like you? We see so many like you, son. We're in that world; we hear it all. We walk with the Rat King to our left.' Now the boy *was* reacting, trying to hide it. He was looking at the bell, clearly not feeling it, but as if he'd suddenly thought it might have some power that could be a threat to him. 'Oh, there we go – the bell's a bit more meaningful now, right? You want to call someone? You reckon anyone official here knows what I'm talking about? You reckon your lawyer knows about it? The law on your side don't know this stuff, but the law on *my* side does.'

The boy shut down, his face a mask. He was breathing hard, though. He hadn't expected this level of knowledge on Costain's part. He was still wondering what the bell might be there for. His eyes kept flicking to it, and he was hunched up a little now, like . . . like he was personally afraid of it, like it was a drugs scanner. Costain carefully lifted up the bell and looked at it, grinned, like he'd taken a reading off it, then looked the boy up and down. Bates stiffened, guilty of something.

'So you see what this means? Your "alibi" means fuck all to

me. I know you got out of here. I know you did those murders. Your blood's at one crime scene; you're caught on bloody camera at the other. They showed you that video, the last lot that were through here, right? Only, they believed you when you said "just someone who looks like me", and I fucking don't.'

Bates tried to front it out. 'So what you do about that, blood? If lawyers don't believe this stuff, how you going to—?'

He hadn't finished his sentence before Costain had leaped out of his seat, grabbed him and slammed his head into the table. He hauled the boy's head back and threw him off his seat onto the ground. Costain moved quickly forwards, as if he was about to start kicking, and stopped to let the boy squirm out of the way, heave himself up against the wall, put a hand to his nose to stem the flow of blood. Costain wasn't actually prepared to take the violence any further, but the kid didn't know that.

He yelled helplessly as Costain grabbed him again, the sound of someone who'd been beaten a lot. There was a tiny sound of Hell in that shout, but Costain didn't let himself care. He was doing this now just so he could get close enough to search him, to catch a tiny hint of something of the Sight about the boy's clothes, to find—

There it was. Costain pushed the boy back so he hit the wall and put a finger between his eyes. 'Take whatever that is out of your top pocket. Slowly.'

Bates hesitated, saw the look in Costain's eye, then reached inside his uniform and produced a stick of chalk, roaring with Sighted power, power that had been weirdly and entirely muted by being inside the kid's clothes. It must be designed that way, thought Costain distantly, as he felt the extraordinary weight of the thing. He put his hand out and Bates reluctantly gave him the chalk.

Costain expected it to be heavier than the slight weight that rested in his palm. Now he needed to know exactly what this was and if possible where it came from, because who knew whether or not Ballard would dish, or even know? But, as in undercover work, to ask was to give away more than you got.

'Right,' he said. 'Clever. You figured you could just keep it on you, 'cos nobody's going to care about this in a search, are they? Nobody's going to nick it either. Where did a nobody like you get hold of something like this?'

Bates had blood on his lip, his tongue flicking to it. He was sizing Costain up, wondering how to get the best deal. 'That'll cost you.' He stepped back as Costain moved as if to attack him again, and his voice got shrill. 'I didn't kill no one. If I tell you, you gonna move against him, finger him for this, not me. I used it, but I didn't use it to go and fucking kill no one. It was him. I can prove it.'

So the chalk *could* be used to get out of here, and to get in and out of the Holmes murder scene, in the same way Ballard had used it.

'Who are you going on about?' Costain asked.

'This bloke. Remand prisoner, I think he was. He was in his own clothes, anyway. You know they go on about this shit in here. Some of them got their fucking religion, and some of them talk about voodoo or whatever. But just a few of them, they really know. You get to be able to tell. They ain't showy about it. You get to know them, and they'll do tricks with it, like passing out fags from an empty hand, and you can see them appear – it's not like some fucking thing on telly.'

That was something Sefton was going to enjoy hearing about, that the culture of the Sight was known to prisoners. Costain wondered if that, like so much about their world, had been a development of the last few years. 'Yeah,' he said, careful not to appear interested, 'this bloke.'

'He was one of them lot, was talking to all the ones like that. He was in here for a few days, told me that he could get me out if I liked. I was all, yeah, sure. He meant it, though. He showed me how to use it, drew a door and walked through the wall of the shower block, did it again, came back, rubbed the mark off before anyone saw. He called it walkthrough.'

'Does just what it says on the tin. No, don't smile at me, son. He gave you it out of the goodness of his heart, did he?'

'No, that's what I mean by proof. Look.' Bates rolled up his sleeve and showed Costain the tiniest of needle marks in the crook of his arm. 'He said he wanted some of my blood in return. I asked the boys who knew about this and they said, yeah, that's the sort of deal they make – he wasn't taking the piss. So I got some works and he took the blood and that's what he fucking used to set me up.'

'What about the CCTV footage?'

'Come on, man, he can walk through fucking walls! He could make that camera see whatever it wanted to, couldn't he?'

Costain admitted to himself that Bates's story was starting to sound plausible, though the boy's idea that a pinprick in his arm was 'proof' was typical prisoner bollocks. 'Didn't you stop to wonder what he was doing in here if he could get out? Bigger question: why are you still here?'

Bates looked incredulous. 'Mate, if you can get out, this is a fucking hotel. Food and bed and your mates. I used the chalk to go out, come back. I thought that's what that bloke was doing too. I thought he had loads of these. I thought everyone was into it, or maybe they'd been in the last place this bloke was inside. I got out after lights out, had a smoke, got laid, back for breakfast. Easy fucking life. But I never used it to kill nobody; this fucker did. He took that blood to set me up for it.'

'What was his name?'

'Dean Michael. No, being serious.'

That sounded a bit like a job name, which was going to make finding the prisoner on the jail's records that much harder. Costain got the relevant dates from Bates, and a description: black, maybe some Latin too; six foot or so; goatee; tattoo of something like a dragon down the side of his neck.

Bates looked worried again as Costain stood to leave. 'Give me the chalk back.'

'Like I'm going to do that.'

'That's my property! I'll tell them you stole something from me.' He sounded suddenly like the frightened child who was underneath everything else he was.

Costain was sure Bates knew as well as he did that the authorities here wouldn't care what he'd taken, especially if the item in question turned out to be a piece of chalk. But what else could the boy do? He was losing the key to his freedom. He took a sudden pace towards Costain, force being his next option. Costain faced him down and he finally turned away.

'You better fucking catch him, then,' said Albie Bates.

After Bates had been taken back into the main body of the jail, Costain went to the prison officer on duty at the end of the row of interview rooms and asked about what this lot called 'the establishment' of the jail. It took him a couple of hours in the office to go through all the records on the C-NOMIS system, and thankfully he found a skilled operator to help him. They kept a specific record of tattoos. No prisoner of the description Bates had given had been through here during the time Bates had been in Wandsworth.

Costain was sure the frightened child inside the no-hoper hadn't been lying to him. Which left him with lots of loose ends to add to the ops board. He headed for the exit and tried not to speed up as he did so.

As he walked the corridor back towards reception, he saw out of the corner of his eye the beaten-down figure of Wilde looking at him from a corner, caring for another lost child. He shook his head and dismissed it.

He could have said something to Bates, couldn't he, told him he could have his chalk back after the investigation? Of course not – that would be letting a dangerous prisoner escape, despite the fact that it had made no difference to the world when he'd been coming and going. Still, Costain was always a stickler for the rules, right?

He got out, reached his car, found he was leaning heavily on it without opening the door. The building behind him mocked him with its weight and his complicity, its shadow lying on his back. It wasn't his job to redeem every prisoner who was a little shit because of the shit done to him and so on and so on back to the start of time, was it? He'd decided a while back to stop living in fear of Hell, and he wasn't planning to return to that, but again he thought about how he was going to bring these new points of information back to Ross, and how she would resent it being him who brought them. How they could never, as it stood, do their job together in peace.

He wasn't a saint. Maybe, though, he could do better about how he was, about the choices he made. He wanted desperately to do better for Ross. He took the chalk from his pocket and wondered about using it to step out of this life and be someone different, someone good. He could just be that, couldn't he? He could just decide to change. He put the chalk back in his pocket, with a question not an answer in his mind, got into his car and drove too quickly out of the prison.

SEVEN

Mark Ballard had been incarcerated on remand in HM Prison Brixton, somewhere Sefton had never previously set foot. He did so now with a mixture of dread and interest, a mixture in which, he had to admit, he'd started to find great satisfaction.

As he walked down the corridors that howled with history, he wished his colleagues could be where he was now, emotionally: explorers in a new world, not victims of it. He hoped this case might still help get them there, no matter how much simpler it suddenly seemed to have got.

Ballard, as the team's reading for Operation Dante had left them in no doubt, was a real piece of work. He made the Keel brothers, those hardcore entrepreneurs who'd forced their peers to start dealing in cash, look like amateurs. He'd profited from the sudden absence of law in hidden London in the last few years, and he'd done it in secret, without showing off, either aware that some new law would come along or anticipating it might. He wouldn't be overawed by anything Sefton could present him with. So Sefton was planning on taking a different approach.

Ballard was lounging in the interview-room chair, in that same expensive suit he'd worn for the bank job, which was now looking a little crumpled. He was sipping from a cup of coffee. Sefton sat down opposite, aware he was a bloke who shopped at JD Sports. He opened his faithful holdall and, without ceremony, put onto the table, still in its evidence bag, the blade that had killed Sherlock Holmes. 'Mr Ballard,' he said, 'we'd like your professional opinion.'

'Yes, I was expecting something like this.' He glanced at the weapon, then looked back to Sefton. 'I didn't think that, having caught me, you'd let me go to waste. Who are you people?'

'We're what replaced the Continuing Projects Team.'

'Who?'

Sefton knew from previous dealings with the occult underworld in London that it had been known there was law out there, but they'd been seen more as a limiting force than a team with a name and a base. Maybe that said something about how they'd operated. Way in the background, most likely. 'We're the new law for our sort of London.'

'The new Shadow Police?'

So some of them at least had given this force in their lives a name. Sefton gave Ballard a few bare details about what they'd done so far. It was enough of the truth, he hoped, to gain some trust. Ballard said immediately he hadn't known anything about what had preceded them, only that everyone had said there was something, and that around the point where he'd started to flex his muscles, everyone started saying it had gone away. 'I wondered what the Mora Losley case was about. I was out of London for the Ripper, thank God. I only came back when I heard the riots were over.'

'People like us, we're always going to come back, though, right?'

Ballard laughed, as if noting Sefton's on-the-nose attempt at fellow feeling. 'Yeah, but who's this "we", kemo sabe? What exactly are you offering me here?'

'I was thinking about the sort of deal sometimes offered to hackers. You become a white hat, consult for us, stop committing crimes. You get to live off your previous immoral earnings, no questions asked.'

'I don't know, I was looking forward to the trial.'

'Yeah, so were we. We got a narrative sorted before the raid that doesn't include anything a jury would find impossible to believe.'

'Whatever.' Ballard's expression remained placid. 'You'd never keep me inside.'

'Because of that stick of chalk of yours? We'd put a watch on what you took in and what got in to you, and, between you and me, if you did a runner, you'd find yourself with some serious off-the-books shit on your tail.' Not that Sefton had anything of the sort at the ready, but he was pretty sure the threat would seem credible.

'Oh. I note this interview isn't being recorded.'

'Damn right.'

Ballard considered for a long time. Longer than anyone would really consider anything. Sefton took that to be a good sign and allowed himself a smile that slowly grew. Finally, Ballard let out a long breath that was almost a laugh. Yeah, he was going to take the offer. Of course he was. 'I'll need to talk to my brief about this. For that, I need you to make a formal offer that anyone reading it who's not involved in our world isn't going to baulk at.'

'We'll get that sorted. Right now, give me something I can tell my chief, a show of good faith. Something about the dagger, something about the chalk.'

'Isn't the chalk obvious? You saw how it worked at the bank.'

Sefton kept a poker face. Ballard sat down again and picked up the dagger. It had already been examined for fingerprints. They'd only found glove marks. Similarly, the envelope and photo had yielded nothing meaningful. 'This is made in London, of course.'

'Yeah, we can read.'

'"Wilkinson and Son, Pall Mall, London,"' Ballard read out loud. 'The company that became Wilkinson Sword. This is a bowie knife, dates from around 1840 to 1860, fake-ivory grip, in very good condition. If you had the original leather sheath, this would be worth a small fortune, but a copper could retire on this as is.'

'We really wanted a bit more detail than you'd get on *Antiques Roadshow.*'

'The stick men carved into the blade aren't an original feature; they look to have been added recently. Nothing supernatural about them, but there is much of interest about the knife itself. I don't have the Sight, but I suspect this object feels meaningful to those that do.'

Sefton carefully didn't confirm or deny his own status. 'Why do you suspect that?'

'Because look at the notches on the grip here. Very small, but each of them will have been cut with a sacrifice and lined with blood. This is a "fetch kettle", an object that's been modified, long ago, to host a particular "spiel", a way of keeping useful sound and gesture handy without having to replicate it yourself. This being a knife, I'd say the effect would probably be activated when it was stabbed into something.'

That was more detail than Sefton had ever previously heard about hidden London, framed in a language of professional use that went far beyond anything his unit had ever come up with. It was, obviously, the tip of a dirty great iceberg of data. He kept his expression steady. So the knife might well have had some sort of ghost-killing power imbued into it, be a 'ghostkiller', as the coded inscription named it. 'What effect would that be? In detail.'

'Ah, no.' Ballard laid the knife carefully back on the table. 'Get that paperwork sorted.'

'And about the chalk?'

Ballard shrugged. 'Not much to tell. I've seen two or three sticks of it in my time . . . pretty rare, but not unique. Don't know where it comes from, just that, with the proper gestures, it works.'

Sefton decided to go with another tack that he'd considered in advance. 'OK, we'll get into that. In the meantime, as a show of good faith on our part, is there anything about unseen London *you'd* like to ask *us*?'

Ballard didn't look incredulous, thank Christ. He considered for a moment. 'It's changing, isn't it?' he said.

'Yeah.' Sefton wished he could have a straightforward conversation with this guy. Maybe before long they would. 'We think something major changed about five years ago.'

'When the old law went away, right. But what about since?'

Sefton had already considered what he was going to reveal. 'Our investigations point to events moving in a particular direction. A worrying direction.'

'Yes.' Ballard waited to hear more, then visibly realized he wasn't going to. He sighed. 'I'd really enjoy having the time and space to work with you. But only after I get my deal.'

Ross had gone to see Ann Stanley, assistant curator at the Holmes Museum, at home at her parents' house in Rickmansworth. She'd been given leave while the museum was a crime scene, and she didn't like it at all. 'It sort of feels like I'm meant to be in shock, or that I did something wrong,' she said, handing Ross a cup of tea.

'There's no reason to think that,' lied Ross.

The museum had shown the main investigation their post room, an office downstairs with a dedicated secretary who answered all the letters that came in to 221B. A standard reply was printed on stationery that bore the detective's profile in silhouette, complete with a pipe and deerstalker cap. As if Holmes would have allowed the use of those symbols in 'real life'. The form letter thanked people for writing and fobbed off requests for help with the phrase 'In his own words, Mr Holmes has given himself up entirely "to that soothing life of nature for which I had so often yearned during the long years amid the gloom of London".' Certainly, a sentient Holmes with an interest in his own mail, assuming he had the power to come downstairs and to lift things, could have found a specific parcel and taken it back to his study.

'What sort of mail did Sherlock Holmes get?' Ross asked.

'People asking if he was real, or if he'd run for president in the US. Sometimes they had mad theories about the books they wanted him to confirm. Some of them were written like . . . like a kid believing in Father Christmas. Sort of half thinking of him as real and half not. Like people you'd think were completely normal write to characters in *Coronation Street*. They asked him to solve crimes too. A lot wanted him to find Bin Laden. That's a bit sick, isn't it?'

Ross didn't express an opinion. 'Were there any ghost stories about the museum?'

Stanley looked puzzled. 'Well, no, but . . . it was me on the evening shift a lot, clearing up after the day, and . . . you heard things. Other people did too. Like there was someone moving around. And things got moved. Small stuff. You'd put something back where it was supposed to be and then it'd be somewhere else. That sounds stupid. You're not writing that down, are you?'

Ross had been. 'Don't worry,' she said. 'That's all useful information.'

When she got back to the Hill, Ross found that Sefton and Costain had returned too. Quill seemed to have spent the time staring at the ops board and making tea. They all listened to each other's stories, and Ross felt she could now just about support the idea of at least a mobile and perhaps a sentient Holmes who might have taken the envelope from the post room. She went to the ops board and added a suspect line between the three murders and 'Dean Michael', which she kept in speech marks to indicate a possible alias.

Ballard's deal was in progress, Quill having put a request in with Lofthouse. Enquiries to the Sherlock Holmes Society and the Baker Street Babes podcast had revealed that Conan Doyle hadn't been terribly precise about what Holmes kept on his bookshelves. Ross suspected that, despite her warnings about secrecy, being contacted by the police for expert advice in the midst of the 'Rache' killings would result in a few stray tweets of glee from those organizations. Of the few book titles named in the stories, none was missing. The museum didn't regard anything as being missing. They had the same number of blank prop books as their records said they'd had before. Recent pictures from visitors to the museum, as seen on Facebook, right up until the day of the Holmes 'murder' also revealed nothing that shouldn't be in the museum, no astronomical charts on the walls, the standard number of books all shoved up next to each other with gaps only left at the end of the shelves.

'Is it . . . just us that can see this stuff?' asked Costain. They went to have bacon sandwiches in the Gipsy Hill canteen and awkwardly showed a photo of the astronomical map to a lid, who, looking puzzled at them, said that he liked to stargaze sometimes, like.

'So,' said Sefton, bewildered, 'did this sentient and mobile Holmes . . . set up his rooms differently after everyone went home, like something out of *Night at the Museum*?'

'That does sound like him,' said Quill, weakly, as if he felt he ought to contribute something.

Ross went back to the ops board and tried to sum that grey area up in a couple of added notes.

After they'd got back to the Portakabin, Quill took a phone call from the main inquiry and reported to them the results. 'So, Bates's girlfriend confirms that she's been seeing him lately, didn't even try to conceal the fact, because he'd told her he was out.'

'Which,' said Sefton, 'using Occam's razor, puts him right back in the frame, whatever story he's telling us. He had the opportunity, and with the chalk he had the means.'

'Which is why,' said Quill, 'I felt obliged to share the first of those details with the main investigation. Not that I could tell them *how* he got out. Still, that'll cause havoc at Wandsworth.'

'He had a frigging staggering lack of motive,' said Costain. 'Nothing was stolen from those two murder scenes, and what's he got to do with killing Sherlock Holmes?'

'Maybe he was working for someone else?' said Sefton.

'So whatever mastermind put together this baffling mystery was stupid enough to hire Albie Bates?' asked Costain.

'Bates was lying about not knowing anything about the Holmes stories.' Ross hated replying directly to him, but at the same time she now felt weirdly able to. It was like Costain was so caught up in the case now he'd stopped having artificial reactions to her. 'His mum's Facebook page includes pictures of him aged eight, in the deerstalker, in his primary-school production of *Hound of the Baskervilles.*'

'Oh, well then, case closed!' said Costain. Ross was amazed he was talking back to her. Pleased, honestly. Maybe they could work together after all. 'Listen, can you imagine our first victim, Christopher Lassiter, even if he was the most un-racist person on earth, answering the door to complete stranger Albie Bates and then immediately having a cuppa with him? Albie doesn't have the gift of the gab.'

Quill had been listening, looking increasingly frustrated. 'Not a good fit, I grant you, but maybe he forced his way in, ordered the victim to make a cup of tea.'

'Instead of grabbing his DVD player and running?' asked Costain. 'Come on, what's in it for Bates? Why leave a word on the wall that isn't in his vocabulary? Bates isn't who did this; Bates is who gets sent down for it when they can't find anyone else, and you know it. Is that what we do now?'

Quill looked for a moment like he was going to bellow at Costain, had to visibly control himself. 'Of course it isn't.'

'So,' said Sefton, moving on, 'if we *assume* Bates is innocent, we should focus on this guy, our new prime suspect.' He pointed to a piece of paper on the board with only a name written on it. 'Dean Michael. If he's real, he could have used the same item, gesture or sound to hide himself from the prison authorities and to create, on that CCTV camera, and possibly for anyone watching, the illusion that he was Bates. That's well within the bounds of what we know to be possible. We didn't see anything of the Sight about Bates on the ladder, but we've seen that people in the know can hide from us.'

'The name Dean Michael isn't in the databases,' said Ross. 'Google offers a number of individuals called that from around the world, but none with any of the indicators associated with our line of work or with London.'

'Say he's pretending to be in the prison system,' said Costain, 'to set Bates up, which, if you can walk through walls, wouldn't be that hard to do. Individual prison officers see inmates come and go all the time – they don't know who's supposed to be in the mess hall unless they're called upon to make a count – and as a remand prisoner, he'd be in his own clothes.'

'He didn't use this "walkthrough" to enter either of the first two crime scenes,' said Quill. 'Just at 221B.'

'Because, in the first case, he had to obtain the victim's trust to use the poison. In the second case . . . well, Lisa noted that means of entry was bizarre. What if he did it that way in order to get his illusion seen by the CCTV camera, in order to fit up Bates?'

Quill nodded. 'Let's get Bates in here with the PRO-FIT software, get a photofit of Dean Michael we can show around.' He called Clarke's office again and requested that Bates be brought over to the Hill tonight, so they could interview him in the morning. 'Another long day,' he said. 'We'll leave it there for now.'

Ross tried to hang about, after Sefton and Costain left, to have a word in private with Quill. He'd done so much for her in the past. Whatever he was dealing with on his own, she wanted to help. When Quill saw her hanging back, however, he just tossed her the keys and curtly told her to lock up, then was away to his own car. Ross watched him go. She wondered if there was something somewhere in Quill's life that might give him a lead on what was weighing him down. She hoped desperately that he could find it.

*

Since getting the Sight, Quill had found the drive home from work really bloody difficult. He'd put the radio on, try to screen out the horrors London offered. Sticking to the same route had, to a degree, made those horrors routine, but only to a degree. He would always wave, for instance, to the same forlorn figure standing in the graveyard near his home. Lately, he'd been making himself do it, because after Hell, he had to make himself do so many small, routine things.

Tonight, however, the drive home was different. It took him a while to feel it, through the thoughts about Laura and Sarah and Jessica that he kept rolling round and round in his head. He gradually became aware that the Sight was trying to tell him about something. Something was behind him, occasionally to one side. He looked in the mirror, couldn't see anything unusual. The feeling persisted all the way home. He parked outside his house, locked the car, then hesitated for a new reason, looked slowly around the leafy housing estate close.

The Sight was giving him a strangely generalized warning. It was very vague, on the edge of being nothing, close to the anxiety that these days infested his every waking moment. He found he was looking at the corner at the end of the close, the pavement in the longer shadows of approaching autumn. He thought yet again, as he looked, of the pavements he'd tramped in Hell. He tried yet again, as he often did, to take comfort in the mere existence of physical objects around him, in being basically comfortable and free from pain, in the weather, even. They were all just sheets draped over what was true. Was that shadow on the corner getting longer? Was someone standing just around there? Quill watched and waited. Eventually, he became uncertain. The length of the shadow had changed with the light.

'Quill?' That was Sarah, standing at the door, Jessica in her arms. 'What's going on?'

He shook his head, turned to her with a broad and artificial smile. 'The great detective was lost in thought.' He went and kissed Jessica, and made to go into the house, but just before he went inside, he looked back again and was still unsure.

'You know,' he said, so, so casually, as he and Sarah made dinner together, 'I think we should try and talk Laura out of coming to live in London.' He hadn't rehearsed this. This was nerve-wracking, on the edge of disaster.

'I know what you mean,' said Sarah. 'What with all you've told me, all that's happened to us. But we're doing OK, aren't we? The people who don't know about this stuff are doing OK too.'

'"OK"?!' Quill felt his heart suddenly racing, had to breathe deeper. 'You think what happened to me is "doing OK"?!'

Sarah stopped, put down what she was doing, nervously wondered how she should reply.

He hated seeing her like that. He took those deep breaths, calmed down. 'Sorry,' he whispered.

'It's all right.' She came over and put her arms round him. 'Quill, I just want to help. Please let me help.'

He disengaged himself. He had to get to his point. 'I meant that it's probably going to get worse. It'd be irresponsible to let Laura move down if, you know, that smiling bastard's going to start something. We don't know what his big plan is.'

She knew he was keeping something back from her. 'Quill, she's never going to believe it. Even if I back you up. She'll think we're mad.'

He suddenly had to control his breathing again. He went to lean on the fridge.

'Quill, please, I know you don't want to talk about it—'

He quickly straightened up. 'Another great detective moment, love. Moving swiftly on . . .'

'Please—'

'Can I try to tell you about my work? Can I please just try to bloody do that?' He was overreacting again. He couldn't help it. He hated not being able to help it. Something inside him kept trying to make that her fault. 'Sorry.'

'You can tell me anything. You know that, don't you?'

He shook his head, ignored what those words had done to him. 'Like I said, moving on. Sharing something from work. Let me put a question to you directly, see what you reckon, just the first thing that comes into your head?'

'OK.'

'Who killed Sherlock Holmes?'

'Arthur Conan Doyle. He killed him off in the stories, because he was fed up with only being known for writing that one character. Are you going to tell me what that's about?'

He did. Tons and tons of it, feeling some relief at being able to share at least something about his work life, in the way he'd become used to since getting the Sight. Every detail, though, felt like it might lull him into weakness, into telling Sarah what he must not tell her, about that sign over the entrance to Hell. 'Conan Doyle,' he said. 'You know, that's not a bad idea. He might be remembered by London too.'

They went to bed. Sarah went to sleep and Quill pretended to.

The phone call came what felt like a few minutes after Quill had fallen into a troubled sleep, but from the clock it was more like two hours. He scrabbled for the bedside phone and heard Ross's voice on the end of the line, and what she was saying made him slowly stumble up and start finding his clothes.

He got to Gipsy Hill around 4 a.m. The nick was in lockdown, and it took him a while to get through the added security to the cell where a boy he took to be Albie Bates lay half on the floor and half across a bunk, his spine arched, his mouth set in a grimace, his eyes staring. Around the body crouched the crime scene examiners, and in the corridor outside, Costain, Sefton and Ross, furious, incredulous. Costain was walking back and forth, his face an angry mask. Behind them, on the wall that led, through a couple of empty cells, to the exterior wall, was chalked the shape of a very small door.

Costain caught Quill's glance. 'I think,' he said, 'Bates was probably telling the truth.'

Quill felt like kicking that chalk shape. He had to will himself not to do so. 'How did he die?'

'Strychnine poisoning,' said one of the CSEs, straightening up. 'I'll need to do tests, but I've seen it before. Administered by . . .' She pointed to just above the boy's right ear, where something long and dark was sticking out of the skin. 'Looks like a thorn of some kind.'

'So was it pressed into him by someone standing out here, or . . . ?'

'I'm betting it was fired by a blowpipe,' said Ross. 'Because that's the murder method in the next Sherlock Holmes book after *A Study in Scarlet*, *The Sign of Four*.'

They all took a moment. They looked at each other, lost. The CSE, judging that this was their private burden, stepped discreetly back into the cell.

'So did they just use this MO because they wanted to shut him up?' asked Sefton. 'OK, so someone's killing people not just like the murders in *A Study in Scarlet* but continuing into the other Holmes books, meaning that nothing was written on the wall in this case. But if the location the murders take place, at least near to where they happen in the books, was important for the first two—'

'That's the worst thing,' said Ross. She held up her phone and showed them a Google map with many pins in it. 'Conan Doyle fans made this map of the locations used in the stories. In *The Sign of Four*, Bartholomew Sholto is killed by poison dart at his home, Pondicherry Lodge. The book doesn't give a street address, but it's in Upper Norwood.'

'Oh no,' said Quill.

'This is the nearest police station. Not only is our killer continuing to murder people in ways that copy the Holmes stories, they just used us to do it.'

EIGHT

Rebecca Lofthouse felt awkward to be in the company of Quill and his team again. Now more than ever, she had to keep her poker face on at all times, to not give away to these people she'd come to trust the dangerous adventure she'd been on. If her husband . . . if whatever had possessed her husband . . . could walk into her communications devices, then he could certainly access theirs. Indeed, if she were him, any sign that she'd told this team what was going on would be the first thing she'd look for.

As soon as she got into the station that morning, she got Quill to brief her on the murder in custody and swiftly got him access to the CCTV recordings of the cell corridor. The small chalked doorways did indeed also appear in the empty cells that led to the exterior wall, and on the inside of that wall. There was a matching one on the outside too. The suspect hadn't bothered to erase it.

'Here we go again,' she said to him as they gathered round the monitor, thinking back to when Mora Losley had invaded Gipsy Hill. The team fast-forwarded the video to the point where they told her they could see a figure in the corridor, then halted it and exclaimed about the nature of the shape.

'Wait a sec,' said Lofthouse. 'I can see it too.'

They compared notes. They were seeing exactly the same

thing. The suspect was not a creature only visible by the Sight. It was a male, who looked to be of subcontinental descent, of very short stature, dressed in a sort of tribal outfit.

'As in the book, ma'am,' said Ross, sounding as astonished as Lofthouse felt. The footage showed Bates asleep as the suspect walked up to his cell. The figure bent to aim his blowpipe, then fired. Bates jerked, convulsed, made what must have been choked attempts to cry out. The small figure, his work done, walked out of frame. They checked the cameras outside the nick. They showed the suspect approaching, looking around to see he wasn't being observed, then producing a stick of chalk, drawing it on the wall and walking through it. Lofthouse felt that, without the Sight, she shouldn't have been able to see anybody walking through anything, and said so.

'Makes sense if you think about it, ma'am,' said Costain. 'If we freeze-framed on the moment of him going through, then maybe you'd get a headache looking at it, or couldn't see the moment of impossibility, but what are you actually seeing there that requires the Sight? Nothing. First the bloke's there; then he isn't.'

'That fucker,' said Costain, with some passion, 'is visible to everybody. How the fuck did he get across the car park without anyone seeing him, looking like that?'

'Maybe he doesn't look like that, really,' said Sefton. 'We were working on the theory that it wasn't Bates who climbed up that ladder, but someone else, creating an illusion of Bates. An illusion the main investigation could see as well as us. Perhaps that's what happened here too.'

'No,' said Ross. She was looking professionally angry, like she hated this puzzle being beyond her, even perhaps hated not having anticipated this. 'Think about the size of the chalk doorway. Only someone really that small could fit through it. So either we assume the suspect has the power to change size also, which is a seriously groundless assumption, or we're looking at a team of some kind, a team that actually includes a . . .

small blowpipe bloke. Why does he even look like the killer from the story, anyway? The killer didn't have to last time.'

'Maybe the fuckers are trying for as much authentic detail as possible,' said Sefton, 'except when something else is more important. For the first murder, they had to gain the victim's trust; for the second one, they were setting up Bates; this time, they were able to go to town. Or maybe what was written on the wall provided enough authenticity on those two occasions, and this time they had to find that in other ways, such as . . . employing a small assassin of indigenous origin.'

'He has got to be on a database somewhere,' said Costain.

They searched on their phones, there and then, because the search terms were so easy. Lofthouse watched that hope crumble. There was nobody on the police databases resembling the suspect, and only two such people on the books as actors, even, neither of whom looked at all like the killer.

'Damn it,' said Ross, switching off her phone. 'We just have a cloud of data points right now. I can't call any of it intel, because we haven't made step one towards processing it.'

They checked the exterior CCTV. Frustratingly, there was no camera that precisely covered the angles leading to that stretch of wall. They went outside and found chalk marks in the shape of a door on both sides of the wire fence, in a darkened corner of the car park where one of the ancient lights had failed. Costain led them along a path between cameras, some of which had also gone out of order and hadn't been replaced due to the continuing austerity measures. It took them a while, but they finally got to the entry point at the wall.

'That would take a lot of figuring out,' said Ross. 'Suspect couldn't have done it on the night; he must have staked out the station, made notes.'

Lofthouse ordered that all the walls in question be checked for fingerprints. She realized that normally she would have expected to hear some words of experience from Quill before now, but instead he was staring at the exterior wall, his fingers flexing, frustrated to the point where he radiated pain. She could see his team glancing in his direction too, not wanting to comment in front of her. Ross said she wanted to take the new evidence back to the ops board across the road. Lofthouse agreed.

As Quill headed out, she held him back. 'James,' she asked, 'what aren't you telling me?'

He shook his head, a nervy smile on his face. 'That's bloody ironic, eh, ma'am? Tell you what, if you tell me yours, I'll tell you mine.' Which was right on the edge of insubordination. But she had to admit he had a point.

Lofthouse kept in touch with the operation all that day. She put out an all-points warning for a killer with a very distinctive appearance. The new commissioner called her to talk to her about this second death in custody at Gipsy Hill within two years, the call being clearly just a warning shot, with pleasantries throughout. Lofthouse told him that a review of security procedures was already in progress, which was true.

At the end of the day, she headed home, and saw Peter's car in the drive. Tensing up, she went into the house and found him in the bedroom, in his dress shirt, putting on his cufflinks, like their life together of thirty years continued as always.

'Hurry up and change,' he said, his voice still with that edge to it that said someone else was in there. 'Everything is normal, remember?'

Christina's birthday party had a lot of their old friends attending, people from the law-enforcement community, London business-people, Peter's mates from the City. They mingled in one of the new apartments in the Shard, enormous tanned windows turning even the descending sun into something controlled. Lofthouse wondered distantly if, had the invitation been to somewhere outside of London, Peter would have refused to go. She'd tried that once, at the start, driving him quickly towards the motorway, but he'd calmly produced a Stanley knife and put it to his wrist. Lofthouse would have found it impossible to keep her calm expression tonight, she was sure, except for the fact she was on a mission. Still, she made sure to look a little burdened whenever Peter glanced in her direction.

She found herself quite naturally in the company of one Jack Glassman, a mutual friend, always in strangely ill-fitting suits, the perfect imperfection of one too rich to care. She waited until his girlfriend headed to the bathroom. 'We don't have much time,' she said. 'I'm not joking. Keep the look on your face calm, like you're listening to me making small talk.'

His eyes lit up. Oh God, he thought she was going to proposition him. 'OK.'

'You're an antiques dealer, right? The leading one in the south of England, I've heard. So I'm betting there's *something* dodgy about you, something somewhere way down in the detail of your properties, accounts, procedures, something you might not even be aware of, that you wouldn't want opened up to, say, multiple dawn raids.'

To his credit, he kept that slight smile, though the sparkle in his eyes became something very different. 'Are you warning me . . . ?'

'No, I'm *threatening* you. Here's another assumption I'm going to make about you: you know what I'm talking about when I say I want to see something that can't be seen.'

'What?'

If he genuinely didn't have the faintest idea what she was talking about, then she'd just threatened a powerful member of the public for no good reason. Then she could say goodbye to her pension, and to her husband's life. It was ironic that Quill's team had in custody, in the form of Ballard, an individual who could, no question, provide her with what she was after. But to access him, to let him out to get what she needed, would require official communications that whatever was inside her husband would doubtless notice. She had to do this through back channels.

'You've seen an enormous number of objects with London history to them. You know there's something . . .' She realized she was on the edge of sounding weak. She moved her head closer and dropped her voice to a whisper. 'Don't you *fuck* with me. You *know* what I mean.'

He did. She could see it. It scared him, and it scared him that she knew. He glanced around the room, and she took the moment to see Peter still chatting away. 'If I did . . . ?'

'Then find me an item that lets the user see things that aren't otherwise there. Deliver it to me at Gipsy Hill nick. Do not email me, do not text me, do not call me. That'll be an end to the matter, and I . . .' She allowed just the slightest hint of possibility into her voice. 'I will owe you one.'

His sudden intake of breath and curt nod were very satisfying.

NINE

'What the fuck are we looking at?' Ross stepped back from the most crowded ops board she'd ever seen. The small assassin from *The Sign of Four* had been added to it, by way of a still from the CCTV camera footage, with a suspect line connecting him to Bates, who was still himself similarly connected to the first two murders. 'It's like every time something new happens, a firework display of data points goes off.' The chart did indeed look like a fractal explosion, with unconnected data pinned everywhere. Added to it had been the news that the astronomical photos and charts had been ordered from an online astronomy shop via PayPal, an account the investigation of which led through several loops to a dead end.

'We're going,' deadpanned Costain, 'to need a bigger board.'

'At least,' said Ross, 'now we know this is continuing, we can stay one step ahead. I've read the next few books. There's an earlier murder in *A Study in Scarlet*, but that's in the US, and my searches find no trace of anything like it in the last five years. There's also an earlier murder in *The Sign of the Four*, as the original's called, but that's in India, and again, no sign.'

'Because if this is about harvesting the power of sacrifice,' said Sefton, 'you'd need to be in a city of the Sight to do so. Probably London, if this is all about Sherlock Holmes.'

'My wife,' said Quill, 'mentioned Arthur Conan Doyle. I mean as a suspect.'

He'd been looking very distracted, twitchy, pacing. It was like he was building to something. It was making all of them nervous.

'Good thought,' she said. She wondered if Sarah, who'd impressed her in the past, was managing to help with Quill's current situation. She printed out a picture of Conan Doyle and added him to the board.

'He would also be a ghost,' said Costain. 'So we've got a ghost murdering a ghost.'

'Wait a sec . . .' Sefton had been looking at his phone, watching the video they'd taken of the flickering corpse of Holmes. 'Yeah, look.'

They gathered round to see. He'd frozen it at a moment when the ever-changing face of the sprawled figure was that of a distinguished-looking Victorian. 'Conan Doyle isn't remembered by London separately. I mean, you know, where would you expect to find him? Nowhere specific. He's not remembered as doing any particular thing apart from creating Holmes, so there he is, mixed up with his creation. He's *part* of the *victim*, and so, therefore, unless we're dealing with something bogglingly existential here—'

'We might be,' said Ross. She didn't want to take the name off the board, but she didn't feel any particular enthusiasm towards the notion, not without further evidence. 'What most gets to me is that Gipsy Hill nick could be used as a factor in this murder spree. It seems to me that the only reasonable possibility is that the killer or killers knew from the outset about our team's existence and what we do, and deliberately caught our attention, purely in order so they could do the double: set up Bates as the killer of victim number two, in order to conceal their own identity or identities, then make sure we're interested enough to bring Bates to a location that allowed his death to fit the pattern.'

'You don't think . . . ?' Sefton had a sudden look of inspiration. Ross gestured for him to keep going. 'They wouldn't have killed Sherlock Holmes just to get our attention, would they?'

Ross found herself making the same sound of horrified realization that Costain did. 'That makes so much sense.' She gestured to the board. 'Holmes is the odd one out, not killed in the manner of a Holmes story.'

'It's either that,' said Sefton, 'or our theory about these murders being payment for killing Holmes is correct, only the payment has to continue. It breaks the law of threes, lead lead up, lead up, then pow. But now I say it out loud, I think that's actually a rule of comedy, not this shit.' He rubbed his brow. 'It's weird what feels natural.'

'What's the next Conan Doyle book?' asked Quill.

'It's not a book,' said Ross. 'It's a collection of short stories, *The Adventures of Sherlock Holmes*.' She went and got from her bag the paperback copy of *The Complete Adventures* that she'd bought. 'The next few stories are "A Scandal in Bohemia", "The Adventure of the Red-Headed League" and "A Case of Identity".'

'Is that publication order or how they are in the book?'

'Both. Nothing like the events in those stories has happened yet. I've got search alerts set up for what happens in the first of those, which should be pretty easy to spot.'

Costain produced his own copy from his jacket. She felt her continuous irritation at him crank up by one notch. It was even the same edition. Like he wanted to check up on her conclusions. She was being irrational, she knew. That was another thing she hated about him. He made her irrational. 'There isn't a murder in that one, though, right?'

'I think a murder or something equally big would be required for a sacrifice,' said Sefton.

'Yeah,' said Ross quickly, 'which is why I've got searches set up for "The Red-Headed League", which also has no murders, and the same for "A Case of Identity" but a whole bunch more for "The Boscombe Valley Mystery", in which someone *is* killed.'

'But not in London,' said Costain. 'That's set in Herefordshire. There's someone found dead in Sussex in "The Five Orange Pips", but then—'

Ross raised her hands. 'I've already got searches . . .' She found the annoyance overwhelming her. She couldn't help it now. This had brought her to a dead stop. 'Look,' she said, 'who's the analyst here?'

'I'm not trying to . . .' Costain put down the book. 'I want us to work together.'

Ross wanted to say he should keep to his speciality and stop trying to cosy up to her. But before she could find any words, Sefton stepped between them. 'If it *is* just murders in London,' he said, 'then we have an opportunity here. The killer or killers need to commit these crimes close to where they're done in the original.' He looked to Quill, addressing the whole room. 'How about we find out where the next one's going to be and just bloody *nick* them?'

Quill watched as Ross spread a map of London out on the table. Something in the back of his head was nagging at him, in that copper way, but he couldn't focus on it, had to hope that the others working the case would bring it to light. Not that anything mattered . . .

He stamped on the thought. He had to keep going. At least until he worked out what he was missing.

'Later on in "The Five Orange Pips",' said Ross, 'there's a drowning in the Thames, from the deck of a ship called the *Lone Star*. That's the next death in London. So let's check the references in the story and online, because the fans will have our job already, and see if we can sort out where on the river such a drowning might take place.'

Sefton looked something up on his phone. Quill saw him react in amazement at what he found. 'The *Lone Star*,' he said.

'It's a real ship. It's on its way to London, gets here in three days.'

'*What?*' said Costain.

Quill found that he had to lean on the table. 'It's like . . . something can make enormous changes to reality.' Was it like he'd said, that the death of Holmes was the start of . . . of the mere possibility of law, rules and meaning all falling apart? 'How likely is it that a ship with that name would just happen to be coming to London, right on time for our murderer?'

Ross was glaring at him like she was going to slap him. 'Enormous changes to reality my arse. Sir. It's not that hard to change the name of a ship, and if our suspect can change reality, they could have killed the victims in the *exact* locations, not just nearby.' She took out her own phone and checked online. 'Government maritime service in Cardiff is what we're after.' After a few minutes, she had the answer. 'Until last week, when somebody bought and renamed it, this *Lone Star* was called the *Ocean Queen*, a US-registered vessel, currently in Ostend. It was bought by a company called Missing Room Ltd, who will have a bloody paper trail that will lead to somewhere close to our killer.' She went to the board and added all this with hard, swift strokes of marker. She stepped back from it and pointed. 'We have just resolved that heap of chaotic shit into not just a solid lead but an opportunity to apprehend.'

At the end of her working day, Lofthouse walked out to the car park with Sally Rutherford, a civil servant out of the Home Office whom she'd got to know quite well. She'd come over today to aid Lofthouse in prepping for a presentation she was due to make on the future of policing at an international law-enforcement conference, the details of which to Lofthouse now seemed ridiculous. However, she also represented an opportunity. A package had arrived for Lofthouse that lunchtime at the Hill, with no return address. It had contained an object she intended to put to use as quickly as possible.

'Sally,' she said, 'I was wondering if you could do me a favour? You see . . . I wish there was some other way to put this . . . I'm having an affair.'

Lofthouse hoped that, should a friend of hers say something similar to her, she wouldn't greet the news with the open-mouthed glee that Sally did. However, that was exactly the reaction she'd anticipated. Her friend swiftly recovered her composure. 'Well, I'm flattered you'd choose to share this with me . . .' She paused. 'Why *are* you sharing this with me?'

'Because I'm desperate, Sally. All my other friends love Peter. They don't know me like you do. They wouldn't understand that things have become . . . difficult.'

'Are you OK? I mean, he isn't . . . ?'

Lofthouse shook her head, as if to say that she didn't want to go into the details. If this worked, she was going to have to spend a long time afterwards working to recover Peter's reputation. Dear God, she hoped she could get to the point where that was what she was most worried about. 'So I want you to text me in about ten minutes, maybe email me too, to say there's something urgent you want to see me about, business, not personal, and then, about two hours later, if you could send me another message, saying thanks for coming over so late . . .'

Sally nodded and nodded, lapping it up. Having set up this cover, Lofthouse reasoned, she could use it several times if need be. If Peter found out what she'd said, she could say she'd needed to explain the tension between them. It was still true, thought Lofthouse, that if you wanted the world to know something, the best person to tell was a senior civil servant.

She waited in her car until Sally sent her the text, then replied to it saying she was on her way, switched off her phone and tablet, and drove quickly to Golders Green. She flashed her warrant card to thankfully the same caretaker and parked in the quad of the apartment block.

She made her way to where she knew the invisible door was,

her briefcase clutched under her arm. She waited until an elderly man with a suspicious look on his face went into his flat carrying his shopping, then took what had been delivered to her out of its packaging. She took care snipping off the layer of bubble wrap that concealed it. Inside was a shape made of paper: a small off-white origami bird. The unsigned note that had come with it had indicated that it had been made in London for the novelist Dennis Wheatley by one Rollo Ahmed. Lofthouse gently took the bird by one wingtip and, in the absence of instructions, held it in front of her as she approached the worrying place where she assumed the door of the missing apartment number 23 to be. She ignored the complex sensations and inched the bird forwards. The key on her charm bracelet reacted as it had before. The paper bird must now be near the door.

The bird suddenly, impossibly, moved. It leaped from her hand, spent a moment moving swiftly up and down, as if aiming itself, then instantly flattened itself again, becoming a white square that seemed to hang in . . . no, not in space, but against a door, which she could now dimly perceive, like a projected image overlaid on reality. It still distorted everything around it, it was still hard to look at, and Lofthouse was sure she felt something creaking, as if the piece of paper was soaking up enormous architectural stresses.

She took a moment to breathe properly. She looked down at a tug on her wrist. Her charm bracelet was being pulled towards the door by the key, which was pointing at it like it was magnetized.

She took a look at the ordinary lock that hung like a phantom in front of her. No great security required, not here, with a guard on the gate. She looked right and left, then took the crowbar from her briefcase, slipped it into the edge of the phantom door and threw all her weight against it. It took a lot of heaving, and she was sure she'd get reported to the gate-house, but what for, exactly? Madwoman, police officer, attacking a wall. Because as she saw with a step or two back, the door was only visible when she was close enough. She returned to her task, and the door finally flew open, leaving the piece of paper hanging in the air in the revealed doorway.

She tried to look inside and found it sickening, then bloody made herself do it anyway. It was like looking at one of those Escher paintings through some sort of stereoscopic viewer. She was seeing at least two things at once. The piece of paper, though, provided perspective. She got the feeling it was sorting out what she could see. She made herself step inside.

It was like falling asleep and starting to dream. Her conscious brain kept trying to haul one part of the room over to join with another part, to make sense, and that kept making her stumble, like she was on a ship's deck that was rocking from side to side in all possible directions. She was inside what looked like images of walls, floor, ceiling, objects, projected onto whiteness, and not sorted properly, hanging askew from each other. Presumably this was the best the piece of paper could do in the face of . . . She could feel it, now she thought of it, a tremendous power trying to erase this place from her mind. It wasn't like being in one's own dream, then, but like being in that of a giant, and it felt like he might at any moment wake up. She looked over to the piece of paper and saw that its edges were starting to char. That must be a visual representation of that power getting to it, using up its resources. She had minutes at the most.

She ignored how skewed her senses were and let her training take over. What sort of place was this? A rich person's grace-and-favour apartment, small but tasteful, now lost to the world. She felt she should recognize it. She must have been here. To think about that would make the paper burn more quickly; she felt that instinctively as her brain pushed at the idea. She dismissed trying to remember. She had to quickly search the place.

Where first? The key on her wrist tugged her towards just one place: the desk. She swiftly followed the call. It was like a blown-apart diagram of a desk, inside out and back to front. She went to it, found the drawers, didn't want to throw the contents out for fear she'd lose them in the void. Just a few mementos. There was a locked drawer, with items inside: she could see them inside the desk. The key was straining at the leash. She broke the desk open and really could see, in a way that she hadn't before. Better. A sheaf of folded papers. The key swung about them like a compass needle. This was all it wanted. She dropped the papers into her briefcase. That was it for the desk.

Was there anything around here the key would fit into? She couldn't see any possibilities. The key was ancient and everything here was modern. There was a wall safe. The key wasn't interested – it had what it had come for – but she was. She went to the safe.

It was closed, a numerical tumbler. Her crowbar wouldn't do for that, and if she had once known the combination, as it seemed likely she might, then she'd certainly be prevented from remembering it now. It was a six-figure combination. Could she apply the same logic she'd used to find the door? The strange pressure she felt in this room seemed animal, blunt; it didn't feel like it could react strategically.

She thought of the first number, trying to remember it as if she'd forgotten it normally. One . . . two . . . There was the smallest jolt of resistance at the thought of three. She could do this; it was like listening to the tumblers in a lock. If she had time. She would see it through. What was the worst that could happen, that she'd be trapped here? Then Peter would be safe, at least, no need to hurt him if she wasn't around to be threatened by it.

She quickly thought through the numbers for each digit, built up a combination of six of them in her head that hurt like an enormous buzzing, that would reach the point of actual pain in seconds, if she kept trying to remember. She put her fingers on the dial, smelling burning paper, hearing the thump of a flame bursting into life. She spun the dial back and forth and heard the clicks. She let each number go from her memory as she did. There would only be one chance at this. She got to the last number, felt the door give and flung it open.

In the safe was a gun. An extraordinary gun. It was ornate, covered in decoration, shaped like a shotgun but with so much more—

She didn't have time. She grabbed it, threw it into her briefcase and turned for the door. The piece of paper was on fire. It suddenly began to sing, the alarm call of a bird. It was dying.

As in a dream, she found it hard to haul her feet across the floor towards the doorway. She could feel the room starting to react to her presence, now the licence the paper had given her was vanishing. The giant was about to stop dreaming her. Her existence was about to vanish. She bellowed with the effort of it, and thought of nothing but Peter, and pushed herself through a roaring gale of nothingness to the doorway. She grabbed it with one hand and heaved herself through . . .

To stumble a few steps out onto the walkway. The spectral door shut like thunder behind her. The ashes of a piece of paper fluttered into her face as she turned, sad birdsong fading with them. She stood there panting. She'd done it. Hadn't she? She was in the normal world again. She could feel the cold air on her face.

She looked into her briefcase. The gun and papers were still there.

She wanted to cry. She would not. She straightened herself up and went to find her car.

TEN

Night on the Thames. Costain was looking along the river from the deck of an unmarked vessel of the Met's Marine Policing Unit. To someone with the Sight, the river was like a cascade of emotions, a restlessness that continually woke all the moments of history and story along its banks, stirred them into loudly restating all the details of their existence. He wondered for a moment why simple water did that, when actually it was only briefly of London, on a one-way trip from some underground aquifer far to the west and then out to the sea.

Oh no, Tony, you're missing an important detail there, old son, he thought: you haven't considered the rain. The water of the bodies of living Londoners evaporated upwards, became clouds, fell back into that river, or into the ground to be absorbed into that aquifer.

Everything they'd found in the Docklands ruins said that the Continuing Projects Team, which had come before them, believed that buildings and other physical objects were mostly responsible for the shape of the occult forces in the metropolis, but Costain's lot, being coppers, knew that everything bad that happened was the fault of bloody people.

They had no idea tonight who they were facing, but it was a relief to, just for once, be one step ahead of the bastards. Since they'd got on to the lead about the *Lone Star*, the team had started to work again, once more all having particular tasks to accomplish. Maybe if they kept that going, things would get better. Unfortunately, in the middle of that there was Quill. There was something deeply worrying going on with him now. Sooner or later, they were going to have to confront him about it.

Costain looked over to Ross, in a life vest like he was, a shadowed shape on the unlit deck. He saw again the beauty of her face in silhouette, the awkward angle of her nose that was so brilliant. He'd been looking at her too often. She'd said a couple of things to him in the last few days, directly to his face. He'd responded normally, because he didn't have the energy or the willingness to deceive her even slightly now. He might get back to a professional partnership with her by doing that, in time, but that wasn't the way to get to where he wanted to be with her. He needed to change, to really change, to deserve her respect. That was an end in itself. She wouldn't take him back when he did, he knew that, though a part of him really wanted that to be the case, like it was in the movies. If he could change, he could be free of needing her so much, they would both be people who stood on their own, and then perhaps she could meet him again as that different person. That was the best he could hope for.

He would act on this. He would demonstrate change. He had a terrible feeling it might involve sacrifice, but OK. He would do this proudly, deliberately. He looked in the other direction, to where the Met skipper, Sergeant Alex Petrovski, was in bemused conversation with Sefton. This hard-surveillance stop was going to be unlike any the sergeant had previously experienced, and Sefton was making sure there was nothing about the vessel they were on that might give it away to a Sighted observer. That process had included quite a bit of sniffing and tasting.

Somewhere ahead of them, upriver, was the *Lone Star*, heading for the point where the attempted murder might happen. They'd heard from the Dutch police, using undercover assets in the port of Ostend, that the ship had taken on a single crate there. Coming up fast behind it by now, showing as few lights as they were, should be a second police vessel, a fast-response Targa 31, with an SC&O19 specialist firearms team on it, trained for tasked interdictions of commercial and private vessels, the vessel crewed and steered by the Marine Policing Unit's Tactical Response Team. The officers involved, from Inspector Patterson of the MPU on down, had expressed interest in being part of a raid organized by Quill's mysterious little squad. Petrovski picked up the radio again and hit the button. 'Marine Four One to Marine Six Eight. Do you have target in sight? Over.'

A confirming voice came from the other end of the channel. 'ETA to interdiction approximately three minutes.'

There were two other MPU officers with them, in uniform, ready with the specialist equipment that would enable Quill's team to board. Costain glanced over to Quill himself, who was pacing the deck, on edge as always now.

Ross stepped forwards to address him as much as the crew. 'OK,' she said. 'For the third time . . .' One of the crew made a humorous clearing of the throat, but that was the extent of the protests. 'The crew of the *Lone Star* on this particular voyage numbers eight, all of them American citizens, three of them with criminal records for crimes ranging from GBH to armed robbery, all of those three plus two more with connections to the Ku Klux Klan.' That detail was as in the story. Whether or not their opponents had the almighty powers imagined by Quill, they certainly had an extraordinary reach in the everyday world to arrange things like that. 'We think they're planning a drowning tonight. We suspect their potential victim is being kept in a crate secured to the deck, as observed by the plain-clothes units we've had trailing the vessel. We don't know where they plan to throw that crate overboard. We think they're now heading for deep water, and perhaps for a moment when river traffic is light.'

'There.' Petrovski was pointing downriver.

Costain picked up the binoculars he'd brought along. The *Lone Star* was a beaten-up-looking sea-going freighter, with a low deck, still running with all the correct lights. There didn't seem to be any activity on deck as yet, but, and this was worrying, he couldn't see the crate, not in the location reported by the last contact from the plain-clothes officers watching the vessel. He reported that to Ross.

Ross took up her own binoculars. 'Hopeful assumption: they must have moved it ready to chuck it. If they'd already done so, I think they'd have scarpered back to open sea.' Petrovski relayed the news to the other police vessel.

Costain hoped she was right. He couldn't imagine the plight of the poor bastard inside. He couldn't feel anything of the Sight about the vessel. They continued heading towards the *Lone Star*. In a few moments, they would be level. The radio buzzed again in the skipper's hand. He listened for a moment, then looked back to Quill. 'Inspector Patterson is asking for go or no go.'

Quill looked relieved to be doing something. 'Go,' he said.

Petrovski relayed the order, increased his own boat's speed and started swiftly turning the wheel, as the crew members readied the boarding gear. They were now closing with the *Lone Star*, coming alongside . . . Costain found himself tensing, waiting for someone on that vessel to notice, horribly aware that he had an urge to prove himself, the sort of thing that got soldiers heroically killed. He desperately wanted to make himself right by reaching for something beyond himself. He would. He would.

They came alongside, and at that exact moment, powerful searchlights blazed from the other side of the *Lone Star*, illuminating the deck as the loudspeaker of the other Targa blared into life. '*Lone Star, Lone Star*, armed police officers, armed police officers. Switch off your engine, heave to and prepare to be boarded.' At the same time, metal ladders were flung over the opposite rail, and the black uniforms of armed officers in flak jackets and helmets leaped over, taking immediate firing postures and trying to acquire targets. Their aim, stated in the briefing, was to dominate and shut down, with the purpose of making the bridge surrender and bringing the ship in to the nearest dock. Suddenly, bright light erupted from the cabin, with a cracking sound like popcorn. One of the uniforms ran for cover; another fell and rolled away, shouting in pain.

Fuck. Fuck.

Costain just had time to look over to where their Targa's crew were pulling hard on ropes, throwing their own boarding ladder over. Quill hadn't bothered with ordering his team to follow, and he clearly wasn't waiting for the armed police officers to secure the ship; he was running for the ladders, because he must have already seen what Costain saw now: that towards the bow of the vessel, in shadow, oilskins were being swiftly pulled from a crate that stood right beside the rail.

Costain ran for the ladder and clambered up it, Quill ahead of him, Sefton and Ross right behind. He wished he had a gun, but that was out of the question with uniforms about: he wasn't authorized to carry. They all had Metvests on under their life vests, but that was the extent of their protection.

He hauled himself over the side of the ship and onto the unfamiliar deck, which was swaying violently. He felt deeply scared about Ross behind him, that she'd be shot and fall, but no, no, for fuck's sake, don't think, just run. Ahead, two men, who still didn't seem to have spotted them, what with all the noise and the lights shining towards them, were heaving at a tall, thin coffin of a crate. They were trying desperately to get it to a point on the rail where its own weight would take it over. Fuck, this lot were professionals, to try to complete their job while their mates were under fire.

The first of them looked up and cried out just before Quill ran into him like a train, knocking him to the deck. The second of them grabbed – not a gun, thank God, not a gun – a crowbar and Costain was on him, full of anger, exulting in it, punching him in the throat and falling with him onto the slippery deck. They rolled and hit a door as it was opening, and out of it rushed two more men. One of them shoved something towards Costain's neck, and he realized a second too late that it was buzzing with an electric arc, and—

Sefton threw himself aside as the shooting started, him and Quill and Ross having to scramble back along the slippery deck, desperately trying to find some cover. He saw in a moment holes appearing in the wood beside him, sawdust and water and bonfire-night smell in his face. There was nowhere to hide. He thought in that moment he was about to die. Then, thank Christ, light and sound from back down the deck, answering fire and the sound of running boots.

'Police officers!' he shouted, in case their own lot fired on them. He had time to look back to where Quill and Ross had their heads down, and now there was answering fire, back and forth, each side trying to keep the other pinned down. The two men Quill and Costain had tackled were inching their way back towards the crate. Where the fuck was Costain? God, had he gone over the rail? Now, one of the men got up and ran at the crate, actually dodging fire. All he'd need to do was throw his weight against it . . .

Sefton found that his legs were actually trying to make him clamber to his feet, to get into the way of harm, and he could feel Ross moving that way too, but beside them, with a roar of something that sounded more like pain than courage, Quill had beaten them to it. He'd pushed himself to his feet and was leaping to intercept the man who even now was hurling his weight against the crate. Once, twice, then Quill was on him, but it was too late. The crate went tumbling over the rail, and in that second the man who'd pushed it was revealed, a shaven head and a black T-shirt under a leather jacket. Suddenly, he jumped back as holes burst out of that T-shirt, and he fell. Quill hadn't stopped moving, he'd just changed direction, and he was clambering up; he was on the rail in the way of bullets, silhouetted against the white light all around them. Then he was over; he'd hurled himself after the crate.

Sefton heard the splash as Quill hit the water.

In the murky waters of the Thames, James Quill plummeted down. He'd had time to take a big breath. He had in his hands a pocket knife he'd brought to cut ropes. He'd landed in the foam of the crate's impact, so he must be right on top of it. Christ, the cold! He swam as best he could, a couple of big strokes, down, down.

There it was, standing upright on the river bottom, illuminated by the searchlights from the boat above. He was calm. This was nowhere near as terrifying as Hell had been. He didn't feel in danger of going back there now, and that was his only measure of risk. Right now, his anger was all he was. He used it. If he could just save one person, he might make his life feel worthwhile. He had seconds.

He saw they'd cut fucking holes in the crate, so it would fill up. The thing must be weighted at the bottom. He saw fingers desperately clawing at those holes. He pushed himself, flailing, towards them. He shoved the knife into the gap between two boards and heaved. The blade broke and fell into the dark. He got his fingers into the gap and broke his own nails heaving where the victim was heaving.

The fingers touched his own. They grabbed his, tried to get him to pull, but there was still solid wood between them. Quill made a last desperate effort and got his legs down, tried to heave them against the top of the crate, and now suddenly there were hands on him, black gloved hands, pulling him away as more of them flocked suddenly at the crate, and he realized these guys were the underwater rescue unit. He had to let out his breath at the second a blessed oxygen valve was shoved into his mouth, and he saw, in that moment, the top being wrenched off the crate.

He saw a dead face staring at him.

Quill had been there at the moment life had gone. It was a man, and all Quill could think of was that he knew him from somewhere. Then he was being propelled upwards and he closed his eyes and let all thought go in a shout of fury as he broke the surface.

Sefton ran to the rail to help Quill scramble back into the vessel, which had only been secured a few minutes before. Across the deck, armed officers were standing above a row of surviving crew members, who were cuffed and lying face down. Quill's expression was terrible to see. 'I . . . knew him,' he whispered.

'You shouldn't have done that.' Sefton looked round, and there was Ross, who'd found a blanket and rushed to wrap it round Quill.

Quill ignored that. 'The important thing we have to find out . . . Did he ever live in London?'

'What? Who?'

Quill gestured frantically over the side. 'The victim. We have to find out.'

The divers were now hauling the body over the side, and Sefton found to his surprise that he too recognized the pale, contorted face of the corpse that was laid out on deck. Petrovski and his officers had organized a stretcher. The faces of the divers told a story of anger and failure. They'd been delayed a few seconds too long by a firefight that had had a greater intensity to it than anyone had expected.

Sefton shook his head to clear it. 'Jimmy, the important thing is to find out what's happened to Tony. The armed uniforms have gone down into the hull; they're searching every inch of the ship—' He was cut off by a shout. Armed officers were marching two more cuffed suspects out onto the deck, and behind them, being helped along by other officers, was Costain.

His face was covered in livid welts and bruises, one eye almost fused closed by them. He saw Sefton and Ross looking over at him and pushed himself away from those holding him up, made himself stand, an impossibly stoic expression on his face.

Sefton looked to Ross. She turned back to Quill. 'So,' she said, too quickly, 'who's our victim?'

The crew of the vessel checked out as those registered to sail her. Three of them were now dead. The rest weren't talking, were calm, even. It looked to Sefton like they felt the danger was over for them now. They were professionals, who'd regarded potentially going to prison as part of what they'd been paid for. He'd met a few like them in his time within gangs. He covertly tried the bell with the powerful sense of the Sight to it on those being held in cuffs, but got no reaction out of any of them. It wasn't likely they'd get much more on interview.

As the *Lone Star* was brought in to dock, Sefton watched Costain accept only the minimum of first aid. He said he was sure he hadn't broken anything. Sefton saw Ross concentrating on the victim's body, taking photos of it, Quill standing beside her, still wrapped in blankets, staring, and finally decided someone should bloody do the decent thing. He went over to Costain. 'So what happened?'

'I got ambushed by a bunch of this lot, took me out with an electrical stunner, I think it was.' He paused to run his tongue round his teeth and wince. 'Not clear about what happened next. I think a couple of them must have hauled me down into the hull, where . . .' He paused to control his breathing. 'You've seen this lot. Swastikas and shit. They thought they had time to take it out on me. One of them held me while the other went to work. Fucking deluded. The armed officers burst in and I was hoping they'd drop one of them, but no, they were good as gold, hands in the air, on their knees, and I wasn't in any state to take advantage.'

'That's so weird, that they'd take the time to do that. It's almost like you were the target.'

'Yeah. So why not you and all?'

'You don't recognize any of this lot, do you?'

'No. Believe me, I've taken a long hard look.'

'You should get yourself looked over by the FME, check you're OK.'

Costain shook his head. 'I want to finish the operation. I want to take this ship apart, make sure we haven't missed anything.'

Sefton's glance darted over to Ross, then back to Costain. 'Listen——'

'Quill's not going to think to bloody stop me unless you get him to. So don't, OK? I need . . . I need to keep working.'

Sefton couldn't bring himself to argue. He put his hand on Costain's shoulder, where he was pretty sure it wouldn't hurt him, then went over to join Ross and Quill. Ross was looking at her phone, hands still in evidence gloves, comparing a picture to the corpse on deck. Sefton wanted to say they should all be gathered together, but seeing the look on Ross's face, he recalled again the enormity of what Costain had done to her and felt like he'd just walked across the deck from one end of a seesaw to the other. It wasn't that she wasn't feeling for Costain, he was sure; it was that she didn't like how much she was. 'What have you got?' he asked.

'I got his name and occupation from his passport, then checked IMDb. This guy is Erik Gullister, sixty-eight years old, a professional actor, been in loads of stuff on US television, everything from *Castle* to *Sons of Anarchy* to *E.R.*, back in the day. I searched for his name in the Dutch media, and, if Google translation is close enough, when he was abducted, he seems to have been in a season of theatrical events staged at seaside locations. No starring roles, no recurring characters, not since the 1970s, when he was the lead in a couple of short-lived series. Problems with drugs, dealing as well as possession, a couple of arrests, according to Google. But he's still one of those guys who's been in so much that you know his face but not his name. It strikes me also that three of these five victims had criminal records, but not Lassiter and obviously not Holmes—'

Quill interrupted her, insisting again. 'Did he ever live in London?!'

'He doesn't seem to have worked here, and . . . Here we go – his passport isn't stamped for the UK. This is his first visit to London. Why is that important?'

Quill just shook his head, visibly relieved.

'But listen,' Ross continued, 'here's the most important thing. One credit leaps out at you.' She scrolled down the screen and pointed.

Sefton was looking over her shoulder now too. 'Sherlock Holmes,' he said. He called Costain, who made his way over as quickly as he could and looked at the screen incredulously.

'He was the lead in *American Sherlock* for six episodes in 1978,' said Ross.

'Bates played Holmes too,' said Sefton. 'You said he was Sherlock in that school play.'

'And Lassiter had been an actor,' said Quill.

Ross looked it up on her phone. 'With the lead in a touring *Hound of the Baskervilles.*'

Costain's face showed the sudden copper pleasure of seeing a connection materialize. 'I'm betting if we ask Duleep's family if he ever played Sherlock Holmes, in an amateur production or something, they'll say yes.'

'This,' said Ross, 'is why the differences in the murders are indicative. Killer or killers are willing to alter, within boundaries, how close they get to the original location, and will compensate for that with other details, because the one thing they absolutely need, the one thing they'll sacrifice other aspects in order to achieve, is this: their victims must have played Sherlock Holmes.'

ELEVEN

Quill got home before midnight. He'd called Lofthouse and briefed her about the results of the raid, got the paperwork sorted, including decent arrangements for the victim. No grieving widow, but there were some grown-up children. No comfort to them that their father wasn't in Hell. Quill had made sure the crew were, as he'd always done it, put in separate cell corridors, so they couldn't get their stories sorted between them.

He'd realized in the car that he should have ordered Costain to go and get his injuries checked out. The sergeant had taken a first-aid kit from one of Petrovski's lot and had retreated into a corner like a wounded animal, to deal with some minor cuts and bruises on his face. He'd still been staggering when he got back to the others, refusing to admit to how much he'd been hurt, not wanting, maybe, to look weak in front of Ross.

The face of that actor kept coming back to Quill: old and lost, not knowing why this had been done to him. He'd been escorted from his hotel room; they'd found out, got into the back of a car all smiles and laughter. What had they said to him? *We're such fans of yours. We know all about your work. Listen as we reel off our research.* Whoever was behind this knew exactly who to hire: not just professionals, but ones that fitted the Conan Doyle story. What enormous organization would it take to fund and carry out something like this, and with such a precise and eccentric aim?

As Quill drove, he kept finding his attention drawn to the rear-view mirror. It was, he realized, like last time. Was he being followed? He never saw the same car, but he kept jerking his head up, hoping to catch one, like it leaped back into the mirror every time he looked away. He pulled up in front of his house in Enfield, switched off the lights and engine, and sat there without getting out, still looking in the mirror. He kept expecting some vehicle, some something, to come round the corner at the end of the close. Once again, there was a feeling of something hanging back.

He got out of the car and stared into the dark, his breath billowing around him. He took a step towards the darkness on the corner, then waited, hoping to hear a reaction. 'Hello?' he called. No response. He heard a noise, a definite noise, and was suddenly running, was at the corner in seconds, saw a change in the shadow as he reached it . . . and found Mrs Epton putting out her recycling.

'Evening,' he said, breathing a bit too hard. 'Did you see anyone else pass by, in just this last minute or so?'

Mrs Epton, looking nervous at why he was asking, said she hadn't, and then he asked again if she was certain, and now he felt sure that she was looking nervous because of him.

He stayed outside for a while, wondering if the feeling of being watched would come back. It didn't, and he finally went inside. Sarah would already be in bed and asleep, and he could hear Jessica snoring. He took out his phone, and making himself not think twice, he called Laura. She'd probably be awake. Indeed, she answered after two rings. 'What can I do for you at this time of night, James?' Her voice, to him, always sounded deliberately soft, like she was consciously trying to cut out the masculine sounds. That apparent carefulness had always charmed him. It was how priests should sound, how he wanted everyone to sound.

He made himself sound calm in return. 'Just something I

wanted to have a chat with you about. Listen, are you sure you want to move to London?'

'Well, yeah. I've got interviews lined up. Why do you ask?'

'It's just . . . things aren't great here these days.'

'I'm a big girl.' Indeed, he'd seen her get abuse on the street that had amazed him. She insisted on going to football and walking wherever she wanted to, which resulted in repeated verbal abuse, and on some occasions physical attacks too. She lived a life the harshness of which would be difficult to get most people to believe. What could he say to her to put her off London?

'I . . . can't tell you why, but I'm serious. There's an enormous threat to . . . I'm calling people I, you know, people I care about.'

'Christ, is it a nuclear bomb or something? I'm not moving for weeks. It's not like . . . What about Sarah and Jess?'

'I . . . I haven't told them.'

'You've had a warning about some sort of terrorist threat and . . . ?!'

'No. Nothing like that. They're not in danger.' If only that was true. 'This is a problem purely for . . .'

'For people like me?'

This had all gone too fast for him to do anything but react, but OK, that would do. 'Yeah.'

There was silence at the other end of the line for a moment. Then she spoke again. 'You're telling me there's been some sort of serious long-term threat made against transsexuals in London?'

Quill found that he couldn't lie about the job. He really should have written down what he was going to say. 'Well, no . . .'

'I can keep your name out of it, but if there's been a threat, there are people I need to tell, to make the community aware of what's going on. Why haven't we been told officially? Are they even planning to do that? Who are we talking about? Some extreme religious group?'

What could he say? There was nothing he could say. He had to say something. 'It's nothing anyone in authority knows about. It's probably just me being paranoid.'

'James, please!'

He felt as if the muscles down the back of his neck had locked. He wanted to tell her everything, but that would mean telling her more than he'd told Sarah. That would mean telling Sarah.

After a moment's silence, she took pity on him. 'Listen, when I come down, you're going to tell me everything about this, all right?'

'Could you . . . could you please not come down?' He didn't know how long a stay would be counted as 'living in London'.

There was a long silence now. Quill recognized it. He was about to say something again, perhaps to apologize, when she spoke up once more, and now she was extremely calm and precise. 'Don't tell me to be a coward, OK? Not when you won't tell me what the threat is. I live with this every day.'

He tried to back down, to say it was probably nothing. She tried a couple more times to get him to tell her what was going on. 'Are you OK?' she asked, finally. 'I mean, is there anything . . . wrong?' *With you*, she could have added. No, that was unfair.

'Of course not. Look, it's late . . .' He tried to downplay it now, made jokes, tried to talk about the football. She was having none of it. He eventually broke down and angrily, desperately, asked her to not say anything about this conversation to Sarah. Laura, now completely lost and very worried, agreed, but like she was going to keep to that.

Quill finally put the phone down and found he was shaking. He wanted to do what someone in the movies did now: drink; smash something; punch the wall and not go immediately to casualty. He was confined by the rules of the world only he knew about, which he didn't fully understand. He sat down, not wanting to go upstairs, thinking of Hell, back in it.

TWELVE

Lofthouse had kept the papers and the gun in her briefcase at home, and had not so much as looked at them, not so much as moved the case. When she'd got into her office at the Hill on the first morning of Quill's team's planning for the *Lone Star* raid, she first made herself check in about the progress of current investigations. She'd discovered, among other things, that the walls of the nick that had been dusted for prints had found only a few, all identified as being from police officers and suspects who'd been in those corridors. That had been a long shot in any case. Someone who'd planned so meticulously to have Quill's team bring a victim to where they needed to be would surely have taken the trouble to wear gloves. Finally, she told her assistant she wasn't to see anyone or take any calls, and had opened her briefcase and inspected what she'd found.

The gun was indeed a functional shotgun, double-barrelled, in the 'over and under' fashion, one barrel atop the other. Lofthouse came from a farming family and knew a little about such weapons. The top barrel was inscribed 'J. Purdey and Sons, London' in gold inlay. That was a firm she had actually heard of, which, this being presumably an item from Quill's side of the curtain, came as a bit of a surprise. The gun had been kept in great condition. The metal of the barrels was patterned, a very fine finish like the wings of a butterfly. It didn't look to be a matter of engraving, but something about the metal itself. Lofthouse wished she could look it up on the Internet, but her every keystroke would be looked at and thought about. A very London gun, certainly, but was that all there was to it? She checked the chambers and found that each was loaded. Oh, terrific, she'd kept a bloody loaded shotgun in her briefcase as she'd jolted along.

Carefully, she removed the cartridges. Now, these looked like nothing she'd ever seen before. They seemed to be made of soft white paper, with something that made a shaking noise inside, a metal cap on one end that bore no inscription. Could these even work in a shotgun? With no supply of ammunition, unless she wanted to covertly buy some normal cartridges, two shots were all she had. So practice was out of the question. Whatever was in these was designed to take down . . . something. There was no way she was going to be able to find out what.

She put the shotgun back in the drawer, the cartridges beside it, and turned her attention to the papers. She wished she'd had more time in the apartment. She was sure she'd have found many other useful things. Instead, she had the contents of one locked drawer, which was what the key had regarded as the most important thing, and the safe.

The papers had clearly been kept folded for many years – they unfolded with reluctance, and the folds left white lines across what was revealed. It was a diagram, drawn in ink by a brush, wavy lines going across the page, then splitting, like the branches of a tree, until several of them, further down the page, led to a big circle. It reminded her distantly of a calligraphy exercise, but there was no writing of any kind. Lofthouse held the page up to the light to see any sign of invisible ink, but there was none. This was what the key had regarded as most significant, but she had no idea, as with the gun, what the piece of paper was for, what it might mean. Apart, that was, from one immediate and obvious deduction. 'You're a map,' she said out loud. 'But to what?'

The morning after the *Lone Star* raid, Ross got into the Portakabin before anyone else. Listening to the radio on the way in had been an education in how the media adjusted a narrative. They were now reporting the 'Sherlock murders' as if they never had been the '*Study in Scarlet* murders'. Although the news organizations had made the connection that Erik Gullister had played Holmes, they didn't yet know that about the other victims. Also, they seemed to think the suspects in custody now were fancied for the earlier murders too, a perception that would probably vanish before lunchtime, when it became clear they hadn't been in the UK at the time. Duleep's family had confirmed he had indeed once played Sherlock Holmes in a local amateur dramatic production.

The money trail to the company called Missing Room had gone cold in a Swiss bank. To buy and rename a ship took a lot of money, but it had already become clear that whoever they were playing against had power in the material world. They'd put together a team that had included the striking individual who had killed Bates, the mercenaries on the ship and Dean Michael, if that was his real name. Who knew how many others?

She was about to start rebuilding the ops board when she heard a sound behind her. Costain had entered. He still looked bruised about the face. Normally these days he'd come in late, to make sure they weren't alone. Oh God, was he going to try some new tactic to get past her guard?

'I'm going to put myself at your service,' he said, without even a good morning. 'We could try to put it all right.'

'If you mean you and me—'

'No, I mean what's most wrong with your life.'

'You're talking about helping me get back my future happiness?'

He nodded.

'Yeah, OK, listen, I'm not some sort of prize, where you work hard on my behalf and then earn the right to shag me.'

Costain's expression remained surprisingly stoic. 'What happened to me down there . . .' He meant inside the ship. 'They *hated* me, Lisa. There was nothing more to them than that. All I could think about while they were on me . . . I wanted to come back out into the light and . . . I just want to come back into the light, OK?'

It was entirely possible that he might come up with some useful idea about how to get her happiness back, considering all the dodgy contacts he had. That usefulness would still be there even if he couldn't live up to his fine sentiments, which was obviously going to turn out to be the case. The next auction of occult London items, when those in the know traditionally gathered to bid cash or barter for objects of power, was on 23 September, the autumn equinox. The auction house now owned Ross's future happiness. They had taken it from her in the form of a liquid and presumably bottled it. She'd sold it to them in return for a chance to get her dad out of Hell. Costain had fucked that up, but Ross had always been planning on going to the next auction, to see if the house was immediately going to sell it on. She'd imagined pleading with whoever bought it, or following them, grabbing it from them . . . but those had been useless dreams. With Costain on her side, she'd have more force to put towards the second course of action, more guile to put towards the first. But still . . .

'I don't know,' she said.

Sefton entered and pointed at Costain. He looked like he'd just been struck by a terrifying idea. 'Have you,' he said, 'ever played Sherlock Holmes?'

'What?'

'Oh,' said Ross, realizing. She should have thought of this. 'He's wondering if what happened to you on the boat was attempted murder.'

'But . . . were there two deaths in that story? Or is the next murder in the stories on the river too?'

'No to both,' said Ross. 'The attack on you was an anomaly. I thought you were reading ahead?'

Costain looked awkward. 'Got a bit bored with it,' he said.

'I'm not saying that Klan members wouldn't just do that for fun,' said Sefton.

'But they did go out of their way,' agreed Costain. 'No, I've never played Sherlock Holmes. I wasn't the sort for school plays.'

They all looked round at the sound of Quill arriving. He looked pale, like he hadn't slept. 'Today,' he said, 'today, I think one of you better lead, because I am just . . .' He looked as if he was appealing to them to say he was unfit for work, to let him off the hook.

They all went to him. 'Jimmy,' said Ross, 'please, just tell us?'

He shrugged off their expressions of concern, shook his head, sat down. 'Could one of you, please . . . ?'

'All right,' said Costain. 'You get yourself together, Jimmy. We're here for you. Next move: we interview the *Lone Star* crew.'

They actually had a one-way mirror at Wapping High Street nick, like in American cop shows. Ross and Quill watched from the next room as Sefton and Costain played good cop and bad cop. Ross had been worried about Costain conducting the interview, but he stayed within the bounds of the law, satisfied, it seemed, to have got a reaction out of the men when he walked in. They hadn't expected their victim. That had been just about their only reaction, though.

'I should go in there,' said Quill. 'I'd fucking show them.'

'No, sir,' said Ross, and after a glare, he backed down. The idea that the mercenaries had powerful connections, plus the previous death in custody, had been enough to sell the Met mainstream on the policy of keeping them in maximum security between interviews, guarded round the clock. It was the only way Ross could think of of guarding against rescue from someone who could walk through walls.

In the end, the interviews were among the most fruitless she'd ever witnessed. Sefton, being black, wasn't actually that great, with these bastards, at being the good cop. He tried the bell trick and established that these gentlemen didn't have the Sight, but that was about all they got.

When they got back to the Portakabin, Ross went to the ops board and looked at it. It was laughing at her. She inclined her head, literally looking at it from another angle. Once again, it was one of those puzzle pictures in which you could feel the shape of something lurking. Had the 'death' of Holmes really been just to get them involved? What sort of mind thought that far ahead? A chess player, a planner. An adversary for her.

She could just about see the edges of who she was dealing with. One person, yeah, someone who employed others, but a mind behind it all. Her thoughts drifted once again, as they had often that day, to her and Costain maybe going to the auction, the possibility of her regaining her happiness. She pushed the idea away. That was going to keep distracting her until she'd sorted it. There were no killings in the next two stories, 'The Man with the Twisted Lip' and 'The Adventure of the Blue Carbuncle', but the one after that included a murder that immediately presented a strategy to entrap the killer, or at least to prevent the next killing.

She set to work on the wheezing office PC and got a notice prepared for printing. The other two were fruitlessly trying to talk to Quill over strong, sweet tea. She picked up the first copy from the printer and read it out. '"Have you ever played Sherlock Holmes? In amateur dramatics, at school, anywhere? If so, we want to hear from you. Production company seeks anecdotes. Big money paid."' There followed the Portakabin phone number. 'Of course, they'll discover there's no money involved when we interview them. They'll have to be content with a police warning to flee and save their lives.'

'Are you going to put this out all over London?' asked Quill. He sounded incredulous, at his wits' end. Ross wanted to get him into an interview room and find out what he was hiding from them.

'No,' she said patiently. 'The next story takes place in a very specific setting, the village of Stoke Moran, "on the western border of Surrey". That's not a real place, but Holmes fans online seem to agree that it's standing in for Stoke d'Abernon, which is just inside the M25, and thus hopefully still counts as London. I reckon we can leaflet every house, get the whole community onside and thus make it extremely hard for our opponents to do what they have to do next.'

'Which is?' asked Sefton.

'Kill someone by means of a poisonous snake.'

Sefton and Costain exchanged looks that said that for them the game was still very much afoot. Even Quill managed a raised eyebrow.

'Whoever we're playing against,' she continued, 'now knows that we're anticipating their moves, so we can do all this in the open. The bastards will still have to try to go through with it.'

'That's where the Chelsea training ground is,' said Sefton. 'Shit. Maybe one of the players once put on a deerstalker for a comedy sketch.'

Ross instinctively wanted to shy away from doing what she was about to do next, but, after a glance towards Quill, she went through with it. She would have to do more than just offer options now, if Quill wasn't prepared to take the lead. 'The other thing that's urgent is that now we know that people who played Holmes are the targets, we're looking at three enormous examples of that who are in danger right now: Gilbert Flamstead, Alice Cassell and Ben Speake. A high-profile kill might be what this is all working towards. I've been emailing their production companies, and getting a perhaps unsurprising degree of cooperation, given all the media attention. I reckon if we can talk to them, we can demonstrate that what the news is now saying is true: that there's a clear link between the victims and them. We might be able to persuade them to go home. Or their insurance companies could.'

'Also,' said Costain, 'if any of them are planning a trip to Stoke d'Abernon—'

'Let's hope they are, and we can stop them, and thus all this.' She suddenly realized that she was now talking directly to Costain again, and that Sefton had smiled to see that. She pressed on. 'So, Jimmy, I reckon the undercovers should go down to Stoke . . .'

'So we don't get to hobnob with the rich and famous?' said Sefton.

'. . . start the leafleting, but also get in with the locals, like undercovers do best. There are details in the short story they can check for any signs of. Our killer or killers obviously don't need to get all the details straight, but they like to when they can. Meanwhile, Jimmy and I will try to get a meeting with the three Sherlocks. What do you reckon?' She looked to Quill for assent.

'Yeah,' he nodded, too quickly, as if he didn't want to think about anything. 'Great.'

That afternoon, Sefton and Costain caught a train out of Waterloo. Sefton was pleased to see it was one with the grimy old sort of carriages that actually still had compartments. He and Costain sat facing each other on the threadbare seats that had that peculiarly satisfying London smell about them, like a particular sort of carpet cleaner was only just fighting back decades of commuter sweat. That smell, for Sefton, was close to being a thing of the Sight. The further he got into this stuff, the more he learned, the better he could see that the everyday things of London were part of a spectrum that led to the hidden world, not cut off from it on the other side of a curtain, as the others tended to say. Sefton threw his overnight bag onto the rack beside Costain's, glad that he'd included his holdall of occult London paraphernalia, though it added to the weight of his share of the leaflets. They sat in silence, watching the construction sites outside Waterloo as the train accelerated. 'So,' said Sefton, 'you and Lisa . . .'

'Yeah.'

'I don't want to pry about you two, but I'm trying to get us all working together again, trying to get the team spirit back.'

'Well, mate, I hope we can, ah, contribute to that.' His sudden grin faded. 'Listen, I don't mean I just want to get with her again. I want to make things right.'

'I know you do.'

'Really?'

'Yeah. I can see both sides. I always have. I know Quill used to think you were still a bent copper, but . . . I know your heart's in the right place.'

'Because of all your' – Costain gestured in the air – 'your hoo-ha.'

'I wouldn't call it that around Lisa. No, it doesn't take any London shit to see you both did what you thought was best. It's not like you used that thing Ross found to save yourself.'

Costain paused, looking taken aback by the vote of confidence. Sefton got the feeling it had been a long time since anyone had said anything positive to Costain. 'Tell me about you and that stuff. How's it going?'

'My hoo-ha, you mean?' Sefton found that he was really kind of pleased that someone other than his boyfriend was asking him about what he did. So, hesitantly, he started to fill Costain in on what he hadn't always shared every detail of with the others, about the mad places he'd gone, just how far out he'd ventured in order to bring back information. Costain was, of course, being a fellow undercover, a great listener.

Stoke d'Abernon turned out to be not really a quaint little village but a commuter-belt town that was still trying to be said village, meaning most of those who lived here went to out-of-town shops. There was a lot of greenery among the winding closes of upmarket estates, and not much in the way of store fronts. The row of shops by the station included a swimming-pool supplier. The endless spirals of housing revealed by Google Maps were going to take bloody ages to leaflet. There was, however, at least a radio car firm on call, so Sefton and Costain got picked up and taken to the Woodlands Park Hotel, a sprawling mansion that had that cosy, clean-carpeted feel of a non-chain hotel in a well-heeled suburb.

Sefton threw his bags onto the bed in his room, went to his window and looked back in the direction of London. This was the furthest he'd gone from the centre since they'd got the Sight. He could feel the enormity of it in perspective from here. It was like a distant storm. He could see, as his experienced eyes sought them out, details in the air above the metropolis: the ghosts of barrage balloons, the nightmares of the Blitz, even now. That memory, of the dead as well as the living, must make it harder for the capital to be as cosmopolitan as it was, must contribute to the creeping fear of outsiders, of difference, that Sefton saw everywhere these days. British xenophobia had mutated so white Europeans with different accents were seen as people who weren't quite people. What wasn't often said, though, was that Britons of colour like Sefton and Costain were also included in that feeling. Too difficult to say, but at the same time too obvious to mention. Speaking of which, there was one factor that Ross hadn't considered in her operational plan, which was how two young gentlemen such as they might be received in the leafy shires. He and Costain, without consulting each other about it, had both come along in smart casual, like they were here for a weekend of golf or an out-of-town stag do.

He went downstairs and found Costain already in the bar, already talking to a couple of local older chaps. He'd put a note of white-collar precision into his voice, was purring about his independent television production company . . . Oh, he was the owner of their cover story, was he? OK, then. He was showing the leaflet around. Oh yes, he was here on business, not just to work on his tan. Big laugh. Christ, were they going *there* tonight? Costain spotted him at the entrance to the bar and beckoned him over. 'This is Kevin, my producer. Shall we get these fine gentlemen a drink, Kevin?'

Sefton shook hands all round and saved a wry glance for Costain, who gave him a genuine smile back. Even if Quill was suffering and distant, thought Sefton, as he headed to the bar, at least the rest of the team were slowly drawing back together.

'Can I get you anything?' The PA was looking at Quill like she'd never seen a real copper before. He wanted to say 'salvation', like he was in a TV show himself. But he wasn't built that way, and that'd also start Ross off on worrying about him again. Ross allowed him only a moment's silence before answering for them, ordering two cups of strong, sweet tea.

They were in a lobby constructed inside the entrance of an old warehouse in Southwark, which was now home, according to the list on the wall behind the reception desk, to five companies, ranging from the rentable TV studios they were visiting today to games developers and design firms. Quill had always loved this part of London, which on the way in had shown even more of itself to him, now he had the Sight. The authenticity of the place had somehow survived it becoming a tourist area, so now the streets were hyped up and utterly London, but real too.

There was phantom detail by every paving slab, and notably in clouds of exclamation around the cathedral, where the flames of the Great Fire raged like shadow puppetry. There had been one of the great annual fairs here, and London seemed to remember those particularly. Southwark had been a kind of Hong Kong to the capital, a place just outside the original jurisdiction, where a certain amount of bad behaviour was allowed. The patterns of money and violence had made a whirlpool here. The Sight sometimes gave one pleasure like this; it wasn't all darkness. But Quill found, to his disappointment, that now he couldn't see the beauty as anything other than meaningless. The thoughts that went round and round kept dragging him down.

He saw Ross looking at him and made a conscious effort to engage. He recognized that it wasn't just Hell and his own depression that were getting to him; there was something going on in his copper brain too. It was working at something they'd missed, but he didn't yet know what.

'Ah, Detective Inspector Quill?' The face of someone Quill assumed he knew had appeared round the corner of an office door. It took him a moment to realize it was someone famous. It was Gilbert Flamstead. Him off the telly, in his long dark coat and very white shirt. Sherlock Holmes.

Once again Ross replied for them, but this time it was because Quill had lost the power of speech.

Flamstead took them to a Portakabin that was rather better equipped than the one Quill was used to, having been made into a production office, with coffee maker, and posters on the walls. He let a beautiful young lady who was some sort of personal assistant do most of the talking. It turned out that Flamstead had been the first to hear of Lofthouse's request for a meeting, from his executive producer at the BBC. He'd taken the liberty of assembling his fellow Sherlocks, which was why Alice Cassell and Ben Speake also soon arrived. Cassell was looking almost deliberately rough, in stressed jeans and hooded sweater. Speake was either still in costume or always wore to police interviews boots, waistcoats and the sort of shirt that got poets drowned. All three of the actors were surprisingly short, and thinner than human beings were meant to be. It was, Quill thought, like addressing a group of Hobbits.

Along for the ride was the executive producer of Cassell's show, Felix Lindt, a clean-cut young man in very new jeans who didn't look old enough to be in charge of six seasons of a top-rated US TV series. The other two had done without entourages, though it was clear Flamstead, the gracious host, was on his home territory, this being where his show rented studio space.

Quill cleared his throat. 'So, as my email said,' he began, 'there is now a clear, if unspecific, threat to your lives.'

'Alice and I have been having a conversation about packing up and going home,' said Lindt, sounding as if that would be much his preferred option. 'If you think that would be—'

'That conversation *ended*,' underlined Cassell immediately, 'with the decision that we only had two more weeks here to finish the three-parter, and that, with extra security, I would stay and get that done. I speak for myself, OK? He's always trying to control what I do.'

'Well,' laughed Lindt, with a lightness that sounded like it was born of bitter experience, 'I am, kind of, you know, your boss.'

She looked shocked at him. 'You said you'd never go there.' She held up a hand to stop his protestations and turned back to Quill. 'I guess he's trying to protect me. Or the studio's investment.'

'Alice, I would never think of you like—'

'I get death threats, threats of rape every single frigging day. Shitheads who think they own Sherlock Holmes, who don't think I should play her. This new threat? Same old same old.'

'Is it . . . Shirley Holmes in your case?' Ross had read up on the respective series and had expressed the view on the way over that a young white woman these days being called Shirley was so bizarre they might as well have stayed with Sherlock.

'*Shy*, usually,' said Lindt, 'Shy Holmes. It sounds more contemporary.' He indicated Cassell. 'Can you believe it? She's Shy.'

'I'm a grown woman. I'm not running. OK?'

'Good for you, Ally,' said Speake. There was something a little Californian in the handsome middle-aged man's accent, a weird transatlantic awkwardness to his East End tones. In the movies, he was full-on plummy thespian. Presumably this was what he thought of as his authentic voice. It was as if he'd literally forgotten what a real British person sounded like. 'Fuck 'em and their ways. We ain't for moving.'

'Well, given you two are so laid-back about it, I *so* completely disagree,' said Flamstead. The others laughed.

'What Gilbert means is that we understand the threat,' said his PA, 'and none of us wants to make your job harder. We'd all like to help.'

'The show must go on,' said Speake, as if he was coining a new truism.

'Did any of you ever work with Erik Gullister?' asked Quill.

'Yeah,' said Cassell, 'just for a few days. He was a grieving father on *Dear Alibi*, about a decade ago. I was his daughter. Good actor. Never had any luck.'

Speake didn't think he'd worked with Gullister, but said he wouldn't necessarily remember. Flamstead just raised an eyebrow: as if. Ross confirmed that, as far as IMDb knew, Cassell's was the only connection. Quill asked if the name Dean Michael meant anything to them. It didn't. Ross, saying it was a matter of form, asked for alibis from all three actors for the times of the previous murders. Speake protested, saying he didn't know he'd need his bloody lawyer present, thank you very much, chums, but Flamstead calmed him down.

'You had to ask, didn't you, Inspector?' said Flamstead, actually giving Quill a wink. 'In the old country, things are still done in the proper way and in the proper order.'

After a lot of humming and hawing, Speake agreed to check his diary. Lindt and Cassell had to compare theirs on their tablets. 'You had that thing,' said Cassell, 'with that girl, on that night.'

'She is not "a girl".'

'Hah! What do you mean she's not? She's very nice.'

Lindt's smile grew more forced every second. He finally declared they'd worked out where Cassell was on every occasion and showed Ross the diary entries. There were a number of people in every case who could confirm where she was every time.

Flamstead's schedule, on the other hand, had a few holes in it. 'You like walking, collecting your thoughts, don't you?' said his PA. Which included the first and second murders, and he claimed to have been asleep in his hotel at the time of the Holmes killing. Ross hadn't identified the victim in that case, of course, just that there was another incident the details of which hadn't been released to the media. That news made all the actors and Lindt nod seriously in a way Quill had only seen during charity telethons.

None of them could have been on the river for the death of Gullister. Speake turned out to have been in the same pub for all of the killings, which he only haltingly admitted. The faces of Lindt and the other two actors betrayed only polite interest.

None of them had even heard of Stoke d'Abernon, and checks with Cassell and Speake's companies confirmed that none of the productions planned to go there. All those involved agreed to send lists of recent threatening messages on social media. 'Good luck wading through mine,' said Cassell.

'I was just wondering, while we're here,' said Ross, and Quill noted that her tone was nowhere near as casual as her words, 'if we could get a look at the set.'

Ross was glad to get the access she'd been after so easily. She and Quill followed the actors, Flamstead's gorgeous PA and Cassell's producer into the enormous open space of the warehouse-turned-studio. A scene was being prepared in Holmes's study. Ross and Quill were able to step past the cameras and the assistant director, who was watching as a prop person checked every detail of the wall behind Holmes's desk against a photo. 'It's not like in the Holmes Museum,' she said.

'Because,' said Flamstead, coming to stand beside her, 'they *so* precisely depict what Holmes's study would actually be like.'

His tone of voice seemed to tend towards irony. She found herself reacting to him. He was a very pretty bloke. He moved in real life like he did on screen, such expressive hands. His presence made her sad, though. Her feeling horny without happiness, without a smile, that was a bit grim. If she was with anyone now, what would that be like? Mechanical, functional. There would be no love without happiness. Unless she could get it back.

She made herself concentrate on what she'd come here for. She'd wanted to get a look at the production team, to find out if any of them had anything about them that drew Sighted attention. Beyond that, though, the deductive part of her wanted to get immersed in Sherlock Holmes, to be able to walk in his (or her) shoes, to add that perspective to the ops board. She was now playing against someone extraordinary, and she needed data. 'So,' she said, 'tell me about your Holmes.'

Flamstead looked pleased by the question. 'As with all Sherlocks, he's a mess of emotions and loves human companionship.'

The gorgeous PA literally stuck her head into the conversation. 'By which Gilbert means the opposite, of course.'

'My network still worries about that,' said Cassell, 'six seasons in. They want Gregory House, but *nice*.'

'They do not—!' Lindt stopped himself, and just held up a hand, excusing himself.

'Charmingly eccentric,' said Speake, as if he was the one who'd been asked. 'He can only do romance by rote, like Holmes does all socializing. He's somewhere on the Asperger's spectrum, but he knows how to *use* emotions; he has mental lists of things he can do to get a result from other people. That's the heart of how I portray the character. Nothing like me. That's what they call acting, mate. Actually, if the Internet is anything to go by, the autism thing really excites a section of my audience. The section living in their mother's basements, I mean. Isn't that a dreadful Yank expression? But so true.'

'He's much more at home in disguise,' said Lindt, having regained the power of speech. 'He can be all these other people with different lives absolutely perfectly.'

'He?' said Cassell.

'I am talking about—' And Lindt had to force himself, once again, not to continue.

'Well, that's so not the case with Shy,' said Cassell. 'So I don't know which Holmes he'd rather be working on.' Lindt just shook his head, keeping his smile fixed. 'She loves her life; she's at home in her own skin. Her big problem is trying not to keep intervening in dear Watson's love life.'

'Some sort of Watson is about the only thing our three versions have in common,' said Speake. 'She's just started shagging her Watson . . .'

'In the *show*.'

'They know that,' said Lindt.

'. . . because "will they? won't they?" has become "yes, they do" – immediate gratification, thank you – and as for us two Sherlocks, we're both shagging—'

'Irene Adler?' said Flamstead. 'I deny everything. Goodness, dear old Irene Adler, such an underused character in the modern media.'

'She's not used very *well*,' said Cassell, pointedly.

Flamstead grinned as if this was the most charming thing he'd ever heard. Speake just shrugged.

Flamstead looked back to Ross. She wasn't just imagining this, was she? He was checking her out. She was pretty sure she didn't have anything to compare to the sort of Hollywood stars he must hang about with. Not even to his PA.

Ross found herself needing to look away, to Cassell. 'Are all of you still into this, or do you feel the urge to play Sherlock kind of . . . dying away?'

Flamstead moved deliberately back into her eyeline. 'Far from it. I have a very straightforward relationship with the viewing public. I adore them.' The other two were busy loudly indicating that they still loved playing the part. It sounded like they, at least, meant it, to whatever degree they usually meant things. Lindt was looking at Cassell with something approaching relief.

'You're all much darker than the Conan Doyle, aren't you? Even your movies . . .'

'Conan Doyle got damn dark,' said Speake.

'Yeah, yeah,' said Cassell. 'I look at those movies of yours and think, Kids can get in to see that? But I think that about everything in modern cinema.'

'You're just saying things that are true,' sighed Speake, 'as if they're important.'

'You have to give the audience what they want,' said Flamstead. 'And these days, what the audience most wants is gritty realism that says something about their lives, inhabited by people like themselves.'

'*Sure* they do,' said Speake.

Ross also felt that, once again, the twinkle in Flamstead's eye said he was saying the opposite of what he meant. She didn't quite know what she was working towards. There was something in Flamstead's expression that seemed to be leading her on, in more ways than one. 'How does deduction work for a modern Holmes? In Victorian London, maybe it was true that there were tight social rules, so you could tell what someone's job was by, I don't know, an ink mark on their hand, but these days that might just mean the suspect had an ink fetish.'

'You still can sum people up by a collection of facts about them. That's what predictive marketing does. That's what every quiz on Facebook does,' said Cassell. 'Oh God, are you saying we're getting it wrong?' She gestured to Lindt. 'Listen to her – this is a detective!'

'*We* have detectives—' began Lindt.

'Don't you think,' said Flamstead, interrupting, 'that character is more important than clues?'

'A lot of Holmes's deductive methods still hold up,' said Speake, as if personally affronted by that idea they might be getting it wrong. 'As Conan Doyle said, "When you have eliminated the impossible . . ."'

Ross sighed. 'Let me stop you right there.'

'". . . whatever remains, however improbable, must be the truth." What's wrong with that?'

She didn't want to say that for her unit, eliminating the impossible was the tricky bit. 'After you've eliminated the impossible, there are still loads of possible things left, and some of them won't be true, so what does that even mean?'

Speake frowned, then looked around, as if there might be another gorgeous PA handy who could take her off his hands. Ross knew she wasn't being fair. She didn't know what she was working towards here. She looked back to Flamstead, who gave her that secret smile. Even if he was trying to encourage her in some way, him fancying her, or trying to impress her, or whatever it was didn't help with anything.

'Question,' said Quill. 'Same thing I asked the wife. Tell me the first thing that comes into your head. Who killed Sherlock Holmes?'

Flamstead looked around for a moment, found his target and pointed. 'He did.'

Ross and Quill turned to see a pleasant-looking middle-aged actor in a tailcoat approaching. 'Who's this?' asked Quill.

The man extended a hand, a wry smile on his face. 'Professor Moriarty,' he said.

This *Alexander* Moriarty, it turned out, was a Victorian investment banker, part of some sort of global conspiracy, played by an actor called Patrick White. Something in the back of Quill's brain was itching. He listened to the actor saying that originally in the stories, Conan Doyle had given the name James to Moriarty's brother, but then had forgotten that detail and given it later to Moriarty himself. So their version had it that that had been part of a complicated scheme of multiple identities on the professor's part. 'My Moriarty loves leading Holmes astray,' White said, 'planting clues, leaving little hints.'

'Mine too,' said Cassell. 'He's a serial killer, so he's an intellectual and leaves puzzles, of course.'

'And also mine,' said Speake, 'though in my case, the clues and puzzles are all a bit more fun. Despite,' he added, seeing Cassell's raised eyebrow, 'all the horrible murders.'

'Unlike the original Moriarty,' said Ross, 'who tried to leave no clues at all.'

Cassell, hearing once again an expert opinion, threw another accusing look to Lindt, one that made him spread his hands in final, utter disbelief.

Quill suddenly realized that he knew what had been troubling him. His heart started beating so quickly he had to turn away, to try to control his breathing. It was so big he didn't want to say it out loud. Ross finished her tour of the facility and took him aside to tell him what he already knew, that there was nothing particularly of the Sight here. He nodded, eager to get moving. He shook his head when she asked him what was wrong. This wasn't something he could share with her, not yet.

He shook the hands of all the Holmeses and the producer and the PA and that blessed Moriarty, and when they got out of the warehouse and onto the street, told Ross to go home, said he'd be fine, realized she hadn't asked, had to stifle a laugh and headed for the Tube station. He looked back and saw her staring after him, concerned. Understandable. He went on his way for a few moments, then stopped, letting the Southwark early evening commuter crowds pass around him. Then he looked quickly over his shoulder. Yes. Someone had ducked back round that corner just as he'd looked. 'Onto you, sunshine,' muttered Quill, and, at a more careful pace, headed once more for the Tube.

He surfaced at Bond Street and walked up the well-heeled streets of apartments and offices until he got to Manchester Square, where he took a right. Google Maps took him to the corner of Welbeck Street and Bentinck Street. It was dark now, with lights on in some of the apartments, the air filled with the noise of cars and the occasional burst of music from them. He stayed on the corner, almost willing it to happen, a ghost van with two horses to roar down Welbeck Street and off down Bentinck, to escape into the night via Marylebone Lane. He waited some more. Nothing. It started to rain. Quill finally, grudgingly, turned right and headed down Welbeck Street, then turned a couple more corners and found Vere Street.

He stood between a Pret a Manger and a Debenhams, both lit and warm. Here he was hoping to be attacked, for a brick to fall from a high roof, aimed at his head. Again, he waited. Again, nothing. He closed his eyes. Perhaps the alternative to what he was feeling was to go to a pub, to let go and really fucking enjoy himself, to lose himself in doing all the things he enjoyed so that when death did finally come, and Hell with it, at least he could say he'd lived fully first. Wouldn't that involve sex too? He couldn't think about that away from Sarah. He didn't want to go to Hell and deserve it. If he got pissed, he ran the risk of telling her the truth when he got home. He realized he was thinking about his own situation again. Nothing had happened. Damn it. He'd been so sure. He started to move in the general direction of Bond Street.

There was a sudden shout that sounded more like a snarl and Quill's eyes snapped open as he threw himself backwards, instinctively, and just had time to see a cyclist all in black racing away from him. Was that some sort of cosh in his hand? If it was, it must have missed Quill's head by inches. The man turned the corner.

'Hoi!' Quill shouted, and sprinted after him, but by the time he'd got there, the cyclist had already vanished into the Oxford Street traffic. 'Oh, I've got you now,' said Quill, panting as he leaned on the corner. He felt himself shaking and willed it to stop. Finally, there was something he could do. Finally, he had something to hold on to.

THIRTEEN

Sefton spent the next two days in Stoke d'Abernon going door to door with Costain, getting a lot of nice conversations, but also sometimes suspicious encounters on the doorstep. Sometimes people failed to come to the door at all, when the twitching of the curtains clearly indicated there was someone at home. At one point, as they were leaving a particularly manicured close, a uniform showed up and enquired what they were doing there. Sefton hung back and watched Costain politely explain their mission here, which resulted in the lid saying, 'Yeah, whatever. Let's just keep it moving along, OK?'

Sefton nearly got out his warrant card and asked who this youth's boss was, but then he noted Costain's warning glance. They didn't want the local nick gossiping about the big-time London undercovers in town, that obviously something tasty was going down. They moved on.

In the evenings, they worked the pubs. They met a lot of genuine and pleasant people. Their skill set was all about getting folk to open up. They heard a couple of anecdotes about friends of friends who'd played Sherlock Holmes, but nobody had played him themselves. In a small town like this, the numbers who had must be tiny, approaching zero. Sefton started to wonder if they were actually seeking a specific individual, a target their opponents might already have in mind.

Someone mentioned the nearby Yehudi Menuhin School of Music, and Sefton and Costain shared a sudden moment of excitement about making the connection between Holmes and the famous violinist, but a visit to the school the next day revealed that none of the current students had done anything like stand in for Holmes's hands on television. The administrator got scared of the warrant cards they showed and their refusal to reveal the purpose behind their questions and clearly started wondering if his school was harbouring the 'Sherlock Holmes killer'. It took a long time to talk him down and make absolutely sure there were no potential victims on the premises. Despite the administrator's promises of secrecy, that looked like gossip waiting to happen. Ross reported that the handful of messages left on the office answerphone hadn't yet yielded anyone who actually lived in Stoke, just people from outside who'd been contacted by mates who'd read the leaflet.

They decided the next day would go more quickly if they split up. Sefton went to a small newsagent's, which looked rather out of place on its leafy corner and which kept a pristine red postbox outside, and checked out that day's local newspaper. If Ross couldn't find anyone in this town who'd played Sherlock Holmes, then their opponents might also be struggling, and might have had to abandon the Internet for local measures such as small ads. Nothing in those today. There also wasn't anything in the cards in the window of the shop.

It was while he was checking those that Sefton heard a voice calling to him and turned to see an old lady coming out of the shop, a newspaper under her arm. She had the look about her of someone who did good works, a satchel over her shoulder, a cardigan with lots of pockets and flat, sturdy shoes.

'Excuse me, but you're one of the two young men, aren't you? Sherlock Holmes? Those?'

'What can I do for you?'

'Well, I hope you're willing to believe something that sounds very strange.'

Sefton grinned. 'Ma'am, you've come to the right people.'

The woman, who said she didn't want to give her name, because 'Enough people around here think I'm batty already', led him to a square of parkland near a garden centre. 'I always get up early,' she said, 'with the lark. One of the advantages of getting old. I take a walk if the weather's all right. Still safe to do so round here. About a week ago – no, you'll want me to be precise, won't you, because you're a policeman? Don't look so shocked. I know people at the Yehudi. They've been talking about nothing else . . . Yes, it was last Wednesday, about six, just getting light, anyway. I was doing my usual circular walk, from my house to that newsagent, and as I came to the edge of the trees here, well, there he was. Sherlock Holmes, standing stock-still in the middle of the park. By the slides.'

'How did you know it was Sherlock Holmes?'

She looked at him like he was mad. 'He was wearing a deer-stalker and a little cape.'

'Did you see his face?' Sefton, not really believing what he was hearing, had got out his special notebook.

'He was quite far away. I got an impression of . . . I was going to say he had a long nose, but I think perhaps now I'm just saying what he *ought* to look like, if you see what I mean.'

Sefton's mind was racing. Was this an encounter with the 'ghost' of Holmes *after* he'd been 'killed'? Had he come back? Or would that be the ghost of the ghost? These days, he had to wrap his brain around thoughts as mad as that. Or was this just someone pretending to be Holmes? If so, here was a poten-tial victim. Perhaps this guy was already lying dead in bed somewhere in this town, victim of a snakebite, his body as yet unfound. Or perhaps this was all just an old lady seeing things, or making something up.

'Why did you say this was very strange?'

'You mean, apart from meeting some random loony dressed like Sherlock Holmes in a park in the first light of dawn? It was what he did next. He started to . . . Well, it wasn't exactly a dance. He saw I'd stopped and was watching him, and he started making these gestures with his arms. Very specific. He would raise his arms in a particular way, then lower them, then walk a couple of paces, then do a different shape. He did it over and over, the same patterns every time. He was like something out of *Monty Python*. When he started, I was going to call out to him and ask what he was doing, but then I got a bit scared, and wondered if I walked off, was he going to follow me? Because all the papers are full of Sherlock Holmes murders. So I was stuck there, rather.'

'What did these gestures look like?'

She bit her lip, clearly upset that she couldn't remember offhand. 'Go over there.' She flapped her hand.

Sefton walked back ten paces. Under her instructions, he raised and lowered his arms, until she was certain of each of the four poses the man had struck. Sefton drew what he'd been doing, then showed the old lady, who nodded eagerly. 'What happened then?'

'He bowed. Honestly. Then he walked off through those trees. I very much went the other way. When I got home a couple of minutes later, I was shivering. It was as if I'd encountered . . . it sounds silly, but . . . something supernatural.'

'Ma'am, you've been really helpful. If I could just take your contact details, my colleague Lisa—'

She shook her head. 'I've told you all I know. I don't want anyone calling.'

Sefton tried a little more persuasion, but it clearly wasn't going to get him anywhere. He'd made several notes about clues she'd given away to where she lived. He was pretty sure if they really needed to, they could find her. He thanked her and, once she'd gone, went over to the gap in the trees. He walked through it, looking more closely at the ground, and beyond it found only a further area of parkland. There was a fence that backed onto a row of houses with alleys in between.

Sefton sniffed the air as he went and kept an eye out for traces of silver and gold. Nothing. He wouldn't necessarily expect anything to remain after a few days, even if those weird gestures had been meant to achieve some supernatural effect. He felt intuitively that rain, of the sort he'd heard on his hotel window last night, would wash this stuff away, but this was another of the many things he didn't yet know. Still, here was something meaningful, something potentially huge, and very weird.

At an isolated table in the hotel bar that evening, Sefton showed Costain what he'd drawn in his notebook. 'Is it a message?' Costain wondered aloud. 'If the ghost of Holmes has somehow come back, why is he here, and not in Baker Street? Here, *is* he . . . ?'

'I called Ross and got her to take a look. He's not back in Baker Street. And I suppose this is one of the locations featured in the stories, but not one where you'd think Holmes would be remembered. Unless there are a lot of people here who specifically expect him to be around, like with all those Losley ghosts that popped up everywhere.'

'Yeah.'

'And why communicate to some old lady who's nothing to do with anything? I'm thinking maybe it's about place and time. I'm going to go over there tomorrow morning and see if he shows up again.'

Costain turned the book in his hands, looking at the four stick figures from every angle. 'Stick figures, like on the blade. Like in that Holmes story.'

'One of the figures performed live for the old lady is a bit like one of the ones from the blade, but the other three really aren't. That one there – the third one, one arm up and the other diagonally down – that's the flag semaphore letter "K", but only because he's got his legs together. In semaphore, only the arms matter, and he's definitely doing things with his legs. That's the only standard coded meaning I can find, and that's pushing it.'

'Ross'll see something.'

'Yeah. I hope.' He found himself smiling. 'You're still so into her, aren't you?'

Costain looked suddenly vulnerable, almost angry, then visibly let it go. 'She's like the sun round my earth, mate. Still. She's way over there, and she doesn't care if she shines on me or not.'

Sefton closed his hotel-room door behind him and called Joe, who was also away from home, at an academic conference in Oxford, where he said his major function was to stand behind his publisher's stall and drink coffee while everyone else was in lectures. Sefton told him a few details about the case, thankful that Quill's rules for their team allowed him to do so, asked his opinion about the stick men. Joe agreed with Costain that Ross would crack the code. 'If you ever meet her,' said Sefton, 'she's not going to live up to your expectations.'

'I do see her basically as Wonder Woman,' Joe agreed. Sefton told him he loved him and they said goodnight.

Sefton tried to read on his phone before going to sleep in the too-tight sheets of the hotel bed. He was making his way through the later Holmes stories, wanting to keep a step ahead. There was a lot of weird stuff here. Having killed his hero and been forced by public opinion to bring him back, Conan Doyle seemed not to know what to do with him. The public wanted him to live, but his creator didn't. Sefton's last conscious thought was that the 'ghost' of Holmes must have been traumatized by that, all the time.

In his dreams that night, Holmes came urgently to Sefton, tried to get a message through to him. There was a telegram, an urgent communication; he had to rip the envelope open, quickly; they may already be too late! But there was nothing inside the envelope. Something was hissing; an unignited gas flame bursting up angrily into Holmes's study. Sefton tried to haul something over it, to put it out. There was a sudden pain in his left arm, a burn!

The pain shoved him up out of his dreams. He flailed around the bed, his eyes opening, realizing there was a weight on his arm, something preventing him as he tried to thrash it away. The pain suddenly doubled into something he couldn't deal with and he saw the thing he couldn't get off his arm.

A snake.

Sefton leaped out of bed and realized he wasn't going to make it to the phone. The pain was suddenly too big again, and it shoved itself up into his throat and head. He managed to yell. He fell and the darkness rushed in to take him.

FOURTEEN

Ross stood at the end of the bed, Costain beside her. He was looking as horrified and empty as she felt. In the bed lay Kevin Sefton, his face covered by an oxygen mask, his bandaged arm still in a splint and hooked up to an IV, his skin deathly pale. Ross had found the number for Joe in his phone. He was heading here, to Walton Community Hospital, five or six miles from the hotel where, hours before, Sefton had been attacked. Ross had taken a hire car out of London, before the trains started. They'd both tried to call Quill, but kept getting his voicemail.

'I heard weird noises from his room next door,' said Costain. 'He was thrashing about; then he yelled, so I called back, got no answer, ran down and got a key off the front desk.' He sounded like he was making excuses, desperately trying to establish a credible cover story for this not being his fault. As if it could be. As if this was about him. 'I found him lying on the carpet with the snake still on him. It had its mouth clamped onto him. The skin around its mouth . . . you don't want to see. It had been chewing. They always say with a major injury don't move them, so I didn't. I wanted to kill the snake, but I thought, Shit, what if that makes it pump more venom into him? So I called 999 and they got there in less than five minutes. They were brilliant. They'd obviously talked to someone on the way over, and they took him and the snake both. I mean, these paramedics, they actually grabbed a snake.'

Ross had seen the snake, still alive, in an empty fish tank in the paramedics' office. An Indian cobra, she'd found out, by comparing it to pictures online. Of course, a small hospital like this didn't have any antivenom. Some was being flown here from London, less than an hour, they said. 'A neurotoxin that will often kill in a few minutes,' she'd read online. The effect was something like a heart attack.

The snake in the story had been a 'swamp adder', but there was no such animal. This speckled, dangerous species, native to India, was indeed, another search confirmed, what several people thought was the closest thing to the snake in the story.

'Right,' she said, determined to do something instead of just standing here. 'We need to find that elderly woman Kev described to you. She set him up to "play the part of Sherlock Holmes" by making the same shapes himself. She must be in on it, one of our ever-increasing gang of suspects. If there was CCTV overlooking that park, we can confirm—'

'There won't be,' said Costain. 'This town doesn't have much coverage.'

'They couldn't find a victim in this town, so they made one. Always the plan within a plan. We have a description, and indications of where this old woman could be found, assuming she was telling the truth. Which is bloody unlikely. Let's get it out to the local uniforms.'

They went to the hotel and found crime scene examiners working the room. There was no bell rope, of course, as there had been in the story, not that snakes could slide down them anyway, apparently. Nor could they be controlled, as the snake in the story was, by whistling. The bed could be moved, not having been bolted to the floor. The snake, it seemed, had actually been introduced through an air vent above the bed. The vent itself was too narrow for a person to fit into, but it led up to a between-floors space in which, crouching, someone could fit. Maybe that had been their short killer again.

The examiners entered the gap through a floor panel that was loose under a rug on the floor above, having been already prised open, and found regular-sized shoe prints in the dust, a photo of which they sent to Ross. Glove marks, no fingerprints. The hotel CCTV did indeed show an old lady who matched the description Sefton had given, delicate lace gloves on her hands, show a surprising amount of sudden heft in heaving open the floor panel.

'Who *are* these people?' said Costain. 'What sort of gang includes old ladies, American mercenaries, prisoners called Dean Michael and South Sea islanders of limited stature? Talk about positive discrimination.'

'The snake will be rare in the UK,' said Ross, 'not something easily kept as a pet. I've put the word out to the reptile-owning community. Let's see if anyone's had one stolen.'

'Can you fingerprint a snake?' asked Costain.

'We'll bloody try,' she said. She checked a message on her phone. 'Lofthouse is coming down. They've stabilized Sefton, but it's still touch and go.'

'Great. If there's nothing we can do for Sefton here, I did think . . . I mean, it'd just take an hour for us to get back into London . . .'

He sounded like he thought she wouldn't like what he was about to suggest. 'What?'

'Ballard's deal hasn't come through yet, but maybe he'd have access to something that could save Kev.'

Ross nodded. 'Let's go.'

'Wake up!' someone was shouting in Sefton's ear.

He suddenly realized what had happened, thought he had the snake on him, leaped up.

He was standing by a hospital bed, looking down at . . . himself.

Shit. Was he dead?

No, he could see himself breathing. He reached out a hand and it passed through his own neck, immaterial. He felt it, though. It was like a sudden cold in his throat. He moved his fingers, experimenting, letting his curiosity help him deal with the fear. Then he remembered that someone had spoken to him, and looked around. Gilbert Flamstead was standing nearby, arms folded, a grin on his face, watching him. 'Ah,' he said, 'that's better. Good morning.'

So was this also a dream with Holmes in it? No. Sefton knew the texture of dreams by now. 'Who are you?'

'I am whoever you say I am.'

'Yeah, no, enough of that bollocks – who actually are you?'

'I'm Gilbert Flamstead, the actor. You may have seen me in such productions as *Richard II* for the Royal Shakespeare Company, a number of blockbuster superhero movies as the ever-so-charming British bad guy, in *Nicholas Nickleby* on Sky Arts and of course as the BBC's current in-period but still rather funky Sherlock Holmes.' He held up a palm before Sefton could reply. 'No, really, I am actually him.'

'Sorry. Gilbert Flamstead, the actor, is aware of me standing by my own body in some sort of near-death experience? Are you . . . what, someone who knows our side of the curtain?' Sefton took an experimental step forwards and peered at Flamstead, who seemed delighted by the attention. 'No, you're more than that. I've had a bit of experience of you lot now. People who know this stuff are all a bit scared. You lot swan about like you own the place. You're one of the . . . I don't know what to call them, the great powers, like Brutus or the Rat King.'

'The Gods of London, you mean?'

'I think I'd like to be the judge of that.'

Flamstead laughed. 'In so many ways, you already are.' He held out his hand for Sefton to shake. Sefton did so, a bit surprised there was something physical to grasp. 'I've been around much longer than Gilbert Flamstead has. I've been called Puck, Mr Punch, Ally Sloper, the Artful Dodger. I was actually one of Lionel Bart's drinking companions when he was composing *Oliver!* He nearly cast me, but I thought, Bit of a giveaway.'

Sefton suddenly wondered if he should be shaking this hand. Flamstead laughed as he withdrew it. 'Which of these gods are you, then? Are you the Trickster figure, like—?'

'Spot on. You *are* learning. I'm the one who always finds the fun. I like pulling the carpet out from under. Everything I say is a lie. Oh, your face! Priceless! Actually, to be honest, I've got a bit bored of saying that now; it just sends people round and round in that ancient loop of logic. Everything I say in the real world to real people is a lie. It has to be. It's just the way I'm made. So here, this not being the real world, you can genuinely trust what I'm telling you. I've discovered that in the real world, being British and sarcastic, I can actually get my meaning across enough to function by just saying the opposite of what I mean. That and I've trained a couple of expert posh-type to media-type translators.'

'So when you say you *are* Gilbert Flamstead . . . ?'

'I had myself incarnated. I decided, towards the end of what had been a terribly serious century, to see if I could have a bit more of a laugh by getting down and dirty with the flesh in the next one. Only to find . . .' He spread his arms in mock despair. 'What a ridiculous bloody audience. It's all getting more serious by the day! What fools these mortals be. I wanted to see what it's like from the other end. You see, when Londoners call on me, it's because they're fed up with how things are. They want improbable dramatic reversals. When reality isn't good enough, they use me to fashion great myths.'

'So you're sort of . . . the software that gets things and people "remembered"?'

Flamstead opened his mouth in theatrical shock. 'I am not fucking "software"! Look at you, deciding who is and isn't a person! Typical bloody human.'

'OK, OK, so you're a god who likes tricking people. Are you and the Rat King related?' Sefton recalled that the God of London he'd met when he'd been searching for answers in the Ripper case had also had a poor opinion of humanity.

'What?! Him with his "bring down the government" malarkey? Honestly, politics! I'm not pro or anti anything, except when it's the right fashion to wear for a while. I'm just having fun. I suppose you could say he and I are all part of the same thing. You've probably decided he's some sort of, I don't know, computer virus or something.'

Sefton looked back to his body on the bed. He felt now like he'd felt the last couple of times he'd ventured into the 'outer boroughs' where these 'gods' lived. That feeling was suppressing the panic that was threatening to well up inside him about the fact that, yeah, he'd actually been bitten by a snake, hadn't he? Standing here right now, he felt like he wasn't experiencing time properly. The quality of light was a bit askew, the dust unmoving in the air. It was as if Flamstead had halted everything at a particular moment. Which was probably a good thing, because . . .

'You're wondering if you're about to die. Well, perhaps, if I don't sort things around a bit, but me visiting you is nothing to do with that. Someone else handles death.'

'London is all about the letter of the law, isn't it?' said Sefton. 'Like it's enough, for whatever's going on here, that I "act" being Sherlock Holmes, just in terms of copying someone who was said to be him.'

'That's what acting is.'

'That's what I mean! Letter of the bloody law! Why is it like that? Go on, tell me everything that's going on here. Just tell me who's doing the murders. I bet you won't, will you? Even if I'm going to die.'

'You've realized that it's the letter of the law for those like me, and especially for *me*, to never give a straight answer. We're not built like that.'

'Of course you're not. Of course. So why are you bloody here?'

Flamstead smiled, as if they were now getting to what was really important. 'Well, you see, in my physical form, as Gilbert, I got interested in that comrade of yours Lisa when she visited us yesterday. I felt around the shape of her in the world and found you, the only one of your lot I could have a sensible chat with. I'm not actually here in this room, a celebrity visitor. That'd cause far too much fuss. Though I must confess, I do like the attention. No, I've taken advantage of your coma to get inside you, and turned this bit of human London into an anteroom to my own borough, just so we could talk.'

'Your own borough?'

'Never mind that now. Let's talk about Lisa Ross.'

Sefton wondered if he was hallucinating after all. 'What about her?'

'There's something peculiar about her. What is it?'

Sefton briefly outlined the circumstances in which Ross had lost the ability to feel happiness.

'Oh,' said Flamstead, a finger to his lips, 'oh, now everything makes so much sense. Just one more thing.'

'What?'

'Is she, you know . . . seeing anyone?'

It took some urgent communication between Ross, Lofthouse and the authorities of HM Prison Brixton to get Ross and Costain in to see Ballard at such short notice, but Ross could hear on the other end of the phone how highly motivated Lofthouse was to get that done. She'd always got the impression Lofthouse liked Sefton. 'Liked' seemed too small a word for how close Ross herself felt to him. With Quill the way he was now, Kev was what kept her hanging on in this job. She'd come with Costain because she wanted to do everything she could, and she couldn't do that by his bedside. 'How do you want to do this?' she asked as they were led through the corridors towards the interview rooms.

'Your call. You've seen a lot more interviews than I have.'

Ross glanced over to the prison officer, but decided she didn't care what they said or did. 'We don't have much to offer Ballard except what's already on the way. Given they were going to share valuable data, maybe he'd care about Kev dying.'

Costain shook his head. 'Even if he did, he'd want to make us pay for it.' He hesitated for a moment. 'You know, when he and I worked together, we got quite close.'

'You want to make it appear to him that you're still dodgy?'

'Yeah, how about I indicate to him that I'd be willing to play you lot for him, maybe to slip him a few items out of Sefton's holdall, in return for anything that'd keep Kev alive? Because I'm desperate for my mate not to die.'

'And what do you do if he plays ball?'

'Turns out I lied to him, but he's not so badly off, with that lovely deal and all.'

'Yeah, that maze of shite is one possibility. Or how about you just beat it out of him?'

He frowned at her. 'No. Because . . . what Kev would want us to . . . Listen, we don't just need Ballard for today, do we? We're hoping he'll be an ongoing source. And . . . I'm trying to not be so . . .' He seemed unable to find the words, threw up his hands.

'OK. Go for your plan.'

He looked relieved, smiled that disarming smile at her. 'Thank you.'

'Don't come on all—'

'I'm just here for Kev, all right?' He didn't even look impatient. Ross considered him, as he looked away from her once more. How much of all that had been for her benefit? The stoic, hurt man, trying to make amends, with no desire for reward. What a perfect disguise.

She let him go into the interview room alone, and once the prison officer had withdrawn, she sat outside the door, plastic cup of coffee in hand. She wondered if, after all, she would hear sounds of violence from inside the interview room. There were none. After ten minutes, Costain opened the door and beckoned for her to come in. Ballard sat across the table, looking pleased with himself. 'We've been having a chat,' he said.

'Fuck you, Hannibal Lecter. What have you got for us?'

'She's the good cop,' said Costain.

Ballard barely seemed to notice. 'I'm told you're an analyst,' he said. 'Is it you I have to thank for getting me caught?'

'Team effort.' Ross didn't like that silky tone of voice one bit. 'We're working against the clock here—'

'And I'm still waiting for my deal, but . . .' He glanced towards Costain and obviously chose his words carefully. 'I've been persuaded to show a bit more goodwill. So. Here's something to help your friend, who I look forward to seeing again, safe and sound.' He wrote down an address and a series of numbers. 'Storage place near Wembley. This code will get you into one drawer of one of my many lock-ups. In it is just one item, instructions on the label. And here's my written authorization to them to let you in.' He scribbled a quick note on another piece of paper.

When he was finished, Ross grabbed both pieces of paper and made to go.

'Wait a moment,' said Ballard. Costain put a restraining hand on Ross's arm. 'There's something very important you should know. That blade your friend showed me: I told him it was a fetch kettle, but I didn't say what spiel it contained. It's this one, and I hope you never need to make use of it. That weapon will allow you to kill what I'd call a figment, but you'd probably call a ghost.'

Ross nodded. So that was something confirmed. It also indicated there was more where that came from. 'I'm sure you'll get your deal,' she said. 'We have to get going.'

They marched with the prison officer back down the corridor. 'That was weird,' said Costain. 'Why did he share that, and why then?'

Ross shook her head. 'Maybe you shook him up so much he thought he needed to give us more.'

'I didn't go hard on him. I went dodgy, like I told you, said I'd sell you all out. Maybe that was for my benefit. Maybe he wants me to get him the knife.'

Ross rubbed her brow. 'Every time I think I've got every data point about this op into my head, something new comes along, something with bits I haven't worked out yet. It's like distraction after distraction.'

'You'll get there.' That smile again.

Ross just shook her head and was silent as they got through the exit procedures as fast as they could. Having checked the alibis of the three Sherlock actors and found them all to be vouched for at the time of the murders, she'd just finished ploughing through the threatening messages sent to them when she'd heard about Kev. She'd become numbed to the torrent of abuse celebrities, hugely and particularly Alice Cassell, got every day, and had found nothing to take them any further, and then she'd been told her friend was a victim. It had felt like payback for her own lack of feeling.

She got her mobile back as they left the building and saw a message from Lofthouse had arrived. 'Fuck,' she said as she read it, wanting to throw down the device.

'What? Is Kev—?'

'A zoo in Kent has reported that *two* of its snakes were stolen.' She heard the ping of the second email coming in and looked, her heart sinking. 'And they've found a body. One Danny Mills, aged seventeen, in Stoke d'Abernon; the snake was still in the room. Uniforms are all over it. There was a window left open.'

'Shit. They got it done.'

'There's a link here, a YouTube video. His parents showed it to the local uniforms; they thought it might have been a suicide note. Or that he might have bought the snake as some sort of prank. He did stuff like that, apparently. Couple of incidents with the police, nothing major. A baby son – bloody hell – who he didn't see much of, bit of a waster.'

Ross started the video playing as they got into the unmarked car Costain had had waiting for them when they got back into London. Costain didn't try to look as he accelerated violently, heading for the Stockwell Road.

The kid on the screen of her phone, a kind-looking youth with freckles and mad hair, nobody's idea of a father, was talking to a webcam, full of energy. 'So, OK, cheating, getting in first. I know about the reality-TV show, OK? I'm not just going to call your number and enter like I'm nobody. The two guys who went round town asking about people who'd played Sherlock Holmes, well, one of your film crew was in the pub, and he said maybe a bit too much, and when it gets out about the prize, you'll have everyone doing this, so, like I said . . .'

'Fuck,' said Costain. 'Fuck, they played us. Again.'

Ross wanted to hit something. Whoever she was playing against kept using her own moves to . . . to kill people. The kid on screen produced, suddenly, a deerstalker hat, which looked like it had been made from folded paper, and slapped it onto his head at a jaunty angle. Then he pulled out a guitar. As he started to play what Ross thought was probably quite a clever song about how he'd always wanted to be Sherlock Holmes, and now he'd got the chance, her heart sank. She imagined this bright, foolish kid, thrashing about, having the same heart attack Kev had had, but his parents too fast asleep to hear him. Parents whose first thought had been suicide by snake. She made herself watch to the end.

'Pub, mates, description,' said Costain, still concentrating on the road.

'I'm sure,' said Ross, clicking off her phone, 'that a description of whoever he met in that pub will add yet another member to the gang.' And, she thought, another spiky data point to her brain. She closed her eyes and tried to get some sleep, but an anger that was growing all the time wouldn't let her.

'Turns out you can't fingerprint a snake.' Lofthouse was standing awkwardly at Sefton's bedside, beside a young man who'd introduced himself as Joe. This was, she supposed, Sefton's partner. Fifteen minutes ago, the doctors had injected Sefton with the antivenom. Lofthouse had heard the air ambulance that had delivered it landing outside, which had been when Joe had entered too. He'd gone straight to Sefton and had stopped, wanting to touch him, but obviously not wanting to disturb the cannula. Finally, he'd just reached out and put a hand to the side of Sefton's face. Only then had he looked back to Lofthouse and introduced himself.

'Sorry?' Joe now looked to her again.

'The local police have confirmed there's nobody of that old lady's description living in the area she said she was from. From what I've been reading on my phone, the Danny Mills murder has confirmed for the media the idea that there's something about Sherlock Holmes going on with all these killings, but thanks to information we've withheld, it's not yet apparent that the victims all *played* Holmes. So some of the killings remain unconnected in the public mind. That could help us later.'

'Don't you want to tell the public? I mean, warn people?'

'It'd be a hell of a public service announcement. "Have you played or do you know someone who has played Sherlock Holmes?" No. You couldn't get people to take it seriously. They'd start daring each other. Bloody people.'

'That's what got him here,' said Joe, looking back to Sefton. 'How weird the shit you deal with is. It's like those people who end up in the "Strange Deaths" column in *Fortean Times*. That's the risk he takes, every day.'

He was making her think about Peter. About how much harder to deal with a bizarre risk was when it was someone you loved taking it rather than yourself. At the end of her working day yesterday, she'd finally found something useful to compare the squiggles on the piece of paper to. She'd ordered some books from the Met archives, mostly stuff one would expect her to consult, but one of them just happened to be a collection of maps of London, and one of those maps had turned out to be what she was after. An inkling in the back of her head led her to a diagram of natural tunnels that ran beneath the surface, alongside the many artificial ones.

Her piece of paper hadn't been an exact match, but it was close enough to convince her. That was what the key had wanted her to find. Whatever its mission, its desire seemed to be to give her more knowledge. It might take her somewhere that would give her access to new objects and powers, something that might give her the ability not only to help James's team but to free Peter. Now she had to find a stealthy moment to buy the equipment she needed to pursue that lead.

A noise from the doorway made them both turn, and in rushed Costain and Ross. Ross was carrying a tiny bottle, the lid of which she was already unscrewing. The bottle was green and covered in the grime of ages. 'The tears of Boadicea, they're called,' she said, not stopping to acknowledge Joe. 'The label says they can heal anything, instantly.'

'Do we know anything about—?'

'No. The label was written in the 1870s. No provenance, nothing I can find online.'

'Only, they've injected him with the antivenom, and if that's a risk—'

'It doesn't seem to be doing him any good,' said Joe. 'They said he'd slowly come round, and he doesn't seem to be. Let him drink it.'

'I'm meant to throw it on him.' She had the rusty cap off now.

'I'm senior officer,' said Lofthouse. 'I say we wait to see if—'
Ross threw the liquid.

Sefton sat up in bed and screamed.

He was reaching blindly for something in front of him, his hands scrabbling, his eyes wide and wild. He sucked in a huge breath. The monitors went wild. Medical personnel rushed in. Ross picked up the empty bottle from where she'd dropped it. Joe was trying to talk to the doctors, trying desperately to ask if Kev was all right.

'I'm all right!' That voice was familiar.

The doctor and nurses stepped back, staring. Lofthouse led her people through them, to see Kevin Sefton sitting up in bed, one hand out to hold Joe's. Kev was breathing normally now, relief all over his face. He started tugging at the dressing on his arm, then, alarmed by the reaction of the medics, thought better of it. Joe was looking worried again, as if Kev might have suffered some sort of brain damage, but Sefton's mania finally left him and he slumped back on the pillow. 'Really, I'm OK.'

'Thank God,' said Joe.

'Well, *a* god. He says to thank him.'

'Who does?' asked Costain.

Sefton looked around the medics who were now checking him over, obviously worried that if he came out with it, they'd start examining his head. 'It's complicated.' He looked over to Ross. 'I've got a message for you too.'

Lofthouse felt such relief she needed to put a hand on the wall to steady herself. She hadn't, it turned out, been present at the death of one of her officers. Someone else, though, should have been here. Where the hell was Quill?

FIFTEEN

Quill had no idea why Sarah was looking at him with such a weird expression. She'd been like that every time she came home from work the last couple of days. She'd kept getting Jessica to go and do something else, rather than help Daddy out with the ops board he'd constructed in the kitchen. OK, so it did get in the way a bit, but where else could he put it?

'So you're not on leave?' she said.

'How many times? I'm working. So I don't need to tell them. I'm working from home. Working on the case. I've switched my phone off. Erased their messages on the home phone. I'm waiting until I can give it all to them in a bundle with a ribbon on top. I'm closer to the case than they are, right now. I just don't want to tell them.'

'Why don't you want to tell them?' What was that weird sound in her voice?

'Because they'd come up with loads of complications, and I need to think clearly, so I took it away.'

'But—'

'Stop making it complicated. Would you, please? Could you?!' He hated feeling angry at her, but every time she'd spoken to him, she'd got in the way. He didn't feel able to cope with even the slightest complication. That was why, obviously, he'd taken his work home, so he could focus on it, narrow it down.

'Are you going to stop shouting at me?'

'When you start . . . just . . . seeing sense! Let me work!'

'OK.' She sat down on the kitchen floor, her back against the fridge. 'Explain it to me.'

Quill pointed to the drawing he'd made of what Holmes had written on the back of the photo. He'd attached the drawing to the cork board by the back door. He'd had to take down all the stuff from Jessica's preschool. 'Yes. Finally. Good to be able to share this with you. Keep up. Here's what Sherlock wrote: "The ultimate crime." He obviously thought the photo must be a clue to it. What's the ultimate crime?'

'You tell me.' Still that same strange, annoying carefulness in her voice.

'I think it's what I got an inkling of when I was in Hell, the kidnapping of people from . . . other sorts of afterlifes, bundling them all into Hell. That seems to have happened a few years back.'

'What? You never said anything about that.'

Quill realized he was on worrying ground here. That had come close to telling her what he couldn't tell her, what he was on the way to sorting, so he would never have to. 'I saw clues about it there; I worked it out the other day. That's the ultimate crime.'

'Well, it *could* be, if—'

He deliberately cut her off. 'Holmes was always about just deserts. What if he started working on that crime, maybe *found a way to solve it* and then was killed to stop him from revealing it?' Before she could answer, he excitedly pointed to the various other drawings he'd put up around the kitchen. Some of them were just sketches, stick figures, some of them he'd tried to put some real work into. Which was a bit unprofessional, yes. He was under a lot of stress; he sometimes needed something to work on, something to distract him. 'The name of the company that hired the *Lone Star*, Missing Room – that's also the name of a 2011 album by a French-American rock band with a meaningful name. There's also an asteroid that shares that name!' He found his drawing of what was admittedly just a field of stars. He hadn't copied every single one from the photo on his phone, but he had copied the index numbers round the edges. 'I'll bet that's pictured somewhere on the star field photo that was sent to Holmes! Dean Michael! The first names of two famous people, one fictional, one real, but both with the same surname!' She was looking like she still didn't get it. 'The same as the name of the rock band and the asteroid! *Moriarty!*'

'Yes, yes, I see what that means . . .'

'Who else recruits gangs of weird criminals? He's meant to have written *The Dynamics of an Asteroid*. That's why he's got one named after him! Sefton said there wouldn't be a ghost of Moriarty, but what if there was, just a tiny one, only it got pumped up by "Holmesmania"? It's had its nature changed by all those people in the audience thinking about it, so it's now someone who leaves clues and puzzles, like those actors said! I'd been being followed, I knew that, so I went to where Moriarty appears in the books and I was finally attacked!'

'You didn't tell me about that.'

'That's not important! Aren't you *listening*?! If Moriarty thought it was worth killing Holmes, because he got too close, then Moriarty must think there's a possibility that the ultimate crime can be solved, reversed!'

'And that would get all those people out of Hell?'

'She's getting it! Finally!'

'But . . . this "ghost" of a fictional character, he can't have been responsible for putting them all in Hell in the first place, can he? This can't be a crime he committed. So why does he care about Holmes investigating it? Why does he even know?'

Quill stared at her. He could feel himself shaking with sudden anger. He was so tired; his limbs felt so tense, like he had an actual burden on his shoulders. He took a moment to walk in a circle, to calm himself. 'They're connected. The Smiling Man and Moriarty. They must be. They might even be the same being. Or maybe Moriarty is some sort of evil force in the human imagination that the Smiling Man used to do it!'

'But Holmes didn't believe in the occult, so most of his media versions don't, so how come he's investigating this?'

He couldn't believe how she kept putting things in his way, when the only thing he needed, what he depended on right now, was a clear path. 'If Holmes got the first idea of what the real London is like, he'd have to start believing in the supernatural, wouldn't he? Like us, he wouldn't have any choice! Why do you keep *questioning* me?'

'Because I'm worried about you.'

'I don't need worry. I need help. Get out of my way. Don't you get it? If I can catch Moriarty, I can find out the secret about the ultimate crime; then I can reverse it. Then Laura can move to London.'

There. He'd laid it all out simply in front of her. Now she would definitely see it.

'Why does that mean Laura can move to London?'

Quill shook his head, made himself sigh theatrically. Oh no, he couldn't go there. He had to cover that by making it look like Sarah couldn't keep up with him. 'Logic,' he said. 'It's all about logic – one, two, three, like dominoes.'

'Logic? OK, then.' She went to his drawing of the star field and looked at the numbers round the sides. 'These say "R.A." and "Dec". I think that must stand for where the telescope was pointing to get this picture. Agreed?'

'Agreed.' He was breathing hard. Let her work through it. Let her see and agree.

For the next half-hour, as Quill paced, Sarah did some work on her phone, making notes on what was left of the kitchen pad after Quill had used most of it for his drawings. 'OK, well, the asteroid called Moriarty is supposed to stay in what they call the plane of the ecliptic, where all the planets orbit the sun, but this picture is of higher up, near the pole, part of the Great

Bear constellation. If these numbers are right, Moriarty could never be in this picture.'

Quill shook his head. 'Lot of numbers there. Can't be right.'

'What about everything else that was at that murder scene? The hole in the slipper?'

'I reckon they fought and the blade caught it.'

'The photo of Irene Adler?'

'A clue left for us that she'd be Moriarty's next victim. Her ghost is probably out there too.'

'The pile of correspondence with the letters snipped out?'

'All sent by Moriarty, full of clues.'

'Even though they were in the museum before? Never mind. Why did he melt the wax head?'

'Holmes set it up as a target, like in one of the stories. Moriarty comes in, attacks the fake Holmes; the real one leaps out; the wax head goes flying, into the Bunsen burner on the desk. Moriarty only has a few moments after the murder to put everything straight—'

'Why bother?'

'Because he knows only the Sighted can see the murder, he wants to leave the majority none the wiser.'

'The curator didn't hear this fight.'

'Do ghosts fighting make any noise?'

'What about the biro lines between the bullet holes?'

'That's another message for us, maybe about the number of forthcoming victims. He's a serial killer in the new versions, so there have to be victims.'

'What about Henry Ward Beecher and General Gordon?'

'Heroes of Holmes's who were victims of the ultimate crime, not suspects, now in Hell unjustly.'

'The missing books would be . . . ?'

'Full of notes by Holmes implicating Moriarty.'

'And where the hell is Watson?'

He stopped, had to take a deep breath again. 'That I don't know.'

She paused, as if she was wondering how she could put something to him. 'You said you were following logic. I know I can get through to you with logic if I keep trying, and I've just proved all this huge pile of "facts" you've put together, it's full of holes—'

Get through to him? He grabbed her arm. Maybe a bit too roughly. 'Look. Look, just come and see it, OK?' He hauled her to the front door, saw Jessica look up from the front room where she was playing, gave her a smile to show her it was OK, and then they were at the step, and Sarah was angrily whispering to him to let go of her, keeping her voice down for Jessica's sake. He opened the door, and now she'd see, and he was sorry if it scared her, but it was necessary.

He pointed to the corner of the close. 'There,' he said. 'There's the shadow. Wait.' She waited, to give her credit. There was that slight lengthening of the shadow. She must have seen it. Had *he* seen it this time? Yes, he must have. It must be there. 'There it goes,' he insisted.

'Quill . . . I . . . Please don't get angry.' She was actually afraid now. Afraid of him.

'Come on, this is me.'

'There's nothing there.'

'You can't see it like I can see it. I should have realized that. I should have got that. Sorry.'

'So this is something you're seeing with the Sight?'

'I . . . didn't think it was, or I wouldn't have shown it to you. But I must have been wrong. There, I admit it – I was wrong.'

'If I put Jessica to bed, can we talk about this?'

He closed the door. 'We've talked about it. You don't listen.'

'For a start, wouldn't it be a good idea to go and see the others, or at least get them to come over here, so you can show it to them? If there's anything there, they'll be able to see it.'

'There *is* something there! I'm being followed! I told you how it all fits together!' He was shouting now. He heard Jessica suddenly crying. He couldn't deal. He coiled round himself, head in his hands. 'Could you . . . could you, please . . . ?'

Sarah went to reassure Jessica, took her up to bed, with a look on her face that said to Quill there was going to be more of this when she got back down, worse and worse. He managed to nod and smile at his little girl, who he was trying to save from Hell. He didn't want his colleagues coming over here and joining in with getting in his way. He got out his phone and called Lofthouse, pleased he got her voicemail, easier. He left a message saying he was going to take some leave. Then, steeling himself for the next conversation with Sarah, he went to sit against the fridge.

He liked the feeling of coolness and solidity against his back.

SIXTEEN

'Jimmy's done what?' The next morning, Ross had been surprised to find Lofthouse waiting for them in the Portakabin. She'd waited until Costain, and, amazingly, a still rather pale-looking Sefton, had arrived before sharing the news. The friends of Danny Mills, Ross had learned on the way over, had given typically varying descriptions of the man in the pub who'd bent Mills's ear about the 'reality-show contest'. Forensicating his room had revealed nothing.

'Does Jimmy know—?' began Sefton, then waved aside the end of his sentence.

Ross shared the sentiment. How could Quill know about what happened to Sefton and not come in? 'I'm going to see him,' she said.

'We all will, I'm sure,' said Lofthouse. 'But taking some time away is Jimmy's prerogative, and God knows he's been under enough strain. It does come, however, at an unfortunate time. Especially considering the fact that I'm going to be away at a conference for the next few days.' Ross didn't remember Lofthouse ever having shared a detail like that with them before, but with Jimmy gone, perhaps she felt she had to stay closer to the team. 'So the detective sergeant' – she nodded to Costain – 'will be leading the investigation. Now, our second issue is, Kevin, should you be up and about?'

'I'm fine. Completely.'

'The healing potion worked out,' said Costain.

'I think you bringing the healing potion . . . if we're going to call it something that makes this sound like *World of Warcraft* . . . I think that was the Trickster's doing.'

Costain frowned. 'But we decided to do that.'

'Or maybe he just wanted me to think he'd done me a favour.'

'So who is this "Trickster"?' asked Ross.

He'd given her just a few details of what he'd seen before Joe had taken him home. Now he related his encounter in detail. Including, incredibly, who the being had claimed to be. Ross's astonishment increased with every sentence.

'He wants to . . . go out with me?' she said when he'd finished. 'Him being not just one of your Gods of London, but also, actually, really, the real Gilbert Flamstead?'

'This is a thing that can happen?' asked Lofthouse.

'First time,' said Ross.

'Yeah,' said Sefton. 'Sorry. He also said that you doing that would be in return for him healing me, so—'

'*We* did the healing,' said Costain, incredulous. 'What, you want her to offer herself up, because . . . ?'

'OK,' said Ross, clearly a bit freaked out by what Costain had just said, 'if this is actually a real thing, not a hallucination . . .'

'It wasn't a hallucination,' said Sefton.

'Then this is worth doing. We could learn loads. How do we find him?'

'I gave him your phone number.'

'You were pretty sure I'd be up for this.'

'I was pretty sure I'd just been bitten by a dirty great snake and was going to die. The problem is, from what I've been reading overnight—'

'You did research last night?' asked Lofthouse.

'I was *fine*. From what I read, this Trickster figure pops up in a lot of the world's religions and he's always trouble. He's usually the villain.'

Ross allowed herself a glance at Costain. 'I can handle trouble.' Costain remained stoic in response.

Lofthouse wished them well and headed back across to her regular duties on the Hill. Costain, a little awkwardly, led them back to the ops board. 'So Mills wasn't a law-abiding citizen, continuing that pattern of the murders, but Sefton, being not just a copper but a fine upstanding one, breaks the pattern, like Holmes did. Maybe that's not a factor in why they're killed. Maybe it's just that these days a lot of people have done a lot of shit.'

'Maybe,' said Ross.

Costain opened his copy of Conan Doyle. Ross found she wasn't as resentful of that now he was meant to be in charge. 'The next few stories are "The Engineer's Thumb" . . .' He looked to Ross.

'No death. And neither is there one in "Noble Bachelor", "Beryl Coronet" or "Copper Beeches".'

'"Silver Blaze" . . .'

'Set on Dartmoor.'

'And "The Cardboard Box" . . .'

'Love that title,' said Sefton.

'The death in that one is in Liverpool,' said Ross. 'The next one we have to look out for is "The Stockbroker's Clerk", in which a watchman is murdered in the City, in Lombard Street, in a building with a big safe.' She went to the ancient PC and found the street on Google. 'The name of the business in the story is Mawson and Williams, but of course that's fictional. It's a pretty short street, but a lot of companies along it could fit the bill.'

'Security guards working there who've played Holmes, though, that's a pretty small Venn diagram,' said Sefton.

'Although,' said Ross, 'we've seen that the victim having played Holmes is the only completely required paradigm – all other circumstances are variable – so we shouldn't limit the possible victims to security guards.' She set out a possible plan, and Costain nodded. It was actually a relief to have that speed of agreement and action once more.

They began to call the companies on Lombard Street, asking to meet with their security representatives in person, as soon as possible. By lunchtime, they had a dozen or so appointments. As Ross went to the kettle to make her fifth cup of strong, sweet tea that morning, her phone rang. Even though she was expecting to hear at some point the familiar, cultured voice on the other end of the line, she still froze up a bit.

After she finished the call, she composed herself and turned to Sefton. 'You weren't hallucinating,' she said. She looked back to Costain, and just for a moment he looked angry. Just for a moment she wanted to reassure him. Then she scolded herself for that impulse and went back to work.

Flamstead had asked Ross to go out that same evening, showing what she assumed was the usual disregard for convention of celebrities and/or gods. By the afternoon, the team had finished calling around businesses and had set up interviews with security staff for the next day. The organizations they'd called had been forewarned that this was to do with the 'Holmes murders', that they should ask all their employees if they'd ever played Holmes, and if the answer was 'yes', not allow them near their places of work. They'd also warned them against contacting the media. As soon as the press realized the connection between the victims, and what the locations were about, the team would find themselves competing with journalists to stake out the next attack.

Then came the awkward bit. Ross got the other two to sit down with her and together they compiled a list of questions for Ross to put to Flamstead that evening, both about their immediate operational needs and more general ones about the place of the 'gods' in London, what exactly the other 'boroughs' were, what the nature of Hell was, et cetera. She would have to see how much of this she could sensibly include in the conversation, but it was better to have a shopping list. Costain seemed just a little relieved at them treating this as an operation, not a date. If he'd wanted to, could he order her not to? If he had, Ross was pretty sure that tonight's events would immediately become a date again, because she wasn't about to miss this opportunity. No, Costain wasn't stupid. She wasn't sure what he was feeling; he was keeping his cards close to his chest. That line about 'offering herself up' had annoyed her. Costain knew how fucked up she sometimes got about sex. Such an adolescent thing to say. It wasn't like she was going to fuck Flamstead, was it? Even if that had been on her agenda, it was none of his business.

That night, Ross wore her only evening-out dress, which frankly needed dry cleaning. She got out of the taxi in front of the Berkeley Hotel, in Knightsbridge, and was both taken aback and at the same time a little relieved to see the familiar figure of Flamstead waiting on the steps outside the rather ordinary brown building. On the way over, she'd tried to call Quill and had left a message on his voicemail. She had gone a bit beyond businesslike in asking him to please come back.

'Well, you look like you got dragged through a hedge backwards,' said Flamstead. He obviously saw that she thought he might be being serious and grinned. 'I tell the truth at all times. This is quite the everyday encounter, eh?' He gestured towards the restaurant. 'Honestly, *I* find it all a bit intimidating.' So, if what Sefton had told her was correct, he lied continually, was incapable of doing otherwise. This was going to be interesting. Or, to use another word, complicated. He seemed nervous, which, given the circumstances, was bloody extraordinary.

'Pleased to meet you,' she said. 'I mean . . . properly.'

He had a table reserved, and everyone was very nice, when Ross was expecting any minute for someone to scowl and say they didn't know how someone from Bermondsey could have slipped through security. Flamstead said Marcus, who was presumably the chef or the manager, was a complete stranger to him. The decor was plush, wood shining, surfaces plum-coloured and polished. There was a warm, hearty smell in the air. She kept her coat with her, rather than give it to the . . . whatever he was called . . . who wanted it. She put it on the back of her chair and saw that nobody else had done that. Flamstead seemed not to notice, which was decent of him, and just showed what a good actor he was. He pointed things out on the wine list, saying they were all terrible, those fingers dancing about. Ross sighed inwardly. The history of deities going on 'dates' with people . . . from what she'd read of mythology, it seldom ended well. Still, if he had got 'incarnated', this was also a bloke, which might explain why he seemed ill at ease, sometimes, in his own skin. She kept her police face on, and so was probably looking much calmer than she felt. Being 'in the field' like this was entirely beyond what she'd been trained for as an analyst. Mixing business and pleasure was taboo also.

'So,' she said, after they'd ordered, 'like you said, this is a bit weird.'

'But not intimidating, I hope.'

'You mean you hope it *is*?'

'Obviously, I don't want to *impress* you or anything.'

'Why did you want to take me out to dinner?'

'For, well, all the usual reasons. Your eyes.' Was that a lie? How could just saying 'your eyes' as a sentence be a lie? This was certainly keeping her on her toes. 'One different than the other. That's the secret of David Bowie's success. As I told him the other day.'

'So you've probably never met David Bowie. Don't you have cosmic goddesses or whatever to go on dates with?'

'You could call some of the actresses I hang around with that, I suppose.'

There had been something puzzling in his tone there, like they were at cross purposes. 'No, I mean . . . Listen, Kev told me everything. I know who you really are.' He looked puzzled. 'You might not have got his name. The one you . . .' She suddenly realized how weird this sounded. 'Appeared in the dream to.'

He was now looking completely bewildered. 'Was . . . this in a play or something? I don't remember him.'

'Sorry, how did you get my number?'

'You gave it to me. When you visited the set with your Mr Quill.'

She was certain she hadn't. She was also now not sure if she was actually talking to someone who always lied. Flamstead was looking so completely lost that she felt like she might have somehow woken up from the nightmare her and her mates' lives had been for the last few years, to a normal life without gods and ghosts. 'Right,' she said carefully, 'so you're just an actor?' This 'date' really wasn't going so well.

'Yes.' He slapped a big hand flat on the table. Finally, something he could answer concretely. However . . . was that a twinkle in his eye? Had he just felt a moment of triumph at having convinced her of something?

She took a second to compose herself. She got the feeling she was being tested. That, at least, was something she understood. She had to go round him, get past him, trip him up. She found she was looking into those eyes, feeling warm inside at the challenge. How bloody awful was it that this couldn't be fun for her? Her body was appreciating his attention, but she herself, unable to feel joy, felt like she was about to take a driving test. 'Listen,' she said, 'what I don't get is why someone like you is interested in an ordinary office worker in law enforcement.'

'Ordinary?' He kept that as a question, which couldn't be a lie. 'Let me see, what would Sherlock deduce about you?' She was pretty sure that any serious actor seeking to impress wouldn't at this point have brought his most famous character into it, like she was a nine-year-old asking for an autograph. Or was he really that useless with women? 'Are you from . . . Bermondsey?'

Was he that good with accents? Maybe that was an actor thing. Or could he have learned that off the Internet? Only with a stalker level of research. She decided to mess with him. 'No.'

'Really? Damn. You're involved with someone . . . No, not anymore.'

She broke eye contact. She didn't like this game. She didn't like what those lies said. 'I have . . .' OK, she decided, she didn't have to be entirely honest with him either. 'I have . . . a medical condition. I can't feel happiness.'

He looked deeply concerned. 'You have anhedonia.'

It hadn't occurred to Ross to look up a name for the state she was in. 'Do actors often know obscure mental health terms?'

'Wasn't that also the working title for *Annie Hall*?'

'If it was, they went with the right one.'

'So . . . was it the result of a trauma, or . . . ?' He was now playing the part of someone who was out of his depth with the issues of someone he'd just met, and was playing it well.

The waiter arrived with their drinks, which gave her time to formulate a strategy. As soon as he left, she went on the offensive.

'It was the result of the relationship you intuited or looked up on Google like you're stalking me.'

'I haven't been!'

Oh God, he had been. She kept him off balance, sticking out her bare arm across the table. 'It's the full deal. Go on, try.'

'Try what?'

'Tickle me. I'm very ticklish.' She raised the arm behind her head, glad her dress was sleeveless and that she'd shaved for this. 'Tickle me under there.'

Other diners were looking over, but she didn't care. Now they were working for her. He'd adopted a rather bohemian pose, after all. An actor couldn't resist causing a bit of a scene. He put on an 'anything once' expression, stood and walked over to get behind her. He smiled to the other diners, making this into a performance, making this OK. She saw them smiling back. He placed the fingers of his right hand carefully just below her armpit, on her bare skin. He did that with only slight hesitancy, maybe apt for someone who'd done weird self-consciousness-erasing shit in stage school, but perhaps also with the arrogance of a god. Then he ran his fingers up her arm, daring for the shortest time to be sensual, and her body reacted again, because she hadn't been touched for far too long. Then he turned it into comedy and went, 'Tickle, tickle, tickle!' out loud as he did so.

She winced. 'Ow,' she said. 'Ow. Ow!'

He stopped, looked aghast at the expression of genuine discomfort on her face, got quickly back into his seat. 'I don't understand.' Was he saying he did?

'I found out about that early on,' she said. 'Without emotional pleasure, the physical pleasure is just annoying, and that quickly kind of shorts out into actual pain.'

He paused, forming his fingers, with a surprising lack of pretentiousness, into a steeple. 'Is that true of all physical pleasure?'

She took a long sip from her glass, keeping eye contact. She watched his gaze darting around her face, checking out her lips. 'No,' she said finally, letting an awareness of what he meant into her voice, a little teasing. 'Most physical pleasure doesn't connect to laughter. Also' – she moved back to serious again, trying to keep him off balance – 'my dad's . . . imprisoned. I used to be able to see him; now I can't.'

'Is he from Bermondsey too?'

'He isn't from there *either*.' She wasn't sure she liked lying to this man who seemed genuinely interested in her situation, even if he himself was lying at every moment. She tried something else, using exactly the same words she'd used before. 'What I don't get is why someone like you is interested in an ordinary office worker in law enforcement.'

He nearly replied exactly the same thing as last time, but stopped himself. That was something her team had noted about the 'ghosts' they dealt with, that they often seemed to use stock responses, like video-game characters. Were the 'gods' the same? 'Only because you're very attractive,' he settled on.

She suddenly wanted to tell him to go fuck himself. Which meant she was getting far too into this. She took a big gulp of her wine instead. There had been an 'only' there, hadn't there?

'Or perhaps it's just because of the case you're investigating.'

'Right, I thought so. You're only interested in the case and want to quiz me about it.'

'I'm not only interested in . . . No, I mean . . .' He had actually tripped over his own need to lie, and now he was getting flustered about it. If he was this Trickster deity, he was also the human he claimed to be, and the human part of him, evidently, could get flustered.

Their first course arrived. She'd ordered a salad, not wanting to have to deal with anything she didn't understand the name of. She tried it. Her palate and mouth gave her signals that once would have been pleasurable, but were now like watching a party from outside the window. She had to exercise harder these days, she'd found, because her body was used to a certain amount of pleasurable satisfaction from food and kept urging her to find it now in quantity rather than quality. She wondered if sex would be the same. God, she hoped he didn't want to go there. Her body, though, detached from her in a terrible way, did. That made her feel . . . ashamed. It made her think of that awful thing Costain had said about offering herself.

'Hey,' he said, gently, putting down his soup spoon. 'You rather left me hanging there; you drifted off.'

No, *he* had. He was now sounding like someone who genuinely thought he was in the middle of a terrible date. Or was that him getting the better of her, another play? 'Sorry. I'm not used to blokes being interested in me.' Which was really a bit of a lie. 'I get lied to a lot.' To that last line she added a meaningful glance.

He sighed. 'I don't enjoy lying to you. I am who I say I am.

Basically, I just want you to feel . . .' He paused, obviously trying to find the right word to insert where 'happy' should go. 'The opposite of comfortable and calm.' Perhaps that was his way of confirming who he really was, that he was indicating that he had to say the opposite of what he meant?

'You mean uncomfortable and alarmed? Or involved and excited?'

He looked sad, trapped even. He *had* just told her who he was, she was sure of it. 'Please . . .' He literally couldn't finish that sentence.

She decided to be merciful. The nature of the Gods of London seemed to be as limited as that of the ghosts. If she was going to hear anything useful tonight, she had to give him something to work with. 'How about I tell you my story?' she said. 'Then you tell me yours?'

He just smiled. Which she took as permission to continue. So, through the clearing away of the first course and the arrival of their main meal, the nature of which, on his plate, she couldn't guess at, but in her case was something with chicken, she talked. She felt a reduction in stress as she did so. That was the closest she got to comfort, these days, hitting the limit of lack of pain. She'd learned to reach for that slow dropping down the scale, rather than the excitement of approaching pleasure. It had made her quiet, confined. She was like an animal who'd started to accept its confinement, to be changed by it. It was bad to think about. It was good to talk about, even using medical euphemisms as she still did now. Although she was pretty sure the man opposite her would know about Hell and deities and ghosts, the diners around her, all straining to hear the celebrity, wouldn't. For that release, and to pursue her list of questions, she would have to wait until they went some-where quiet. She wanted, she was pretty sure they both wanted, him to be honest with her.

He listened attentively, nodding when those nods could be taken to be the opposite of agreement. He listened like a god who still needed to learn about the world. Ross skipped past the details that were impossible, and avoided anything of operational significance. Over dessert, for which Ross chose, relieved, treacle pud and custard, only to find it was a very small treacle pud on a huge plate, she reached the present day.

'Is your detective inspector all right?' he asked. 'He seemed entirely sane.' She told him about Quill's leave of absence, but didn't feel loyalty allowed her to describe his erratic behaviour. 'So you're left with this man Costain in charge? It's not like you talk about him at all. Sherlock would say—'

'Sherlock's not here.'

'Sherlock would say you're not at all sensitive about this.'

'Sherlock wouldn't, because all of his supposed deduction was about physical clues, not about how *random* most people are, and besides, Sherlock can fuck right off.'

He laughed, took the bill from the hand of the waiter that proffered it, dropped a card into it without looking, handed it back. Ross had decided before she got here that, much as she'd like to go Dutch, she'd let him pay for food she wasn't capable of enjoying. 'Would you like to go on somewhere? Dancing? I think I'd like to distract you from your current investigation.'

Somewhere loud, where she couldn't ask questions? No. She felt emotionally like she was anticipating a swim or a run. Her physical arousal was moving her away from her baseline of comfort, though. She wondered if they could find a way to talk that was about ease rather than excitement. 'How about we go back to mine?' she asked.

Once again, he just smiled.

SEVENTEEN

Joe had been incredulous about Sefton getting back to work so quickly. 'So they can just snap their fingers and do that, then? Get poison out of your system, miraculously, like proper gods?'

Sefton had said they obviously could. Joe had replied that it'd be a good thing to get one of these gods on Kev's side permanently. Then his expression had gone all trying not to cry, and Sefton had held him. They ended up laughing in relief at him having come out the other side OK. Sefton, as always, did his best to reassure him.

The next morning, before getting into his car, he tried to call Ross, half interested in the answers to their work questions, half in a 'so, girlfriend' kind of way, but he only got her voice-mail. Immediately he clicked off, his phone rang again. It was Sarah Quill. Sefton was the only one of his team she had managed to get hold of. She hadn't left messages for the others; she didn't want to say what was going on. She asked him to come over as soon as he could.

So here he was, at Quill's house, which he'd last seen with the shadows of an urgent investigation hanging over it. Now it felt bad in an entirely different way. Sefton could feel the wrongness as he walked to the door, feel that now this place was . . . haunted. Sarah answered; she had that trying-not-to-cry expression, but with it was a great determination and anger. 'He's in the kitchen,' she said.

Sefton felt Quill's presence before he saw him. He'd never experienced this sensation of the Sight before, to feel a place haunted by a living person. Quill was squatting by the fridge as he entered, drawing slowly and carefully on a piece of paper. He looked up and nodded. 'Yeah, good, now's the right time for you to be here.'

Sarah looked anguished at Sefton. 'I called him, Quill.'

'Well, good for you. What do you want, a medal? Just because for once you haven't put something in my way, just because you accidentally got something right. Kev, never mind her, look at this.' He was drawing, Sefton saw, what seemed to be a star map. 'She says the asteroid couldn't be in that part of the sky. I say it could, millions of years ago. We may be dealing with a crime that old. Logic, you see?'

So Sefton asked, and heard the whole theory, which jumped over many lapses of logic with phrases like 'That must mean . . .' Sefton called him on this the first couple of times, only for Quill to become suddenly furious, to say he was getting in the way like Sarah was.

Oh God. Sefton looked back to Sarah. She must have been putting up with this for the last few days. 'Right,' he said, 'I've got all that on board now. I'll just go and get my notebook and write it down.' Quill nodded, pleased, and went back to his drawing.

Sefton led Sarah into the spare bedroom upstairs, where he was sure Quill couldn't hear them. 'I'm so sorry,' he said. 'You should have called us earlier.'

Sarah was trying desperately to keep it together, a hardness about her eyes and mouth, not giving in to collapse just because help was at hand. 'I kept waiting for it all to make sense. I mean, what he's saying isn't *so* mad, is it? At least, not all of it. Not with what you lot have been through. It's the anger I can't deal with. He doesn't show that to Jessica – he doesn't let himself do that – he just . . . keeps it for me. She's in nursery now. He's got so much worse today. I don't want her seeing him like this. If you could just take him back to the nick and all talk to him, maybe you could . . . persuade him that's not true?'

He was sure she knew that was hopeless. She just didn't want to think about what the next stage would be. 'I think . . . we need to get some qualified medical people involved.'

'I don't want him dragged off and locked up in some . . .' She was crying now, keeping going through it, so determined. Sefton put a hand on her shoulder, amazed at her. Sarah had gone through the trauma of having Quill die and come back, and now this, and was somehow still on her feet.

'It won't be like that. We'll make sure it isn't.'

'I don't want him on drugs either. I want him able to find his way back to that mind of his. This is all because of what he saw in Hell. He never told me everything. It's still in him; he's never going to get away from it.'

Sefton was sure that was the case, especially the bit about Quill not telling her something. 'They'll start by talking to him. Maybe that's all it'll take. Do you want me to make the call? I mean, to Lofthouse, because I have no idea who else to contact, but she will.'

Sarah visibly forced herself to nod. 'Please.'

Sefton started hitting buttons on his phone. 'And then I'm going to stay put, OK? You can go for a walk, get a coffee or something. I'll look after—' There was a sudden noise from down the hallway, a door slamming, then fast footsteps down the stairs. Sefton ran out, saw Quill wasn't there. He ran downstairs, out through the front door . . . just in time to see Quill's car speeding off into the distance. He stood there for a moment, desperate, wanting to yell after him.

Ross lay in the curve of the arm of the sleeping actor. What a strange thing to wake up and see a famous person on your pillow. She was steady, calm, set for now at an absence of all pain and stress, the best she could feel. He had been objectively lovely last night, very interested in satisfying her, but urgent about his own needs too. She had been trying, as they undressed each other, to ask him some of the questions her team had prepared, hoping his human body's needs would overrule his desire to be careful.

He'd swatted the questions away, claiming to be only human (meaning he wasn't). He also claimed to know nothing about Hell, only that he was sure whoever was in charge knew what they were doing (interesting). He also said he knew very little about Sherlock Holmes, and nothing about the current killings (the first part of which was surely to let her know that the second part was untrue). As they'd lain there afterwards, she'd asked him to tell her about his life, in return for her tale in the restaurant. She'd mentally translated his lies. His Holmes, he said, was about to get more happy-go-lucky and more asexual. So darker and sexier, then. He'd come out with a few inverted barbs about the audience. She'd drifted to sleep to the sound of his voice lying to her.

She hadn't intended to do this when she'd left home tonight. Had he somehow used his powers, whatever they were, to trick her into his bed? No. She'd wanted this. She'd initiated it. Having a one-night stand, or a fling or whatever this was going to turn out to be, was a lot easier without happiness. If she'd been capable of being happy, she might have worried about consequences, about unhappiness.

Somewhere on the carpet over there was a knotted condom containing, well, the cum of a deity. Ross was on the pill, more to help with her periods than anything else, but when he'd produced protection, she'd considered what she was dealing with and let him go for it. The mythology about that part of human-deity interaction was also pretty damn terrifying.

She was sure now that he was a real human man. She was also sure he was something much more than that. Had she 'offered herself' for information? She felt guilty, of course she did. She would never have been able to do something like this without guilt, and in her current situation she couldn't even say she'd done this for fun. He'd wake up and leave immediately, wouldn't he, throwing a few lies in her direction that she would see through right away? She had to make herself think about something else, about the shape of her ops board right now, to stop the self-hating accusations going round in her head. She was practised at that. How was she going to talk about this to Costain? She didn't want to be the sort of person who deliberately hurt an ex. She didn't have to tell him how she'd got these data points.

She realized Flamstead had opened his eyes and was considering her. 'Hey,' she said.

'Hey.' Which could not be a lie.

'So, do you want to get some breakfast?'

'Shall we call ahead for reservations?'

'Er, I meant do you want some toast?' She realized as she said it that he'd just declared that he didn't want to stay for breakfast.

He must have seen the wince. 'Oh dear.' He stepped out of bed and stretched, scratched his balls. She wanted to find a way to test how he was feeling about her, about last night, that wasn't a question. As she opened her mouth to struggle towards that, he kissed her, first gently, then, as she let him, passionately. 'Don't be calm,' he said. 'Feel agitated and distracted. What do you want this to be?'

'I don't know.' She had trouble imagining a relationship with someone who couldn't tell the truth, no matter how hard he was trying to communicate. She also couldn't imagine a relationship without happiness for her to share. Her body wanted more of him, though. She wanted that calm too. She wanted the answers to her questions.

'Well, then,' he said. It was a non-answer that he was obviously practised at, but the smile that went with it completed the meaning. 'Got any porridge?' He wandered towards the kitchen and she watched his arse, feeling passionate and dispassionate all at once.

Ross got in for work only a couple of minutes late; Costain was already at the Portakabin. She found herself making immediate eye contact with him. She felt, ridiculously, like she'd been caught sneaking in. 'I tried to call you last night,' he said.

'Well, you know, I was out with Flamstead. I got a load of data for the board.' She had, too. She'd made a list in her notebook sitting in her car outside her flat. He'd asked if he could go back to bed, and she'd found she had no problem with leaving a god in her home. She hadn't anything sensitive on the computer there, apart from the stuff that was to do with her dad, and if he wanted to look at that . . . well, he might suddenly decide to help, even. She had the feeling he wanted to help her. She didn't want to betray his trust by doing anything weird and underhand like take that condom for Sefton to analyse. She'd left it for him to deal with. She realized that she'd drifted off for a second. Her body still felt like it had had a satisfying workout, then a very refreshing sleep.

She looked back to Costain and found he had a locked expression on his face, like he was keeping extreme control of his emotions. 'I mean I tried to call you late.'

'Well . . .' She couldn't find a response. None of his damn business. 'OK, here's that list.' She started to reel off the points, writing them up ready for Sefton to arrive. She carefully listed every single thing she'd learned, not editing what might be important.

Costain frowned. 'He said his version of Sherlock was going to get darker and . . . more sexual?'

That was his first question? Way to approach what he really wanted to know from out of left field. 'Yeah. Well, he said the opposite, but that's what he meant.'

'I don't know why they can't leave well enough alone.'

Costain sounded actually angry. About a TV show. She would have laughed at that, she suspected, if she still found things funny. Or maybe she wouldn't. She was hoping not to be cruel. Was he going to ask directly about her and Gilbert, or wasn't he? 'You think he's this . . . god. This Trickster. Why do you trust anything he says?'

'Because of a system of communication we—'

'If he's a trickster, isn't he obviously setting you up for something?'

Like you did, she wanted to say. But he was right. She was aware that another shoe was, at some point, bound to drop. That was half the interest for her. With no happiness at stake, she didn't feel like she was risking anything. 'Right. Be interesting to find out what, eh?'

He turned away, frustrated. 'I don't know how to act, what to be, to treat you right,' he said.

She could tell he meant it, and after all last night's mental adjustments, the directness was actually refreshing, but it still annoyed her. 'Don't treat me like anything,' she said.

He took a moment more, then straightened up, turned back to face her, in control once more. 'Absolutely. We still on for the auction on Wednesday?'

She hoped this was all there was going to be to it. Good on him if it was. They were acting like colleagues again, pulling together while Quill was on leave. 'Yeah, if you are.'

He nodded just as Sefton entered, looking grim. 'I've put the word out about Jimmy,' he said. He saw they didn't know what he was talking about, and proceeded to tell them the terrible story of his morning so far.

Ross felt guilty all over again, for no good reason. They immediately started to call around some obvious places where Quill might be, and Ross, with a terrible feeling in her stomach, made sure that all the authorities who could search for him were doing so. Lofthouse called, full of apologies for just having caught up, and said she'd made sure everyone knew to look out for Jimmy. They'd hear the second anyone saw him. Finally, all three of them had to admit that they'd done everything they could and had to get on with today's urgent business, which was to head to Lombard Street and begin their interviews with heads of security, as well as locating businesses with big safes. Costain made a gesture towards making the decision himself, but Ross could feel the sudden lack of leadership in the room. She quickly briefed Sefton on what she'd learned last night, and thankfully, distracted by Jimmy's situation as he was, he didn't ask for all the details in front of Costain.

As Costain drove them to Lombard Street, Sefton found himself taking comfort in their preparations. Jimmy had taught all of them to work outside their specialities. It was teamwork, sharing the burden, that saved their mutual sanity. It should have been pretty obvious that if one of them was going to lose it, it would be Quill, the one for whom responsibility meant he couldn't lean as much on the others. Especially after Hell. Who could come back from that and try to lead a normal life again? If they could find him, perhaps this would turn out to be the best thing that could have happened for Jimmy. Perhaps.

Sefton got a call from Ballard, who'd just walked out of remand, a free man, Lofthouse's deal having been officially made and accepted. Sefton put it on speaker. 'I owe all of you a great deal,' Ballard said, 'and I will repay.' Sefton got the feeling, somehow, that he was laughing at them. He wished he felt able to ask Ballard if he had anything to help find Jimmy, but he didn't trust him enough for that. He instead outlined, without giving the whole game away, their current operation. Ballard said he perhaps had something that could locate a particular individual. That, thought Sefton, might be useful for any one of this gang, or for Watson, whose absence was still a closed book to them, but also might especially help find Quill. He'd be in touch.

Lombard Street wasn't that long, a narrow grey street of

imposing buildings with arcade lanes of shops leading off on both sides. It turned left off Moorgate, just past Bank Tube station, and swiftly became Fenchurch Street. They'd agreed that, given the flexibility they'd previously shown, the killers would probably settle for the death of a Holmes anywhere within a quarter-mile. There was a Pret a Manger and a Sainsbury's Local, lunch places for office workers, fashion and fitness stores. There were also still three major banks with offices nearby, one with a branch entrance on the street itself, the others with less obvious offices back along the side streets, and a corporate finance company, which also, they'd found out, had a safe.

Costain parked on the narrow one-way street in front of doors that said they were in use at all times but led to a brown-field site, and propped his logbook in the window to deter traffic wardens. It was a cool autumn day. Sefton registered sunlight as he got out of the car, looked at Costain and Ross's grim faces, and wondered if they would find hope anywhere.

They split up for the interviews. Sefton went to the corporate finance company and talked to a smart fortysomething woman called Emily Jacobs, who had, to his surprise, after having received his call, read forward in the Holmes stories and knew exactly what he'd be looking for from 'The Stockbroker's Clerk'. 'I agree that the "watchman" who gets beaten to death in the story sounds most like a modern-day security guard. I called round all our security personnel personally this morning, those on shift and those off, and I have one who thinks he might have once gone to a fancy-dress party as Sherlock Holmes. He asks does that count?'

'Let's assume it does. Being a security guard, he's not going to have a criminal record, right?' Although for their victims to have a criminal record seemed a preference rather than a neces-sity for their killers, it was a detail that might serve to make one victim more attractive than another.

'Well, no actual record,' said Jacobs. There was a 'but' she couldn't say out loud, but communicated to him with pursed lips.

'Can I talk to him?' said Sefton.

Johnny Horner had a carefully tended quiff, sideburns that showed he'd had a haircut after getting a tan, and described himself as 'a little bit wa-hey, a little bit woo', the geezer character straight out of *The Fast Show*. He'd been in this job two weeks, and his attitude, an in-your-face and rather forced cheekiness, made Sefton wonder if his employers were regretting the hire and waiting for the end of his six months. Background checks revealed nothing dodgy, though. When asked, Johnny had a lot of big talk about knowing the bad lads when he was a kid, and that was probably true.

Sefton checked in with his colleagues, who'd found just one other potential Sherlock, an upstanding citizen in the rather dull way of most security personnel. They'd agreed earlier that actually putting a deerstalker on someone and deliberately making their own target was unethical. So, all in all, Costain decided Horner was their best option as bait.

Costain brought over a map with the locations of various large safes marked on it. Ross arrived, and together they got Jacobs talking to the owners of a small, and relatively lightly defended, investment broker's nearby. The company owned, as a relic of their building's history, a truly gigantic safe. Horner, to give him credit, was immediately up for their plan. He and the other potential Holmes would be given leave until next Thursday, indeed ordered not to come anywhere near the street. Then, on Thursday morning, the main investigation having liaised with Costain's team in a truly enormous stake-out operation, Horner would take his place as guard near that safe. He was to tell everyone on social media that he was off for a couple of days, and exactly when he'd be back.

'Cushy job,' he said.

'With a very brave bit at the end,' said Sefton.

Horner shook his head. 'If you catch this nutter, then I'm just looking out for my mates. Besides, nothing's going to happen to me with all you lot hiding in every corner, is it?'

Sefton looked awkwardly at the other two. 'Tempting fate, we call that,' he said. He didn't add that in their business there might actually be a fate to tempt. They said their goodbyes to their new allies, returned to their car and, as they'd been reflexively doing all this time, once more checked their messages.

Nobody had seen Quill.

Quill kept wanting to explain to someone exactly what he was doing. It could, he was sure, look a bit unusual to someone on the outside. He'd kept his phone switched off after he'd abandoned the car, and made sure to change as soon as possible out of the clothes he'd left the house in, into the civvies he kept handy for just such a moment as this. They'd find him if he switched the phone on, even just for a moment to look at Jessica's picture. It wasn't Sarah's fault; he kept having to remind himself of that. She hadn't been deliberately getting in his way, had she? *Had* she? No, he couldn't believe that of her. This Moriarty he was chasing, he might be some sort of cosmic power, but Quill didn't think he could have got to Sarah. He'd realized, a couple of hours after he'd left the car behind, and was walking past White Hart Lane, on his way into town, that he wasn't going to be able to sleep in a bed tonight. If he used his cards to get a hotel room, or took cash out, they'd be able to locate him. Still, a night's discomfort wasn't too much to ask of someone who'd gone out on a limb to solve history's biggest crime.

He was still surprised by how small London was. Even keeping off the obvious ways, where they might have uniforms or doctors looking for him, the walk into the centre of town only took four hours. It was teatime before he found himself looking up at Centre Point. He stopped at the Starbucks on the corner of Charing Cross Road and Oxford Street, and felt the first nip of cold through his coat and waited.

Yes, he could hear them, distantly, the sounds that had pursued him since he was in the car. They were trying to find him, slipping through the narrow lanes between these dark buildings. The sounds were of a carriage driven by urgently spurred horses. Amazing, to think that was possible, to think that only a couple of years back if someone told him they were being followed by such a thing, he'd have said they were mad.

The way the buildings were changing, revealing their real faces to the Sight, that was indicative too. He could see Victorian detail even in Centre Point, as if it was a gigantic rookery of slum apartments. Up into the sky went the washing lines from it out to other great buildings, the sky itself brown like a Hogarth cartoon, full of flying scraps, the contents of buckets, the vapours of noxious exhalations, disease.

Had he ever left Hell?

He realized it would be such a relief if he hadn't. It would let all this be OK. It would mean only he was at risk. It would mean all this awful hope had just been a trick. No, though, he could feel the Sight telling him this wasn't Hell. Not yet. This was just a place that was becoming more like it. These opinions he had about what was going on, what he had to do, they weren't a cry for help; they were who he was now, and they were concrete, they could be proven. He was going to do it. But those hoofbeats were getting closer all the time.

He would soon have to find somewhere to spend the night. That didn't matter very much. All that mattered was the pursuit, him of it and it of him. He tried to explain all this to the old lady standing beside him, but she moved off before he got a few sentences in. He held in the anger he felt at her, and turned to walk again through the maze the city was becoming.

EIGHTEEN

Sarah Quill hadn't shared her husband's often changing but usually low opinion of Tony Costain. He'd always seemed to her like the sort of bloke who was trying to project all sorts of things about himself because he couldn't face his own vulnerability, a vulnerability she'd found herself liking. Now, his presence in her home was especially welcome. He'd brought his colleagues over to interview her, to go over once again any details Kevin might have missed.

'There was something he wasn't telling me,' she said as they sat in her living room. She could hear Jessica on the baby monitor, talking to herself upstairs, talking about Daddy. 'Something that was getting to him. He kept talking about Laura moving to London, as if he's so scared of this place now . . . Well, I don't blame him. But it's OK for millions of people.'

'Yeah,' said Ross, whose calm surface had come as a surprise, such a change from the intensity of the last time Sarah had seen her. She had also been altered by this insane job the four of them did. 'We all got the feeling he wanted to speak up about something.'

'We should have given him the chance,' said Sefton.

They went over everything, managing to get a pretty accurate idea of what was in the bag Quill had put together and hidden from her. 'If he calls,' said Ross finally, 'please tell him we want to listen.' Sarah had to close her eyes, resenting the implication that she hadn't told him that, though she doubted Ross had meant it that way.

After they left, Sarah listened as Jessica talked herself to sleep, then lay back in the sofa and looked at where she would normally expect to see Quill. She couldn't do this alone. That lot were wrapped up in their usual horrors, the ones that were one day going to eat them like they'd eaten Quill. She needed family; she needed someone who could help, who knew Quill. She picked up the phone and made the call. 'Laura,' she said, 'listen, something's happened. Could you come down to London a few weeks early, live with us for a while? We've still got the spare room.'

At lunchtime on the Wednesday, with nothing to do at the Portakabin except monitor the build-up to Thursday morning's operation and wait for news about Quill, Ross accepted Flamstead's invitation to come for a walk in Hyde Park.

Flamstead smiled at the passers-by who recognized him, signed autographs. Ross wondered if pictures of them were going to end up in the tabloids. She finally told him, not regarding it as an operational matter, all about Quill. He listened, concerned, upset. Were those emotions lies too? Surely not. How could any being function like that? 'How's Costain taking it?' he said, out of the blue.

Ross didn't like that he'd asked. 'Costain? He's trying to make out it's not hurting him, being stoic. He says he doesn't like where your version of Holmes is going. I don't think he'd have had an opinion before. This isn't some sort of pissing contest for you as well, is it?'

'Now, how can I possibly answer that?'

She should know better than to ask him direct questions. 'I'm going to one of the London auctions tomorrow night. Do you know about those?' She wanted to say, ridiculously, that as well as perhaps having a chance to get her happiness back, they might find something to help with their current operation. That was a distant possibility, however, and she was talking here, she suspected, to someone who could spot half-truths a mile away.

'Ah. Alone?' His tone indicated he knew what she was talking about.

'No.'

'What does Costain stand to gain by accompanying you?'

She was pleased at his insight. 'My trust, I guess.'

He took her arm in his and put a gentle hand on it. 'Ah,' was all he said again.

The location for the auction was, as always, somewhere special. That Wednesday night, Costain and Ross took the train out to Greenwich, threaded their way through the bohemian streets, still packed with tourists and summer food vendors, and, having been given the nod by an oddly shabby-looking security guard at the locked gates of the park, made their way up the hill towards the Royal Observatory.

As they climbed the incline, Ross looked down on London, lit up on this clear night. The Sight made Greenwich into somewhere that smelt of the sea, and overwhelmed you with the knowledge of time. She could feel, in this hill, the small weight of her own years, the steady decay of everything, how short a while was left to her. From the hill she could see, above London, constellations, a web of lines actually drawn in the sky, making the stars feel trapped. As they walked higher, the feeling got more and more intense, like they were inside an enormous clock, and she knew it was about to strike the hour. It felt like the grandeur above them was locked, by this hill, into the notion of Britishness, that here was somewhere that connected the eternal to Empire. This feeling was still at play in London below, but it was complicated, worrying. Here was displayed, for all to get nervous about, one of the grand certainties that nobody felt certain of anymore.

She looked to Costain. He remained stoic, seemingly not as affected by the experience as she was. She remembered how he'd described the night he'd looked out at London from the

Downs, how left out of the memory of the city he'd felt. This would surely be making him feel the same way. This time, however, when he saw her looking at him, he managed a smile. He was trying so hard.

The location this time had only been vaguely advertised as being at the observatory itself, but none of the old red buildings that vaguely reminded her of Battenberg cake looked big enough for the crowd that had assembled last time.

The whole cluster of buildings, including one with an observatory dome and one with a red ball on a mast on the roof, was lit up, as if this were an official event, and she supposed, given the connections that must be in place to have let the last auction happen at the Tate, it might be. Then, as they got to the main gate, she noticed figures standing in the shadows of the buildings, and a familiar one setting down a wooden crate across the line of metal on cobbles that marked the Meridian itself. It was Miss Haversham, the host of the last auction, still in her dilapidated gown. Ross could feel the Meridian, stark in her senses, like a vein or a wound, pumping time and pride around the world. It connected directly to the glowing compass that was all the sky above them.

. There was a modern metal sculpture of some kind on the line, one artist's own suggestion of compass points and great circles. It felt like a sliver moving inside one's finger. Haversham glanced over and saw them approaching, and gestured for someone else to come and see. From out of nowhere stepped, wearing exactly the same garb as last time, her assistant, Bernie the Bitch. He reacted to seeing them with a clownlike, exaggerated sadness.

'The ones oo've been 'urt,' said Haversham, in her carefully chosen accent, 'they're the ones oo come back soonest.'

Ross and Costain entered, having seemingly chosen the right moment, as the crowd started to gather, latecomers running up to the gates. A lot of them had reason to make their way here carefully, to avoid old enemies, though there was a truce in place on the grounds of the auction themselves. They were the people of hidden London, in ancient clothes, many of them threadbare. Those individuals were deliberately emphasizing their poverty. They came here to yearn for items that might make their marginal lives better, or, in the case of those in suits and ties, to vie for objects that would increase their power. The division between those who'd brought money to pay for their wins and those who intended to barter by sacrifice in the older way was more evident than last time. The groups tended to gather together, even. The influence of money had swiftly spread into even this shadow of the transactions of the metropolis below them.

A fine mist of rain blew suddenly through the buildings, clouds suddenly scudding across the sky, the side of the hill becoming, in seconds, even more maritime, and the crowd responded by raising umbrellas, many of which were patched and one of which was a mere skeleton. Just like last time, Bernie produced the lectern and the big book from thin air. Ross recalled being taken into what had seemed like a room behind the stage last time, where no time passed. The lists of items up for auction tonight were passed out, again printed on some ancient mechanical machine, in faded purple type.

The crowd, muttering about what they were after, or exchanging gossip, came forwards in the rain as Haversham stood on the crate and repeated, word for word as far as Ross could remember, her introductory speech from last time. She saw a number of glances towards her and Costain, and had to swat away a series of occult attempts to learn more about her with the 'blanket' gesture Sefton had taught her. She saw that Costain wasn't bothering. She looked at him incredulously and he looked back, calm and proud. So tonight he was letting them know he was a copper? Maybe this was another aspect of his latest attempt to be an upright citizen. She expected someone in the audience to react, but nobody did. Perhaps this lot had heard now that there was a new law in town. When she got hold of a copy of the list, she swiftly looked down it and found it: 'A lifetime's happiness.'

It was the third item to be auctioned. As they came to it,

Haversham's expression became concerned. 'We 'ave some miraculous melodrama in the miasma for you tonight, ladies and gentlemen and others, so we do. A lifetime's 'appiness was put to the risk, and now 'ere's the young flower, seeking to set things right. Am I correct?' There were cheers and catcalls from the crowd. Ross quickly nodded. 'What am I bid, then?'

The bidding began with the usual newbies whose small offers of personal pain or money were mocked. The desperate looks on their faces haunted Ross. The use of money for a bid didn't elicit as much anger this time round. Someone bid £10,000, and that wasn't taken lightly by the crowd.

Ross decided now was the time and raised her hand. She'd thought long and hard about what she had to offer. 'An obligation from Mark Ballard, collector of London items,' she said. She was pretty sure she could back that up, given a bit of horse trading. Thank God, the crowd seemed to regard that as a serious offer. She looked to Haversham, who nodded, a tiny smile crossing her face. Hers was the leading bid.

'Twenty thou,' said a voice from behind her.

Ross looked to Haversham, who took the moment she always took to use whatever internal measure of value she had, then, horribly, nodded to the new bidder. Money, so rare in this community, now had one hell of a rate of exchange compared to barter. Was £20,000 all a lifetime of happiness was really worth?

She turned to find the bidder, a tense-looking Caucasian male, fifties, about 180 pounds, balding, a frizz of white hair on his head and chin, a knotted brow, wearing a raincoat that looked like it would have been fashionable in the 1960s. He was nodding urgently, as if his nod could change worlds, as if it had to.

'A favour from the Trickster,' she said, sure she could get that too. The audience made noises that said this was serious business. Haversham nodded to her.

'Fifty thou,' called the man.

Haversham nodded to him instead. She looked back to Ross. She looked to Costain, but he had nothing to suggest. They had played all their cards. Ross felt the crushing despair once again descend on her. Did she now have to face up to a lifetime of this emptiness? No, she threw the despair out of her mind and took anger instead. She would not cry. She would do something about this. For now she shook her head.

She had to listen as the angry-looking man bettered several increasingly desperate offers from other bidders and ended up purchasing Ross's happiness for £200,000. 'Cheap at the price,' said Haversham, pointedly. The man was invited to join Bernie beside the crate, and in a moment vanished and then appeared again, head down, immediately walking away, through a crowd that muttered at him angrily as he shouldered his way through it. Ross didn't get to see in what sort of vessel her happiness was now contained. Costain made to follow, and Ross was close behind, but Haversham called at them from the stage. 'The truce is in place. Nobody can find anyone leaving who don't want to be found, dears. Better luck next time.'

'Fuck better luck,' said Ross as she watched the angry man literally disappear as he reached the edge of the crowd. 'Let's work this.'

She found some faces in the crowd that she vaguely recognized from the Goat and Compasses. A couple of them turned away, not wanting to speak to them or busy with items they were interested in, but one old lady in the remains of a pinstriped suit and bowler was willing to tell them who the purchaser was. She said she'd liked how Costain had stood up to the Keel brothers. 'That's Nathaniel Tock. Heart and soul of this community, some say. Used to be dead against money coming in and changing things, but it looks like he's changed his tune. Maybe it's 'cos now people have started to deal in it, he has so much of it. He's got serious connections, they say. The big lads. He sells artefacts and land of special value to us, and runs regular gatherings of our lot. I don't know if you'd enjoy 'em, being newcomers and all. They're a bit stuffy if you ask me.'

Ross asked where and when, and was told they were held in

a hotel near Heathrow. There was always one the first weekend after an auction. So this Saturday, then.

'I used to quite like him,' said the old lady, recovering from a cough that sounded worryingly serious. 'You know, he's a rough diamond. Gives cheek to everyone. But these days, oh, he's pissed so many people off, got into some serious fights. He's started to call himself the King of London, people say, and that used to be a real title, but nobody's had it rightly and undisputed for over a century now. Look at him tonight, though, face against the wind as always. He don't care. Admirable, in a way.'

Ross asked if they could just show up at these events of his. The woman stifled a laugh.

'No, dear, he's very serious about that. You don't get in without a ticket, and he tries to control who gets them. A friend of mine is here tonight, though; we were going to go for a pint of porter after. He's got tickets to all things.'

She led them through the crowd to her friend, who was in what Ross took a moment to identify as a polished wooden wheelchair, a sort of combination of kitchen chair, church pew and wagon. It sang of the Sight, an impression of calm decency, of trustworthiness. That, Ross thought, must be entirely deliberate. The old lady's friend was sheltering under a tattered golfing umbrella inserted into a hole in the back of the chair, and had on top of the rug on his lap a series of envelopes. He wore a fisherman's cap, and his neat white beard and ancient eyes confirmed the impression that here was a son of the sea. Again, though, what could be more likely to gain one's trust in this location? He listened to the woman's introduction, couched in formal language that Ross tried to remember for noting down later, and asked what they wanted a ticket for. The price to attend one of Tock's conferences was a hundred pounds or some small sacrifice.

'I keep those reasonable, like,' said the man in the chair. 'Some of us don't think it's fair, this devaluing lark.'

Costain put a hand in his pocket, then stopped, considering the man for a moment. Suddenly, Costain put a hand in his own mouth, made a sound that was halfway between a roar and a cry of pain, and held up, still bloody, one of his own teeth. 'Been wobbly for a while,' he said.

Ross watched incredulously as the man took the tooth in a gloved hand and slipped it into a paper bag. He handed Costain, who was wiping his mouth on his handkerchief, two of the tickets, and Costain immediately passed one on to her. They were ornate jobs, fine paper covered in watermarks, the words describing the location barely visible among all the security measures concerning forgery. She looked back to Costain, who was wincing, laughing at what he'd just done. They gave their thanks and headed down the hill.

'You didn't have to do it,' she said. 'I could have found that sort of money.'

'I thought that'd impress him a bit more.' And her as well? He hadn't said a word about Flamstead tonight. 'I thought about getting three, because there might be tons of new info for him to work with, but I had to weigh up between us needing him to know about that and . . .' He was struggling with everything about this.

'And the possibility we might have to do something dodgy.'

'Yeah. I *want* to get your happiness back . . . ethically. *Legally*, even. But if we end up going the other way, I don't want him implicated. We can record what we find, let him know afterwards . . .'

'And hope he'll forgive us?'

'Is that OK?'

Ross continued to look at Costain as they headed back towards the lights of Greenwich, the sky overhead still proudly standing for something a little hollow. 'Actually,' she said, 'I was going to ask for that.'

NINETEEN

On Thursday morning, Sefton stood where Lombard Street became Fenchurch Street. If the Sight made him aware of police officers, he thought, he would be watching a sea of blue dots, with out-of-uniform members of DI Clarke's team walking up and down this and every side street and on guard in every office where there was a safe, and with uniformed and Armed Response back-ups in vans at convenient intervals. Costain had played a blinder over the last couple of days, staying on top of his new leadership role, keeping in touch with the search for Quill, and thus allowing Sefton and Ross to focus on the work.

There had been some discussion as to whether their own team should be here, but Costain had decided that of course they should be. The killers knew they were on to them, knew they were aware that this must be their next target. It was only natural they'd be up and down it. What they didn't want to reveal was how much support they'd brought along, or their connection to Johnny Horner.

The security guard had taken perfectly normal leave, and so it was perfectly plausible that here was a person who'd played Holmes who the police had missed. Besides, the killers *had* to have a go, and Horner was now their only target. All Costain's team had to do was be ready every moment Horner was near this street. The only problem was, how long could Clarke justify keeping this massive back-up operation in place?

Even a small team, though, would have a chance now, given how they'd secretly narrowed the odds in their favour. This was the sort of trap, thought Sefton, that Holmes himself might have set.

He wandered over to Clement's Lane, where the corporate finance company Travail Ltd had their headquarters. Horner was inside, currently enjoying the company of three officers in security guard uniforms. That big safe, like the one in the story, was a floor above. It was eleven twenty-five now, some office workers starting to go for early lunches, a few smokers gathered outside their places of work. Horner would knock off and go home at six. Surely soon, maybe even today, their opponents, with their incredible means of entry and getaway, were bound to have a go? All they had to do, they'd be thinking, was whack Horner round the head with a poker, just like in the story.

Sefton walked on past; he had to stay away from that building, show no particular interest in it, look as if he thought it was one of the banks that was the target instead. Costain was in the RBS building, further up the street, making a big scene of checking the walls for chalk, as if they feared one of the gang had got inside already. Ross was in the command van with DI Clarke, ready to send forces rushing in to grab the assailants. A bucket of water and a window cleaner's shammy were ready under Horner's desk, the officers there bemused to be under orders to use it on any chalk marks. The gang could get in, but would then find their expected retreat cut off.

Sefton heard the sound of a distant alarm down the street. The passers-by paid no notice, of course. Was there a Holmes actor they'd missed? It seemed possible, but unlikely. Besides, today, every security guard, no matter what their thespian inclinations, was on alert. He heard another alarm, and another, and another, all from nearby streets, and from this one. The pedestrians were noticing now, laughing and saying things to each other about an earth tremor setting them off. Not likely, but given how nervy Londoners were these days, who'd bet against the foundations of their world starting to shake? Sefton called Ross.

'Whole bunch of alarms going off. Team here thinks it's some sort of computer worm,' she said. 'Costain's called in. He's going to run between several of them, see if any of them represents a real situation, because the one at RBS doesn't. Main team' – that was the one with Horner: they didn't want to say anything over the phone that'd indicate they knew his name or building – 'have nothing to report. You're to check on the following . . .' She gave him three potential targets. If this was a feint, it would be good to indicate they were falling for it. Sefton jogged between two banks and a bonds-trading firm, and found, having gone inside and right to the door of the safe in each question, no sign of a chalk door, nothing unusual.

He was running back towards the Fenchurch Street end of Lombard Street when he became aware that all around him, others were reacting and starting to move in the same direction. The plain-clothes guys, it must be. He felt a buzz from his phone and found a single-word text from Ross: Home. That meant converge on Travail Ltd. By the time he got to Clement's Lane, he was part of a rush of uniformed and non-uniformed coppers.

He burst through the doors and was surprised to see Horner standing, his hands raised, puzzled by the attention. 'Nothing going on down here,' he said.

Ross and Clarke entered together, Costain just behind them. 'But something is upstairs,' said Clarke, looking at her phone. She led Costain's team up to the first floor. There, in the large Victorian room, stood the enormous door of the safe, magnificently decorated with brands and commendations. Beside it stood two of the plain-clothes officers who'd been stationed downstairs and a handful of scared bank workers. The door of the safe was slightly open. 'I . . . heard something from inside,' one of the bank workers was saying. 'So I opened it and . . .'

Sefton went to the safe and opened the door further with the toe of his boot. Inside, not even filling the space, lay the body of a large man, his face turned away. On his head was a deerstalker. On the back wall of the safe was drawn a window-sized chalk square. Costain stepped forwards, having donned evidence gloves, and gingerly removed the deerstalker. The back of the man's head had been smashed in, leaving a mess of hair, bone, blood and grey matter. The movement made the body fall to one side, and in that moment, they all saw who the victim was: Mark Ballard.

Sefton had to turn away to restrain himself from kicking at a door that would have definitely injured his foot.

Dr Piara Singh Deb, forensic pathologist at St Pancras Mortuary, was not willing to be taken for a fool, and so he had promised himself that he would never again deal with DI Quill's team. This evening, he had been startled, therefore, to find that his boss had done some sort of deal with Detective Superintendent Lofthouse. Every case of theirs was to be brought here until further notice.

Dr Deb had considered making himself unavailable as a protest, but his boss had taken him aside and said that these were good people, who seemed to be under a lot of stress, and who seemed to have a high regard for Dr Deb's skills. Dr Deb had remembered how they'd seemed last time. That couldn't have been acting. They too must have been fooled, at that point, by the, it must be said, incredibly similar corpse that had been provided in place of their friend and leader, James Quill. Surely they too must have been kept in the dark about whatever deep undercover operation had led Quill to pretend to be dead.

That thought had made him feel rather better about having not been trusted with such secrecy, and so he had scrubbed up and gone down to the labs, and had proceeded to examine this latest corpse. Now, he faced only three of Quill's team, Quill himself apparently being on leave. He saw what his boss had meant. The intelligence analyst, so stricken with grief last time, now had something cold about her, and there was palpable tension between her and the detective sergeant, who was leading the team.

'Victim,' he said, 'was struck on the back of the head several times by a metal implement, smooth and with a sharp point. You can see here how this depression in the brain is created by the point having slipped into the wound. The force used in the attack was considerable, but not wild. There are no wounds anywhere else on the body. This was a deliberate, precise assault. Cause of death was sudden-impact trauma. He'd have been unconscious after the first or second blow, but his position doesn't seem to have shifted, so he wasn't in a position to fall. I'd say he must have been tied up, but if he was, there's no sign of rope marks. Also, there's something unusual about the musculature. It was stiff long before rigor mortis should have set in, because time of death, from the blood clotting, is only ten minutes or so before the body was found.' He kept one eye on their reactions, hoping one day to spot something that gave him some clue as to why this team in particular brought him such extraordinary cases. He wanted to ask them what they knew, because it was obvious what he was saying made sense to them, had been expected even, in the way one expects the sky to fall. They had no obligation to answer any such question, unless he had a professional need for the answer. 'You can still see that rigor on the face: the muscles are tight, as are the leg and arm muscles. I think it's possible he may have been suffering severe cramp immediately before the attack. No trace of anything unusual in the blood, so that isn't a result of that tribal poison you mentioned in the notes.'

'Any indications as to nature of assailant?' asked the analyst.

'Strong, muscles like a sportsman, with a good aim. Taller than the victim, if that muscle locking indicates the victim as somehow standing up.'

'Could he have been held by the others?'

'It's possible, but it strikes me that to hold someone so still that their muscles protest in this manner would take . . . well, too many people for one person to get such clear access, or, if there were that few, they'd have to be incredibly strong.'

Once Deb had completed his report, the sergeant thanked him and he watched them go. Perhaps, he decided, he was glad to have in his life the highly unusual cases this team brought him, even if they themselves made him want to take them home and feed them.

Ross had a full-on headache. She found herself looking at an ops board that now took up three A3 sheets of paper and covered the corkboard under it. Sidebars had stretched onto the walls, fixed there with Blu-tack. She could imagine this case reaching a point where it covered the interior of the Portakabin like wallpaper, with no two data points seeming to relate to each other. She was literally living inside chaos.

'Ballard,' she said, going over once again what she'd added to the explosion of fact, 'used a fake ID to sign on as a security guard with a company who weren't used on any of the premises.'

'The mere fact he was genuinely a security guard seems to have been enough for the ritual element of this,' said Sefton. 'He didn't have to work there. This is so much about rules and specifics, it's like someone's determinedly ignoring the emotional side of the power of London and is getting OCD about the details.'

'He did that within hours of getting his freedom,' said Costain, 'like he was planning something new even while he was in custody. Him suddenly deciding to look into being a security guard is a hell of a coincidence otherwise.'

'It's a hell of a coincidence that it was what suited our opponents,' said Ross. 'So I don't think it is a coincidence. But I have no conclusions to draw beyond that. The back of the safe, after a very thick wall and several security devices, all of which were knocked out by the same untraceable worm that set off those burglar alarms, leads to a storeroom of the money-transfer company next door. What CCTV there was went down at the same time, but a chalk doorway of the same size was found there, and some blood splashes. It's being forensicated now, but I'm betting we'll find that's the murder room. So Ballard and assailants walked in there, either through the front door or using walkthrough, the chalk from which was then rubbed away. On this occasion they had time to do that. Perhaps Ballard did think he was being consulted about a robbery, came along to help out. Having dumped the body, they must have walked out of the safe using walkthrough, then out of the front of that building next door. Again, CCTV was down.'

'The muscle-locking business is interesting,' said Sefton. 'I reckon some sort of artefact was used on Ballard, maybe one of his own, to hold him in place, maybe force him to act out being Holmes. Ballard followed the news like anyone else, and knew of our interest in the Holmes murders, so he wouldn't have done that willingly.' He let out a long breath. 'Shit, he would have reacted as soon as he saw the deerstalker.'

'Upon which there is no trace of anything but Ballard,' sighed Ross.

Rebecca Lofthouse hated that she was going to be out of touch with both Costain's team and with the continuing efforts to find James. Her own task this weekend, however, was, in the end, more important.

She'd confided about her 'affair' to Sally Rutherford specifically because she was the organizer of a conference in Coventry this weekend. That had seemed at the time Lofthouse had decided on it to be an opportunity to dig deeper into the mysteries of her own past, but now the date had come around, it was actually a chance to go even further. She'd called Sally from a payphone and told her a ton of romantic nonsense about the man who was going to take her away from her cruel husband. They were going off to Paris together, when Lofthouse was meant to be in Coventry. If anyone asked, would she mind . . .? Sally agreed, with only slight and required protest, to be her accomplice. The powers of the entity that was possessing her husband, Lofthouse reasoned, only extended as far as London's boroughs, and certainly not to Coventry.

Having set up her cover, when she was supposed to be heading for the train, she actually went to a supplier of caving equipment and put the manager of the shop through a swift interrogation. Working from a position of complete ignorance, because she hadn't been able to research this beforehand, she quickly discovered exactly what she would need. She left with a rucksack full of equipment and a how-to book. She'd had to dress this morning to suit a meeting, so she bought a change of clothes as well, aware all the time of how weighed down she was going to be.

Finally, as the first late-afternoon gloom set in, she headed for Tower Hill. At the end of a street that was rather wonderfully called Petty Wales, along from the Tower of London ticket office, she found the little brown turret of a building. Stern lettering round it declared, 'London Hydraulic Power Company, Tower Subway, Constructed AD 1868'.

There were a great many tourists wandering past, many of them stopping at the ice-cream van that, even this late in the season, stood nearby. The power company in question had bought the tunnel under the Thames when Tower Bridge had opened just downstream, making this subway unprofitable. The company had closed the system in 1977 and had itself been put up for sale. Its right to dig up London streets made it attractive to Mercury Communications, a cable company. They'd become part of Cable & Wireless, then been bought out by NTL, then sold on to NPower. Lofthouse had arranged a visit to NPower's London offices on the pretext of addressing their security concerns in light of recent fuel-poverty demonstrations. Once inside, she'd gone to the toilet and passed on the way back a little office, the door of which was open. Inside it hung a particular bunch of keys. Those were now in her handbag.

She walked up to the little tower like she owned it, used the keys on the multiple locks and, once inside, locked the door behind her.

The circular stairway smelt of metropolitan engineering and damp. It was lit with tiny bulbs in cages. It led by way of a short flight of steps to a narrow tunnel, alongside which ran the rubbery bulk of enormous cables.

She walked quickly along, looking at the opposite wall for the access point she sought. She took out the piece of paper with the drawing on it that she'd found in the intangible flat. Her researches, conducted in snatched moments in libraries and never online, indicated that what she had in her hand might connect to the world . . . right here. She was looking at a door-sized metal plate in the floor, bolted down. She'd expected something fixed by ancient decay, but those bolts looked . . . greasy, with silver in the black, recently used.

Now she'd found it, she took the opportunity to change into boots, trousers and pullover, and pack up her work clothes. Then she took her tools from her bag and got to work on those bolts. She felt the key on her charm bracelet start to react. She was doing the right thing. Thank God. As she worked, she thought of how she'd got that damn key, of all the hurt and wonder it had brought into her life.

TWENTY

Five years ago

Rebecca Lofthouse had always been famously hard to wake up. Her husband said only duty could wake her, because when the phone rang in the middle of the night, only then would she be instantly aware and reaching for the notepad she kept on her bedside table. It was a blessing for a copper, she'd always thought, that facility to switch off.

So this morning, when she woke to the sound of the alarm at six, felt Peter stir beside her, reached under the pillow and found something there, it seemed entirely plausible to her that what she'd just laid her hand on had been placed there without her knowledge. She slid it out and looked at it.

It was a key, very small, with a hole in the fob. It was ancient, made of metal, smoothed by many hands over a long time, but its tiny teeth looked unaffected, viable. The overall impression was that it was something from archaeology that had been put to modern use. To sharpen those teeth like that, surely that was doing damage to a relic?

Handling it, she suddenly felt the most tremendous déjà vu, but as always that feeling faded with the application of reason. She knew she'd never seen this object before. She rolled over, the key balled in her fist, and embraced her husband. 'What's this?'

He made a questioning noise, and when made to wake up and focus on the key, he looked puzzled. He'd never seen it before, he said. With a slight sinking of her heart, she believed him. He wasn't one for romantic surprises.

That morning, as she dressed for work, she kept going back to the key, picking it up, looking at it, rolling it between her hands. It felt somehow . . . urgent. There was, of course, the matter of how it had got under her pillow. Could she be sure it hadn't been there when she'd gone to sleep? No. Was it something a cleaner had done, some sort of charm, a wish for good luck? Nice thought, bit creepy. A conversation with her cleaner yielded only puzzled denials.

She put the key in her bedside drawer, but every time she went to bed, every time she woke up, and sometimes in the night when she'd been dreaming about something tense and violent and woke up sweating, she could sort of . . . feel it there. So she moved it to the study, but still she could feel it. It was like it was demanding something of her. Some days she felt that she should remember what this object signified, why it seemed so important to her. The feeling it gave her made her go to her doctor, nervous about the onset of some degenerative brain condition, but that had been a red herring, thank God.

So, one day, she did what she did with everything that made her feel vulnerable: she brought it closer to her. She opened her old charm bracelet and slipped the wire through the hole on the key, and damn well wore what worried her. 'From now on, Sonny Jim,' she said to it, 'I've got you where I can see you.'

It turned out to be a good idea. Every now and then, when she was dealing with a case where a decision had to be made, she would suddenly feel the weight of her bracelet and note that the key was swinging in one direction or the other. She always found that direction implied a particular choice.

For a long time, she fought off that conclusion about what was happening. It made her feel like a bloody 'psychic', like she was dowsing. In the end, however, after so many good calls, she couldn't deny the reality of it. She decided that *she'd* made the key into what it was, that it was just a focus for her concentration. After all, it didn't have an 'opinion' on every case, just a peculiar, seemingly random selection of them.

In the next year or so, the main focus of Lofthouse's role as a detective superintendent started to be the pursuit of that most obvious and miraculously non-jailable of gang leaders, Rob Toshack. One morning, she sat down with a blank piece of paper and started to plan an operation to finally have him: multiple undercovers, 'strangers' from up north; a very long game. She'd need a solid London detective inspector to lead it, either Jason Forrest out of Belgravia, who she knew . . . God, no, just the thought made her feel ill, for some reason. Why was she suddenly reacting like that? There was nothing wrong with Jason. She realized she could feel the key swinging at her wrist, but that emotional reaction that had come with the movement, that was new. OK, then, what about someone she didn't know, James Quill, who'd been recommended to her? What if she asked him?

Her heart leaped with something fierce that felt like love.

She grabbed the bracelet from her wrist and threw it onto the desk.

She stared at it in shock for a moment, then put it back on, ashamed of herself. She was blushing, and furious at the same time. She had no feelings for this complete stranger other than a distant admiration. This feeling from the key had gone far beyond a hunch. This was like a bunch of cheerleaders had rushed into her brain screaming support.

All right, she was going to test this. She'd been aware for a long time, had kept in her back pocket, that there was an intelligence analyst building a reputation up north who had a personal connection to the Toshack family. Damaged goods, undoubtedly. Maybe even a mole for Toshack, because he had to be doing something incredible to keep avoiding jail. Should Lofthouse include this person who'd named herself 'Lisa Ross' in her as-yet-unnamed operation? She put the question concretely to herself.

Yes, came the answer from the charm bracelet, in the form of a definite movement and a little frisson of pleasure, like the memory of a good day out with the children. She found herself feeling tense at what she was about to do, but she did it anyway. No, she thought to herself, I can't possibly do that. I *won't* use Ross or Quill—

She burst into tears. The sheer despair that that decision had caused to explode inside her. She stumbled to the wall and leaned against it, sobbing helplessly.

Could it be this obvious? Why were the key's reactions to this particular decision so much more intense?

OK, OK, so she was going to include Ross and Quill in the team . . .

Endorphins flooded her body. She fell back into her seat. Such immediate bliss, such release from pain.

She grabbed her handkerchief and angrily wiped her face. She ripped the bracelet from her wrist, put it down on her desk and actually spoke out loud to the key. 'You bastard,' she said. 'I know now, don't I?'

She wasn't going mad. This was real. This thing *wanted* her to choose Lisa Ross, *wanted* her to choose Quill. Somehow.

So when she'd gone to meet Ross, she'd gone with the same expectation she'd had when she met James Quill, that perhaps this person would know something about the key. She'd played with it in front of Quill, as she asked if he felt he was drawn to this job. But he'd just been enthusiastic to get Toshack, in an everyday way. She'd worried about the key making her behave ridiculously in his company, but it turned out as long as she was on the right track, as long as she *behaved*, it left her alone. At least its conclusions about what was best for the operation seemed to match her own.

When she finally met Ross, Lofthouse found her much stranger than Quill. She looked like she'd seen some shit, with her nose askew and one eye a different colour to the other. Lofthouse asked her if there was anything she felt she couldn't tell her. Ross denied there was, but Lofthouse never quite lost the suspicion that she was lying, that here was someone who might have seen some things as strange as her key.

Initially, she left the selection of the two undercovers to Quill, but, at the key's prompting, again intervened about his choices.

When Toshack died in custody, Lofthouse waited until she was sure she couldn't be overheard, then threw the charm bracelet against the wall. 'What are you working towards?' she demanded. 'Are you some sort of . . . curse on me? I will drop you in the sea! I will be free of you, because what use are you?'

She put a hand to her head, convinced she was going mad, but once again she forced herself to deny that possibility.

'In the next few days,' she said, 'I'm going to come up with a new operation, and this time I want you to bloody sing along at the top of your voice, or you'll be taking a swim in the English Channel.'

Lofthouse woke the next morning with a genius idea fully formed in her brain. 'This is genius,' she said to herself in the bathroom mirror while brushing her hair. 'This is absolutely brilliant.' It took until she was brushing her teeth for her to realize the truth. She stopped, and stared at herself in the mirror, foaming at the mouth. 'It's not *my* idea,' she said, looking to the bracelet on her wrist and the key on it. 'I asked for your help and you've come up with something and you've planted it in my head like it's my own idea. And it's *bollocks*.'

She tried to decide against it, and in consequence spent the morning wracked with such depression and fear that she couldn't leave her office, until at last she told the key she'd go along with it, and once more experienced immediate relief.

She stood nervously as the second undercover entered the hotel room where she'd gathered Ross, Quill and the first undercover, Costain. Kevin Sefton was his name, and he reacted exactly as Costain had. He was terrified at his real identity being suddenly revealed to a whole team of people, certain she was mad. Now, however, Lofthouse felt she'd made her choice.

What followed was like a nightmare unfolding itself into the waking world. Quill and his team uncovered a serial killer who became known to the media as 'the Witch of West Ham'. Like Toshack, Mora Losley seemed capable of impossible escapes. When Losley suddenly appeared somewhere that didn't fit with where Quill's team had just encountered her, Lofthouse forced herself to face the possibility that if Losley really *was* a witch, then perhaps Lofthouse really did have a key that wanted input in the planning of operations. That a key was interested in catching a witch indicated a whole unseen world of possibilities.

Whether or not that meant Quill and his team had any knowledge or experience of the impossible stuff, or whether the key had just put together some ordinary coppers to bring down Mora Losley was a question Lofthouse asked herself every day. She kept failing to find a safe moment to ask them questions that would make her sound insane. The key, annoyingly, seemed satisfied with how things stood.

Then, weeks after the end of the Losley case, Lofthouse heard that Quill and his team were exploring an empty area of Docklands. The key screamed at her to go and see.

Something that looked like her husband walked onto the

screen of her computer. He started to tell her she was indeed connected to impossible events, and that the one thing she must above all never do was to try to remember.

TWENTY-ONE

Quill couldn't quite remember how he came to be watching the sun set with his back against the door of an access stairwell, on the roof of a tower block, somewhere in Docklands. This was a bit like being drunk. Everything in his head was in a different place. His memory was here somewhere. He couldn't find it. Just . . . *being* felt like hard work, all the time. It tensed his muscles; it made his heart race; it made him breathe too fast. He shook his head, kept shaking it, until the clarity was gone. He was angry, almost all the time. He was sitting here, panting, and he didn't know why.

He could just about see what had been following him. He *could* see him. He stood over there; yes, that wasn't a shadow now; that was a figure standing outside the shadow of that air vent. He was watching Quill. The silhouette had a top hat on, and a long coat. He had his hands together in front of him. All cleverness was in that figure. He was whole and satisfied and comfortable. He had arranged everything so Quill was not.

He had to stop Laura from moving to London. That was why he'd come up here. How that fitted together . . . he didn't know, but he might remember. There was a long list of connections that made that plan work, somewhere.

He slid up the door, until he was upright, leaning on it, then let his weight tip him forwards, until he was standing. He was in a warm coat. He didn't know where he'd got it. It smelt terrible. How he smelt now was not important.

He pointed at the figure. 'Hoi! You! Moriarty! I got your number, sunshine!'

No response from the silhouette. Quill took a step towards it. It didn't move. He was getting angry again, too angry to speak.

He ran at it.

It was gone. Had he gone straight through it?

He was at the edge.

He scrambled to a halt. He was teetering. There was London below, Hell below, all the old buildings growing among the new, over the new. He watched the tiny people below, the damned, between the toes of his boots. They wouldn't see him up here. He could piss on them. He could join them.

No, fuck Sarah. Fuck Jessica. What help had they been to—?

He was crying again. The tears got in the way of him seeing where he was. He lurched. He couldn't find anything to grab.

Oh, he could feel that sod behind him now. So he'd re-appeared? That was the plan, was it? He spun suddenly, trying to take him by surprise. He landed on the gravel of the rooftop, and for a moment wondered if he'd landed on the concrete below. No, there was that familiar air vent again.

There was the figure again. Moriarty. Quill smiled, pleased at how in control he was now. Oh yes.

Ross attached a new victim thread from Ballard to their enormous horizontal range of suspects. It was dark outside now. 'Clearly,' she said, 'our attempts to set a trap for the suspects have now also been used by said suspects to further their aims.'

'Fucking *clearly*,' said Sefton.

'Hey,' said Costain.

'Sorry.'

Ross felt it like they were all feeling it. Everything they did seemed to be part of the plans of their enemies. It made them feel small, and compromised. As if their actions were now actually making things worse. Nothing helped. She was fucking a god and *that* was not helping. Quill was gone; Lofthouse was completely absent. Their backs were against the wall and soon now the Met mainstream would start asking questions about their startling lack of success. Clarke would take some of the heat, but she wasn't a charity that helped weird units with questionable budget allocations.

Sefton walked in a small circle, then deliberately began again. 'We're not being bugged,' he said. 'I'd swear to it. Last time I set up defences around here, I thought about that.'

'The next Holmes stories,' said Ross, 'are "The *Gloria Scott*", outside London, "The Musgrave Ritual", which has a murder, but is also outside London, "The Reigate Squire", outside London, and "The Crooked Man", same again. So the next point where we'll have a chance to intercept is "The Resident Patient".'

'What happens in that one?' asked Sefton.

'A mock trial and hanging,' said Costain. 'The target will ideally be a private doctor who once played Holmes, or who now could be *forced* to play him. It'll be somewhere near a medical practice in Brook Street in Mayfair. The main inquiry are all over this and are already staking out the options.'

'How many stories are left?' said Sefton.

'Thirty-six, and two novels, and that's assuming they're sticking to the Conan Doyle, 'cos there are lots of other authors who then wrote Holmes stories,' said Costain.

'There's a major point in Holmes's life coming up soon,' said Ross. 'We're getting close to him going over the Reichenbach Falls, seemingly to his death.'

'Tough for him to do,' said Costain, 'considering he's already dead.' He looked down at a message on his phone. 'The warrant to search Ballard's premises has come through. So that's our last thing before the weekend.' Ross thought for a moment she saw a flash of guilt on his face. This weekend, they were going to leave Sefton behind, at this lowest point of their investigation, and pursue her own selfish ends. The look was gone again a moment later. Costain was too good an undercover to show his true feelings like that.

She turned back to the ops board. If only she could say the same.

Ballard had said he had many homes, but the one Costain had the warrant for was the one he'd claimed as his main address, an apartment in the Heron building at Moorgate. Looking up at the black-and-white, chilly facade, which was like a pile of metal packing crates, shining industrially against the night sky, Sefton was once more reminded of how being a copper was to continually be a beggar at the feast, an unwelcome visitor to places in which one could never hope to live.

They entered the building, found they were facing, weirdly, an enormous fish tank and took quite a while to find someone they could talk to about their warrant.

The apartment took up a whole floor of the building, the twenty-eighth. The elevator opened onto a lobby area, and the key cards they'd been given operated both the lift itself and the door on the other side of the elegantly designed space. It already looked like the home of a collector, with what looked like some sort of fossil shell perched in front of an enormous picture window, and paintings, all of London subjects, on the walls even here. The weight the Sight gave to what lay beyond was the total of what Sefton had felt on approaching the building. He'd felt it above him as they'd entered the tower, and all the way up in the lift. 'He's got some shit in here,' he said.

They donned evidence gloves and opened the inner door. Inside, it was immediately obvious that the place had been searched. Drawers were open; a desk had been taken apart. There was no wreckage. The door of the wall safe, unhidden, obvious, was still closed. In the movies, such searches were often meant to have happened at speed, and for some reason those searching usually seemed to have just broken things for the hell of it. This one looked to have been thorough and to have time taken over it. There must have been some sort of ticking clock, though, or why leave evidence that it had been done at all? Unless the searchers were so confident in their power they just didn't care. Sefton quickly went to one of the inner doors and listened. Was anyone still in here?

Costain came over, listened himself for only a moment, then opened it. It took just a few moments for them to be certain they were still alone. 'Any sign of walkthrough?' he asked. He went to the walls and started to look for signs of a chalk door, then stopped himself. 'Of course not – we're on the twenty-eighth floor.'

'Don't beat yourself up about it,' said Ross. 'Sooner or later we're going to encounter a suspect who can fly. But, couple of steps less amazing, if they can walk through walls, maybe they can also hack a key-card system.'

'It's weird,' said Sefton, 'that Ballard didn't have better defences.'

'When I was with his lot,' said Costain, 'he was always saying about how few people knew about this shit, how he was just about the only big boss left. Though he may have been deluded about that. Besides, we only learned where this was when he had to give an address on arrest. He never told us lot about it.'

They started to examine what had been searched. 'There must still be significant stuff here, or what are we feeling with the Sight?' said Sefton.

'So maybe the searchers weren't Sighted?' said Ross.

'Good assumption, but noted as one.' Costain knocked her familiar caveat about assumptions back at her.

Sefton closed his eyes and let his sense of balance lead him across the floor to where he felt the Sight was indicating the greatest power was, through into the bedroom. There was something under the bed. Feeling a bit vulnerable once again, Sefton looked under the bed and saw, as well as a collection of what looked like bondage gear . . .

He could feel the presence of something beneath the polished wooden floor. He swept away the cuffs and straps, and found, with his Sighted fingers, an indentation, a panel. It didn't give at his touch, of course.

With the help of the others, he moved the bed aside. Sefton felt out the dimensions of the anomaly. It felt like it was hiding rather fearfully, like it was thin. He'd never before found himself ascribing emotions to planks of wood. This was how the Sight was changing him. In their business, you couldn't even rely on what was under your feet not to have an opinion. 'Fuck it,' he said. He stood up, raised his boot and brought it down in the middle of the spot. The floor broke. They were rather more careful in excavating the pieces, making a pile of them, still with their evidence gloves on. In the shallow compartment beneath was a single piece of paper. Ross picked it out and read.

It was a list of artefacts, with locations given beside them, including the 'draft for healing once' with the location given, Ross confirmed, being the lock-up where she and Costain had found it.

'Jackpot,' said Sefton. 'One item on this list was kept in this apartment. I wonder if they found it.'

The item was a 'bastard scourge'. It was meant to be in a hidden compartment in the desk. They found the compartment, but it was empty. 'This list is a major step forward, anyway,' said Ross. 'There's no reason to think our opponents know about these. Does anything on here sound like it could help with the current operation, or in finding Jimmy?'

They studied the list at length. Most of the names of the objects were pretty straightforward descriptions of their function. None of them sounded like an item for finding anyone, which meant that Ballard had either been lying about his capacity to do that or had still more caches elsewhere.

Ross finally sighed. 'I don't think anything here is of immediate help.'

'In that case,' said Costain, 'rather than rushing about now,

I'll spend Monday and Tuesday visiting these locations and bringing the haul back to the Hill.'

'We can help with that,' said Sefton.

Costain shook his head. 'I'm keeping the grunt work off you two. I think that's what Jimmy would do. I hope it is, anyway. I hope at some point we find a whole bunch of stuff to crack whatever this gang of murderers shit is, and something to get Quill back and make him better, and then . . .' He finally gave way to a grin. 'Then I can stop bloody trying to lead.'

Sefton put a hand on his shoulder and smiled back. 'We're all,' he said, 'looking forward to that.'

Lofthouse was glad of her torch. She was picking her way down through absolute darkness, in what she was sure now were natural caverns, carved by water. The path she followed, however, had been made by the erosion of feet. What could it have been like for the first person to do this? When would that have been? Would they have been from some tribe, seeking to go into the earth for their religion? Was that religion anything to do with what Jimmy's team encountered these days?

Her mind was going to wander, she realized, and she better let it, because otherwise she would only fret on the multiple risks she was taking. If she was lost down here, nobody would ever find her, and that bastard inside Peter might hurt him out of spite. Beside the path, at intervals, had been left offerings, long-crumbled sprigs of plants, rings and coins all snapped in two. There were things written on the walls too, like tourist graffiti, but of a very specialist sort, some in English, but also in German, Spanish and in Japanese characters. Some of the writings replied to each other, like a conversation carried on over decades. 'Not long now until the drop.' 'Don't hack your karma like that.' 'Fuck the Rat Queen.' 'Is that an order?' Most of what they referred to was gibberish to her, but Kev Sefton would love this stuff. Her map had turned out to be only a very rough description of the terrain. Of much more help were the path itself and the urging of the key on her bracelet, which she could feel straining on her wrist like a terrier heading for the park.

She nearly slipped, despite the spikes on her boots, at a sharp curve of the path. The air was getting very cold, and damp. You could tell you were in a cave. The path opened out, after a little while, into a wider gallery, and the path now had an edge to it, a slope of scree, which led down into a plunge the depths of which her torch couldn't penetrate. On the wall now were desperate warnings, big letters: watch your step.

There were also stalactites and stalagmites, but the colours, she saw as she washed the torch beam over them, weren't the pale hues she associated with caving. Here were rust reds and bright yellows, and sick-looking greens. These, she realized, were stalactites of industry, chemicals from human work that had managed to seep deep underground. She wondered how long that process had taken. Lost in thought, it took her a moment to recognize what the latest shape her torch had caught actually was.

A face! She stepped back for a moment, hearing the echo of her gasp, and then she realized what she was seeing, the torch beam having held firm: a skull, atop a skeleton that had been propped up against a wall and had now been moulded into it, its bones covered by the process that had formed the stalactites. The chest of the skeleton had been caved in, as if from some sort of impact. It looked like something an animal might do. Or had people fought on their way down? Just beyond the skeleton was a plummet into nothingness, as if the slope had eroded under him. A sign on the wall beside her had a big red arrow pointing to him. According to it, his name was Boney.

She had, of course, no idea what she'd come down here to find. All she knew was that for her to follow the map was what the key wanted above all. She had gambled everything she loved on something impossible.

Quill had walked a long way in the dark, pleased at how the act of walking allowed him to bring his theories back to mind again, to make sure every detail was correct, this tremendous bedrock he could rely on. He'd memorized them, like songs, rhythms to walk to. Some of those songs would just wander into his head and he'd be their instrument for a while, and that was, well, he didn't know if that was great or distressing. He was quite glad nobody was asking him how he felt.

He'd come to what seemed to be an empty suburb, a modern group of houses, nestling in the Victorian wonderland that had grown up all around. This was a new development in Hell, avenues and closes with pristine two-bedroomed semis, new builds, with tended lawns, but no cars outside, nobody living there.

He walked past a security office with a light on, and a sign that had said something about the houses being on sale, but the sign looked like it had been there a long time. He walked into the middle of an island of grass in the midst of a circle of houses, a sapling at its centre, and turned, seeking even one light in all these would-be homes.

This place was blank to the Sight too, a nowhere where nothing was remembered. Why was nobody living here? He realized that he'd heard about this place, or somewhere else like it. The developers thought it better to keep the houses empty than to drop their prices. A bunch of squatters had been removed from somewhere like this. So could he live here, then, while he pursued his enquiries, or while they pursued him? Why not, old son? He had enough stuff in his bag now to begin a proper diagram of his operational theories. He tried a couple of back doors. He found one open.

He walked carefully into the house, then forgot the idea of walking carefully and marched into the kitchen, shouting that he was moving carefully, that he was an armed police officer. He laughed that he wasn't. He could hear the sound, he realized, of a television.

He wondered if he'd returned home, if Sarah and Jessica were going to be in the lounge. There was the light of a telly under the door. He eased the door open, finding enormous pain inside him at the idea of the joy of seeing Jessica again, enormous difficulty at the idea of seeing Sarah, of what that would mean he had to face.

They weren't in here. There was an armchair and there was a television, tuned to static, and nothing else in the room. In the armchair sat the Smiling Man. He was beaming at the fuzz on the screen. He turned to look at Quill.

Quill wasn't afraid. Or he wasn't much more now than he was all the time these days. This was to be expected if he was in Hell. If there was going to be punishment, he wished they'd get on with it.

He had all sorts of questions he wanted to ask. He wanted to check his theories.

The Smiling Man held up a remote control, a signal not to talk, and pointed it at the screen. The image changed to a picture of Laura, in her pyjamas, entering what Quill recognized as Jessica's room. She was in London. She was about to sleep in London. To *live* in London, to stay several days, if that was what that meant, and it must be, mustn't it, or why was he being shown it? She was about to qualify for Hell. Jessica would be in bed with her mum: this is what they always did when they had visitors. This should have been OK, because they were all already in Hell, but it wasn't, it wasn't.

Quill realized this might be a lie. He had a way, though, to check if it was true. Fumbling, he got out his phone, switched it on and hit the app that showed the image on Jessica's baby monitor. It was the same as what was on the telly. He switched it off again. The Smiling Man kept looking at him, asking him a silent question. He was asking Quill to accept, to agree, to find peace.

Quill didn't know what his answer was. He left the question hanging, turned and walked away. He would need to come up with an answer. He walked out into the ghost estate of ghost houses and saw the dark figure standing there, in the shadow of the Victorian buildings of Hell that hung over them. It was almost a pleasure to see him. He wasn't the Smiling Man. He was Quill's Moriarty. Quill nodded to him.

After a moment of hesitation, the figure nodded back.

Saturday morning. Ross felt way awkward to be in the car with Costain, driving down to the maze of roads around Heathrow, her using the map on her phone to finally find a long, straight run of hotels. She'd checked in with how the main investigation was going and found they'd already done a house-to-house in Brook Street, compiled a list of medical practitioners and asked everyone to be on their guard. No former Sherlocks had been found, but with their quarry's seeming ability to now control someone's actions, that had ceased to be a factor.

There was nothing more she could do right now, but her duty, she knew, was still to the ops board, to the working over of data that might lead her to some new insight. Instead of which, she and Costain were going off piste again, perhaps about to risk everything for her selfish desire to be whole again. Even if they were successful, what would he want in return? Still, she supposed they might also find something that could be useful for the op, or to find Quill.

Costain was looking like he hadn't slept, but his driving, his calm control, gave no sign of that.

They walked into the rather eccentric lobby of the Radisson Edwardian Hotel together. The decor made it feel a bit like entering a jewel box. In front of them was an eccentric double staircase in what looked like marble. The Sight was saying things about ancient memories of fighting and fucking and drunken extremity and most of all deep, deep nostalgia, which made the shine of the stone and the tiles all the more baroque. There was also a smell in the air that Ross had never encountered before, a polish unique to this hotel. In the lobby were gathered people that suited these surroundings, in an odd sort of way, in that they had the right eccentricity, but were also a contrast, in that they wore the tatters and affected poverty of the London occult underworld. There were, however, occasional details with this lot, Ross noted, a nice belt buckle or a very new pair of bronze goggles, which bore witness to the money that had entered that community. There were now haves alongside the have-nots.

Ross and Costain had agreed to dress down for the occasion, but what they'd brought for that was still in their suitcases. They went to reception and checked in, and then went over to a table in the foyer with two ladies in medieval peasant gear behind it. Ross deflected their enquiry gestures with her blanket, and they took that, with a smile, to be a sign that here were two of their own. Costain just gave them his best poker face and didn't bother with the blanket, like he hadn't at the auction. They looked away, found something to do. This lot were still a little awkward around people of colour. Costain was the only such person in the room. Whatever they'd learned, they didn't see fit to comment.

Perhaps this changing culture was starting to accept the idea of police among them. Ross handed over their tickets. They got in exchange a stamp on the back of the left hand. The green ink mark was something like a postmark, a circle with some sort of unreadable lettering. The mark felt Sighted, a slight weight on her skin. 'I'll bet,' she said, as they headed for the elevators, 'this doesn't come off with soap.'

Costain was looking at a programme he'd picked up at the table. 'The theme of this year's event,' he said, 'is finding something to rely on.'

'Brilliant,' said Ross. 'Here's hoping.'

TWENTY-TWO

When he got back to Joe's place on Friday evening, Sefton, as he always did, checked in to see if anyone had sighted Quill. He was kind of surprised that nobody had. Jimmy must be actively hiding, or one of the services would have found him by now. He also couldn't be making use of medical facilities or hostel accommodation. Or . . . No, Sefton didn't want to consider that yet. He didn't like to think what losing Jimmy twice would do to Sarah. He resolved that this weekend he would do at least two things to possibly help both the investigation and the search for Quill.

Sefton had said to Costain that he'd leave searching the locations on Ballard's list to him, but what the hell, he could make a start. He spent Saturday morning checking out a few of the closer hidden locations. He was disappointed to find that none of the three he visited still held their treasure. Even if whoever had searched the apartment hadn't found that list, they must have had some other way to discover the dealer's stashes. He got back to Joe's to find him still in his bathrobe, listening to Danny Baker on the radio. 'Listen,' he said, 'do you want to try something with me?'

Joe raised an eyebrow. 'I thought you were knackered.'

'I mean . . . my sort of stuff. Something that might get the investigation moving again.'

'How can I help with that?'

'I have something in mind.' He got a big pile of purple art paper out of his holdall and started putting sheets of it down on the carpet to make a square. 'I've been reading up on this. A simple summoning.'

'Of what?'

'Of who.' Sefton took a stick of ordinary chalk – well, ordinary with a bit of London about it, coming from the South Downs – and, having found the relevant book he'd been studying and propped open the relevant page, started copying the symbol, much larger. 'An important witness who's gone astray: Dr Watson.'

'What are you drawing?'

'This is the symbol of the Worshipful Company of Parish Clerks, who are, for all intents and purposes, one of the ancient Livery Companies of London, the trade organizations that trained and represented the people in their professions. Except this lot don't have a livery, a sort of official insignia, of their own, and don't have a place in the order of precedence, all of those guilds knowing exactly which one is more important than whichever other one, because of some sort of dispute in the sixteenth century.' He'd now finished copying the symbol and stood up.

'Interesting.' Joe being Joe, he meant it. 'So if they don't have an insignia . . .'

'Not officially. This is what they use in secret, if my reading is right. I suspect that off the books they're the guild that handles our side of the street. I really need to find a parish clerk to ask about this stuff, but you know: busy. Anyway, this sign is what you're meant to draw when you're a Londoner trying to summon something up from the collective memory. Not that that's the sort of language the book uses. It's from the eighteenth century, and so it's all about there being thirty-eight different classes of ghosts and revenants and other tormented souls being kept out of the afterlife. OK. We stand in the middle' – he indicated for Joe to come and join him – 'and we need to, sort of, power it up . . .'

'How do we do that?'

Sefton kissed him and slid his hand down his stomach, and after a moment of surprise, Joe got the idea and got into it. 'How far do we have to . . . ?'

'All the way, but hold your horses.'

'Is this what your book says?'

'No, it talks about blood sacrifice, but there were also lines in Latin about gentlemen knowing of alternatives to blood. They also indicate the ladies of Covent Garden would understand enough to be employed in helping. It took a while for me to work out what that was all about.'

'Still holding my horses. The history lesson is helping.'

'We need to sacrifice you to the four points of the compass, places in London, to something called Leeging Beech Gutter in the north . . .'

'Charming. Should have been Cockfosters.'

'To the Adam and Eve on the Uxbridge Road, which I assume is a pub.'

'I think being sacrificed is kind of horny. Am I sick?'

'To Saint Peter and Saint Paul in Chaldon . . .'

'I'm sure they'll appreciate it. You're going to need to hurry.'

'And the Liberty of Havering, which you'll be pleased to hear is now . . .'

Joe gasped, trying as hard as he could to hold back.

'. . . Hornchurch.'

Joe came, and Sefton quickly moved him round in an anti-clockwise circle, keeping him coming for the whole turn. 'I like your world,' he said, as they kissed again.

'You can go back to watching now. I've got my sacrifice.'

'Why aren't they all like that?' Joe had found some tissues and was heading back to the sofa.

'Because almost everything else takes a lot more . . . energy, or whatever it is . . . than just wanting to make a ghost appear.'

'You could get a lot of blokes to jerk off together.'

'I don't think the Met would approve. Now shut up – I've

got to concentrate.' Joe gave him an expression saying he felt used, and settled down to watch. Sefton found the shape of the air in the room was ready now, somehow, and made the gestures he'd learned from several different lines of research. 'I'm thinking of Watson,' he said, visualizing the various actors who'd played him as he said it, 'Watson, Watson, Doctor Watson, elementary, my dear . . .' He grabbed the weight of what was around him and pulled it, shaped it. He found that one part of it suddenly led off out of the room, and he heaved on that part. He realized as he did so that the line didn't feel right. It felt like it was vibrating to some different . . . feeling that he didn't associate with London, like Watson was off the London grid completely, somewhere else. But it still felt within reach. Sefton kept speaking his mantra aloud, concentrating on the images, kept his hands dancing, miming pulling on a rope, adding his own arousal and strength to what was already in the—

Suddenly, the line pulled back.

Sefton found himself flying across the room.

He just had time to throw his hands up and instinctively grab the atmosphere of the room into some sort of cushion—

He hit the wall.

He hit the carpet a moment later, yelling at the pain in his arms and chest. He'd managed to get something in the way. He tried to step outside of the pain, but there was nothing left in the room to help him do that now. He realized he was having trouble breathing. After a few moments of panic, he found that he could take shallow ones. He wasn't going to die.

Joe was crouched beside him, shouting. Sefton grabbed his hand and finally found he could speak. 'OK,' he said. After a few moments, with Joe's help, he managed to stand. Nothing was broken. Sheer luck. That attack had been deliberate. Something hadn't wanted him to find Watson.

So finding Watson must be very important.

*

'He's a bit of a rough diamond.' Ross had fallen into conversation with an old lady at the cheap tea stall that had been set up in the hotel's extraordinary atrium, on the first floor, where a slim white bridge crossed a lighted expanse of glass that reminded Ross of a fish pond without actually being one. She had wondered for a moment if you could pay for your tea with a small sacrifice, but it seemed practicality ruled at least some aspects of Sighted life. Still, the cost of a cup of tea was only six pence, the result, she suspected, of the price once having been a sixpence coin. The presence of the ancient urn and wheeled stall on this level of such a modern hotel was the sort of visual clash she'd come to associate with this lot, which she found kind of charming. It had been easy to find an excuse to talk about Tock. From what she gathered from this woman, this particular subset of their culture revolved around him.

'Normally when someone's called that,' Ross said, 'it means they're a complete bastard.'

'Yeah, well, he is sometimes, to some people, but to others he's golden. A bit gruff, doesn't suffer fools gladly. Mostly, I think he just believes in the rules. And thank God. Where would our lot be without rules?'

Costain wandered over. She'd watched him putting his undercover skills aside and just walking up to people and asking questions, in the way UCs weren't supposed to. It was working this time, though, because these nervous people seemed glad to see newcomers among them. That wasn't the impression she'd got from any previous gathering of this lot. 'Opening ceremony's in five minutes,' he said, which she took to be a request to talk privately beforehand. She made her excuses and left the lady to her tea.

'They're scared,' he said, as they headed towards the main hall, joining a drift of others in the same direction. 'This lot have a bit of money now, not much by mainstream standards, but that makes them different in their community. They've adapted to it more quickly than the others, which seems to be down to Tock. They're worried about how they're seen. Tock makes them feel better about that, having made a packet pretty quickly.'

'Yeah, every third word that lady said was about rules and tradition. This lot talk so much about that because they're worried they've stepped outside it. All of which sounds like the sort of thing organized crime families go on about.'

'I think there's a bit of that to Tock as well. From what the woman at Greenwich said, it sounds like he's connected that world to this one. Hard to see how he made all this cash otherwise.'

They entered the dark, civilized expanse of the hall, with raggedly garbed audience members filling it up from the back, rather than rushing to the front. They found seats somewhere in the middle. At 9 a.m. exactly, to a smattering of applause, Tock walked onstage and went to a lectern. He was wearing, Ross realized, a reasonably normal tweed jacket. It was a look that, unlike that of anyone else here, wouldn't have caused raised eyebrows in the street.

He made a few words of introduction, then swiftly came to the point of the gathering. 'We know,' he said, 'there used to be law for our lot, but we know next to nothing about what it was. That troubles many of us. Well, me too. I don't like the idea of there being any law over people like us, but I like even bloody less the idea that there was some such authority and it went away without us knowing about it, somehow.' That last word he underlined. It caused widespread mutterings and wry laughter. That question was obviously an issue of great and possibly angry debate in this community. 'That's part of why I chose the theme of this year's event. This is the eight hundred and twenty-fifth annual Circle of Hands Convention, but, I think we can safely say, the fourth since whatever happened . . . happened.'

Ross realized, worryingly, that the event they were attending might be about the disappearance of the Continuing Projects Team, the lack of any memory of them, and the void that had been left. Maybe they could learn something, but she felt like sticking her hand up and saying she and her mates were doing their best to be the law in London now. She had a terrible feeling now that some of the panel discussions she'd read about might be about *them*. If there was a slideshow of how to recognize them, or something, they'd be buggered. She and Costain had agreed that they weren't here undercover, as such, but they weren't going to admit what their job was unless there was some emergency. They didn't want to end up as obvious targets at a convention full of people who traditionally hated the police.

'The other big thing that seems to have changed,' Tock continued, 'is the nature of sacrifice to London. Does it really feel different now? I think so. I know a great many of you do, and I know that was a realization that took a long time to sink in.' This lot knew, in their gut, about the Smiling Man's take-over of sacrifice in London, though they weren't aware, from what Ross and her colleagues had seen so far, of the Smiling Man himself. 'I know, for me, like for most of you, even discussing change is . . . anathema. We're in the middle of it now, though, having been infected by filthy lucre.' It was only half a joke, and got half a laugh from the crowd in response.

'Listen. Either we deal, in every sense of the word, or we fall.' There were a handful of boos. 'I know, some of you lot disagree. That's all right – you're allowed. At the moment.' He was too hard a man for the audience to take that ironically, though that was probably how he'd meant it. 'I've had to change more than most of you. I've had to reach out to powers our forefathers had no dealings with. Earthly powers, I mean.' Another slight laugh, nowhere near what he'd probably been hoping for. This lot were too worried for that. 'Today's sessions will start to explore the nature of whatever's out there, getting in the way of, responding to, accepting the sacrifice of, summoning. Those sessions will lead to the themed central summoning tonight, as we attempt to contact and re-establish the pantheon.'

As he started to go into detail, Ross made eye contact with Costain. She hadn't expected there to be a practical element to today's events. What if they summoned the Smiling Man himself? Would this lot have any way to deal with him?

'Doing this without Mags . . .' Tock had suddenly become emotional, and from the expressions on the faces of those nearby, Ross could see it was an emotion the audience shared, 'it's always difficult. She'd want us to do this, though. She'd want us to find a way through, bring everyone into the tent and get 'em all pissed together.' He said a few more things about cheap lunches being laid on, where the toilets were and how children weren't encouraged, and then departed the stage, not even making eye contact with the woman in a ragged fur coat who tottered on to present the first main hall item.

Ross got up. 'I want to have a word,' she said.

'Is going straight for it really the best idea?' Costain was following her.

She put a hand on his arm to restrain him. 'I don't care.'

She caught up with Tock in the hallway. He turned and his face immediately registered a kind of smiling, resigned aggression, as if to say, *Yeah, the world did get as shit as this, and you can only smile at it.* 'I know why you're here,' he said. 'The answer is no.'

'You don't know what I'm going to say.'

'I know what you have to offer, 'cos I heard it all at the auction. It's not enough. Nothing could be enough. OK? Does that satisfy you sufficiently to leave me alone now?'

He couldn't know she was with the police. He just saw her as someone pursuing an obsession. 'It's my future happiness. That's what you've got—'

He held up a hand and marched off. Not listening. She tried to keep her expression neutral. She'd been dangerously out of control there. What had she hoped for? That he'd simply give it to her? She'd just needed to look him in the eye, to appeal to a shared humanity that didn't seem to be there.

Costain arrived by her side. 'Hard case,' he said.

Nobody was in earshot. 'So. Do we . . . do we start thinking about finding some way to steal it?'

'That would be a criminal act that could end your career.'

'I know.'

'Besides, he'll be so prepared for that.'

Ross found, as she often did, that her brain had been thinking without her. Something she'd heard in the conference room had now connected with something else. 'When the Continuing Projects Team's headquarters was destroyed, nobody felt it at the time, did they? Like he said onstage, they just slowly realized over the next few years that something had changed.'

'I guess.'

'But when Sherlock Holmes was killed, Sefton was shocked by it, saw it in a dream, like a signal went out. Have you heard anything from this lot about the death of Sherlock Holmes?'

'Not yet.'

'If this lot knew about that, wouldn't it be big news? Someone would have said something. There'd be a bloody panel discussion. I think maybe that signal, about Holmes dying, was sent straight to Sefton. Straight to us.'

TWENTY-THREE

The morning and afternoon of the Circle of Hands Conference consisted of panels, debates and what this lot called workings. Some of them were on such a small scale that, having put her nose round the door, Ross got the feeling they were done more out of group habit than anything else.

In one of them, three people were sitting in a small conference room, chanting over an old London bus-route map. Ross had considered the ghost bus they'd encountered, and had stayed for a few minutes, but nothing practical was revealed, and she'd eventually decided she had to get a taste of as much of the programme as possible.

She'd let Costain go and nose around in his own way. She'd found a lot of formal sacrifices being performed. Phials were sterilized before the taking of blood, with rules read out at the start of panels about bringing one's own instruments to extract it. She saw many acts of self-inflicted injury, performed offhandedly. To her surprise, through open doorways, she saw acts of what should have been sexual ecstasy from which all passion had been drained, orgasms for both sexes performed while holding a conversation about something else, or reading a book.

Several of the panels featured people talking about stuff that was familiar. There was one about Mora Losley that she couldn't resist sitting in on. The panel was mostly about how Losley was a fake who shouldn't feature in the ancient annals of true practitioners of the craft. It made Ross so angry she had to leave before she said something. We risked our lives against that 'wannabe', mate!

These attendees had paid a lot to be here, but they still lived pretty frugally. Lunch was about taking one sandwich, one packet of crisps and one can of drink, with a real-ale bar made of a table with two barrels on it and plastic glasses. She really fancied a pint, but she was, if not officially, on duty in her own way. Once again, she felt like she'd like to be a part of them, was hurt by the distance she had to maintain. Wouldn't it be good to all explore the unknown together?

At dinner time, Ross found Costain in the bar, drinking water, and got a Diet Coke. 'What have you found?'

He produced a piece of paper, the writing on it the product of an ancient typewriter. 'The schedule for tonight's summoning. There's a mass event; then they're going to split up and work into the early hours trying to contact them separately. They don't know who's in the pantheon: several of these have question marks beside them.' Ross ran her finger down the list:

Bard
Boadicea
Brutus
Consumption (?)
Dick
Eros
Gap
Lud
Morningstar (?)
Other (?)
Rat King
Rat Queen (?)
Trickster

'Sefton has met three of those,' said Ross, surprised. 'Do you reckon this is a complete list?'

'You've met one too, or one who says he is. I don't know. It'd be unlike this lot to have a complete list of anything.'

'It's unlike them to have question marks, if everything's stayed the same. There must have been a meeting about the question marks.'

The 'mass summoning' event was in the main hall, and nothing was scheduled opposite it. 'They've been in this hotel for decades,' Costain said as they headed in, having had dinner at the hotel and talked little and awkwardly. 'From what I've read, they regard this hall a bit like . . . a major sporting auditorium. It has history to it, things have happened here, and if you've got the Sight . . .'

Ross was about to say she hadn't felt anything much in here earlier, but now, as she entered, she felt it, suddenly, big time. It came on as she opened the door to the venue, as if that door was made of lead shielding. It was the feeling of being a child at the cinema, magnified a hundredfold. The curtains behind the stage, the sheer tallness of those curtains, the careful pools of light by the lectern, the smell and feel of the seats, the details of the ceiling . . . here was where the saints had trod. They knew some way to muffle it in the daytime, but now they'd let it out. It grabbed her heart and made her ache. Such community, and she hated that she wasn't a part of it.

A young man and a young woman in waistcoats and bowler hats pushed onto the stage a pile of wood. A bonfire. 'All contributions prized and recognized!' they called together. People started coming forwards from the gathering audience, lining up down the aisles with wallets open, bags pulled from pockets. This was to be a giant sacrifice. Thank God nobody got their cock out this time. All Ross had was money, which this lot seemed OK about burning, judging by the coins that were being thrown onto the pyre. Not a lot of notes. Costain reached in his pocket too, and she gave him hers. He went up, and when his turn came, threw the cash into the pile.

Onto the stage had come a large, middle-aged woman in a long, flowing white dress. She looked solemn, determined. The two acolytes grabbed her and hauled her towards the bonfire. She fought them, or rather she pretend-fought them, making a lot of flailing gestures but not actually trying to escape. Ross was suddenly afraid. She looked to Costain and saw him watching the stage too. This could be, given how calm this lot were about the extraordinary, absolutely what it looked like.

One of the acolytes was now dowsing the bonfire with petrol, as the other made to bind the woman's wrists to a stake that had been brought onstage so late in the proceedings that Ross thought that had probably been a mistake. The bonds looked like they were made of . . . That was newspaper, wasn't it? The woman stood on the bonfire, the petrol being sloshed carefully away from her feet, and suddenly red lights played on the stage, missing their target initially, then illuminating the woman properly. She cried out, the stage faded a little too slowly to black, and Ross could see her being freed and helped off. The bonfire was lit and proved to be just a low fire, not some huge blaze. Ross could feel it being kept in check and the smoke being led away, presumably to avoid setting off the fire alarms. The audience rather dutifully applauded.

'Health and safety nightmare,' sighed a man in a top hat a couple of seats along the row.

'They like their gestures,' said Costain.

Onto the stage walked a series of figures, thirteen in all, each clad in a robe of different colours. The seventh, in the middle, was Tock, dressed all in black, no, with little silver highlights. Ross looked at the list and wondered if they could be in alphabetical order. 'Gap' said to her the Underground, as in 'Mind the gap', but Tock's costume reminded her of the livery of a London black cab.

'Maybe he bought it at the Gap,' said Costain. Some of the

other colour schemes seemed to fit the list. The first figure looked like she was dressed in red leather, like a bound edition of plays, for 'Bard', and yeah, gold and silver like armour fitted 'Boadicea'. 'Brutus' was thus pure white with a slash of purple, which fitted Sefton's description of the toga that god had worn, 'Consumption' was glittery blue, 'Dick' was felt black – and that could have been worse – 'Eros' a shabby bronze, 'Lud' a dull brown, 'Morningstar' silver on deep blue, which seemed logical, 'Other' a bright green, 'Rat King' russet, 'Rat Queen' a silvery grey and 'Trickster', worn by someone who really didn't fit that part, if they were indeed playing parts, a rather dull grey. That seemed odd until he turned, at the moment they all did, and Ross caught a glimpse of a bright red lining.

It occurred to Ross that all these symbols were just a rather desperate attempt at control, a search to impose meaning, or find it. They were being honest with the theme of their event; this lot really did need something to rely on. Didn't they all? The bonfire was now blazing. The acolytes would every now and then make a discreet hand gesture to rein it in. All the robed figures started making gestures too, complicated ones, at odds with each other, a chaotic anti-dance in which, nevertheless, sudden patterns would emerge and then vanish again.

Ross looked round and saw the audience were taking part. She felt the gravity of the Sight surging around her, pulsing like the smallest, most precise underwater currents, around the auditorium, between the seats, then straight at the stage. It was building and building. She looked to Costain. He was clearly worried. He didn't know how to take part any more than she did. Nobody was paying them any attention, thank God.

Onstage, some of the robed figures were wavering, as if the air between them and the audience had become warmed by the bonfire, no, much more than that. Sefton might have had words for what was happening. The shape of the room and everything inside it were being changed. Ross felt as if she was standing at the edge of a cliff, but also, she'd never felt more in London.

It was like the metropolis had been taken out of context and put on the stage, at a sudden, scary distance. The room was warping around the call that was being broadcast from the stage.

'I think they're trying to summon all of them, at once,' whispered Costain.

It didn't feel like they all wanted to come. There was resistance in the air. Ross found herself hoping they didn't come, or not all of them. The shape that had been Tock was particularly worrying, something like a black hole. One of what was being summoned definitely wasn't coming. The man representing 'Morningstar' was gesturing pointlessly, looking frustrated, while all the other robed figures were transforming. Ross was interested to see what 'Trickster' would appear. That figure was blurred, but seemed to have only got so far, a formless cloud that showed no sign of becoming clear. 'Other' was quickly settling into a seated shape. The vision of her suddenly leaped forwards, and Ross was teetering above her, feeling like she was about to fall, her arms flailing, held up only by the trivial forces of physics. 'Other' had become a black woman in a wheelchair, only a fine sheen of hair on her head, her ears opened by rings, a stud in her nose, her eyes those of . . . Ross had been about to say an animal's, but it was Ross who was the animal and she was something more. For a moment, she was different, green with purple spots. 'You have to *do* something,' she said, her voice clear and angry. She was saying this to the whole room, Ross realized, not just to her. 'You have to do something before it's too late.'

There was somehow a feeling of agreement from the rest of the swirling mass. 'Other' raised a hand, a stump, and suddenly the vision leaped back and to the right, and they were all craning their necks towards the gravitational heave of . . . the top of St Paul's Cathedral, she was sure it was, that familiar dome. It was suddenly clear, in the room with them now. Every other building in London, every spire, every skyscraper, was leaning precariously towards it. On the steps of the cathedral stood a figure, the Smiling Man. This was a vision of him in the future.

He was laughing: a bellowing, vomiting laugh. From the sky was falling . . . snow? No. It was a fine white dust, and it was in her mouth and nose, and she coughed it, and thought for a moment it must be ashes, but no, it smelt of . . . electricity, straight into her head. It was cocaine. It was raining cocaine.

Around her, she could hear sobbing, cries of anger. She felt the rest of this community beside her, these wonderful, vulnerable people, and she realized they weren't in this future. They didn't have a place in it. By this point they were all gone. What about Ross? What about her friends? She didn't know how to begin to search for them. Sefton could do this, maybe; she couldn't. They were seeing all this, and they had deliberately left Sefton behind!

She felt the intensity of the vision growing and growing. It had taken over everything else. 'Other' was still sitting there at the edge of it, but now she was making wild gestures, as if it had got out of her control. The audience were tumbling out of their seats now, trying to hang on as the auditorium upended itself, and they were grabbing things, trying not to fall into that huge laughing mouth, which was getting bigger and bigger.

An enormous sound.

The slamming open of a door.

Ross fell back and so did all those around her. They were panting, tears on their faces. Beside her, Costain carefully and slowly relaxed back into his seat. She looked back to the stage, where the robed figures were staggering, trying to support each other, sitting down.

'You must excuse me.' The familiar voice came from the back of the room, theatrically loud. Ross turned to look. Standing in the central doorway of the auditorium was Gilbert Flamstead, in a grey jacket with a red silk lining. 'Could anyone tell me where I am?' he asked. 'I'm here completely by accident.'

Lofthouse wouldn't normally have elected to go to sleep at eight o'clock in the evening, but she was exhausted. The key on her wrist was urging her to keep moving, but that was beyond her. She used her torch to look long and hard at the cavern she'd come to and found nothing in the graffiti to suggest it was particularly dangerous. There was a sheer drop nearby, but not so close that she might roll into it in her sleep. She started pulling the sleeping bag from her pack. She'd have the first portion of her rations. She had four more packs: supper tonight and three square meals tomorrow, because whatever happened, she had to be out of here by Sunday night.

She tensed at a sound from deeper down the tunnel. She waited, but no further sound came. Water would drip. Rocks would fall. The silence would never be complete.

She ate some of her Kendal mint cake, drank some of her water, curled up in her sleeping bag, still fully clothed, and switched off her torch.

She waited in the darkness. Was she going to be able to get to sleep? What else could be down here? She realized that the texture of the silence had changed. She heard . . . voices? Yes, definitely voices. She sat up, fumbled for the zip on her sleeping bag, found it and slowly, deliberately tugged on it, needing her legs to be free. The voices weren't speaking English. The language sounded sibilant, like nothing that could be made by a mouth. It was like hearing water talking.

She got slowly to her feet, trying not to make a noise. She picked up the bag with the gun and found her torch. There was definitely movement at the end of the passage, between her and where she would be heading tomorrow. Something big and slow . . . a cluster of them. A smell came with them, something like rotting fat. She found the cartridges and started to load them into the shotgun. If these were animals, the noise in this space would . . . also do permanent damage to her ears, yes. She pulled the cartridges out again. If these were animals, the torch might prove just as shocking.

She prepared herself, aware that all that was keeping her hands moving in the face of sheer, physical terror was a sense of something beyond herself, of duty. She aimed the torch towards the mass at the end of the tunnel and switched it on.

She got a glimpse of three enormous pink men, or something like men. They were naked, vastly obese, with enormous hands, small eyes, large, flaccid genitals and . . . long, elephantine proposces instead of noses. These were not, incredibly, beings one needed the Sight to perceive, she realized in that second. There was something about them that looked hungry.

They screamed through their trunks and flung up their hands to cover their faces.

They screamed as they rushed at her.

A thought was in her head to go forwards, not to flee. She ducked past the first set of flailing arms that grabbed for her and dived towards the end of the tunnel. One of them spun and the back of a wet red hand sent her staggering. Her feet slipped on the sudden wetness of the path. She was going to fall. She tried instinctively not to let go of the gun, threw a hand out to steady herself.

There was nothing there. She fell. She hit a wall. She was in darkness. She screamed. She fell once more.

Ross had expected the audience to realize that here was the Trickster, summoned by their ceremony, but among those all around her getting to their feet, none of them seemed to be doing that. A few close to Flamstead had already risen to engage with him, some of them star-struck, shaking him by the hand, answering his question, some of them berating him for interrupting this ancient ceremony. Ross looked back to the stage. Tock was sitting there, his gaze flicking suspiciously to Flamstead as the other robed figures talked to him urgently. They had gained a vision, but the interruption meant they were wondering if they could have seen more. There seemed to be no question of starting again. The acolytes were spraying fire extinguishers on the blaze, and it was already reducing to smoke, which impossibly flattened and rushed back into the pile of blackened wood.

'Him,' said Costain.

'Yeah,' said Ross, 'you got a problem with that?'

Before he could answer, Flamstead, with a shout of surprise, had come trotting over. 'What a vast surprise to find you here! You shouldn't really come for a drink with me, should you? Or can I persuade you?'

Ross took his hand and allowed herself to be helped out of her seat, and kissed him hello. She looked deliberately back at Costain. 'I'm buying,' he said.

They went to the hotel bar, which already had in it a handful of the audience from the summoning, those willing to stomach the prices in search of something to fortify them after that. Flamstead just said, 'Anything,' when Costain asked him what he wanted to drink. Ross wondered if that actually meant nothing, but it seemed, considering the long gulp he took of the pint of lager Costain gave him, that not expressing a preference meant he didn't have to lie. She stayed on the Diet Coke.

Costain rather aggressively clinked glasses with the actor. 'So,' he said, 'obviously it can't be a coincidence you're here – let's get past that.' Flamstead made a sad clown face, emphasizing that any comment he would have made had been cut off. 'And I know asking you questions isn't a good idea. So. Most of this lot don't get who you are.'

Flamstead smiled. 'The ones who do trust me implicitly.'

'Meaning that the ones who realize who you are don't want you here.'

'Because,' said Ross, joining in, 'he represents lies, and they're after the truth.'

'I've never done them any harm!' laughed Flamstead. 'Or caused any of them to stumble on the path. Or thrown any of them from windows or anything like that. Not at all.'

'They probably don't like your tone,' said Costain. 'I've

known people like you all my life. It's all fun, until somebody loses an eye, and then it's still fun for you.'

Flamstead simply bowed. Then he looked to Ross. 'Don't think I'm here for you, young lady.'

She felt suddenly scared again. If he was here to help her, then she must need helping.

'Oh, just leave it out, OK?!' Costain had put his pint down and was suddenly in Flamstead's face. 'I do not intend to allow you to . . . I can't just frigging . . . You can't have her without . . . !' His fury seemed to be getting in the way of his speech, his head actually jerking back and forth with each wrench of indecision. 'Fuck it!' He lashed out with his hand, not at Flamstead, but towards the table, and sent the pint glass flying, causing the barkeeper to start yelling that he'd pay for that. But Costain was out of the door.

'I wouldn't dream of paying for the damage,' said Flamstead to the barkeeper, doing just that.

Ross realized she was shaking. God, she hated that that had been about her. Did making her own choices really have to end up with blokes acting like that? That had gone beyond all normal behaviour. Was Costain cracking up too? 'He . . .'

'Knows what he's doing, and yet he doesn't.'

'Hey. That has to be true.'

Flamstead scowled as if caught out. 'What are you to him, do you think? A prize to be fought over? An individual whose wishes are to be respected? A lady to look up to? A colleague, a source of anger, a regret, a foul temptress? Do any of these words set off anything in that brain of yours?'

There was a shout from the doorway. Tock, back in his normal attire, had entered, and with him were several more of those who'd been onstage. They were all looking angrily at Flamstead. 'You're not welcome here,' Tock said. 'I can tell this bar not to serve you. You know you're banned from this hotel.' Flamstead just smiled indulgently. 'You' – Tock pointed at Ross – 'you should know what happens to those who worship him. Have you made a sacrifice to him?'

'More the other way round.' She'd meant it as a joke, but they obviously understood what she meant and, to her surprise, backed away slightly. She recalled what had been said at the first auction she'd been to, about not giving up oneself to London or any other power that got sacrificed to. Was she wrong to trust Flamstead? She looked at him now, and still felt that sense of baseline ease. She would, after all, always know when he was lying.

'Fucking whore,' said Tock. 'I don't use those words lightly.'

'Fucking cunt,' said Ross calmly, and took a sip of her drink. 'Me neither.'

'I bought your happiness fair and square. You know what I'm planning to use it for? I'm going to give it away, as a sacrament, something to share out at the end of this convention, something to hold this culture together, in the face of that vision we all saw just then. We know what's coming now. We're going to swear to stay together, to bind ourselves to solidarity by all drinking from the same cup, by all feeling uplifted for a moment. So go on, call me the bad guy, when I'm doing that and you're fucking that thing.'

Ross wondered if he'd been so unpleasant before the death of his . . . wife, partner, whoever 'Mags' had been. There was something about the bullish set of his shoulders that said yeah, probably. 'Are you going to throw us out?'

'Are you going to behave?'

The bartender looked up from his phone. 'Erm, actually, Mr Flamstead can stay,' he said. 'The manager says that's policy from now on.'

Tock stared at him for a moment, so angry he couldn't speak. Then, without a word, he turned on his heel and left. The others followed him, glaring back at Flamstead as they went.

Costain entered again as they did so, stepping carefully away from the men storming out. He looked contrite, in control again.

He raised his hands. 'What I said before—' he began. Then, at a wry glance from Flamstead, he stopped, decided instead to remain stoic. 'I heard what was happening. I went round the corner to the hotel front desk and showed my warrant card. I said you're with us.' Then he went to the bar and started apologizing.

'He's really keeping it together,' whispered Flamstead, his tongue in Ross's ear, 'a straightforward character with no contradictions.'

Quill had found an empty space in one of the houses that seemed to be intended as a bedroom. It was freezing. The heating didn't work. Of course, these weren't real homes, but at least he was out of the wind. The question the Smiling Man had left him with sat in his stomach like indigestion. He would need an answer by the morning.

Just accept, and then all hope is gone. Great! Done! Sorted! Ignoring the cold, he got his notes from his bag and started arranging his ops board around the room. He stopped after a while. None of the connections seemed to connect. He looked to one of the windows, with no curtains, and saw the lurid lights of Hell outside. They could become solid, something to depend on, if he agreed. That would just be for him. For nobody else. Not yet. Against them, on the close outside, stood the silhouette of Moriarty.

Quill realized that another figure was visible against the lights, had seen him and was now approaching. Shit! He leaped into the corner and pulled his coat over him to hide.

He heard the sound of the door opening. Someone entered the room. He couldn't face whoever it was being a copper.

A hand pulled aside the coat. Quill scrambled away and saw who it was. It was Laura. She was looking as calm as ever.

'Hi,' she said.

'Have you moved to London?' Quill leaped to his feet. 'Have you?'

'No.' Her voice was careful as always. She had the sort of face that clearly had once been that of a man, but somehow her transition had added something to it. Whatever it was that had been added, some hard-won sort of compassion, maybe just the result of all the shit people had flung at her, Quill found himself relieved to see it now. 'Why do you ask?'

He made himself be calm, to match her. 'How did you find me? Did one of my lot use . . . stuff you don't know about?'

'Nothing like that. You switched on your phone. Sarah has "Find My Phone" set up for you. She asked me to go to see you first, because . . . well, she's afraid of you. And she's afraid *for* you.' Quill was biting his lip hard. 'I was hoping we could talk, and you could tell me what was wrong, because Sarah thinks some of it is about me.'

Quill had to force out the words. His own voice sounded to him like that of a scared child. 'You wouldn't believe me.'

'Sarah also said that, within some limits which she set out for me, I should believe what you say. She told me about what happened with Jessica last year. About her being taken by Mora Losley. About . . . what Mora Losley really was.'

'And you believed that?'

'Yes.' It was the quickest, most unqualified reply he'd ever heard to that question. 'I know Sarah. I also know the truth when I hear it.'

'That was all she told you?'

'Yes, and to be honest, that was enough to scare the fucking crap out of me, Jim. I can see why you don't want me to move here. I'm having second fucking thoughts myself.'

'She didn't tell you the hard bit.'

'She said you wouldn't tell her.' She sat down opposite him and waited.

He paced for a while. 'There's stuff she doesn't know. Big stuff. It rips up everything you rely on. It makes all this' – he gestured around him – 'into a joke. I have to tell you, though, so you can save yourself. Then I'll have saved one.'

'By me not moving to London?'

'Yes! That's all you have to do. I can't tell you why. It's about a threat that's been made. More than a threat, a certainty. It's someone Sarah's probably told you about. We call him the Smiling Man. It's too late for the rest of us. We're doomed. Sarah and Jessica. They don't know. That's why I'm . . . Because they don't know and I can't tell them! You can save yourself by not moving here.'

Laura nodded. 'All right,' she said. 'I understand.'

'So you won't live in London?'

'I'll live where I want to. This Smiling Man of yours doesn't get to tell me what to do.'

'But I've told you! You don't know—'

'This is harassment. You give in to that, that way lies madness.' She went to him and put a hand on his arm. 'You've done your best to save me. Now it's up to me.'

Quill could only look at her. 'I'm sorry—!'

'Listen. What do you most want to do?'

As they walked out into the cold night air, Quill stopped. He could still see, he realized, Moriarty, standing next to what must be Laura's rented car in the empty close of houses.

Him being there felt different now. Not a threat. Quill felt that Moriarty was something to do with him, that he almost had a responsibility towards him. There was something about him that made Quill think . . . perhaps here there was even something that might help him, though help still felt a long way away.

He didn't know what he was doing. Acting on instinct. Still ill. 'Can you see someone over there?' he asked Laura.

Laura remained deliberately calm. 'No.'

'Great,' said Quill. 'Here, you!' He marched towards Moriarty, who reacted like a scared cat, but Quill made calming gestures. 'I'm going home. Do you want to come too?'

TWENTY-FOUR

Lofthouse lay on the ground, panting. She was in absolute darkness. She'd bloody well left her pack on the other side of the chamber when she'd run at those things. She had her torch, and what was in her shoulder bag . . . Yes, it was still here . . . and she'd kept hold of the gun, thank Christ. She felt like her ribs were bruised down her right-hand side, where she'd landed. She'd taken some of the impact on her knees, which also felt fucked. She'd hit a few lumps of rock on the way down too. Her fingers and palms were ripped from trying to grab for dear life. She put out a hand and found a rock wall, the cool of the wet rock against the heat of her skin. She found purchase and used her better leg to push herself upright. She experimentally put some of her weight on her other leg, and just managed to stifle a cry of pain.

She lay against the wall, breathing deeply. She was going to die here. She was going to die far beneath the earth. She would just vanish. They'd say she was having an affair. The thing inside Peter might think she'd taken action against it and Peter might be tortured, might be killed. She let the panic take her for a while, her breathing turning into gasping, but then that turned into coughing, and she slowly calmed. The fear had nowhere to go. She felt a familiar sensation and searched for her charm bracelet. The key was indeed still pulling steadily in one particular direction. She found the torch and switched it on. There was

261

a narrow path ahead of her, another sheer drop to her right. She'd hit without rolling, thank God, or that might have been the end of her.

Was she making herself believe it, or was the pressure of the key slightly more insistent, as if she was closer to her target? No graffiti here, but feet had clearly worn down the way. Too scared to test her weight on her damaged leg, she started to edge along the wall. She was blazingly thirsty, but she had no water now. She tried licking the stone, and after a while, that helped a little. She had no option. She would keep calm and carry on.

Quill entered his own house again slowly, carefully. He looked at Sarah, who was standing in the hallway, her own expression careful, non-committal. The weight of just seeing her again. If he started to apologize, a crack would burst wide open. He was going to do more than that, though, wasn't he? He walked into the lounge and saw all the familiar furniture, another room with lots of things in it. What he had to work his way back towards was meaning, for himself and between him and Sarah. He went and deliberately sat down in what he distantly knew was 'his favourite chair'.

Sarah entered with half a smile on her face, probably at how serious he was looking, but that look faded. Laura said she'd go to make some tea, but Quill called her back. He was going to go for this straight away.

Moriarty looked around the lounge door and, unseen by the other two, swept in, with a little snarl of contempt at the accommodation. He had suddenly become a bit of a pantomime villain, Quill realized. Maybe he could only be a monster when he was hidden. Now he was in plain sight, the clichéd details of him felt harmless, even homely. Quill had felt such an urge to gather him up, to bring him in from the cold. This connection he felt to Moriarty, it was as if he himself had . . . created him.

That was an interesting thought. A weirdly clear thought. It felt like the first inkling of something better. But never mind that now. There was something urgent he had to do.

'There's a sign,' he said to Sarah and Laura, 'over the gates of Hell.'

He said the next sentence. He told them what the sign said. He wondered if he was fantasizing about doing this. No, here he was. Here was the weight being entirely lifted from his shoulders. He couldn't feel it going. The look on her face wasn't scared yet. That would take a while.

Laura looked to Sarah, interrogating her about whether this was true, or part of Quill's delusions. She'd had some time to think about what the revelation might be. She had the perspective to get scared. Quill was relieved, sort of, to see that Sarah believed him. She came to sit closer, opposite him, and took his hands in hers. He started to sob at the touch. 'No,' she said gently, 'listen, listen. You don't just have to tell me. You can't. You have to tell your lot. Right now.'

Ross, Flamstead and Costain had stayed in the bar, her talking to Flamstead, Costain keeping his distance, talking to anyone and everyone else, starting up conversations with that easy undercover charm. God, this was like being at school. If she left with Flamstead, would Costain make a fuss? Which version of him would prevail? She felt her phone vibrate, saw who the call was from and scrambled to answer it.

That familiar voice on the other end of the line. Quill. It wasn't quite him; he talked very weirdly, as if there were pressures on him she couldn't understand. He asked her if she remembered that he'd been to Hell, and she was saying, 'Well, bloody of course . . .' when he came out with his bombshell.

She had to sit down. He repeated it. 'I heard,' she said. 'It's everyone who ever lived in London. They're all in Hell. We're all going there. That's . . .' She struggled to find the right words for a moment. It was too big to process. Except with a part of her mind that was always processing things. Which had suddenly realized. 'That's something I can *use*.'

She made sure Quill was with people who were looking after

him, talked to Sarah for a moment and said she thought what he'd said was probably true, yeah. Her mind was racing. She finished the call, then called Costain over, turned to Flamstead. 'We're all going to Hell. You knew, didn't you?'

He just looked sad at her.

'What?' said Costain.

She repeated what Quill had said. He looked like he couldn't process it either. 'This is such leverage, but the three of us can't bloody use it. This lot won't believe you or me. Who would they believe? Wait. I know.' She grabbed the programme out of her pocket, found where the room was and before either of them could ask her what she was talking about, she was on her way out of the bar.

There were five people in the panel room, kneeling in a circle under the light of a PowerPoint presentation, the single slide of which said, 'Other (?),' against a bright green background, a pile of small sacrifices being burned in a brazier between them. Ross and Costain quickly joined them. Flamstead stepped into the middle of the circle, causing one of these middle-aged ladies to scream and the others to start shouting. He threw an enormous wad of cash onto the brazier. It erupted into green flame. 'Come on, then, you irritating bitch,' bellowed Flamstead. 'This is *me* calling!'

When he spoke to others of his kind, Ross noted, he spoke the truth.

She appeared without fanfare – not there one moment, there the next. Her smell was of exotic spices . . . travel . . . dirt . . . Ross realized that the scent itself was dragging her Sighted brain towards horrors, that she would get to thinking of something terrible in just a moment, and consciously hauled her attention away. The figure that sat where the brazier had been had a furious scowl on her face. She was looking angrily at Flamstead. 'They have to understand,' she said, 'you only ever help them for your own ends.'

'They know that, Brent. Or should I say Mother?'

'You just told them my *name*!'

'I suppose I just did. They'll find a good use for it.'

The goddess turned to the circle, looking only slightly less angry. 'I told you before,' she said, 'I keep telling you, every time I'm summoned, the things you must do. You never *do* them.' Her voice was a mixture of Jamaican, Eastern European; it again started to lead Ross to thoughts of terrible suffering. She brought an awful awareness of that suffering with her. It would be tough, she realized, to keep this goddess around for any length of time. She looked to Costain. He was back to his stoicism, his defence against all things.

Ross turned back to address the summoned goddess. She dared to use the name that Flamstead had just revealed. 'Brent . . .' She saw the others in the circle looking at her in awed horror. 'Tell them what's on the sign above the gates of Hell.'

The appearance of the goddess visibly warped. She was trying, Ross realized, to get away. 'They mustn't know. It'll crush them. My people most of all. They will think their lives are for nothing.'

'Right now they are!' shouted Ross.

'You're bound by the circle, Mum,' said Flamstead, 'by the size of that sacrifice.'

'The sign says that everyone who has ever lived in London goes to Hell,' hissed Brent. 'It's true, though it hasn't always been. It all changed when Lucifer was murdered and something else took his place. There. Now nobody can be happy!'

A couple of the people in the circle stood up. One of them ran for the door. The remaining ones had started to weep, to ask urgent questions. The truth was out. Christ, what weight had Jimmy carried all this time? No wonder he'd broken and fled.

With a great yell, Brent threw up her hands in a gesture of disgust and vanished. The brazier fell, and smoke burst into the room. The fire alarm sounded, and water started to pour down from sprinklers in the ceiling. 'How dare you compromise her like this?' yelled Costain. 'Get her away from this downpour!'

Ross was utterly bemused as Costain squared up to a pleased-looking Flamstead, both getting sodden with water. That was so different from his normal way of speaking, and he now didn't seem to need the slightest cause before charging into battle on her behalf like a smitten teenager. What the fuck? But she had much more urgent things to worry about. Coughing, she allowed Flamstead and Costain, actually shouldering each other for the privilege, to lead her out of the room. 'I need . . .' she coughed as they all stumbled out into the corridor, the alarm lights flashing around them, 'I need to find Tock.'

He was in the car park, as was everyone else as they streamed out of the hotel. He was being surrounded, Ross saw, by a swiftly growing crowd of people, all of whom seemed to be telling him and each other the terrible news. Some of them actually ran up and made to attack Flamstead, as he followed Ross and Costain, but he shouted to them about whether or not they believed Brent, and him knowing her name held them back.

Tock glared as Ross reached him. 'So this isn't a trick of his?' He was pointing at Flamstead.

'The Other said it,' an exasperated woman shouted beside him. 'She was bound by the circle: she had to tell the truth.'

'All right, all right.' He ran a hand over his thinning hair, like a gorilla making a blunt gesture of aggression. 'Well, we're fucked, aren't we? That's what happened a few years back – that was the big change, our souls all being chucked into the shitter. We had our conference and we got our answer.'

'You don't know who we are,' said Ross.

'I don't want to know who you are, love.'

Ross looked to Costain, who hesitated, so she reached into his jacket and grabbed his warrant card. '*We're* the law now,' she said. 'We're part of what you're having this conference about.' A reaction spread through the crowd: angry, mixed up, not understanding.

'I'm on their side!' called Flamstead.

'You heard him lie then,' said Ross. 'He's not with us, he's just helping us with our enquiries. We have access to the Continuing Projects Team's files, some of their equipment—'

'You're lying,' said Tock. He pointed to Costain. 'He doesn't use blanket. We check for coppers, and he isn't one.'

'I realized after failing to use blanket a couple of times,' said Costain, 'that I'm safe without it. I guess I give off a vibe that's more . . . criminal.' He looked a little lost to Ross. 'Now you know. I didn't want you to. I would give anything in the world for you not to—'

'It's because he was an undercover,' she said, cutting him off before he went on and on. It was a working theory, but still it left questions to answer. Later for that. 'Listen, our boss is Detective Inspector James Quill. He went to Hell and he came back. He nicked Mora Losley. He put the Ripper back to bed.' Neither of those were strictly true, but it was all close enough to satisfy the crowd around her, who were busy slapping her with gestures to check her veracity. 'Our specialist is Kevin Sefton, who's met with Brutus and the Rat King.' She was talking and talking. It was time to move away from detail and get to people. 'We want to be the law for you lot. We know how much you used to hate us. And "used to" for you lot takes a long bloody time to go away. But' – she gestured around her at the increasing size of the crowd, the rising feeling of panic – 'you know now how desperate the situation is. You need someone to be a respected and recognized authority that you consent to, that you want in your lives. And we need you in return.'

'That's a nice speech—' Tock began.

'Yeah.' She stepped into his face, desperate now. 'Yeah it was.' He was, she was sure, one of these blokes who needed to be able to say he liked people who stood up to him, when that was just his mechanism to save face when he lost. She had to give him that way out.

'We don't like being told what to do. We don't like someone having a hold over us.'

'That's not how policing works. Police should be answerable. *You* should have some hold over *us*.' She realized as she said it that her own needs and the needs of her team had just at that moment come together. The size of what she could grab here staggered her. She ploughed on, kept talking. 'You reckon you're going to spread a little bit of happiness among this lot? How far will that go, compared to guaranteed Hell? Wouldn't you rather have a friend in law enforcement who's working the crime of the afterlife?' She looked him in the eye, hoping against hope that this was going to come down to being about *people*. 'Wouldn't you rather I owed this whole community an enormous debt?'

He thought for a long moment. Then he reached into his jacket. Of course he'd have it on him.

He took out her happiness in a small clear bottle with a gold cap. He held it up in front of her. He taunted her with it. 'You're going to owe us big time,' he said.

She held out her hand. 'That's always the deal,' she said.

He made her feel it, that enormous hole in her life, for a second more. Then he gave her the bottle.

She didn't look at Costain or Flamstead. She had no idea what her colleague would think of her speaking for the entire Met like that, but she had meant what she said. At least this was a debt she was prepared to repay. She unscrewed the top of the tiny bottle. She fixed her lips carefully round the top. She poured the liquid onto her tongue. Suddenly, there was much more of it than could fit into her mouth!

It erupted, not out of her, but into her, into her head and her body. She sucked on the bottle like a teat, feeling it, oh, feeling it, the difference, so much! She drained it. She lowered the empty bottle. She stumbled.

She wiped the back of her hand across her mouth.

She started to laugh.

TWENTY-FIVE

As soon as he got the call, Sefton went over to Quill's place. Sarah opened the door for him, a woman she introduced as her sister, Laura, with her. It was close to one in the morning, but as Laura said, nobody was likely to be getting any sleep.

Sefton went into the lounge, to find Quill drinking very carefully from a cup of tea, his hands shaking. He looked up, nodded, hesitant to do more, as if Sefton might not be real. Sefton marched across to hug him, but then jumped at a sudden movement in the air between them. 'What is *that*?' He was looking at a dark, somewhat hunched individual who'd leaped into existence as he crossed the room. Its beady eyes were sizing him up.

'My Moriarty,' said Quill, without humour.

'I should think,' said Sarah, 'you'll want a cuppa yourself?'

Slowly, Quill managed to talk about everything that had happened, both in Hell and since he'd fled. Sefton asked questions like this was an interview, and Quill seemed calmed by the process, allowed himself to be led. Sarah and Laura listened, the latter sometimes holding on to her sister's hand, Sarah sometimes trying to restrain her tears, sometimes failing.

The idea they were all going to Hell was too big to deal with. It seemed slight and distant, almost, compared to Quill's pain. Still, every time they got back to that, they fell into silence. Quill took his story back to what they could use in their current operation, and Sefton tried to make that as easy for him as possible. 'All those clues at the murder scene,' Quill whispered. 'I worked them. They worked me over. They all have to mean something. Don't they?'

Sefton wondered if he could safely answer that. They were in professional mode, though, so he felt he had to. 'I'm not sure, Jimmy, but I think maybe most of them were put there deliberately to distract us from looking for what wasn't there: Watson.'

'An orgy of evidence. That's what my old boss used to call a crime scene like that, a room that had too much in it.' Quill sounded like he'd just been slapped around the face. 'It was all for . . . for *nothing*!' He realized he'd shouted. He put down the cup of tea. His hands clasped the arms of the chair. He tried to control his breathing, his eyes closed. 'What about that cyclist?'

'I think some bolshie courier carrying a package that might have looked like a cosh . . .'

'Oh fuck,' said Quill. 'Oh fuck.'

Sefton looked over to Sarah. This was so hard on her. Sefton almost didn't want to vocalize his next thought, because it felt like it might lead Quill the wrong way, but it also said that not everything he'd done was meaningless. 'But I also think some of the clues you found *did* mean something.' Quill's eyes snapped open and he looked afraid at this sudden hope. Like devils were going to rush in. 'For a start, that blade really did have the weight of something Sighted about it. It probably does have a "spiel" attached. Some of the other stuff you worked out, that was the old Jimmy Quill brain still doing its best—'

'Don't!' snapped Quill. Then, a second later, more calmly, 'Just tell me.'

'Missing Room Ltd, that really was a reference to a rock band called Moriarty. Which might be an amazing coincidence if not for Dean Michael, which also genuinely points that way, his name being the first names of two famous Moriartys, one fictional and one an actor. Putting those two names that way round seems deliberately chosen to cue us towards thinking it wasn't a real name, because he could equally have called himself Michael Dean, and there are probably loads of those. I would also agree about the astronomical photo, except that, like Sarah said, it doesn't show the right bit of the sky for the asteroid named after Moriarty to be on it. What that means I don't know, but still . . . I think someone sorted out that room to firstly set us off on a lot of wild goose chases – which had a terrible impact on you – and then, as we got deeper, to get diverted into suspecting Moriarty.'

'Just the sort of thing I would do,' chuckled Moriarty.

Sefton looked at him in shock.

Quill looked over at his new friend. 'I didn't know you could talk.'

'I heard it too,' Sefton quickly said to Sarah and Laura, to reassure them. 'He's sitting right there.'

'So relieved,' said Laura.

'I think I've worked out what he is,' said Sefton. 'Jimmy, you've said you started to believe you were being followed.'

'I started to believe a lot more than that. I thought someone was watching me from the end of the close here. Then I thought it must be Moriarty, and then when I had a near miss with that cyclist . . . in the right place . . . I was so sure. I ended up being followed across London by—' He had to stop for a moment. 'Sorry,' he said. 'I can still feel it. It's like I'm going to slip back into that. I will, you know. I'm sorry when I do.'

Sarah sat down with him, held him.

'You're doing better now, though,' said Sefton, 'and I think I might know why.'

'It's him, isn't it?' said Quill, pointing to Moriarty.

'I think so. You put all that belief into an image of Moriarty in your head, belief that London fed on. Like when all those extra versions of Losley appeared, because people thought she was everywhere. So for those of us with the Sight, this Moriarty became real. You *made* him.'

Quill couldn't say anything.

'How does that help?' asked Sarah.

'In two ways, I reckon. First, all of Jimmy's paranoia is standing right there, and he looks to us a bit, well—'

'A bit stupid,' said Quill.

'You've actually given your pain not just a name but a face, a body, dialogue. While he's over there, he's not in there.' Sefton pointed to Quill's head. 'Secondly, I think this might give us a way forward. You made Moriarty by getting obsessed with him, by focusing on the clichés about him. Maybe you could do that with yourself. Jimmy Quill, all the stories they tell about him. The more you can make up who you are, healthy and happy, the more you can project that at London, the more London might go along with it.'

'Yes,' said Sarah quickly. 'Yes, and we can help with that.'

They all tried, talking deliberately about Quill's previous exploits, Sefton deliberately inflating them until Quill told him to stop, said he'd never find himself if what he was after wasn't true. In the end, with Laura and Sarah's help, he reduced what he wanted to remember to a couple of whispered sentences, which he repeated over and over. 'It's helping,' he said finally, 'a little. Just enough to . . . keep me anchored here. I can feel it. I just have to try and believe in . . .'

'In yourself,' said Laura. 'In who you really are.'

'It's not just you, though,' said Sarah. 'We all believe in Jimmy Quill.'

Sefton didn't want to watch his boss start to sob, so he went into the kitchen and made them all tea.

Ross sat down in the middle of the car park. She looked around, pleased at all the people out here, delighted at how newly multifaceted her feelings towards Costain and Flamstead were. A bit too big to deal with, honestly. Pain in there too, which she'd been protected from because it had been wrapped up inside happiness. But never mind that now! She felt the future ahead of her. There it was. There were tough times ahead, but the sudden rush of possibilities, of hope, had smashed into her like a river bursting through a dam. This was what people lived in, all the time, and it was so brilliant!

She saw Tock looking at her, that empty sadness in his eyes. 'Yeah,' he said, 'enjoy.'

Everything she wanted to say to him would make him feel worse. She turned instead to Flamstead, who was laughing along with her, and kissed him. 'Well,' he said, 'I want to be with you forever. I'm definitely committed to this relationship.'

'What?' She took a step back. She couldn't quite believe he meant the opposite.

He took her head in his hands and kissed the top of her skull. It was a brother's kiss. 'It's not me. It's you.'

She knew him breaking up with her right now was the best possible time anyone could have done it, but she would have so appreciated the chance to have a relationship now she could once again enjoy the emotional pleasure of it. She would also have appreciated him doing this in private. 'You got together with me just to get me to this point, is that it?'

He smiled, which she took to be the only agreement he could make. 'To exactly this point,' he said, 'and no . . . further.'

So there was something else he felt she should do? Solve the case, presumably, but surely she was nowhere near doing that tonight?

'The gods make long-term plans,' said Tock. 'There'll be some advantage to him involved.'

'Can't advantage sometimes be mutual?' asked Flamstead.

Costain stepped forwards to meet his gaze. 'You didn't have to hurt her. You could have been a lot more direct about all this.'

'Yes,' Flamstead agreed gleefully, 'I could.'

Ross couldn't help but feel saddened, maybe a bit used, but it still felt to her like Flamstead had been thinking of what she needed. Also, the whole experience, looking back, had been inside the anaesthetic of her lack of happiness. And come on, it had been a few good shags and some walks. Any sadness right now was of a beautifully limited nature, and there were roomfuls of happiness beside it, and she couldn't help but laugh again. She'd never known him properly. She'd shagged a god, and it hadn't been all that. On impulse, she kissed him properly, and he let her. He didn't mean it, though. Then with a wink at her about old times and a little ruffle of air, he was gone.

She looked to Costain and he met her gaze. Now she could see clearly the suffering that was going on behind that face. It looked like he was holding her responsible.

Sefton was too knackered to drive back home, so he texted Joe and lay down on Quill's sofa. Across the room from him, Moriarty was glaring at him, his fingers formed into a steeple, his back hunched forwards, plotting, or pretending to plot. When they'd all retired, Sefton had wondered if this creation would follow Quill up to bed, but scheming somewhere nearby seemed to be the iconic look Moriarty was going for, rather than glaring down at a married couple. Sefton was sure Sarah was glad about that. He wondered if the two of them would get any sleep, or if Quill would feel he had to keep muttering his new mantra. At least Jimmy was home now.

He found that Moriarty sitting there gave him an idea. He got out his phone. If the immense, misguided belief of one brain could generate a Moriarty, then couldn't something similar, with more people involved, do something to help their cause? He found the email addresses for the three production companies involved in the Holmes series and began to write. 'Time,' he said to them, 'to make your fanbase very worried.'

In the early hours of Sunday morning, Ross lay on the bed of her hotel room. Her sheer relief at being able to feel happy was keeping her awake.

She heard a sound from outside her door and went to the spyhole to see what it was. There was Costain, pacing outside her room. He was going back and forth, a focused, utterly obsessed look on his face. If they hadn't been shown his credentials, security would surely have come for him by now. This was so extraordinarily unlike him. Her first impulse was to open the door and tell him to go away, or at least to talk to her, but she was too scared of that look on his face, of what he might be capable of. She was amazed they'd now got to a place where she could think of him like that. What did this jealous, possessive man, desperately trying to hold himself together, have to do with the person who'd hurt her terribly by making tough, decisive choices? This person was seeing her as an object he wanted to possess. That person had been focused on the needs of others, and had hurt her, whom he'd truly loved, as a result.

The comparison had said it to her, and her newfound happiness agreed: the old Costain really had loved her.

She sat down, her mind going back to what Flamstead had said. He'd wanted her to get her happiness back. He also wanted her to do something more. But he felt he'd already done everything necessary to . . .

She suddenly had an entirely new idea in her head, a horrifying one, an enormous one, formed out of connections she'd already seen, but hadn't put in context before. She saw it whole, at once, every part of the hypothesis. It made her slowly lower her hands to the bedclothes and grasp them in horror and exultation. She finally knew who she'd been playing against. It was what she had been missing, what they had all been missing, and it had been in front of her all the time.

TWENTY-SIX

Monday morning. Sefton parked up beside the Portakabin and was surprised, even pleasantly so, to see all three familiar cars already there. He walked cautiously up the steps, but before he could open the door, it had burst open, and Ross ran into his arms, hugging him . . . and laughing!

He stared at her, amazed, not letting himself believe it, had to step back from her. 'Hey! What happened?!'

'I'll tell you all about it,' she whispered. 'But I came out here mostly to say big stuff is going down this morning and I'll need you to back me up, OK? No questions. Don't say anything.'

'OK,' he said, now worried as well as bemused. She led him inside, and there was Quill, still shaking, a cup of tea beside him, and with him Moriarty. Costain seemed to have accepted the presence of the sketchy, dark shape completely, pacing, tense, but not giving the creation a moment's attention.

'So . . . yesterday morning, you told me that you'd started doing something . . . that might progress the investigation,' said Quill to Sefton, not his old self by any means, but trying to lead. From the looks on Ross and Costain's faces, they'd already tried to have a joyful reunion with him and quickly found themselves feeling like Sefton, that Quill shouldn't have come back so soon. The atmosphere in the room was well weird, not matching the slight hope he felt at them all being together again.

'Yeah,' Sefton said, 'and with the support of the three Holmes productions' social media departments, it's really taken off. It should get even bigger today, now we're past the weekend. They've each let it slip to their fans that one, or all, of their Watsons might be killed off.'

'And of course,' said Ross, 'that's generated a lot more media interest than the deaths of all these real people.'

'Of course. So there's now a lot of London memory space being devoted to Watson. That interest, getting London to remember him, could act as a hook when we next try to summon him.'

'I've tried to talk to Lofthouse.' Quill sounded as if he hadn't listened to what Sefton had just said. 'She's not back at work. Her office says she fell ill at a conference and is staying with a friend. What else have we got?'

Sefton listened with interest to Ross and Costain's report about the occult London conference. Interest and annoyance. Something from his speciality and they'd gone off on their own? He made himself keep a poker face, which turned into a genuine smile as Ross got to the bit about how she'd got her happiness back. She'd asked him, a few moments ago, not to ask awkward questions, so he didn't. Also pleasing was the idea of a culture who'd provided them with a few indications of interest in offering leads, who'd expressed the start of a grudging interest in being policed by consent. 'We also,' said Ross, 'heard about another site where Ballard left artefacts that might—'

'We did?' said Costain.

'I meant . . .' Ross looked suddenly awkward. 'I forgot to tell you. It was one of . . . you know . . . one of those things Gilbert . . .'

'It's OK,' Costain said quickly, as if protecting her virtue.

Ross took a piece of paper from her pocket and handed it to Sefton. On it was written, 'Don't let anyone else see this.

Pretend it's an address. Say you'll go over later.' He kept his expression steady and pocketed the paper. 'Right. I'll go over there later.'

'There's meant to be a few things we might be able to use, including some sort of hat that lets the wearer see through all pretences. But not that item Ballard talked about that can find people. I think Gilbert really wanted us to go get this stuff.'

'How's the "Resident Patient" scenario going?' asked Quill. He'd been muttering his couple of sentences about himself under his breath at intervals. Sefton could see him holding on, and it was about just holding on.

'Uniforms haven't reported anything unusual around Brook Street this weekend,' said Ross. 'Jimmy, how would you feel if I laid out suggestions for what our aims should be today?' She started making a list on the board. Costain was to go down to Brook Street and liaise with the uniforms; Sefton was to leave Ross and Quill instructions for what needed to be assembled for the summoning of Watson, then go to the address she'd given him.

'On it,' said Costain, and headed out.

'OK,' said Ross, 'moving forward . . .' Then she paused, as if waiting for something. Sefton heard the sounds of Costain getting into his car, starting it up, driving off. He looked to Ross, puzzled. Her expression had suddenly changed. 'Follow him!' she yelled. She grabbed a bag from beside her chair and shoved Sefton towards the door. 'Quickly!'

'What's going on?' Quill called from the back seat. Sefton was driving at high speed, just about keeping Costain's car in sight. Costain was moving fast, ignoring the lights, which, thank Christ, turned to green just as Sefton got to them. Moriarty had just flashed into existence beside Quill, Sefton saw in his mirror.

'If we lose sight of him,' said Ross, 'that's our only chance gone. If that happens, we call the uniforms, get warrants across the board, get them to search every building near Brook Street, but I think by then we'll be too late.'

Sefton shifted gears and found himself weaving in and out of traffic to follow the car way ahead.

'Too late for what? Why are we chasing bloody *Costain*?' Quill sounded like he was questioning reality again.

'You think, what, someone's controlling him?' asked Sefton.

'Listen,' said Ross, 'this is what I've worked out. We've been assuming we're after a team of criminals, but if I'm right, that's not the case. Just about everything we thought we knew is wrong.'

As Sefton and Quill listened, at first incredulous, then horrified, Ross told them about her theory.

Costain drove north, crossed the Thames over Vauxhall Bridge, up Park Lane and round Speaker's Corner. The traffic stopped him from losing them. To Sefton's relief, he hadn't shown any sign of trying to, was hopefully unaware of them following. He did indeed seem to be heading for Brook Street, which made sense, thought Sefton, with what Ross was telling them. What she said made keeping him in sight terrifyingly urgent. Costain parked not on the street itself, but turned to enter Brook's Mews nearby. Sefton left his car in a non-existent space on Davies Street, the front end up on the pavement, police logbook in the window, and they got out and ran to the corner.

'If he's going to liaise with the uniforms,' said Ross, 'he'll head this way for the control van.' She looked round the corner, and Sefton could hear the tension in her voice. 'Go on, go on . . .' Shoppers were walking past them, glancing curiously at them. 'Oh, you beauty. Come on!'

She led them at speed to a door on the mews, what looked to be a private home with the black door of a garage beside it. Sefton took the stick of walkthrough that Ballard had used in the bank raid and drew with one long sweep the rough oval of a door. Quill dived at it so hard that if it hadn't worked, he'd have injured himself. Sefton and Ross were right behind him. They heard shouts not from the stairwell, not from the kitchen, but from a door that must lead to the garage. Quill, as if desperate to be decisive about something, threw himself forwards.

The three of them rushed into the garage space to witness an extraordinary sight. Costain spun from where he stood beside a chair. There was a noose above, tied to a beam on the roof. He'd been about to kick the chair away and kill his prisoner, who stood there helplessly, his hands tied.

The prisoner was also Tony Costain.

TWENTY-SEVEN

Ross pulled the knife she always carried and leaped forwards to cut the rope.

Quill rushed at the figure by the chair, but that Costain was too fast, throwing himself against and through a wall that already had a door drawn on it in chalk. Quill attempted to follow, but bounced off the wall with a shout of pain. 'He's got something to switch that off!' he yelled.

Sefton got to the door, but, looking up and down the street, there was no sign of where the other Costain had gone. By the time he got back down to the garage, Quill and Ross were helping what Sefton took to be the real Costain down from the chair. He was panting with shock, a look of abject horror on his face. He'd lost a lot of weight; his cheekbones were stark. 'You found me,' he whispered, looking as if they might vanish at any moment.

'When did they take you?' asked Ross. Concern and awkwardness were mixed in her expression.

'The *Lone Star*. Those bastards . . . put me in a crate. I was in there for days. He only opened it up in here. Where are we?'

'Brook Street. Did he make you recite some lines from Sherlock Holmes?'

'Yeah. Just the other day. He used one of those electrical

stunners to threaten me. I went along with it, didn't see why not.'

Ross sat him down and took his hands in hers. She calmed him when he jumped as Moriarty flashed into existence in the room, reassured him that he was with Quill. 'The guy who held you captive was someone who can create impossibly perfect disguises. We thought we were looking at a team of criminals, but he was every one of them, even the native and the old lady. He's someone who gets freaked out by sex and romance, who knows detectives can get lost in meaningless clues and endless connections. But he knows nothing about astronomy, not enough to successfully plant a clue about it, anyway. Plus, he's got form for faking his own death.'

The man stood panting in the alley. He would need to quickly find somewhere to change his appearance yet again. He carried all that was required on him. He was looking at himself in a puddle, examining his now slightly tattered appearance. He had always seen himself as the man, singular, the consciousness about which all else orbited. Now, however, he was so many, and it burdened him so much. He had so little time left to use the chance that had been given him, his only chance to be free to carry on serving. This fallen London he found himself in now felt like Hell, but he knew it was real. So many criminals, degenerates, suspicious foreigners, so much that was new and contradictory forcing its way into his head. Where was meaning? Where could one begin one's deductions? By finding oneself. But finding oneself, for him, was absurdly difficult. He must continue to try, though, for only then could he help others. He would have to activate his back-up plan, quickly find his next selected victim.

He grabbed at his face and pulled from himself the ridiculously excellent mask he could inhabit so well in this protean form. Underneath, he was cycling still between all those different selves that demanded him to be them. He would triumph over them, he yelled silently at all the images. He would become himself once more, no matter how much death and duplicity it took. No matter how many men he had to kill.

He was, and would always be, Sherlock Holmes.

The great detective tried fruitlessly to calm himself and, with a cry of desperation, raced off into the streets that now so perplexed him.

TWENTY-EIGHT

Lofthouse no longer knew how long she'd been stumbling through the dark. It must now surely be Monday. She had no idea how long Sally Rutherford's interest in duplicity would keep her own lies going. Perhaps Peter was already suffering; perhaps he was already dead. She put that thought out of her head as she inched along, unseeing. She couldn't go back, so she had to keep going. She thought she could see the faintest change in light ahead, but maybe that was her eyes playing tricks. Her body kept telling her she needed medical attention, but she was past the point where she felt her life mattered. She had managed, despite the pain in her chest, to squat to shit against the wall, yelling as she slid down, yelling as she stood again. She'd had to lie against the angle of the rock for several minutes afterwards, controlling her breathing, before she could continue. The only thing that led her was the tug of the key. It didn't care what her physical condition was.

She realized the path she was on had started to head downwards, and she felt the shape of a step. Then another, a clean one, cut in the rock. The key grew more insistent. She managed to make good, slow progress down them. She could hear something moving, smell a new freshness, feel a new cold on her face. Was she nearing a large body of water? It would be stagnant down here, wouldn't it? No, it might be an underground river. There was definitely light ahead, far below, and as her eyes adjusted, she realized just how far the steps descended. She kept herself flat against the wall, one foot down, then the other, shuffling like a crab, in pain with each step. If she fell now, that'd be it. The stairwell felt enclosed: she couldn't fall off, but if she fell down, she'd be a useless heap at the bottom. The light was round the corner at the bottom, a clear light, illuminating the last few steps. She got to the bottom and slid round the wall.

It was an ancient, dusty light bulb, fixed to the rock ceiling in a white mount, with no sign of any cable. She found she was laughing. She felt like the laugh might become a sob and stopped herself. Round the corner at the bottom of the steps, the cave opened out. Keeping against the wall, she hobbled to see more. Inside this cathedral of a space, the roof of which rose out of sight, there was an enormous lake, which again extended back further than she could see. There was a rocky beach on this side of it, which swept round out of sight. The steps opened up at the edge of the beach, water lapping at their base. Further along, she could see other cave entrances.

Closer to her, formed out of the beach, was a sort of barrow, a rounded shape that looked like it rose out of the rock. The presence of human artefacts in this space that had been formed by nature spoke to Lofthouse of ritual, like the deep caves where archaeologists found drawings and remains.

Before she investigated anything, she needed water. The key was tugging urgently at her wrist, agreeing with her. She should get to the lake. She swung the bag on her shoulder to balance her and set off from the wall, hobbling on legs like stilts across the shale. This body of water might flow down further into the earth, or it might be a reservoir.

These deductions appeared in her mind uselessly. How many small humans had found themselves in places like this and had meaningless thoughts? She was as alone as someone on the moon, with less hope of getting home.

No, don't let your big thoughts flatten you, human. Body first. Water first.

She thought about how to sit, and did so, hissing between her teeth as she lowered herself to the cold stones at the very shore. She was already cold through to her core. She put her hands into the water, lifted it to her mouth and drank, slowly, then blissfully. The water tasted strange, like it was full of exotic minerals, but that didn't matter. Was it making her feel a little . . . drunk? That must be the dehydration. It was still the best thing she'd ever—

She turned at a sudden sound.

The rocks had moved. She could see nothing along the silent, illuminated beach. Then more sounds; she could hear them but couldn't see them. She'd expected to encounter something she couldn't see, that she would have needed the Sight to see, but shit, not here, now, when she was so vulnerable. She rolled from the water, scrabbled to get the gun out of her bag, fumbled to get the cartridges into it, made herself concentrate on doing that, rather than on the sound of something . . . a number of things . . . running at her now.

She'd readied the gun. She stood, bracing it, looking around helplessly for a target. The sounds were almost on her. Her training and experience made it extremely difficult for her to fire randomly. Unconsciously, she took a step back, preparing to do just that, her finger pulling on the trigger.

Her foot found a sudden absence of support.

She toppled towards the water. Her other foot missed the edge and she plunged down into the lake.

The sudden deep cold hit her. She felt like she was going to die.

She desperately held on to the gun. She hadn't taken a breath. The pitch-dark water was going up her nose. It was deep, so close to shore. A reservoir, not a lake, thought her monkey brain. Pain yelling through her she saw light above. She had nearly lost sight of which direction life was in. She pushed up towards it. She wasn't going to make it. She was too weak. She had to take a breath. Her muscles screamed.

She hauled water into her lungs. No, not water, not all of it. There was something else too, something even more terrifying. It was rushing into her head.

She burst out onto the surface, but she wondered giddily for a moment if she was in a different place. She'd surfaced in a new world. Standing on the shore, bellowing at her were . . . What were they?

Three enormous pigs. Giant albino hogs with combs of wire hair along their backs, blazing pink eyes and sharp tusks. She felt them, somehow, as much as she saw them. She felt their strength, how much this was their home. She hacked hard, water bursting from her lungs. She stumbled forwards, in great pain.

The ceiling above her was illuminated by garlands of golden braid, leading upwards into infinity. The water she was in, full of gold and silver, streamed impossibly upward too, a river that defied her sense of perspective. She was immersed in it. It was inside her. Yelling, she made herself get to her feet. She was covered in silver. She could feel it running from her eyes and nose and mouth. The sense of weight, of presence, of where she was, was suddenly huge.

She realized what had happened, what this had all been about. She had been immersed in the river and gained the Sight.

The pigs bellowed again and her attention snapped back to them. They didn't seem to want to get close to the water. Lucky her. One of them made a swift foray forwards. OK, they were hungry enough to risk it. In a moment, they'd decide it was worth coming at her. She shook the tension out of her hand from where she'd been gripping the gun so hard. She was shivering so fiercely, the cold as far inside her as the Sight was now. She raised the gun, made sure to aim. She found the trigger. She would squeeze lightly. She wanted to keep one shot. She only hoped that the water hadn't ruined the gun or the cartridges. Were such things designed to be waterproof? It certainly felt dependable to her now, its invincibility and potency flaring golden in her hands.

The pigs ran at her. She squeezed.

One of the pigs flew backwards, blown apart. The other two creatures screamed and fled, afraid of another shot, down the beach, down one of the other tunnels and away, their shrieks fading. Thank God. Thank God they had been animals.

Lofthouse stumbled up the beach. The key was still tugging at her wrist, she realized. It wanted her to head towards the barrow. Shelter would be good.

The barrow was made of rock, but there was a metal door to it. On it was a bronzed lock that looked to her now to be momentous and historic and secure against anything. This was a lock and she had a key. She found it on her wrist, and it was willing. She put the key in the lock and turned. She felt the key die, spent, its mission accomplished. The door swung open.

Inside, the barrow was illuminated by another impossible light bulb. There was a rough table, upon which sat a book, a row of pegs on the wall and two stools. That was all there was. It was, however, much warmer in here, as if the bulb could provide that much heat.

Lofthouse went to the book and opened it. It was an ancient volume, a binding of older documents, medieval manuscripts that showed people being immersed in the water, of it flooding specifically into their mouths and their noses, to the point where the figures panicked and cried out. Latin tags explained what was going on. Lofthouse didn't need much in the way of explanations. She'd just lived through it. She'd breathed in the water. Drowning in it was the only way one got the Sight.

She picked up the book and put it in her bag.

She sighed to herself, picked up one of the stools, took it to the door of the barrow and sat down. Here she had the warmth, but also the view of that magnificent cave and the impossible river that ran through it in many surreal directions.

So this was all the key had wanted. It was something enormous, to be sure, but, as far as she could see, it wasn't a way to help Peter. She was sure she had done something that whatever had possessed her husband would not want her to, but that was a double-edged sword. If she managed to get back home, how could she conceal this?

She realized that against the dripping silence of the cave, she could hear something. Sounds were coming from the stairwell. Sounds of movement. Someone was stepping calmly, confidently, down it. Someone whose mere presence suddenly, like a great shadow falling over her, felt more enormous and frightening than anything she'd seen in these caverns.

She stood up to see more clearly. A real shadow now stretched from the stairwell. The darkness of the shadow seemed to change the beach where it fell, infesting it, polluting it. What was coming had never been here before. She felt a strange sense of connection to what was coming and realized that the Sight was telling her of things she couldn't naturally know.

It was telling her that what was coming had followed her down here.

He stepped into the light. A nondescript man in a suit. He was smiling at her. Something about his face reminded her of the expression of her possessed husband.

He brought up his hands and began to clap.

She understood now. She had thought she had found the map despite him, but it was because he had wanted her to. He couldn't have got to it, hidden as it had been. He had motivated her to come on this quest in order to follow her and find what was down here.

As she watched, he took from his jacket a bottle. It reeked of decay. Its foulness was indicated by colours that leaped from it into her eyes, and a hiss like a firework about to go off. The Sight illuminated so much extra meaning. He turned from her and headed calmly towards the reservoir. He was going to put that into the water, she realized. He was here to poison it.

'You'll have been watching me,' she called to the figure, 'so you must know about this gun I've got.' She pulled it from her bag once more, found the trigger, brought the gun to her shoulder and aimed it at his back. 'If you weren't certain it couldn't hurt you, you wouldn't have let me keep it.' She could feel his mockery from here, from the angle of his shoulders as he started to bend. She felt how meaningless he thought her to be, just a pawn he'd duped. All that cruelty to the man she loved, just for this trick. 'That's the logical deduction, isn't it? That this can't hurt you, so I won't fire.'

Something in the sound of her voice made him pause and turn to look back at her.

'I think,' she said, 'that if I've got this gun, I should bloody well use it.'

She squeezed the trigger. The Smiling Man was blasted off his feet.

He landed out in the water. The bottle landed with him. Something broke as he hit. The bottle, yes – that evil erupted, corrupted the water; there was no stopping that – but something else broke, hard.

She'd broken his concentration. It wasn't the shot that had done it, but the impact of what he'd fallen into. The Sight had rushed into a being who was so in control, who had everything balanced on a knife edge. What had Sefton told her about erased memories? That it took enormous energy and concentration on someone's part to keep people from remembering? She could feel the letting go, the tremendous size of what he'd let go. It took a moment to fall from his grasp, to drop back into the world. Here was the shadow of it falling on her; here was the enormity of it, coming at her—

She remembered.

TWENTY-NINE

Five years ago

'Has it never occurred to you,' said the smiling politician, 'how odd a thing the placebo effect is?'

The crowd laughed. Chartres was there among them. He looked around, surprised. But he shouldn't be surprised.

'No, seriously! A doctor gives you a pill and, with all his authority, tells you it's going to cure you. And simply because you believe that, it does. Even if it's just chalk.'

The crowd was now a little more quiet. Perhaps he was trying to reach for a serious point. They didn't like that so much. Chartres nodded at the interesting conjecture.

'That suggests a relationship between the mind and the physical world that should stagger you with its implications. But it doesn't, because you're used to it. Imagine that applied to physics. The airliner you're in is falling out of the sky, but the captain calls from the flight deck and tells you it's not . . . and so, suddenly, it's not.'

The crowd looked questioningly at each other and waited for the politician to draw some sort of conclusion. But he just sighed at them, because they didn't yet understand. 'Thankfully,' he said, 'you've all got an appointment with me.'

*

Then he woke up.

Sir Richard Chartres, RIBA, KCBE, opened his eyes, sat up and started to laugh at the ridiculousness of his dream. He reached for his journal, contained in the old satchel he kept beside the bed. In the old days, whenever the satchel wore out, he would purchase a new one of exactly the same design. But they'd stopped making those, so currently his satchel had holes in it and his books kept falling out. When he'd finished noting down the dream, with some extra annotations concerning his own silliness, he went over to the window of his grace-and-favour apartment in Golders Green. He was allowed to live here rent-free for life because, as with so many things, that was just how the world ticked along. He opened the curtains and looked out at another beautiful sunrise in London. There was nothing at all to worry about.

He had an appointment this evening.

The meeting chamber stood at the end of the garden annexe, a hundred paces to the east of the De Souza and Raymonde skyscraper in Rotherhithe. Everyone commented on how different in style the chamber was to its parent building, but nobody, Chartres was sure, not even all the prize-winning architects who passed it while walking across the courtyard between the tall shadows, could identify exactly what that style was.

It could have been a relic from when Rotherhithe was still proper docklands, when there were warehouses and pulleys and damp brickwork. But it would have stood out as looking old then too. It was low and square, with a dome gleaming so white that it looked like it had never been rained on. That was because it hadn't.

To get to the door of the meeting chamber, Chartres had to pass through the rest of the 'Dessandarr' building – these days, a nightmare of open-plan workspaces – and then go out under the canopy, with its visible cable supports, into the 'Space for Free Thought', with its water feature and sundial. The chamber stood awkwardly at the end of all that, not relating to it, but connected by a gravel path. Chartres, as a young man, had once felt part of the firm, merely seconded to this strange assignment. Nowadays, even as a full partner, this strange assignment took up all his time, and the firm was something through which he was obliged to walk. To get into the meeting chamber, one had to be a member of the De Souza and Raymonde Continuing Projects Team. Each member of the CPT had been given, by Chartres, a key to the meeting chamber, cut from his original, itself made smooth by centuries of handling.

It was Halloween tonight, Chartres thought as he approached the little building, the old key in his hand. What a lovely smell of winter in the air.

Inside the chamber, the illumination came from a cubic lantern/window in the centre of the ceiling dome. When it rained outside, the light cascaded down the four walls like those present were encased in a genie's lamp.

The chamber smelt of the old books that were stored under the floor. The shelves were made of wood polished only by age, otherwise kept pristine by the precise climate inside the chamber. They were accessed by tugging on a loop of rope to slam open a slab of the stone flooring, then cranking a metal lever fixed on a post. The wooden shelves would rise up out of depths, notch by notch. The crank needed special oil to keep it running smoothly, which was kept in a special oil flask.

Files of maps and index cards were kept under other floor slabs, on great spindles that were eased out from underneath through a spinning action. The initial heave took some doing, but there was a knack to it, rather like that of pulling on a bell rope. Chartres could send the stacks flying towards the ceiling with a ratcheting sound, and also stop them, at a touch of his elbow.

Each of the five members of the team had a place at the round stone table in the centre of the meeting chamber. The table top was etched so that each position had two fine diagonal lines leading to it. The table had been made smooth by use, shaped by the hands of Chartres's predecessors.

The floor was made of the same granite, and remained rougher than the table surface. The same pattern was inscribed under the table as was on it. Every chair was different, made of old oak, fashioned in Rennes, specially to suit the body shape of each team member. The journey to Brittany on the Eurostar, to be measured and complimented on one's posture, and fed fine wine and cheese by those who knew of the debt the world owed to these fine upholders of tradition, was one of the perks of the job. Nobody would ever even mention money in connection to any of this. Similarly, new members were first prepared with the right words and gestures made over them in this building, then taken deep under the earth, for a ceremonial procession through some picturesque caverns that was, with typical melodrama, called 'the ordeal', before being baptised in the river of gold and silver, and thus given the Sight. There, words were said over them in Latin. Chartres knew the linguistic meaning, but not the significance. That had been lost. The Sight was what made them special. The ceremonial pouring of a handful of water into their mouths and noses gave them a sort of vague sixth sense, a slight difference in how they saw the world. More importantly, that gave them the ability to see what they were doing when they used word and gesture to do miraculous things within London. The great book that stood in the barrow made the process look a lot worse than it was. It called the whole ceremony, ridiculously, 'the drowning'. The progress down there took so long that Chartres was glad he'd only ever presided over the blessing of one such newcomer. The Sight these days seemed a pale thing compared to what their predecessors had described. Chartres put that nagging thought from his mind now. Perhaps it was just that in this modern age, there was less for the Sighted to see.

For most of its existence, which stretched back, under various names, over at least a thousand years, the Continuing Projects Team had assembled in this meeting chamber on one evening each week. In the last six months, they had taken to meeting every night, but obviously that situation wouldn't persist.

The team was not chosen by a human being, but by a protocol. When any member of the team died, usually of old age, the protocol was read out, which produced a name, in letters on small stone tiles, taken from a bag, and a location. The chair of the team (since 1968 Chartres himself) then set off to find that person, who always turned out to be from the same field of expertise as the former member. Then there would follow a somewhat difficult conversation, mitigated by an excellent lunch, whereupon the chosen one always, it was said, turned out to be interested in taking up the post. They always turned out to be people of the right sort, with accents, manners and modes of dress that allowed them access to the corridors of power. Chartres knew from his reading that centuries ago the bag had been given to a commoner, for them to pick the tiles, that some of his predecessors had said that those who held the bag influenced the identity of the candidate. That didn't seem to be a problem, though. The current system was working out excellently. Like so many things the team used, someone might once have known how that protocol worked. But theirs was no longer to reason why. The interior mechanics of the ways of the world were often great mysteries, and their business was no different.

The five members of the team represented the five foundations of civilization: academia, law, government, the media and the Church. The longest-serving member was always the chair, who, as a partner in the firm, had to at least pass muster as a professional architect. Apart from him, the current team included: Patrick Kennet-Fotherington, LLB, a criminal defence lawyer from a firm in Chancery Lane; Felicity Saunders, the permanent secretary at the Home Office; Adam Fletcher, senior producer of current affairs at the BBC; and Rev. Michael Watson, chaplain of King's College, London.

The team also regularly consulted with people on the ground, in the various London institutions, who knew the truth about what they did tangentially, in smaller or larger doses depending on their prestige or position. They had a particularly useful connection in Scotland Yard. Chartres had shown the officer in question, one Rebecca Lofthouse, whom he regarded as a friend, around the meeting chamber. He had demonstrated their equipment and operational approaches to her. She had kept visiting, here or even at his home in Golders Green, bringing leads to anything inexplicable from her own line of work. She seemed to prefer to do it in person, not wanting a paper trail. She was, he suspected, hoping to glimpse something of the unseen world. It was a pity that since she was not a member of the team, he couldn't gift her with the Sight.

He sat down at the table in the meeting chamber and laid out his pens and notepad, as he always did. Before the others arrived, he used the Lud Vanes to check on how everything was ticking over. The Diana Prime felt like it was pumped impossibly high, while only yesterday all had seemed fine. He next tried the Vanes over a map and found the DP was hitting the Apollo Prime head-on at the Eye . . . whatever all that actually meant.

What it amounted to was that there would be mummified cats whispering up chimneys tonight. There would be telephone calls from the dead. There would be fatal collisions between long-lost twins driving the same model of car. This sort of thing had been happening quite often lately. It was irritating. Never before had they had to sort out so many inconveniences at once. At this time last year, the biggest problem had concerned the Wetherspoons chain buying up another old pub, renaming and redeveloping it, and even that had been a simple matter of balancing things based on the standard layout of the new building. Until very recently, the 'terrible things' that were supposed to be 'out there in the dark', if they existed at all, had stayed there. (The majority of the team had always said they believed such things to be metaphors for the consequences of bad civic planning.) But perhaps now that was changing. It would have been enough to make any lesser man slightly worried. Chartres now put the Vanes away, and as the others arrived, he made sure to look calm and methodical. He called the meeting to order, and they sat down at their designated places round the table.

As he looked at the steady, wry faces of his team, a little amazed that they were back here yet again tonight, Chartres blinked at a sudden mental image: a surgeon, with hands wobbling, something going wrong in the middle of the operation, blood spilling on the stone of the table. They were his hands and his shakiness. He even saw the table split in two.

He managed a smile. What was he thinking? There was no credible record of anyone ever having any sort of foreknowledge about events in London. Whatever was going on, they could deal with it. He called for order again, just for form's sake. But, as he did so, there was a sudden sound from outside. A muffled crash and then childish laughter. Sniggering arrogance. For the third night in a row, youths were hanging about in the court-yard between the skyscrapers. 'Penny for the guy', that would be their latest excuse. Security hadn't so far been able to appre-hend anyone.

Chartres sighed. 'Let's look at London tonight, shall we?' He went over to the wall and inclined his head slightly. The light changed as the lantern/window in the dome above moved into the correct position. Chartres moved his hands into a pleading shape to match with the new angle, as he had so many times before, and vast shadows flapped across the walls as some-thing huge and real settled across the room.

An instant later, it was laid out on the stone table, the greatest privilege his team enjoyed: the entirety of the two cities of London and Westminster, and all the surrounding boroughs of Greater London, wrapped round the river, and standing solid on the stone. This display was produced by a 'rare visual protocol'. The records gave no indication of what 'rare' meant, but the vision portrayed the real thing, the actual place, at this very moment. Chartres, or any of them, could reach down with a finger, and make the buildings grow huge around them, and pass right through them. They could only observe, however, using this protocol, not make anything happen.

At this hour, the city was illuminated only by the lights of the buildings themselves, rather than by the small representation of the sun that would have been visible on the wall of the chamber for any daytime scene. The brake lights of tiny vehicles glowed on the streets. Tiny aircraft, stacked in spirals above Heathrow and Gatwick and London City airport, blinked red and green, while orbiting sublimely through the heads of the team. The entire vision was full of movement. It didn't display artefacts of artificial vision, flares and wobbles, like a camera view would. Instead, it felt actual, alive.

Chartres flicked the air with his finger, and now they could see the grid displayed across the buildings. It was an indication of potentialities, of where things might happen. It was a mesh of white lines, as was used in modelling buildings. In an area where only the normal laws of physics applied, it would be flat, the lines evenly spaced. In the midst of the sort of extreme architectural problems that sometimes concerned the team, it could be warped into extraordinary shapes. Nevertheless, it was still vaguely based on natural geography. Therefore, looking only at the grid, one would still have been able to tell where the Thames was, where the smaller rivers ran and the basic shape of the hills and valleys and underground features. Population density tugged on it too, presumably because more people meant more buildings.

As the grid appeared this time, he felt the others react at the same moment he did. The grid was horribly stretched, like some enormous weight was pushing down on it. Everything was leaning towards one particular point. 'It's like a whole new borough has moved into place,' Chartres said, trying to sound merely interested. 'Outside the map, but . . . influencing it.'

'That's not possible,' said Saunders calmly.

'Of course. You're right, obviously.' He wished he felt as confident as he sounded. It was absurd, but he was actually getting nervous. He recalled his nightmare. What had the man said? Something about the opposite of the placebo effect, that if you believe something bad will happen . . . he saw again his vision of the broken table, and the blood. He pulled himself together. 'Let's see what's at ground zero, shall we?' He made a tapping gesture in the air, and London reared up at them again, and they were standing in a street in what turned out to be Paddington, in the early evening dark.

People nearby were none the wiser about the team's presence. They swarmed like ants between the station, the snack bars, the rows of cheap lodgings, the gleaming monoliths of the big hotels. There were full litter bins, and piles of discarded cardboard outside cut-price electronics shops. There was a feeling of pleasurable expectation in the air. It would soon be Christmas.

'We'll approach the epicentre slowly,' Chartres said, ignoring a man selling chestnuts as he walked through him. 'If this is a real effect, and not some error in the model, we'll need to do something about it.' And who better placed for that than the five of them, the quiet hands upon the rudders, from all five branches of the establishment? Chartres calmed himself. There was nothing London's hidden architects could not look into, define or fix.

They came to the central point where most pressure was being put on the grid. It was a pub at the corner of two enormous traffic thoroughfares. The pub itself was one of those deeply British concoctions whose facade reminded one of so many cultural reference points: the keel of a man-of-war; a music-hall bill poster; a decorative cash register. So many signifiers, each one of them pointing to another golden thread of British life. To look at a pub, to look at any building, was to see meaning made flesh. This pub was cut off from any neighbours, the buildings behind it having been demolished. There was a wire fence round the brownfield site, and a sign announcing construction. In the sky above it, the grid was being tugged down in ominous, heavy arcs. Something huge was waiting for them inside.

Like they owned the place, like they were really physically in this street, they marched in through the wall.

They found themselves in what could still be called a parlour. It contained photographs and items on the wall that genuinely belonged to the history of this building, rather than having been chosen by some design office at the brewery because of their carefully meaningless eccentricity. Deep russet wallpaper, the gold highlights faded to black with old smoke. Somebody's trumpet with dents in it. The floor was swept clean, but the boards were old, and in places nails had come away, and there would be a creaking noise near the burnished golden-green rail running along the bottom of the bar.

The pub was mostly filled with office workers, young men and women in suits, who had seized every table after having got out of work early for the weekend. They were still coming in, shrugging water off shoulders, folding umbrellas, pushing their way towards the bar. Chartres noted Eastern European construction workers, an Indian man and his wife eating either a very late lunch or an early dinner.

Chartres's people split up, moved as phantoms between the customers. It was Watson who first noticed something unusual. He called them over to where he was studying a photograph on a wall. It was of some explorers, sometime at the turn of the previous century. They looked happy and shaven, with piles of provisions and equipment on the dog sleds behind them, every inch the sons of Empire about to set off into the wilderness. Watson put his finger on the picture.

'Watson,' he said, touching the chest of one man. The name was indeed written in longhand, in faded ink, under the picture together with all the other names. He slid his finger down diagonally to the left. 'Fletcher.' Across the middle row to the right. 'Chartres.' Up diagonally to the left. 'Kennet-Fotherington.' Then down diagonally to the bottom. 'Saunders.' He turned to look at them and met their astonished gazes. Under the picture was written one word, in the same longhand.

History.

'Does it mean us?' whispered Fletcher.

Chartres felt a knot in his stomach. 'This isn't about architecture,' he said. 'This is enemy action.' He headed back into the middle of the pub and the others followed. He was about to say something else, to try and find the words to calm his rising panic—

But then he bumped into someone. The man's glass went flying. It hit the ground and shattered. The man spun and stared at him in shock. Chartres looked round and saw everyone in the pub was staring at them. They looked afraid, terrified. They started to yell, to scream, to back away.

'They're seeing us as ghosts . . . as the sort of things we prevent!' yelled Fletcher.

'The protocol,' said Saunders. 'It's been . . . What's that word?'

'Hacked,' said Chartres. 'The protocol's been hacked.' He didn't like the way the fear was building all around them. They were now contributing to what they had always previously merely observed. Where was all this fear *coming* from? It was like there was a reservoir of it lurking somewhere underneath everything, something that they had never dealt with.

History.

Chartres made a quick series of gestures, half expecting them to fail . . .

But they didn't. They were out of the pub instantly, and thankfully standing above London once again, looking down at it. In the same moment, they saw the grid burst upwards from that pub, like a trampoline being released. It was their being there that had set it off. Ripples raced out from it in concentric circles. Those ripples hit other waves within the grid and rebounded, set up interference patterns that bounced off the nearby buildings. There would be worse things out there tonight. Poltergeists and terrible ironies and bedroom visitors. But now . . . now all clearly motivated by an enemy. It was like a tune suddenly appearing out of white noise. Or maybe it was a voice.

This had never happened before. Or it had been happening for a long time and they had failed to notice. Chartres waved his arms. He kept waving and waving until they were higher and higher above the city, watching as the ripples and pulses within the grid resolved themselves into lines of coincidence and impossibility flashing outwards in a great star shape, building with every interaction . . .

'That's impossible,' said Kennet-Fotherington. 'Energy declines; it doesn't increase!'

'Oh,' said Watson, 'science. I had been thinking maybe one day we should employ a scientist.'

'Our enemy is pushing the wheel,' said Chartres, 'somehow adding energy to this. Whatever "energy" means in this case.'

He dropped his hands and they were back in the meeting chamber. They stood round the stone table.

'Do you think that photo in that pub is really there?' asked Saunders.

'I suspect,' said Chartres, 'that it's only there in this model of ours. Our enemy, whatever it is, has placed it there, as a sign that they have interfered, with this, and with who knows how many other protocols of ours.'

They stood silently, horrified by those implications. There came a noise from outside: that same high laughter. Chartres went to the intercom and called security. There was no answer. He turned back to the others. 'I had a dream—' he began.

Something slammed against the door.

Everyone stopped and looked in that direction. The impact came again, the door bulging inwards.

'My God,' said Fletcher.

They backed into the chamber, looking around for something to help them. Chartres stared at the door. He knew now that this had all been part of a plan, that whatever was out there, it wasn't children or criminals. Could the door hold?

The door burst off its hinges and fell into the room. Through the doorway strode a figure. It seemed to grow as it came, its feet treading imperiously on holy ground. It was only half formed. There were parts of it he couldn't see. It demanded something of him, wanting to be filled in. He tried to stop himself from filling in those details, because they were too terrible.

Saunders tried a defensive protocol, one not used in centuries. But what she was trying to say failed . . . or she got it wrong.

Chartres couldn't think of a single word to say. He had been told all of this in his dream, he realized, and yet had still come here.

The shape solidified for him, against his will. It was a smart, well-off-looking young man. Of course it was. He was smiling all over his face. Of course he was. He raised his hands into the position that caused the model on the table top to spring into life.

They were suddenly amid London again, and zooming in, zooming in, to Rotherhithe. To the De Souza and Raymonde skyscraper.

'No,' said Chartres. 'This is one of those things tradition tells us we must never do. We must not look at ourselves. We must not ever be part of what we observe. There isn't anything, when you look too closely, don't you understand? There isn't *anything*!'

But the model kept expanding. They flew towards the meeting chamber. Straight down at it, faster and faster.

'It's not about the map,' said Saunders, and with a start Chartres realized that she was saying words their enemy wanted to be said, with something like the same voice he'd heard in his dream. 'It's about what's underneath it. The time of abstractions

is past. Time itself is nearly over. What's inside the people you looked down upon from a great height is enormous, and it's terrifying, and you missed it. All things now tend towards *me*.'
She raised a hand to point towards the smiling man.

The man started to laugh. It turned out his laugh was the same high laugh as that of the youths outside.

Chartres felt that he was participating in a dream again, someone else's dream. All the history and information and power and tradition that his team had represented was about to vanish.

Their vision of London sped them into the wall of the meeting chamber . . . and through it, and there they all were. They were now standing among themselves. They couldn't help it; they looked. Chartres looked at himself, who was looking at himself, who was looking at himself. Those selves vanished to a terrifying collapsed point in the distance, a hole that he realized could look right back into him and—

He had a thought, just before the moment when all thought would be dragged out of his body and sent somewhere terrifying. That thought was about his duty. He had no hope. So it was time to activate the final protocol, the one that had been drummed into him by the last chair of the CPT, from his deathbed.

He put his hand into his satchel and found his key. He remembered the syllables he repeated every Thursday teatime and spoke them aloud, while making the gestures with his fingers. Suddenly, he was spinning gold thread from the air. He wrapped it swiftly round the key, a bundle of it, containing everything of the team, the pattern and the shape of them, a description of what the five of them did, how they fitted together, the news about what had happened tonight. It was a crude, desperate attempt to preserve their legacy.

He threw his hand open, and to his amazement, he made a solid thing vanish. The most he had ever done, right at the end. The key was gone.

Then he was overwhelmed, and made to see the entirety of himself, and was put in his place and made to halt. The nothing that he was now swallowed him.

Judgement passed over the building.

The Smiling Man stood at the centre of London. He spread his hands wide and drew his people and his monsters in from the darkness in which they had been exiled. The real London was coming back, alongside poverty and tuberculosis and history. The civilized consensus was over. The future was not going to happen. Tonight was just the start. He would have to do this many times, to keep the wheel turning backward and backward, widdershins. He opened his hands again, and for the first time in centuries, they were free.

The next morning, when the shadows were still short, people arrived for work in the courtyard between the high buildings. The cleaners arrived first, then the new shift of security people, who heard of nothing to report from the old shift, and then the workers themselves, and the visitors, some of whom looked across to the garden annexe and saw . . .

Nothing. Just bare pavement. Where there now actually stood a ruin. People were already walking among it like there was nothing there. It, and the people who once worked in it, had been forgotten.

THIRTY

Lofthouse couldn't move with the shock of the huge mass of new information that was suddenly inside her head. She had remembered everything, so much, so fast. She felt like she wanted to write it all down, but no, she didn't need to, she knew it. The whole history of her time advising the Continuing Projects Team . . . those were proper memories, those had happened to her. She remembered being charmed by his culture, and worried by how amateur the organization he ran seemed to be.

The new memories in her head, though, what she'd just seen, events she had not been present at, those were what had halted her. She found herself stumbling towards the barrow as the weight of it hit her. Where had this knowledge come from? From the key. She'd seen Chartres send it to her at the end, with that final gesture. It was that key on her charm bracelet, the one that had appeared that very same night under her pillow. It had been supposed to tell her all she needed to know, but then that attack on the Continuing Projects Team had erased them from everyone's memory. She'd been left only with the feelings the key gave her, a subconscious urge to create a new team to take their place.

There was a noise from behind her. She turned to see that the Smiling Man, the creature who, she now knew, had slaughtered her old friends, was rising slowly from the water. His smile remained fixed. She made eye contact with the thing. She wanted to say she and Quill's team would find a way to stop whatever its plans were. She wanted to say she was going to do whatever it took to bring justice to its victims.

Before she could say anything, the Smiling Man raised his hand in mocking salute and then vanished.

Lofthouse sagged with relief. She put the gun back into her bag. What had been in those cartridges? She might never know. She had to get back to the surface, to find out about Peter. She now remembered Chartres telling her of an easier route back up, of a flight of many steps. The ordeal, slight as it had been for his initiates, was meant to be over at this point.

Slowly, she hauled her pain-wracked body off across the beach towards one of those other entrances.

Tony Costain looked slowly around the Portakabin. The others had first taken him to see the doctor at Gipsy Hill, then, at his insistence, back here. He didn't want to go home and be alone and recover. He wanted to hear what had happened, to be with his colleagues again. They'd been putting food and drink in his hands since he'd emerged, blinking, into the light of Brook Street.

The man who'd kept Costain prisoner, who looked exactly like him, hadn't let slip any information about who he was or why he was doing this, although he had asked him a load of questions about Quill's team. Costain had refused to answer. He'd spent his time in captivity feeling weak, unable to summon the strength to fight back when his captor had taken him from his makeshift cage, put a pad of what must have been an anaesthetic over his face and dragged him to a waiting vehicle. The next thing he knew, his neck had been in a noose, and, miraculously, his friends had come bursting in. He couldn't offer any clues as to where he'd been kept. His captor had been meticulous.

'Yeah,' said Ross now, 'you'd kind of expect that.'

'Holmes can drive?' said Sefton.

'He can learn new skills very rapidly,' said Ross, 'and now there's the Internet.'

'If only we could put out a description,' said Sefton, 'for a bloke with a changing appearance who can do perfect disguises.'

'I'll tell them to throw uniforms into the area around Brook Street,' said Quill, 'and go house to house, get everyone aware of empty properties, who's doing what and where. It might slow Holmes down, at least.'

Costain still couldn't get his head round it. 'So I was held prisoner . . . by Sherlock Holmes?'

'Yeah,' said Ross, going to the ops board. 'So what is up here is a fuck ton of lies.' She started unpicking images and erasing lines. 'He gave himself away not by any specific clue, but by . . . how he behaved. Specifically towards me.'

'What?' Oh God, had he hurt her?

'Later for that. That was enough to bring a whole lot of odd little details colliding together in my head, after Flamstead hinted to me that I already had all I needed.'

'What, Gilbert Flamstead, the actor?'

Ross gave him a sad smile. Which was the greatest thing. 'You've missed a lot.'

'Yeah.' Costain turned to find Quill had sat down, calming himself by muttering something under his breath, Moriarty beside him. He looked across the way to see Sefton had gone to the kettle to make tea for them all. 'Thank you,' he said, loudly, 'all of you.'

'Biscuits,' said Sefton, and threw the packet over.

Costain caught it. 'What did he do when he was pretending to be me?'

'He played us,' said Ross.

He so wanted to talk to her. Just the two of them. Now wasn't the time. He went over to the board, where she was now writing frantically, and the others joined him there.

'He faked his own death,' she said, 'to remove himself from suspicion. He created that orgy of evidence to distract us, not only from Watson, but from the idea that he might not be dead. He also planted clues so that if we saw beyond that, we might get diverted into the blind alley of thinking our prime suspect was Moriarty.'

Moriarty made an impatient noise and flounced away.

'You know,' said Costain, 'that's going to get on my nerves.'

'At that point, he'd already committed two murders, in disguise as a friend of Christopher Lassiter, and then as Albie Bates, having been Dean Michael when setting Bates up as first a patsy, then a victim.' She went round the walls, angrily ripping down the notes from the extra boards. 'He killed the latter in the guise of the short killer from the novel, showing just how perfect his supernatural power of disguise is.'

'In the books,' said Sefton, 'he fools his best mate, who's looking right at him. The memory of London thinks of this ghost as being able to impersonate *anyone*, so he can. The knowledge of character isn't perfect like the disguise is, though. Holmes didn't realize Costain had read the stories, for instance, and covered that up by saying he'd got bored.'

'Then he set us up with the *Lone Star* – the organization of which took immense planning – had Erik Gullister killed, kidnapped Costain and planted himself among us as him. He'd obviously aimed this . . . exquisite, amazing, brilliant plan . . . at us from the start, anticipating what we'd do and using us to do things like get Albie Bates out of jail. I suspect the idea to use us might have come from Holmes realizing during his preparations that we were based at Gipsy Hill and thus could bring Bates to where he needed him to be. Holmes knew once he'd messed with us, we'd get after him, that we might surprise him, so part of the plan was for him to hide among us, to allow him to keep an eye on us, to react to what we did and change the details of what he was doing should he have to.' She looked to Costain. 'I should have realized it wasn't the real you so much sooner.'

'Thanks.'

'I mean because he treated those supposed wounds of his on the deck of the *Lone Star*, away from us. He joined in when we got the idea about the victims all playing Holmes because he knew we'd have got it anyway. In his Tony Costain guise, he arranged the handling of the contents of the ship, and I guess still had some goons handy to take the crate with you in it away a couple of hours later.'

'Oh, I thought you meant because he didn't share my charm.'

She brushed straight past that. 'The first thing he did was to try to distract me, big time, to get me interested in going after my happiness again, to get me lost in irrelevant detail outside of my speciality on the eve of his big score. I suppose I ought to be flattered.'

'That Sherlock Holmes doesn't want you in the game?' said Costain. 'Damn right.'

This time there was an awkward smile. Which then vanished. He was so pleased that she could do that again now. 'I think he tried to distract the rest of us too,' she said.

'Didn't need to in my case,' whispered Quill.

Costain was amazed and horrified by the change in him. They needed to talk one-to-one too.

'He got me to talk about my work,' said Sefton. 'On the train. Everything I'd learned about the London occult shit. Maybe he picks things up fast, like you said, the king of Google, but he didn't know anything about that.'

'Then,' Ross continued down the new board she was swiftly sketching, 'he tried to kill you, having set you up in another typically showy Holmes disguise as that old lady. He killed Danny Mills . . .'

'He said he'd stayed at my bedside,' said Sefton, 'but if we asked the hospital staff, I bet we'd find out he was away for hours.'

'. . . and when he and I went to talk to Ballard, I reckon he must have said something to him when I wasn't there, made a private deal . . .'

'Probably didn't have to break character to do it,' said Costain, before anyone else did.

'. . . because Ballard then went out of his way to tell me that the blade that we thought killed Holmes had a spiel on it that could kill a ghost. So I doubt that was true. It was just to keep us certain in our belief that Holmes was dead.'

'He was telling the truth before then, though,' said Quill. 'The bit about the fetch kettle.'

'Fake Costain realized Ballard hadn't played that bit well,' said Ross, 'so he pointed it out afterwards, used it to build up my sense that Costain was the real thing. He also used the occasion to find one of Ballard's lock-ups. Plans within plans, the brilliant bastard.'

'So the spiel on the blade must have been designed to do something else,' said Sefton, 'like, for instance, to create an image of Sherlock Holmes for the Sighted and broadcast a message to me about his death.'

'Then he went with me to the auction,' said Ross, 'and felt able to pull out one of his own teeth, which now I think about it might be because that was just a bit of his disguise.'

'Sometime around then,' said Sefton, 'he must have gone to find Ballard again, to set him up for being found in a bank vault. He got Ballard to sign up to be a security guard, maybe by making some sort of offer concerning another bank job. Then, when Ballard shows up at Lombard Street, ready to scope out the target, he's forced to put on a deerstalker and play Holmes, before being held still to be smashed across the back of the head. Holmes set up the computer worm—'

'Sherlock Holmes can *code*?' asked Costain.

'We've seen,' said Sefton, seized by a sudden idea, 'if that image he left of himself at Baker Street was accurate, that this Holmes is *all* of them, every version, including all the modern ones. He doesn't have to learn how to drive or code; he just knows!'

Ross pointed at him, correct, and erased a line of her new scribbles.

'He'll be up for the supernatural too,' said Costain, 'with Conan Doyle in the mix. He believed in fairies.'

'But,' said Quill, and him speaking up made them all stop, 'I reckon that'd be a problem, because everyone knows Holmes didn't. Put that and Conan Doyle in the same body, put all these different versions of Holmes in the same body and . . . something's got to give.'

They all took a moment to think about that. Quill sounded like he knew what he was talking about.

'Holmes had time alone,' Ross finally continued, 'to get Ballard out of wherever he was stashed, probably in a vehicle, and into that room beside the bank, where he was killed.'

Sefton nodded. 'I reckon then Fake Costain raided Ballard's apartment, maybe had even been given a key, or just got it off him, though they'd have let him in as easily then as they did afterwards when we both went over. He'd heard Ballard had a device to find anyone, which would be a major threat to him if we got hold of it, but it wasn't there. Not being Sighted, he didn't find the list under the bed. He just came away with the "bastard scourge", whatever that is. When we did find the list under the bed, I think he had a quick look at it and was relieved there was nothing on it that would make us immediately go after the stuff. That night, though, he got there first, more as a box-ticking exercise than anything else, because there was nothing that could help him much either, thank God. Otherwise we'd be playing against Sherlock Holmes armed with tons of exciting devices.'

'No wonder he looked knackered by the time we went to the conference,' said Ross. 'No wonder he couldn't use the blanket spiel to hide his identity. I wonder why the ones who checked him out didn't realize who he was.'

'If they're looking for a copper, he isn't one,' said Quill.

'And if it goes deeper than that,' said Sefton, 'I doubt it

comes back with a name. You'd just get a feeling of something like him being a complicated private eye, which wouldn't have set off the alarm bells like police presence would. Or if there was a flavour of Victorian to what they found out, then from what we've seen, that would have reassured them.'

'At the conference, Flamstead arrived to play against him,' said Ross. 'He put the sort of pressure on Holmes that would have got to any Victorian gentleman, pushed him so hard that his perfect disguise started to crack. I'm going to say a few difficult things now, Tony, OK?'

He was pleased she'd asked him. He nodded. She proceeded to fill in the details of how she'd had a fling with this bloke, this God of London. All Costain could think was that it was a pleasure to have been asked if this was OK to talk about, that he liked how she and him were being with each other now. He took care to nod along.

'I think Flamstead . . . let's call him the Trickster . . . got . . . involved with me in response to Holmes trying to distract me,' said Ross. 'He offered me a . . . shit, a very simple, calming relationship, in which he encouraged me, and pushed me towards the finish line of getting my happiness back a lot faster than Holmes wanted. He couldn't tell me outright about Holmes. That seems to be against the rules for the God of Lies.'

'For all the gods,' added Sefton.

'He was hoping I'd realize, and in the end I did. Still . . . caring about me . . .' She looked to Costain. 'That was initially part of Holmes's perfect disguise. The Trickster played on it, though, made him get into a competition, made it an appeal to his sense of chivalry, made it all very Victorian and love-triangly. And deeply, deeply shit. When I saw you . . . the person who I thought was you . . . pacing outside my hotel room, that obsessed, that Victorian . . . I realized it wasn't you.'

Costain found he was smiling. 'I didn't find that story so difficult.'

'You pissed me off, a few months back, by doing something

you felt strongly about, against what I might have wanted. You took my choice away from me. But you didn't try to manipulate me.'

'Do you feel Flamstead also manipulated you?' He asked the question gently.

She paused for a moment, making eye contact with him, her tooth biting her bottom lip. 'I don't know how I feel,' she said finally.

Sefton made an ahem noise. Moving on. 'It's not just Flamstead who's limited by his nature,' he said. 'Fake Costain—'

'Couldn't we just call him Holmes?' said Costain.

'He told me that Ross was the sun that went round his earth. I'm sure he wanted to set up those astronomical photos to point to the asteroid called Moriarty, but because it's emphasized in the books that Holmes knows nothing about astronomy, because none of his versions do, he would never have been able to get that right.'

'You thought I didn't know that about the sun?' said Costain.

'I thought . . . you'd stumbled over a romantic turn of phrase.'

'Yeah, right.'

'Why,' said Quill, speaking up again, his hand shaking as he visibly tried to hold on to his point, 'is Sherlock Holmes killing people? What's the motive?'

Ross wrote 'motive' on the board and attached it to Holmes. They looked at it for a while.

'What did Fake Costain *tell* you?' said Costain. 'He'd be as good an undercover as I was, so he wouldn't have asked that many questions, unless he had an in-character reason to do so, but what could you tell about what he *wanted*?'

'He said,' said Ross, 'that the murders might continue after they'd run out of works by Conan Doyle.'

'So that's a lie, then,' said Costain, remembering occasions as an undercover when he'd planted just that sort of misdirection. 'He's looking at the end of the Conan Doyle stories as a finishing line.'

'Or . . .' said Ross, 'there's another obvious end point. Assuming he tries for another victim near Brook Street, then there's the murder in "The Greek Interpreter", nobody dies in "The Naval Treaty", so that's the last one before Holmes is "killed" and brought back to life in "The Empty House".'

'It could be either,' said Quill. 'If this was a real person . . .' He ran a hand down his face and had to pause to control his breathing. 'We'd say he was a bit like me, wouldn't we? That he'd had an *episode* of some kind, changed his character. 'Cos Sherlock Holmes, what does he stand for, above all else? Upholding the law.'

'In the books,' said Sefton, 'he often lets people off, if he thinks they deserve it. But, yeah, Jimmy, he doesn't go the other way.'

Ross moved her finger quickly down the list of victims. 'Wait a sec. We noted how most of these had criminal records, except . . . Lassiter, and you two.'

'No amount of research could tell him I was a bit dodgy,' said Costain. 'At first, when I was his prisoner, Holmes spoke very politely to me, like this was an awful duty he didn't enjoy going through with. Then he suddenly went all cold. It was like he learned about me.'

Sefton looked awkward. 'I think I said something about that when I talked to Fake Costain on the train.'

'Oh, ta for that. Until then, I reckon he was planning to let me go.'

'So Holmes prefers to kill criminals,' said Ross. 'But it was him trying to off Sefton that knocked us off this train of thought in the first place.'

'Victorian values!' said Sefton, a sudden realization. 'Oh, you homophobic shit, Sherlock.'

'*No* shit, Sherlock,' said Costain. 'That was a crime back in Oscar Wilde's day, and of those inner Sherlocks, most of them are Victorian.'

'What about Lassiter?' Ross looked back to the man's records on the PC. 'His disability was chronic fatigue syndrome, a condition that definitely wasn't recognized in Holmes's day. Making him a malingerer and a scoundrel, someone taking money away from the deserving poor.' She ran a line between all the victims and wrote the word 'criminal' beside it. 'We have a new limiting factor. He tries for the location and circumstances of the original deaths, he needs victims who played Sherlock Holmes, and he insists, in his broad definition of the term, on them being criminals.'

'We still don't know why,' said Quill.

'Then now we should summon Watson,' said Sefton, 'and ask.'

THIRTY-ONE

Sefton checked the many Sherlockian blogs and message boards, and found that everywhere now the outrage was the same. Although, to his surprise, a significant majority of fans wanted at least one of the three current Watsons to die, a vast number of those following Holmes were horrified and furious. There were petitions. There were calls for the shows' runners to be hunted down and murdered. The calls for calm from more moderate sections of the fandom had only started a new cycle of horror and recrimination.

Many of the fans had already worked out, and this surprised him too, that the three production offices were behind what had been designed to be seen as leaks. That made them even more angry. 'I think,' he said, standing up from the wheezing office PC, 'we're on. Last time I tried this, I used a bit of an . . .' He decided he didn't want to mention the details. 'Easy sacrifice. This time' – he looked around the group. He'd already decided that Costain, Quill and Ross had suffered enough – 'it's got to be something more serious, and it'll be me who does it.'

Costain watched as Sefton used chalk on the floor of the Portakabin to produce a new map of the boroughs of London, with certain features emphasized. Had Sefton, he wondered, been pleased at him seemingly reaching out to him on that train journey? Holmes, with his perfect disguise, had obviously thought that wouldn't seem outlandish. The moment of togetherness he'd felt with the rest of his team was being undermined by something, though, something he noted whenever Ross or Sefton looked at Quill. Finally, he squatted down beside Sefton and whispered. 'Kev,' he said, 'you two know what's getting to Jimmy, don't you?'

Sefton stopped what he was doing. 'Yeah,' he said.

'It's something huge, right? Tell me. I'm back. I can handle it.'

Sefton hesitated only for a moment. 'OK,' he said, 'it's about Hell.'

Lofthouse stood outside her house. She had emerged, an hour ago, at the top of a circular stairwell on a disused platform of what had turned out to be Mornington Crescent Underground station. She'd had to throw herself, many times, against a wooden shutter before it had broken, and had finally stumbled back into a corridor full of commuters who didn't look twice at this wreck of a woman who smelt of shit. The force of what the Sight had revealed all around her had staggered her, had become more and more overwhelming as she'd headed for the surface.

She'd taken her warrant card from her bra and waved it to get her past the turnstiles. She'd managed to stumble out of the station and had had to wave her card again at the taxi rank to make a driver listen to her. She had slept all the way home, despite there being no angle at which she wasn't in pain. The psychedelic nightmare outside seemed muffled by the confines of the taxi.

The door opened. Out stepped Peter, looking at first puzzled at her appearance, then shocked. He opened his mouth to ask some awkward questions, but before he could do so, she was in his arms. The Smiling Man, it seemed, when it had ceased to be necessary, had stopped his cruelty. 'You know,' she said, 'I've rather missed you.'

*

Costain was glad to know the truth. The other two had watched as Sefton had told him. Then he'd gone straight over to Quill and just bloody held him, and Jimmy had held him back. They were that far gone now. Then he'd stepped back. 'We'll find a way to change things, right?'

'Yeah.' Sefton and Ross had nodded at once.

'They're saying we'll sort it,' said Quill, still askew, his gaze searching Costain's face. 'I don't know.'

'One step at a time,' said Sefton, taking a scalpel from his holdall. 'Starting with the job in hand. OK?' They all agreed. 'This is from a very London teaching hospital. So.' He went to his map and cut his thumb, then squeezed a dot of blood onto the major points he'd scrawled on the floor. 'The way this works,' he said, sounding like somebody doing nothing more dangerous than building a train set, 'is that the shape will demand the blood it needs, so I can start small and then, well, it might get serious.'

'Kev—' began Quill.

'This is the least I can do. So let me handle my speciality, OK? OK.'

They let him. He finished the map. He got them to each stand at one of the main points of the compass; then he started to call to the points in between, listing London locations, many of them completely obscure to Costain.

As Costain watched, the map started to become alive, to take on aspects of London itself, to bloom with greenery and moving people. Sefton started to call to the streets around Baker Street; then he listed the buildings of Baker Street itself, then 221B; then, his voice sounding more demanding, he called out for Dr John H. Watson. He called him in the name of all the online communities he'd got thinking about the man, in the name of some of the most outrageous commentators, who in their horrible passion had demanded real suffering for a fictional character. He named them all. He offered his own blood aloud and then winced as some more of it was obviously taken into the map. They had to stay where they were, Costain realized, too far from him to help.

Sefton made a final effort. 'I break the bonds that hold you, which were inexpertly made, made by device, when here I call by blood.' He yelled as the map bloomed once again, and then, suddenly, a figure stood on the space where Baker Street was drawn.

He was flickering, like Holmes had been, between so many actors and drawings, but this image seemed to have a little more stability than the one of Holmes. There was so often a moustache that this image had one, and the face stayed humane and friendly. 'My friends . . .' he said, and his voice was similarly odd, modulated across so many different accents at once, 'for I may, I think, call you that, have you saved me from imprisonment?'

'I don't think we can do that permanently,' said Sefton, sounding like he knew he couldn't keep this going for very long. 'We're police officers. Please, quickly, tell us all you can.'

The figure looked around the room. 'You will have to forgive me. I am not used to discourse with . . . anyone, entirely. My friend Sherlock Holmes and I have lived in a sort of . . . I suppose you would call it a dream world, a vague existence without the detail and volition I experience in this, what I can only imagine must be the . . . real world? I gather we were . . . it taxes the mind even to say it . . . fictions? This we never imagined.'

'When did that change?' asked Ross.

'A few short weeks ago. I still do not have a clear idea of time. There came a moment of . . . awakening, when the world around us suddenly gained undreamed-of clarity and solidity, and my thoughts were suddenly not those of a fever but . . . my own, jumbled and unexamined as they are. Every time one seeks to consider one's own . . . being, one finds such a muddle now, as if the exterior has been clarified to exactly the same extent that the interior has . . . become confused.' His expression was anguished, though, with clear effort, he was keeping his voice steady. 'Holmes quickly understood our situation, pointed out many extraordinary differences between this new world outside our window and the one we had inhabited. He made forays downstairs, then outside. He solved some cases, extraordinary as it may sound, at a distance, simply through his reading. He provided the police, anonymously, with solutions to several major crimes.'

'No wonder the Met's been doing so well lately,' said Ross.

'Holmes also realized something else, however. To his vast surprise, he discovered, in his close examination of the modern city into which he had awoken, the existence of the supernatural. In my memory, he usually has no truck with theories of that sort, although, sometimes I feel that . . . Forgive me, my memories of him are confused also. It took time for him to convince me of it, but convince me he did. He read so much, so fast. He used the devices in the office downstairs to move through page after page of information, searching and cross-referencing, making conclusions at a lightning pace. He communicated with many in distant parts; he set up deals using monies that he found he had at his disposal. He became the spider at the centre of a web of . . . I feared for him when he spoke one night of the sort of people he was employing. He began studying how to make best use of what he discovered about London. He brought to our rooms objects and books. He . . . experimented. Awful sacrifices. Animals taken from the street. This was against everything he stood for or believed in. This was not *him*. I *begged* him to stop. I used every iota of moral certainty that I had to tell him this was wrong. When he wanted to go further, I even threatened him with force. He finally gave way and ceased.'

'You're his conscience,' whispered Quill. 'No wonder he had to lock you up.'

'He finally made . . . an individual . . . appear in his study. I think, though I hesitate to say it, this individual must have been . . . that being which our culture and religion has always known as Satan.'

'Description?' Ross now had her notebooks out and was writing at speed.

'A man in his mid-thirties, thinning hair, dressed in what we would regard as too shabby a style for business but which seems to be the way in this world, always with this same foolish grin on his face. Yet I knew, in my bones, this was the evil one himself.'

'We learned at the conference that he's not Satan,' said Ross. 'He's just a very naughty boy.'

Watson looked puzzled at her. 'In any case, they had a conversation to which I was not privy. Upon his departure, Holmes shook the man's hand. Which I saw with great trepidation. After the man had gone, my friend would not talk to me, or look me in the eye. He went out and returned with a strange dagger, about which he would say nothing. He ordered a parcel to be delivered downstairs, astronomical charts and photos, about which he consulted me, though I knew too little to advise him.'

'Even with the Internet,' said Costain, 'Holmes *can't* learn anything about astronomy.'

'Once it had arrived, he began, in the space of one night, a weird campaign against the fittings of his study, changing many things in odd and startling ways. He asked me to trust him, said all would be well when he had completed his bargain, that no innocents would be harmed, and many more saved with . . . what would come to pass.' Watson visibly hesitated.

'*What* would come to pass?' asked Quill.

'When we would both find ourselves "whole and real forever". Those were his very words. When we would be no longer subject to the whims of the public imagination and could save this rotten new London from the crime and disorder it seemed to revel in. I told him none of this meant anything to me, that I did not believe his caveats. He told me he would see me as flesh and blood in the empty house. Whatever that means.'

'Oh Christ,' said Ross, 'that's what he's doing. That's the motive. He wants to become a real boy.'

'Holmes and Watson were made solid, made real, by "Holmesmania",' whispered Sefton. 'By those three productions all happening at once, by so many people being interested. London's got to a point where its memory can do that.'

'But Holmes wants to go further,' said Costain. 'He's deduced that when the furore dies down, he'll go back to being a ghost, and he can't have that.'

'So he's made a deal with the Smiling Man,' said Quill. 'This series of ritual murders, a media sensation to keep London scared, to keep it moving in the direction he wants, like with Losley and the Ripper. In return Holmes gets continuing real life.'

'And he's trying to source it ethically,' finished Ross.

'He told me,' continued Watson, 'he would summon me again when he had "done what he had to do". He produced an object that he had on his person. I didn't see much of it in that moment. He flung me, with all the skill of a master of bartitsu, and the great strength he sometimes displays, backwards. I had a moment to glimpse that I was being flung not to the floor but through some sort of hole. A hole in mid-air. I landed in an empty version of our rooms, with a view outside of a London that, as I discovered in the next few days, was empty of all my fellow beings. I felt the pull, on one occasion, of something in the air, and assumed it was him summoning me home, but that sensation ceased.'

'That was me,' said Sefton. 'Best not get into the details.'

'The next thing I have to report is you bringing me here now. I thank my saviour that you are the police, and that you know enough that you may prevent my friend from undertaking whatever terrible course of action he has planned.'

'It sounds like he put you in a tiny "outer borough" of his own making,' said Sefton.

'Could you . . . tell me what he has done?' asked Watson.

They were all silent for a moment. Then Ross began to tell him. Watson closed his eyes, his face a picture of horror. 'This is . . . not my old friend,' he said, when he'd heard it all. 'He always thought he was above the law, yes. But he is a good man. I have seen him, in the last few weeks, become so . . . changed. As if he was dragged this way and that, and, caring little for himself, did not see it, and could not cope.'

'I got that bit right while I was doolally,' said Quill. 'What Londoners believe *can* change the nature of a ghost.'

'Yeah,' said Costain. 'With those three very different Sherlocks in the public imagination, with *all* of them over the years . . . our boy is definitely a little confused.'

'He was always one to understand how circumstance could make a man a criminal. Please, if you care about my wishes, I implore you, offer him the same courtesy.' Watson looked suddenly around, as if aware of some change in his situation. 'I feel the pull failing. Can you not free me?'

'Sorry . . .' Sefton was leaning against a table, on the verge of collapse. 'I'm guessing Holmes will have sorted things so you get out if his plan fails, but I can't . . .'

'Then no matter. I trust it to your hands. I have told you all I know. Save Sherlock Holmes.' With that he vanished. Sefton fell.

They all went to him. Costain made him some strong, sweet tea, and he took some iron tablets with it. He actually kept a supply in his holdall. 'I'll be OK in a couple of days,' he said, falling into a chair, exhausted.

They all turned at the sound of the door opening. There stood Lofthouse, on crutches, bruised and battered. 'Would one of you,' she said, 'please answer your bloody phone?'

THIRTY-TWO

Sherlock Holmes sat in an upstairs meeting room of a property just off Brook Street. He was in disguise as an eighteen-year-old woman, a temporary secretary. The fact he now had to exercise no skill at all to make such transformations still disturbed him.

Those chasing him would almost certainly have been able by now to contact dear Watson. What would he tell them, that his friend had gone mad? Well, yes, he had. His thought processes, every time he tried to examine them, were a cacophony of voices that came from the wild variety of impulses inside him. In his past, dreamlike existence, when he had been merely a literary character, he had enjoyed utter clarity.

Now he was so many different people, all at once. As Watson would no doubt by now have told Inspector Quill, Holmes wanted himself and his friend to be entirely real and whole. He wanted this in order to bring order to this chaotic world, the outward appearance of which matched his inner turmoil. He also wanted to see if being a true, living native of this world would bring an end to the inner voices, an end to the many different selves who fought to be in charge of him. He hoped that to be real here allowed one to attempt to be in charge of one's own character.

Here he was, committing murders, being the opposite of himself, in order to be more fully himself. The irony wasn't lost on him. Why did these new fictions about him have to be so dark, so extreme? They, especially, had pulled him in all directions. When he had been created, interpretations of a part were just that. Now there seemed to be multiple worlds, the possibility of an individual being so many different things, each version too soon after the last, and sometimes all at once. How could the public believe in them all, and with such passion?

He was now aware, of course, that the victims of murderers went to Hell. That weighed on him, also. Still, what he was doing would benefit more people, in the long run.

He had, as part of him, his creator. That was the worst voice of all to contain. His creator hated him. His creator wanted him dead. He contained a sudden wince at the thought, a sudden doubling-up as if around a physical pain. His disguise aided that containment. To think such thoughts was out of character for young Alanna.

He wanted nothing more than to bring down the entity with whom he had made this bargain. That would be his first aim when he was made real. It had become obvious the Smiling Man was not, as he had initially thought, a traditional Satan. Indeed, he was a suspect, if what he had heard at that conference could be trusted, in the murder of said Lucifer. That would be a case worthy of Sherlock Holmes.

Worse still, however, was what that actor who had played him had turned out to be, one of the Gods of London, devoted to chaos. He stood against everything Holmes believed in. He had not quite managed to break Holmes, and next time the boot would be on the other foot. He was fortunate indeed that an actor in this era could make little difference to the character he was playing at such short notice, or who knew what extremities Flamstead could have added to his inner turmoil. Still, Holmes felt Flamstead's version inside him, felt the twist of the personality of a god inside that. He wanted, once again, to groan in pain.

Once he had finished and had Watson by his side again, once

they were whole, then he would make all this right. Watson would upbraid him, would rail against him. He would welcome it.

He realized that the door was opening. Into the room, for what he thought was an assignation, suggested by Alanna by text message, stepped young Ben Gildas, a very junior employee here. Gildas was a habitual user of narcotics. Holmes had once had the same habits, but, curiously, a great many of his inner selves thought those habits, even carefully monitored, to be a great evil. Gildas was, by any modern measure, a criminal. Holmes reached under his chair and picked up the rope he'd adjusted to a specific length. He approached Gildas, swinging it playfully. None of the people he was liked the thought of what he was about to do.

Quill and his team had looked to their pockets, found that all of them did indeed have messages left in the last half-hour and had made their apologies. Lofthouse, who had a uniform with her whose job seemed to be to open doors and pick things up, ignored their questions and led them across the road, back to her office on the Hill. With painful slowness she sat down in her chair behind her desk. 'Look up Richard Chartres,' she said. 'Or any of the Continuing Projects Team.'

Ross did. She was amazed to see public records appear on her phone. 'We wouldn't have known,' she said, 'because we didn't have any memories of them in the first place. How did—?'

'I went and found my memories. Brought you back some presents.' She put onto the desk a large, ancient book, some folded papers and an ornate shotgun.

'You've been busy,' said Costain, as Sefton, who had asked for a chair himself, immediately started to leaf through the book.

Lofthouse told them her story, and they filled her in on theirs. Ross urgently wrote down all the details in her special notebook, with Sefton interjecting at points about which he wanted more clarity. Ross noted that none of them volunteered their new knowledge about that sign over Hell.

'Well,' said Lofthouse finally, 'we've all been in the wars. Now, though, I have the Sight. Which I suppose I was always meant to have. Richard chose me to send the key to, a sort of supernatural USB drive, containing everything I needed to know about his team, and how to create a new one in their image. It might have worked too, apart from everyone being made to forget that team. The key feels like it's done its bit.' She held it up, limp on her charm bracelet. 'Now it's just a key.'

'Thank you,' said Quill, 'for telling us. I understand why you couldn't. Is Peter . . . ?'

'He's fine. He has no memory of the times he was possessed. He seems to have done some excellent work at the office during that time. I'm telling him it's a medical condition. Is that wrong? No, sorry, shouldn't have asked that. I'm in charge, and it isn't wrong.'

'Five is better than four,' said Sefton, 'like that fortune teller once said to Ross. When I was in that longbarrow I was told that five was the knot, the knot that catches things. What you just told us about that Halloween where the CPT got erased from memory, there were so many data points . . .' He took Ross's notebook and flicked back through the pages. 'Like what Chartres called the Lud Vanes. I reckon those are what Jimmy took off that bloke who had a go at him at the New Age Fair, the same ones that led us to the Docklands ruin in the first place.'

'I immediately thought there must be such objects everywhere. The first thing I did was to search my house, but there's nothing Sighted there. I suppose that's not surprising. I think this might be why I like to touch the buildings I'm in. I've hung around too much with spooky architects.' She sighed. 'They thought it was all about buildings, and not at all about people. They'd lost so much good practice over so many years. I *felt* they were vulnerable, even back then. I wish I'd known enough at the time to say so. I've been watching the reaction, in official circles, to the return of the memory of them as individuals. It's muted, as you might expect. A file here and there is no longer blank. There'll be a whole constituency who'll now be wondering if, a few years ago, they had a stroke. Friends and relatives will start talking. It'll be fascinating to see that pattern, all those impossible memories, come to the surface, whether or not anyone will realize that something extraordinary happened to anybody but themselves. What the CPT really did was a secret, so I don't know if the people in your world . . . I should say *our* world now—'

'They'll know,' said Sefton. 'Those who encountered the old law, or even researched them, will remember what they found out.'

'They might see it,' said Ross, 'as an indication we're getting the job done.'

'And now the CPT are back in human memory,' said Lofthouse, 'we stand a chance of finding anything else they hid away, any records or objects that weren't plundered from the ruins in Docklands.'

Sefton seemed to have a sudden thought. 'Did the Continuing Projects Team often use the word "protocol"?'

'All the time. One of their euphemisms, for what anyone else would call a spell.'

'A spiel.' Sefton corrected her.

'Don't you start. Why do you ask?'

'When we first saw her, Mora Losley told us there was a protocol "on" us. You say you had strong feelings about which of us to pick for this team. I think the key had already picked us as its chosen successors to the CPT, placed on us something like whatever spiel was said in the ceremony for new recruits in that Docklands HQ of theirs, preparing them for immersion in the lake. The lake was meant to be the power source, but we didn't have one.'

'Until we touched Losley's soil,' said Quill. They all remembered that moment when they had gained the Sight, by touching a pile of earth in the home of that terrifying witch.

'I bet we'd have seen the protocol as tiny golden strings of information,' said Sefton, 'and what was in Losley's soil as the silver fluid, if we could have seen it with the Sight before we, you know, we actually *had* the Sight.'

'And I must have had that protocol on me too,' said Lofthouse, 'also given to me by the key. Because I got the Sight when I went into the lake. God, we have to go back there. We have to see what that poison did.'

'Later for that, ma'am?' said Ross. Lofthouse calmed herself and nodded.

'I think, ma'am,' said Sefton, 'that you didn't get the Sight when we did because you were out of range.'

'I was in Birmingham for most of that day.' She sat back in her chair, astonished all over again. 'I don't know whether to be grateful or angry. The things I saw on the way here . . . how do you live with this?'

'It gets easier,' said Quill. 'Mostly.'

'I hope—' Lofthouse suddenly yelled.

They all spun, to find that Moriarty had appeared, reacted to that reaction and scampered into a corner. They explained. Lofthouse tried to stand, winced, thought better of it. 'You know, when I first got you together, we had a round table. I must have had a feeling in my head for where the Continuing Projects Team had sat at theirs, because I even got you to sit at particular places. Well, now I hope I qualify for a seat at that table. If I'm meant to be one of you, at least now I can help directly, share what you experience and try to find some way for you all to get the bloody Police Medal.'

'I would not turn that down,' said Costain.

'The next thing I should do is try to use my authority to shut down the Sherlock Holmes filming.'

Ross was pleased at the speed of Lofthouse's deductions. That was actually top of their list of actions to be taken immediately.

Lofthouse made the calls as they sat there, Sefton being kept supplied by her secretary with cups of strong, sweet tea. 'Damn,' she said finally, 'none of them are willing to stop production when they're nearly at the end of their schedule, not without solid evidence of some sort of practical connection between what they're doing and the murders, which we can't provide.'

'I'm sure your Gilbert would be up for staging a walkout,' said Costain to Ross. She searched his expression for any sign of bitterness, but found none.

'Yeah,' she said, 'but that's just one of three. I doubt he could convince the others, and anyway, it's not like Holmesmania would stop overnight. If anything, the news of a walkout would make it increase. As things stand, Holmes has at least a week or two to complete his mission.'

Lofthouse answered her phone. She listened for a moment, looking grim, then put it down. 'One Ben Gildas has been found hanged in an upstairs meeting room at a property off Brook Street.'

'Fuck it,' whispered Costain.

'If I go along with you,' said Lofthouse, 'I'm going to see all sorts of horrors, aren't I?'

'It sounds like you already have,' said Ross.

'I'm not complaining. I just want to be ready.'

Quill looked like he couldn't keep it from her any longer. 'You're one of us now. As we drive over to Brook Street . . . there's something we should share with you.'

THIRTY-THREE

The crime scene yielded only the sickening things that Quill expected it to. A startled-looking young man in a business suit, struck down.

He saw that Lofthouse felt it so much more than they did. The distance she had had as a police officer had been taken from her by the Sight. Plus, she now had the burden of the knowledge of Hell. She put a hand on the wall to steady herself and nodded along, staying in command, as the main investigation, led by DI Clarke, came through, with their crime scene examiners.

They found nothing of note over the course of the night, and Quill sent his people home, himself included.

He found Sarah asleep, which was probably just as well, given the long conversations that remained to be had between them. He still wasn't right in the head, despite Sefton's mantra. All it was doing was dealing with the symptoms, holding things off. His thoughts still kept wandering to terrible places, and that made it hard to express himself. The anger was still there. With it would come the crushing anxiety. At least now he was home, and back at work. He got out of his clothes, slipped in beside Sarah and repeated to himself that he was Jimmy Quill, that London should know that, that here was a whole list of what he was. He tried hard to believe it. Thank God, Moriarty stayed downstairs. Finally, Quill slept.

He got in bright and early the next morning to find Lofthouse had joined them once more. Sefton was there, looking pale, but keeping himself fortified with biscuits. Ross was already at the ops board, Costain working beside her. 'Given that we know how specific his targets have to be,' said Ross, 'if Holmes didn't have such an incredible intellect and resources, we'd have had him by now. Ben Gildas was on work placement with a medical insurance company, which only touches on the subject matter of "The Resident Patient". Still, we're now sure about our limiting factors. So for the next story, "The Greek Interpreter", Holmes will be looking for a location in Beckenham that he can seal up to burn charcoal to kill his victim, who should at the very least be Greek and/or an interpreter with a dodgy background. If he's going for authenticity, he'll be capturing him or her ahead of time and starving them first.'

'Sealing a room isn't that hard,' said Costain, 'not these days. You could do it with any modern building, though I'd pick a small room.'

'All I've got about Greeks in Beckenham,' said Sefton, looking up from his phone, 'is that there's a restaurant called the Taste of Cyprus that has a really good rating on Trip Advisor, so a vague estimate of number of possible targets is "some". Wait a sec . . . finding a census page. OK, more sensibly, it's less than a thousand.'

'But there are going to be a ton of interpreters,' said Lofthouse. She looked like she hadn't slept. 'You get language schools all over London.'

Moriarty flashed into the room and swept darkly into a chair. Quill suddenly realized that his presence had given him a very troubling idea. 'What if we could find him before all that?'

'How?' Ross sounded wary.

'When I was . . . very ill, I saw some stuff. I think it was real stuff. I was letting it in, attracting it, being made to see it, whatever. Listen . . .' Haltingly, he outlined what he was thinking.

He watched as their expressions got very worried. Then he looked to Lofthouse.

She considered for a moment. 'I'm new at this,' she said. 'James, are you sure?'

Quill nodded.

Lofthouse looked up as the team approached the Heron Building in Moorgate on foot, startled all over again by the extra detail and meaning the Sight gave her. The way the architecture toyed with the history of this place seemed . . . insulting, askew. That meant bad things could happen here. Given that, and the ongoing situation with Peter, who had insisted on going to work as always, but was going at some point to start asking some really awkward questions, and what James had told her about where they were all going when they died . . .

She felt like she had given her all in pursuit of saving something and lost everything as a result. Was it sheer duty keeping her going? No, it was that here were four people who were in the same boat.

They negotiated their way to the twenty-eighth floor, the building's management thankfully deciding they didn't need a warrant for a 'routine follow-up' about a deceased resident, and probably wondering just how many more police officers were going to come barging through here. Ballard's apartment was how Sefton had described it. Ballard's will was still being worked out.

Lofthouse watched as Quill went to sit down in one of the enormous armchairs, looking uncomfortable as he sank into it. Moriarty appeared in front of him, looking around as if trapped. Here, she thought, was an example of what they called the Uncanny Valley. He had all the soul of a cartoon, creepily trying to be a person, but clearly not alive. 'OK,' said Quill, 'I've been doing what Sefton here told me to, reinforcing the idea of who I am, letting London do some of the heavy lifting by remembering me. Doing that has let me hold on. Just about. It's allowed me to stop seeing Hell all around me. Now, I don't think that was a hallucination. I think I was being allowed to see something underlying everything, a real connection between this world and the other. So what if I stopped trying to hold that back? Don't try to talk me out of it. I'm ordering you not to. I'm going to try it now.'

He closed his eyes.

Lofthouse saw the others all wanting not to allow him to do this, but at the same time wanting him to keep his dignity, to let him have this moment of leadership. She could have stopped it, but hadn't Quill said it was only just about working? Could whatever Quill was planning be anything that might truly harm him?

Then the walls of the apartment began to change.

Quill knew he'd been fighting off this illness that was also part of him by repeating comforting lies. He'd been bigging himself up. He'd been OK with that, because surely it was what just about everyone did. Most people in London thought death was the end, and yet they still found reasons to do things while they waited for the inevitable. Others expected pleasant afterlifes of their own. These were the colours they added to the black and white of life and death.

But come on. He knew better.

He made himself consider the futility of everything. He would die and go to Hell. Sarah would die and go to Hell. Little Jessica would die and go to Hell.

He imagined what would become of her there. He remembered what he had seen being done to children.

That made him angry, made him want to fight, but there was no fighting something as big as this; he let himself realize that. It was like fighting the weather.

The anger got inside him, into all the places it had been getting into lately. He hated having senses. He hated having a real body in the real world. He hated being conscious. He hated that useless cunt at home with her meaningless gestures of support. He hated his child, the burden always round his neck. When they went to Hell, it would be even more painful than when he did. He hated everything and everyone and himself in the face of that. He hated the fear that was everything he was. The fear and the hate were the same thing.

He let all these bad thoughts flood back into him and have their way. Because it was all still there. He'd just been holding it back.

He wasn't in control of any of it. Objects were just objects. People were just objects that *knew*. There was no extra meaning colouring any of it. There was no hope.

He was aware that he was sobbing, bawling like a baby, for the same reason a baby bawls when it enters the world.

He opened his eyes and there was Hell.

'Oh my God,' whispered Lofthouse, 'I can see it too.'

'We all can,' said Ross. She, Costain and Sefton were staring in horror at what James was doing to himself. They were experiencing once again, Lofthouse realized, what she was understanding for the first time. She could *feel* the ghostly tensions wracking Jimmy. She could also *see* . . . what?

The ultra-modern interior of the apartment had become something like a Victorian gentleman's club, all statues and brown surfaces and plants and trophies. Quill sat in one of its decadent armchairs, his face contorted, his mouth working soundlessly. Moriarty had become a vague ghost, Quill's paranoia, Lofthouse realized, having returned to its owner. The surroundings, relatively normal as they were, shook Lofthouse to the core. They came with a smell that was like something on the edge of childhood memory, of the moment when the idea of fear had first come to her, in a nightmare. The smell said that under everything real was horror. It was the decay at the bottom of the world. She could see the others reacting to it also, Costain especially. He was looking around, waiting for some threat to leap out.

Into the room staggered Mark Ballard.

He was dressed in Victorian finery, almost too much of it: a coat so heavy it seemed to be weighing him down, a collar so big his neck was lost in it. Attached to him, leading out of the door behind him from under his clothes, ran many tiny chains. He was staring in shock at Lofthouse and the others. 'Don't trust him!' he suddenly yelled, pointing at Costain. 'He . . . he killed me!'

'We know,' said Sefton, quickly.

It took a few moments of persuasion for Ballard to calm down, but his anger was swiftly replaced by a desperate hope. 'So . . . have you come to rescue me?' He ran up to them, wincing as the chains held him back. 'Please, do it now. I have my examination soon. There's some sort of lease system. I haven't enough money. It's not about justice here.' His voice was suddenly that of a child. 'I want to see my mum and dad. My proper ones. Not the ones who are in here.'

'We don't know how to free anyone yet,' said Sefton. 'Tell us how to find Holmes and we'll keep working on it.'

Ballard looked horrified that he wasn't going to get immediate help. 'No, no, please, you don't understand. You don't know what it's *like* here. Are you real? Listen, I can't get up the inverted tower; I can't see the world; they won't let us see London. I don't know how . . .'

'The person you thought was this guy here.' Sefton pointed to Costain. 'Tell us what the deal you made with him was, give us some reason to help you. What about that knife we showed you, for a start?'

Ballard looked confused for a moment, like he was wondering if this was some new trick of Hell. 'It was a fetch kettle, like I told you. I was holding back on what spiel it held, hoping for a deal, but Tony there . . . I thought it was Tony . . . when he was alone with me, he told me what to say, offered me cash . . .'

He proceeded to confirm what they'd already suspected about the weapon.

'You said he offered cash. What did he pay you with?'

'Gold.'

Lofthouse realized that Holmes's money would now be just as real as his clothes. That power of agency was part of the concept of Sherlock Holmes. 'For anything else,' she said, 'how easy would it be for someone in a perfect disguise to get credit?'

'Once I'd got my deal, he came to visit me. He said he was interested in buying some items from me. I thought I was dealing with a corrupt copper who'd got himself into the best possible place to prosper. He said we could scratch each other's backs. I showed him the Bastard Scourge. He pretended that he didn't know much about this stuff, then grabbed the Scourge and used it on me. He made me dance like a puppet, saying lines like I was Sherlock Holmes. I . . . I got what he was doing then. I have never been so . . . not until now, all the time now . . . He made me walk downstairs and get into a car. Then he made me sleep. When I woke up, I was in another room. It might have been quite a long time later – I don't know. God, I don't like to think about . . . He used the Scourge to make me stand absolutely still, though every muscle was . . . and he picked up this . . . spanner, and . . .' Ballard started to sob, looking at Costain, shivering.

'Fuck,' said Costain.

'It was after the second blow that I . . . went.'

They told him what they thought had happened afterwards, that their suspect had raided Ballard's apartment.

'He only got the list under the bed?' said Ballard, his despair for a moment turning into surprise. 'Then he *hasn't* got everything.'

'That is what we were hoping you would say,' said Sefton. 'Where's the item that can locate a particular individual?'

'You promise you'll get me out?'

Lofthouse took a deep breath. She was about to negotiate

with the dead. Not the sort of thing she normally found on her day planner. 'We'll do our best. You have my word as a senior officer: if we ever discover we can save *anyone*, we'll save you.'

Ballard wrote down the details and then, horribly, tried to keep talking, to say anything that could delay him going back to Hell. Lofthouse looked to Quill, not wanting to let this continue, but then something started to haul Ballard backwards on his chains, which skittered across the floor, and he squealed like a pig. Lofthouse and the others ran to Quill. 'James,' she cried, 'come back to us, please. We're all here for you.'

He opened his red, sore eyes and glared at her with an anger that was only tempered by how lost the rest of his expression was. Sefton went to him and started to whisper urgently to him, to make him say his name, over and over, to recall past adventures. Gradually, the trappings of Hell started to fade. The screams of Ballard as he was dragged down the hall outside vanished into the distance. They were back in the apartment, even though now, to Lofthouse, it felt more like a stage set. Quill wouldn't speak when prompted. He just kept shaking his head. Moriarty seemed to have revived a little. As Sefton kept talking to Quill, he gained in structure and presence.

Finally, when they thought he was able to move, they supported Quill between them and got him to the elevator and out to the car.

Costain drove them to Marylebone station, and Ross and Sefton went to lost property. They had been rehearsing what Ballard had written for them to say. Costain and Lofthouse stayed in the car with Quill. Costain hated seeing that look on Quill's face, that damage that Hell had left in him. 'After we've got him,' he said, 'Jimmy, will you do me a favour and get some help?'

Quill looked up at him and couldn't seem to settle on any gesture or expression. 'I'm sorry,' he said.

'You have nothing to be sorry about.' Costain took his hand.

The car doors opened, and Ross and Sefton got back in, Sefton carrying a bow and a single arrow. The wood of the bow looked extraordinarily old, the sort of thing a museum would have to keep in controlled conditions. The arrow had a flint head, and there were just the sticks of faded feathers as flights.

'I don't know what this is,' said Sefton, 'and what Ballard wrote down is very basic.' As he nocked the arrow, and with no skill at all aimed it up and out of the passenger window, Ross started the engine and pulled on her seat belt.

Sefton let fly. The arrow shot into the air, higher and higher, out of sight. It stayed, however, in Costain's mind, in his Sighted idea of where things in London were.

'I've got it,' said Ross, and turned the car to speed away from Marylebone, and then southwards.

'Faster!' cried Moriarty, gesturing dramatically towards the windscreen. 'We may already be too late!'

THIRTY-FOUR

Ross had no specialist driving experience and couldn't help but wish that it was Costain behind the wheel as they raced down Bromley Road, into the heart of Beckenham, a proper high street in what looked to be a nice commuter town. Mind you, Costain had no specialist training either, just years of experience driving for gangs. She had had to adjust to having in her head a sense of direction being provided by something else, the arrow that she kept imagining plunging towards the earth somewhere in front of her. Several times on the way here, particularly as they'd got closer, she'd had to change course away from it, unable to follow it as the crow flew, and had felt it pricking at the edge of her eye, insisting she pay attention to it, which had nearly made them run into the back of a lorry.

She kept trying to find a left turn, and finally took the corner beside a pub called the Oakhill, going way too fast, only to have to pull up almost immediately in front of a row of bollards. 'It's right there,' she yelled. She could actually see it in the sky now, forever descending, heading down onto the roof of a house ahead and to the left.

She pulled the key from the ignition and leaped out. The others followed. Sefton, still weak from loss of blood, was managing to stumble along. Quill came too, a grim, furious expression on his face. They ran past a barber's shop, and the arrow suddenly speared down and went through the upper-floor window of a little house with a neat garden, seeming to do no damage as it went. Had they found Holmes this time before he'd found a victim? There was a front door and a window. Next door, someone had left an old chair out to be collected. Before Sefton could take the stick of chalk from his pocket, Quill grabbed the chair, barely held on to it, ran at the window and rammed it through, smashing the glass and setting off a blaring alarm. Then he clambered up and leaped through the frame, sending more glass flying.

Ross made herself follow, her shoes slipping on the sill, forcing herself to ignore the shards biting into her hand. Then she was through, and following Quill, the others right beside her, as he pelted up the stairs. Quill wasn't shouting anything about being a police officer, so she was glad when Sefton did.

The arrow was on fire, sticking at an angle out of the carpet on the landing. It burned to dust in the second she set eyes on it. Where was Holmes?

She burst into a back bedroom a second after Quill did, to recoil, coughing, at the taste of the air. An ancient charcoal burning stove was sitting by the bed, and on that bed lay an emaciated, unconscious figure, his face covered – true to the story – in sticking plasters. Quill went to the window, found it locked and smashed it open. Lofthouse went to grab the body. Costain and Sefton at the door were turning, wondering where in the house—

Holmes burst out of another room, a handkerchief over his nose and mouth, a knife in his hand, very possibly the one that had killed Richard Duleep. His appearance was flickering wildly. He leaped forwards decisively, precisely, trained in the use of the weapon. Costain put his head down, ducked under his swing and ran at him, barging into him at the top of the stairs. The knife went flying. Holmes took up a boxing posture, hands up in front of his face. Costain grabbed both his hands and kneed him in the groin, then kicked the crumpling figure down the stairs.

To their surprise, Holmes bounced neatly down like a tumbler, leaped to the door, flung it open and was out and away. With a bellow of rage, Costain raced down after him, got to the door, ran out into the street.

After a few moments, they caught up with Costain. He'd stopped, looking around. 'I couldn't see him,' he said, panting. 'I just picked a direction. We lost him.' Ross, ridiculously, looked around, as if she might see him hiding in one of these perfect gardens.

'And that arrow's a one-time deal,' said Sefton.

Lofthouse ran up to them, her phone in her hand. 'I hauled the victim out onto the landing and opened all the windows,' she said. 'He's still breathing. I've called the paramedics.'

Quill sat down on the street, oblivious to the people now coming out of their houses, looking out of their doors. 'Lost him,' he said. 'No, no, no.'

Moriarty stepped forwards, as if speaking for Quill. 'Follow him!' he bellowed. 'Follow him, for he is fixed on his course now and he will strike! Stand clear or be trodden underfoot!' He turned and raced off down the street, back towards the car. Quill looked up, as startled as any of them, then scrambled to his feet.

'Go,' said Lofthouse. 'I'll take care of things here.'

By the time they got back to the car, Moriarty was pointing frantically. 'Follow!' he cried again.

'I think,' said Ross, as she opened the door for Costain to drive, 'we may have found an expert in tracking Sherlock Holmes.'

Cara Lavey was a production assistant on the BBC's ratings-winner Sunday-night *Sherlock Holmes* series. This was, she wanted her friends to know, not all that glamorous, and was a lot of hard work, mostly consisting of carrying things and making coffee, for actually not very much money, although there was a London living allowance.

After she'd had a few drinks, though, she would admit she

liked getting to know the actors. Today was the midway point of filming on the last block of the last episode in the season. Filming in the Southwark facility was coming to an end, and everyone was a bit thousand-yard-stare and sleepless, with mucking about on set answered not by laughter but by brusque calls to concentrate. She'd been employed counting out properly hallmarked copies of the script, taking a brunch order for the assistant director and finding a floor plan of the consulting rooms set to discover 'which fucking marks are still here from previous shooting days', as the director had put it. All of which was exactly what she'd signed up for, the hard yards she was utterly willing to put in to get noticed, to be given more responsibility and work her way up.

'Cara, you useless fuckwit, how's it going?' murmured Gilbert Flamstead as he wandered to the edge of the set, a grin letting her know that she was being complimented. Just for once, she thought, it might be nice if he simply said nice things.

She would never dare insult him back. 'Excellent.'

'What terrible news. I don't suppose anyone has seen my talentless fellow?' They all suddenly turned at a shout. Onto the set had burst an extraordinary figure. It was Sherlock Holmes. Meaning it must be an actor, or an impersonator, someone in cosplay? He looked bloody good, though. He had the face for it. Such a clean-cut look, like he was someone famous she didn't recognize. He was running towards them, security guards chasing him. Was this a comedy thing, a DVD extra they hadn't been told about? Or, shit, was this a fan? A couple of the blokes with tool belts tried to grab him, but he spun, hurling them aside with ease. In his hand now was something that looked like the handle of a whip. He brought it down with a motion like he was miming lashing at something too.

Flamstead was glaring at him, unmoved, as the rest of the crew either retreated, hoping for the security guards to catch up, or stepped forwards defensively. 'The Bastard Scourge won't work on me.'

'Then try this!' The man pulled a revolver from his coat and Cara suddenly thought it must be real. That he was going to kill them all. The man leaped forwards, grabbed Flamstead round the throat, the gun against his head, and started backing away. Now, to Cara's amazement, he looked like an entirely different excellent actor playing Sherlock Holmes. 'I will finish this!' he called upwards, like he was calling out to God. 'This surely must be enough! I will complete my side of the bargain!' Cara watched, helpless, as he started to drag Flamstead away.

By the time Costain had brought the car skidding to a halt in the car park of the Shoreditch warehouse, Quill's team had no more need of the shouted directions of Moriarty. The hostage situation was all over the news. Local uniforms had arrived outside, where stood a large group of employees, being pushed back behind a barrier. The media were also arriving from all directions.

'Are you up to this?' whispered Sefton as Quill got out of the car. The emphasis on Moriarty seemed to have done him some good, but Sefton would have preferred it if Quill had let them do this without him.

'I have to be, don't I?' said Quill. 'I have to try what you told me to do, only big time. Give me a sec to get into character.' He took a deep breath, then pulled out his warrant card and marched through the crowd, the others following him. 'All right, the cavalry's here. Move your arses.' A combination of dropping the names of Clarke and Lofthouse and sheer loudness got them to the centre of the developing operation, Quill being the highest-ranking officer so far at the scene. The top floors of the warehouse complex had been cleared. Holmes had taken Flamstead to the roof.

Quill established that his team would report in with the uniforms keeping watch on the stairwell, ask about the latest developments and then come back down to await the arrival of a senior officer assigned to manage the siege situation. When they got out of the lift at the floor with rooftop access, Quill went straight to the two uniforms waiting at the stairwell door and asked them the situation like he *was* that officer. Having heard there'd been no contact with the suspect in the last ten minutes, he nodded to them and walked straight up the stairwell. Sefton made himself adopt similar confidence and followed, Costain and Ross beside him. Worryingly, Moriarty, invisible to the police officers, came too. 'I'll try and keep him on his lead,' muttered Quill. 'He's got form for trying to throw Holmes from a great height.'

They emerged onto the blustery rooftop, the Thames stretching in front of them, to find two small figures at the other side of the expanse of roof, air-conditioning ducts between them. They were against the far edge, just a low wall, with, behind it, a fall of five storeys to the street. Holmes, flickering between multiple appearances at an even greater rate, still had his gun, Flamstead remained in his grip.

'Why hasn't he killed him already?' whispered Costain.

As they stepped closer, what Holmes was shouting offered one possible answer. 'Is this good enough?' he yelled at the sky. 'Will I have my freedom?'

'He knows who Flamstead really is,' said Ross. 'He must know this would be an enormous sacrifice.' She was being entirely professional, showing no sign of having a connection to the hostage. Well, no sign apart from a helpless look back to Sefton as his gaze met hers.

'*Can* he be killed?' asked Sefton. 'He said he got incarnated.'

'Which I suppose means he's mortal,' said Ross. 'Or at least some part of him is a person, or something. Anyway, do you fancy just letting him die?'

Sefton took that to be a rhetorical question. They made their way slowly towards the two figures and stopped when first Flamstead and then Holmes saw them.

'If you try and stop me,' called Holmes, 'I shall shoot him. I have no choice.'

Quill took two paces forwards, his hands raised. 'Yeah, but you're not . . . you're not sure, are you? We wouldn't all be here otherwise. You trust that smiling bastard to hold up his end of a deal, do you?' Quill was visibly not, now, the caricature of himself he'd forced himself to be to get up here. His voice and hands were shaking. He seemed almost as desperate as Holmes.

'If he does not, then I shall have at least tried. My existence is necessary to redeem this infested, degenerate, fallen London. I must do whatever it takes to save it.'

'You'll be a little cog in the wheel of order,' shouted Flamstead. 'That smiling bastard is using you, first to create chaos in this world, then to clamp down on it when this world is his. I need this world to operate; I need a background of real life in London to play tricks and dramatic reversals against. I also need some free human beings around to be tricked. I do not need either his near future or his outcome, and yes, I can tell the truth to you because you are not yet, sir, a *person*!'

Holmes just looked to the sky again and shouted. 'Is he enough? Will you be content with him?'

'I think it's a delaying tactic,' said Costain, moving close enough for only Sefton to hear. 'His better nature is still in there, and he's finding reasons not to finish this now.'

'We talked to John,' Sefton called to Holmes, stepping forwards.

Holmes lowered his gaze and looked furiously at them. 'I kept him away from this,' he said. 'He knows nothing.'

'He's horrified at what you've become, Sherlock. He's sure this isn't the real you. You're afraid because you've been influenced in every direction, by everyone who's got their own version. The stress of that, it's warped you out of shape. You were willing to kill me, even though I'm a police officer. That isn't Sherlock Holmes.'

'You're . . . a degenerate! Or enough of one for the rules I have set myself. I'm—'

Sefton didn't want to hear his apology. 'Except that a lot of people now see *you* like that too. A lot of people think you and John are a couple. And if that's part of what you feel inside, if that's part of what you hate—'

Holmes jerked his revolver in their direction and fired.

They dived for cover behind the nearest duct.

'Would you please *not* try to out Sherlock Holmes?' whispered Costain.

Quill stood up again, ignoring the others trying to pull him back. 'It's all part of the same thing,' he called. 'You feel you're torn apart; you don't know what to believe in; you don't know who you are? Well, look at me!'

Before Sefton could stop him, Quill had walked right out of cover and had started marching towards Holmes and Flamstead.

'That room full of meaningless clues you put together, that led me to Hell. Are you willing to send me back there, right now? Is this version of yourself you're trying to live with able to do that?'

'I also have no criminal record,' yelled Flamstead, his chin shoved up by the gun barrel. 'As a human being, I am utterly blameless. Don't you see what you're doing to your reputation, your good name? Do you *want* to be the man who killed Sherlock Holmes?'

'I think maybe he does,' whispered Sefton.

'You're looking to be a real person,' called Quill. He stopped a few feet away from Holmes and Flamstead. 'Haven't you thought that maybe all this horrible confusion is what that's like?'

Holmes looked desperately around him, looked back over the edge of the building.

'He's thinking about jumping,' said Costain. 'I'm not letting that fucker off that easily.' He got up out of cover, leaving Moriarty as a shadow behind the vent, and went to stand beside Quill. Sefton felt Ross get up beside him as they marched over too. He couldn't stop looking at the gun, at the small object that might suddenly be turned in Holmes's hand and kill any of them.

Holmes looked desperately between them. 'Everything has to mean something,' he said, as if starting a lecture. 'Logic states that the movement of every particle may be deduced from the movement of every other, that were we able to observe every action—'

'We'd still know fuck all,' said Quill. He took a step forwards. Because he did, they all did. 'When you wrote about the "ultimate crime" on the back of that photo, did you know what you were talking about?'

'I wrote it merely to send you astray. I regret you have fallen so far. Perhaps when I wrote, I sensed there was a wrongness in the world, a fault in all our stars, and that informed my deception. I am not used to not knowing what occurs in my own depths, how it seems to surface in surprising ways.'

'You've got to be careful with that,' said Quill. 'It's easy to get deluded when London's helping you along. Sometimes a cyclist is just a cyclist.'

'Well,' said Holmes, lowering the pistol from Flamstead's chin, 'I shall try to be myself at the end, at least. I may be in the wrong place, using the wrong methods, and I have chosen a blameless victim. But the latter I can remedy.' He raised the gun once more and this time it was aimed at Costain. 'Perhaps you will balance my scales.'

Sefton looked to Ross. Her expression was a mixture of fear and fury. He looked back to see Costain readying himself to leap forwards.

'Hey,' yelled Flamstead, as only an actor could.

But Holmes was not to be distracted. His finger squeezed the trigger.

'I'm glad I got your happiness back,' said Flamstead.

Before anyone could react, Flamstead grabbed Holmes. He wrestled for half a moment with that enormous steely strength. Then he flung their combined weight towards the wall.

The two men fell together.

*

Sherlock Holmes fell. The god who was in disguise as an actor fell with him. He was laughing at him.

In the few moments available to him, Holmes thought about the crime scene he'd created.

He wondered where all the ideas had come from. Some of it was to aid his deception, of course. There had been logic in the lettering on the blade, in the shaping of a spiral to make Quill think of a previous case. There had also been an attempt at logic, which had failed because of his innate character, in the choice of astronomical photos. Then there had been something he could not avoid, in the presence of the chalk outline. Once the 'deed' had been done, he had to leave, and, since he was becoming more solid all the time, there was the possibility the assistant curator might have seen him. The rest, though, the rest! He had casually pricked out the eyes of a woman many of those inside him had loved, as if she must not see what he was doing. He had taken snippets from his letters, books from his shelves, even melted his own head as if to signal that he was uncertain as to the contents of his mind. The symbol of his sovereign, 'V.R.', written in gunshot on his wall, he had drawn lines across, connecting those dots as if to spell out something else, as if hoping to live under a different power structure. He had arranged his own corpse to point towards two men who had always inspired him, like Michelangelo had arranged Adam pointing to God, without, Holmes had thought at the time, any idea in his head other than to confuse. However, those he pointed to were someone who wanted to emancipate every one of those enslaved, and someone who had died in the service of many, overwhelmed, but had become a hero in so dying. Were they both indicative of some greater purpose, the potential for which was as yet locked in the multitudes he contained?

Below him, Holmes glimpsed, in his last moment, the being with whom he had made his pact. He was looking up at him, smiling as always. He was anticipating where Holmes was going.

Holmes dedicated himself to his God(s) or none, in that moment. He also dedicated himself to a new mission. *The ultimate crime. He must solve it.* He was going to try. It would be some time before he saw his friend again. If he ever would. He had arranged for Watson to be freed into fiction once more. But the empty house would remain empty.

The laughter ceased and Holmes managed not to cry out in the moment.

Ross and the others elbowed their way through the crowd and found, lying on the kerb, Flamstead's body. He was a smashed corpse, far beyond help. A little way back from Flamstead lay the body of Holmes. Every form he flickered through was crumpled, his limbs at awkward angles. The gun lay nearby.

'What are we looking at?' Sefton said, gazing down at the body. 'What are they going to bury?'

'Something that wasn't enough of a human being,' said Costain.

Quill put a hand over his eyes as officers started to run up, demanding his attention. The other two quickly yelled at them to back off and started to lead Quill away.

Ross squatted beside the wreck of Flamstead and tried to see the god. She hoped part of him was still alive somewhere, and that there had been only a moment of pain. She touched his face and felt a little better to have made that gesture, whatever it meant.

THIRTY-FIVE

James Quill went home. He got there just after Jessica had gone to bed, which was a relief, because he didn't feel able to pretend to be normal, not even for her. Sarah met him calmly, desperate to say and do the right thing. He hated that desperation. He hated the anger that rose inside him in reaction to it. Laura stayed a little back from both of them, wanting to stay to support her sister, but also, Quill supposed, wondering if she should leave them to talk.

'Thank you for coming after me,' he said.

'Get better,' she said. 'Then save us all. No pressure.' She looked to Sarah, got a nod that it was OK, then kissed Quill on the cheek and left them to talk.

Quill went to sit at the kitchen table. Sarah put the kettle on and sat down opposite him. 'I'm sorry—' he began.

'Quill, you're not well. You don't have to be sorry.'

He made himself not slap the table. Moriarty appeared beside him, and that eased the pressure, a little. 'I'm sorry for what I've been thinking about you and about Jessica. I'm ill, and I can't heal myself, and I can't use London shit to do it. I need proper help.'

Sarah pulled from her back pocket a notepad and put it on the table. 'Here are some numbers to call.'

He wanted to cry. He decided to let himself. He found he was already. 'It's going to take a long time.'

She went to hold him. He let her. 'That's OK.'

One bright October morning, Rebecca Lofthouse went across the road from her office at Gipsy Hill to watch as Lisa Ross unpinned the ops board. Quill was on compassionate leave, so marking the end of Operation Game was her job. Her injuries had begun to heal. Physiotherapy was giving her a new lease of life, at the same time as the Sight had put dread into her morning commute. Operation Game had been brought to a conclusion, but, uniquely in the annals of police work, they would have to wait to see if their prime suspect returned from the afterlife. With the death of Flamstead, media interest in Sherlock Holmes was at an all-time high. It would take months, maybe years, to fade. So there was the distinct possibility that Holmes might reappear once again as, in Sefton's words, 'a ghost with benefits'.

If so, would that ghost again attempt to become real? Sefton was looking in on 221B Baker Street on a daily basis. There was as yet no sign of either Holmes or Watson. The crew of the *Lone Star* had been extradited back to the US, and various other of Holmes's paid henchmen had been uncovered and arrested. That was a process that was going to take a while to complete.

Lofthouse looked down the list of operational aims. They had, in the end, ensured the safety of the public, gathered evidence of offences, identified and traced the subjects involved, and destroyed them. They had not discovered a means to arrest those subjects.

Costain saw where she was looking. 'About fifty-fifty,' he said. 'For us, that's a result.'

Ross turned to glare at him. 'Jimmy's on the way to getting his sanity back,' she said. 'The boss here got her husband back. I got my happiness back *and* I beat Sherlock Holmes. And you're back.'

'Cheers,' said Costain.

'So,' said Ross, 'better than fifty-fifty.' She turned back to the board.

Lofthouse looked to Costain and saw he was smiling.

'For people who are meant to be devastated by the revelation that we're going to Hell,' said Sefton, 'we're doing OK. We've now got an idea of our cultural history, and we're starting to make inroads into community policing.'

'Yeah,' said Costain, 'but the news about Hell is going to do the damage it's supposed to. It's like the Smiling Man's given a case of depression to the whole occult community. Plus, there's what he did to that underground reservoir. No more giving out the Sight.'

'Also,' said Lofthouse, 'from what I saw happen to the Continuing Projects Team, Halloween may be a special day for the opposition, and we've got that coming up soon.'

'I don't know why,' said Ross, taking the piece of cardboard with the name of the operation on it from the board and putting it into a drawer, 'maybe it's just getting my normal brain chemistry back, but . . . I can't help but feel hope.'

When all the paperwork, such as it was, was finished, Lofthouse let them all go home, prior to taking a few days off.

In her car on the way back to Catford, in the early evening darkness, Ross thought about the challenge ahead of them. They had it from several sources now that every single Londoner being headed for Hell was a recent development. Lofthouse's story of what had happened to the Continuing Projects Team on Halloween five years ago made Ross wonder if that had also been the moment that change had been made. It was certainly the moment everyone in the occult underworld looked back to as the big alteration to their world. Brent, the Other, Mother, or whatever she wanted to be called, had said that moment of change had been when Lucifer, whatever that God of London had been like, had been murdered and something else had taken his place. Was that something else the Smiling Man?

Was there anything four coppers and an intelligence analyst could do in the face of cosmic horrors like that?

She closed the door of her flat behind her and relaxed against it. She wanted to sleep right now. She could, incredibly, if she wanted to, spend the next day in bed. She could literally not remember when last that had been the case. She'd been a different person then. She went to make herself a cup of tea. As the kettle was boiling, she tried again to feel sad about Gilbert, tried again to mourn him. Everyone on the Internet seemed to be doing so; the media were in a frenzy about him, about the sacrifice he'd made to save some brave and thankfully unnamed police officers. She wanted to feel loss, but she was afraid she was enjoying her happiness too much to do that. She'd seen his body, seen someone she'd been intimate with terribly hurt, but she couldn't rid herself of the feeling that he, like Holmes, was still out there somewhere. He'd made his sacrifice for London, and he was such an appropriate Messiah for the world they were in now, the Prince of Lies who'd given himself for his love's lover. Complicated.

She was about to raise the teacup to her mouth when, from immediately above her, she heard a sound. It was like something grinding, trying to get through the roof. Was that a running machine or something in the flat above? Then a familiar smell came to her nostrils. She lowered the cup, in shock. 'Dad?' she said.

He burst through the ceiling, bringing the light of Hell with him, dangling again on the end of the noose that had killed him. He was panting, exulting, a huge fatherly smile on his face that was red with exertion and real in every wrinkle.

She threw the cup into the sink, where it smashed. She pulled out her knife. This time she would at least try to cut him down.

But he was shaking his head. 'No, love, you won't be able to cut it, and they'd notice. Two friends of yours, they sorted it, found a way for me to pop back when nobody's looking. I can come see you here now. They wanted me to say, for a while at least, they're staying. You have friends in Hell.'

She realized he must mean Holmes and Flamstead. She remembered an illustration she'd once seen in an old book, the Harrowing of Hell. If they could arrange for her dad to get out to see her, then surely there was hope for them all. She recalled, once again, what the fortune teller at the New Age Fair had told her, that her dad would also bring her hope in autumn. She held her father to her and smelt for the first time his familiar scent over the stench of the pit, and they talked about nothing important and everything important for three precious minutes before he had to go.

Kev Sefton was now officially sick of steak and liver, and wanted just a salad tonight, thanks. He'd told Joe about Hell, first chance he'd got. Joe had taken it in, nodded. He'd been brought up in a religious family and had faced that prospect himself as a child. That was another mental airbag that people in the know all over London would be using to cushion themselves against the news. Sefton told him once again how amazing he was. He agreed.

A couple of days into his leave, Sefton decided to go into the city centre, just randomly shop, get an Xbox game and some new trainers. He was walking up Tottenham Court Road, seeing the horrors of the Sight these days like they were the weather, noting those little guys in the hoods running about, as free of care as anyone going to Hell could be, when he realized there were large men walking beside, behind and in front of him. He stopped on a corner and they stopped too, and all turned round to look at him at the same moment. He thought he recognized some of these faces. Old lags. Fiftysomething gangsters. Old school. Facial injuries, receding hairlines, a lot of muscle gone to seed. The sheer bulk of their black coats hemmed him in. He stayed silent. Not much they could do with all these people walking past. Well, not much they could do and get away with it. He tensed, ready to do some damage in return, though he was hardly on fighting form right now. 'We represent,' said one of them, 'the King of London.'

Sefton frowned, remembering the briefing Ross had given about the various new players they'd encountered in the last couple of weeks. 'You mean Nathaniel Tock? What does he want?'

'To ask you a question. Whose side are you on?'

Surely they must know he was a copper? 'You know who I work for.'

'Yeah, we wondered if you got what this was all about.' Through their ranks walked a hard-looking man in a black leather coat. This, Sefton realized, must be Tock himself. 'When your mate Lisa said you lot now owed me a favour, I don't think she quite realized how concrete an obligation that was. Or how soon I'd ask for that favour. The end of October is approaching. It's when we all have to pick a side. When hits are made and taken. We're getting five black cabs ready. We're setting up a Halloween job.' He put a finger to the end of Sefton's nose. 'In a couple of weeks, you lot will be working for *me*.'

Acknowledgements

I owe my research sources, as always, such a debt. Those that are comfortable with being named are the following:

Robbie Bourget; Simon Colenutt; Sarah Groenewegen; Sophia McDougall; Seanan McGuire; Simon Morden; Cheryl Morgan; Frank Olynyk; Mike Scott; Andrew Smith; Adrian Tchaikovsky; Bruno Vincent.

Thanks, everyone!

www.panmacmillan.com